MW01490015

Etania's Worth

Daughters of Tamnarae, Volume 1

M.H. Elrich

Published by M.H. Elrich, 2018.

This is a work of fiction. Similarities to real people, places, or events are entirely coincidental.

ETANIA'S WORTH

First edition. December 8, 2018.

ISBN: 979-8201987442

Written by M.H. Elrich.

Table of Contents

Thank You To:

My best friend and editor, C.E. Stone

My childhood best friend and inspirational author, C.M. Fritzen

My husband, for speaking the truth

My mother, for encouraging my dream

"A wife of noble character who can find?
She is worth far more than rubies."
-Proverbs 31:10 NIV

.

Chapter One

Eighteen-year-old Etania Selali took a deep breath. She scanned the small crowd, blowing at the brown wisps of hair that fell in front of her face. She pressed her toes against the wooden floor of the chapel and looked over the crowd of Nova citizens.

He wasn't there.

She shouldn't be surprised. She shouldn't be disappointed. Yet, her heart felt like a hard rock in her chest.

"He'll come, Etania," her friend, Grace Stegel, said comfortingly.

"I hope so," Etania said, but her heart prepared for the worst. Her father never came to anything important. As she was about to look again, Priest Alfred began his speech.

"Today we have come together to celebrate our sons and daughters. From the time they were five, they have learned how to read, write and do basic computations. I have personally had the pleasure of teaching not only them, but my own daughter as well." Priest Alfred looked over at Grace, who blushed and curtsied at the compliment.

"Now," Alfred continued, "We will have the parents present their children as adults, honoring their achievements and announcing their future plans." Polite clapping and cheering rang out at this announcement. "Before we begin, let me pray a blessing over us." Everyone dutifully bowed their heads and closed their eyes.

"Deo," Alfred said, "Thank you for giving us the blessing of children and enabling us to educate them in a time of peace. We are so grateful you sent your son, Melchizedek, to be a sacrifice for us and to put an end to the Long War. You then blessed us with your Mark, so that we know you are always with us. We come before you today to present our children as adults so that you may bless their futures. May it be so."

Etania looked up eagerly. She prayed with the others, but only as a recitation, rather than a personal plea. Priest Alfred called out each new adult's name, and their parents came to the stage to join them and say a few words. This process was repetitive, so Etania barely paid attention to it.

"Etania," Grace whispered, "has Melchizedek told you about your future?"

"No, why would he?" Etania asked.

"He cares about us," Grace replied.

Etania shrugged. Deo and Melchizedek, if they were anything like her father, were too busy to pay attention to her. She looked again, hoping a second glance would reveal her father's black hair.

"So you've never been Marked?" Grace said.

"You have, right?" Etania replied, trying to divert the subject. "What did Melchizedek say when he marked you?"

"He told me that I must endure some trials, but if I trusted him, it would be alright. Do you have any idea what trials he might be talking about?" Grace asked.

"Isn't that what your father is for?" Etania answered, looking over at Priest Alfred.

Grace crossed her arms over her bust and huffed. "I asked you."

"Okay, fine," Etania said, with a slight smile on her lips. "Everyone undergoes hard times of some sort, so he must be talking about that. Did he say anything about your decision to become a seamstress?"

"Yes, he said I will make more than clothes. I have no idea what that could mean," Grace replied. Etania shrugged again.

"Sorry friend, I don't know either," she said.

"Next is my lovely daughter, Grace Stegel," the priest announced, breaking their conversation.

As Grace and her mother took the stage, Etania continued to search for her father. Even though she knew she should pay attention to what Priest Alfred was saying about her friend, she was distracted. Her father was nowhere to be seen, and she was the next one to be called. She found her mother, Tala, in the crowd. Her mother met her gaze and shook her head, and Etania felt her heart harden like stone.

Where is my father this time? She wondered.

JAKIN SELALI SCANNED the horizon, trying to spot any movement of branches in the thick forest. He listened for the crunch of leaves, sensing that the Skazic were out in the brush. He was as certain of it as he was that the Skazic were fallen humans from the races of Tamnarae. There were even rumors that the Skazic had sold their souls to Malstorm in order to become more powerful beings— twisted versions of their previous selves.

"There's nothing here, Lehrling Jakin," Keyel Evant, his apprentice, said.

Jakin grunted in reply to his title, one given because he was part of the original twelve who served Melchizedek during the Long War. Though the war was finished, his personal hunt of the Skazic wasn't. In addition to being a hunter, he was considered the voice of Melchizedek to Southern Tamnarae, advising King Toren and his people regarding Deo's will. After training Priest Alfred and other priests scattered across the country to be that voice, he had established King Toren in his role, and focused on the hunt. He hoped to be done with the Skazic swiftly so he could attend Etania's adulthood ceremony.

"Maybe they can transform into trees," Keyel suggested.

"Some of them can, but not the ones we're hunting," Jakin explained.

"What are we hunting?" Keyel wondered.

"A Soacronis," Jakin replied, referencing the type of Skazic.

"I don't think we've hunted one of those before," Keyel said, narrowing his blue eyes to scrutinize the brush around them.

"The last time I saw one was years ago, right before you joined me," Jakin said.

"Is that what you were doing near my house?" Keyel asked.

"Yes," Jakin replied with a smile. "As I recall, a young man interrupted my hunt by jumping out and asking to be my apprentice."

"That was very rude of me, Master," Keyel stated.

Jakin laughed. "I was just joking! Smile a little, will you?"

But Keyel didn't smile. In fact, Jakin had only seen the man smile a few times since he'd trained him. The man was so tight-lipped that Jakin learned most of Keyel's past from his mother.

Jakin sighed. As much as he wanted to continue hunting the Skazic, he felt the Soacronis would continue to evade capture. A fallen member of the dragon race, the Soacronis had wings, so it might have flown away. He couldn't miss another event that was important to Etania and his wife, Tala.

"Come on, Keyel. We should teleport home," Jakin said.

"We're leaving so early? I'm surprised," Keyel replied.

"I have an important event to attend," Jakin explained. "I will drop you off and we will resume our hunt tomorrow morning."

"Yes Master," Keyel said.

That's what Jakin liked about the Leici. His previous apprentices questioned his whereabouts, wondering where he personally lived. Keyel respected his need for privacy and didn't prod for further information. Perhaps Jakin was a bit paranoid to hide the fact he had a family from most people. Yet, if the Long War had taught him anything, it was to be protective of the people he loved.

Gripping Keyel's hand, Jakin concentrated as his flame Neuma, or power, flickered within his heart. The amethyst flames flowed from his heart to his hands, and twirling around Keyel and surrounding them both. Jakin pictured his house in Khartome, the capital city that sat on an island in the middle of a lake. In a blink, they were gone.

When they reappeared, they were standing inside his house in Khartome. This house, close to the castle, served as a perfect place to rest when he had late meetings with King Toren. Once Keyel was safely secured inside, Jakin used his flame Neuma to teleport again to his family home in Nova, the small town located beside the lake that contained Khartome. He made sure to teleport to his room so none of the townspeople could see him. There, he quickly pulled on a hat and changed his clothing, putting on colored monocles. The double monocles, which were secured by chains, were for covering his purple eyes—an abnormal coloring that designated him as a Lehrling. He walked downstairs and was about to leave when his butler, Barick, stopped him.

"Lord Jakin," his butler began.

"Yes?" Jakin paused.

"They just finished. The bell was tolling at the chapel," Barick said, "so you might as well wait for them here."

Jakin groaned, placing aside his colored monocles and hat.

Tala is going to kill me.

ETANIA SIGHED AS SOON as she said farewell to Grace. Even though her mother had praised Etania's hard work and personally unbraided her hair as the ceremony required, it wasn't the same without her father present. At least he didn't have to hear Etania's choice for apprenticeship: becoming a librarian like her mother. With Tala, Etania would keep the historical records of Melchizedek preserved and make copies of them for others.

Etania followed her mother inside their house and stepped back as her father swept her mother into a hug and a kiss. Her mother pushed against her father.

"That's enough of that!" Tala said breathlessly. "You promised you would attend Etania's ceremony and you didn't! You definitely don't deserve any kisses."

"But I want some," Jakin replied, pouting by sticking out his lower lip.

Etania rolled her eyes and tried to navigate around the couple, determined to reach her room before they started arguing.

"Wait just a minute!" Jakin said, putting his finger up.

Sighing, Etania turned from the first step of the stairs and looked at her father.

"What do you want?" she questioned.

"I want to make up for missing your ceremony!" Jakin exclaimed, picking up two cloth bags from a side table. He handed one to Etania and one to her mother. Etania wanted to toss the bag out the window, but her mother began to smile.

"What is it?" she asked.

"Open it and find out," Jakin replied.

Tala looked at Etania and both of them untied the cloth bags. Her mother pulled out a necklace with a heart amulet, the delicate silver glistening in the fading sun.

"It's beautiful," Tala gushed. "Help me put it on, will you?"

Jakin assisted his wife as Etania looked at what her father had given her: a dagger with an amethyst stone in the pommel.

"What do I need this for?" Etania wondered.

"For becoming my second apprentice!" Jakin replied.

"Second?" Etania repeated. She knew nothing about another apprentice.

"Yes," Jakin said, as if that one word explained everything. Etania put her hands on her hips.

"I am not going to become your apprentice!" she declared. "I'm going to be mother's apprentice."

"What!" Jakin exclaimed. "Why?"

Because I don't want to be yours! Etania thought, but bit her lip to keep those words from slipping out.

"If you were at the ceremony," Etania said, "you would have learned that I was near the top of my class in reading and writing."

"Really?" Jakin said. "Wow, that's impressive."

"I know!" Tala agreed. "I'm so excited for her to join me tomorrow for the first day of apprenticeship."

"Tomorrow? So soon..." Jakin let out a breath. "Well, if my daughter and wife are happy about this, I guess I have no choice, do I? Besides, I'm not sure how my first apprentice would feel about having another one."

"Great, it's settled," Tala said. "Let's get something to eat."

Etania's mother ushered them both into the kitchen, where Barick and his wife, Serena, were setting the table for food. Etania sighed. Her mother was always good at sweeping aside potential conflict and making sure fights didn't break out. Personally, Etania was grateful for her mother's skill, wondering how she might ever react to her father without Tala's presence. Dinner was civil, filled with conversation about Tala's latest project and her father's latest hunt. There was no mention of the apprentice. Etania asked to be dismissed, and left the table, heading upstairs to her room. Her bedroom was across from her parents' and simply furnished, with a wardrobe, desk and bed. Placing the new dagger and its sheath on the desk, Etania changed into her nightgown before flopping onto her bed. As she pulled up the covers, she considered her father's words.

Jakin wanted her to be his second apprentice. She wondered briefly who the first apprentice was, but dismissed the thought. The mere fact he wanted her as his apprentice surprised her. If he didn't care enough to make it on time to her ceremony, why try persuading her to be his apprentice? It didn't make any sense, and she smiled at the thought of even trying to become a fearsome warrior.

That will be the day! She joked to herself, yet sobered when her mind fled to Grace's question. *Have you asked Melchizedek about your future?* Etania snorted. Her choice to become a librarian was her own, and it suited her. She loved books, so it naturally made sense that she should apprentice under her mother. With that justification, Etania went to sleep.

FIRST DAY AS AN APPRENTICE. Etania tried not to let that thought scare her as she sat with her mother in a wagon going to the castle of Khartome. The wagon bumped along a dirt road leading to the bridge that connected the mainland to the island capital. Traffic stopped on the bridge as the King's guards, or Praytor, checked paperwork at the base of a tower. The tower was stationed at the bridge's beginning and had a gated tunnel running beneath it, through which all traffic had to pass. Once they were permitted through, the wagon continued along the stone bridge until it passed by the open gate of a second tower, which sat on the bridge's opposite end. They passed underneath this tower and, within minutes, they were at the foot of the island. The wagon then brought them through the city, winding in a circle uphill, until they reached the castle at the top of the island of Khartome. The wagon pulled up to the castle gates, and the passengers stepped out.

The portcullis was drawn up to allow the castle workers entrance and Etania looked up to see the sharp metal ends of it as they passed beneath. Most of the servants went to the keep, stables, or kitchen to attend to their duties, but Etania and her mother went to the library. It was located within one of the large, round towers of Castle Khartome. Three levels of the tower were devoted to the library, while two levels were dedicated to the defense of the castle. Double oak doors allowed access from the inside of the castle grounds, and the Praytor checked their papers before allowing them inside.

Etania smiled wide as soon as she stepped into the spacious library. In front of her were stairs that descended to the first floor. To her right the second floor continued in a circle, and to her left was a stairway that went to the third floor. Everywhere she looked were scrolls, tightly rolled and shelved, as well as leather-bound texts. Sconces with candles provided ample light. There were slits that let in light as well which archers could use for the defense of the castle as needed. Etania followed her mother downstairs.

The first floor was different from the others. In the center were tables where the royal scribes would organize books and scrolls. Librarians, recorders, and academics bustled around the floor, moving from table to table. There were ink stains on the tables, and several inkwells standing by pieces of stretched paper, anxiously waiting for words to be pressed upon their blank surfaces.

"Come, I'll show you how to use our organization system," Tala told Etania, leading her around the library and explaining the meaning of the placards.

Priest Alfred spotted them both and came hustling toward them. Not only was he the Priest of Nova, but he was the Head Librarian at the castle.

"Tala, Etania, I'm so glad to see you! We are in need of some scribes to copy some scrolls. Are you ladies ready to get to work?" Priest Alfred asked.

"Yes!" Etania exclaimed, and her mother seconded the declaration.

Priest Alfred handed them both a piece of paper. Etania glanced down at the titles: *A Historical Commentary on Melchizedek, Son of Deo by Davi Jesh* and *The Mysteries of Melchizedek's Disappearance by Ezik Turnis.* She felt a grin tugging at the corners of her mouth.

"Tala, yours should be on the second floor, and Etania, yours should be on the third floor," Priest Alfred explained.

"Alright!" Etania exclaimed.

She kissed her mother's cheek before heading back to the library entrance,where the stairs were. She walked slowly, the wood steps creaking beneath her feet until she reached the top. There was a railing to her right and, if she peeked over it, she could see both the second floor and first. On her left, shelves were packed with scrolls and other books. Etania looked at the top of the shelves to read the placards and find the location of the manuscripts she needed. Scanning the last names of the authors, she suddenly felt like eyes were watching her.

She looked behind her. There was nothing there but stacks of scrolls that hadn't been filed yet and a Praytor standing in the corner. No wonder she felt like eyes were watching her! The Praytor was probably observing her.

Pushing aside her feelings of unease, she found the scroll by Davi Jesh and pulled it carefully from its place. When she did this, she heard a loud crash. She looked over and saw scrolls and books scattered across the floor from the shelves on her right. The Praytor bent down to pick them up.

Etania joined him, gathering the papers together, and then she straightened, handing the papers back to the Praytor. As the Praytor put them back in place, he asked.

"Are you the new apprentice, Etania Selali?"

"Yes," Etania replied with a smile. "Word must travel quickly. I only told those in Nova about it yesterday."

"Daughter of Jakin, the Lehrling?" he questioned.

Etania tilted her head to the side. Most people didn't know she was the daughter of the Lehrling, as Jakin told few people about her. Yet, she couldn't lie.

"Yes," Etania replied.

As soon as the words left her lips, the Praytor attacked her. Hands covered in scales squeezed around her neck in a chokehold, cutting off her windpipe. She coughed as he lifted her up and smashed her face against a bookcase. His eyes, yellow slits, were emotionless behind his helmet. Etania flailed, struggling, as scrolls came loose and bounced behind her. She panicked, trying to think.

Thoughts faded as her assailant smashed her head against the bookcase again. Everything spun, and a headache began to form in her temples. A trickle of blood, warm and hot, slid down her cheek. If he smashed her head against the bookshelf one more time, she might die. She had to get free...she had to...

She pushed against the Praytor helplessly, hitting him with her fists to no avail. If only she had taken her father's dagger from home, instead of leaving it out of rebellion!

Stop. She thought, and the word became louder in her mind: *Stop, Stop, STOP!*

A bright light burst from her fingertips, striking her assailant and knocking him back against the railing. He slumped into a pile, unconscious. Etania breathed hard, her body tingling. Somehow, she'd made him stop!

Falling against the bookcase, her vision fading, she stared at the senseless Praytor. *Why?* She wondered. *Why would he attack me?* Before she could think of an answer, she lost consciousness.

A VOICE WHISPERED HER name, "Etania."

She opened her eyes and found herself in a meadow. Wildflowers stretched beyond what her eye could see: red, orange, yellow, and pink. Their honey-like aroma swept into her nostrils and she picked one of them, holding the soft stem against her cheek.

"Etania," the voice said again.

This time she looked, and she saw a young man. He appeared her age, with loose brown hair and kind eyes. His skin, tanned from the sun, was a perfect color.

She laughed at herself. She must be dreaming of her perfect man!

"Etania," he said again, and she noticed his eyes change. They looked older—ancient. All thoughts of romance disappeared.

"Yes?" Etania replied.

"There is great darkness coming, Etania," he said. "I need you to dispel it."

"Me, dispel darkness?" she scoffed. "I think you've got the wrong woman."

"You are the woman I have chosen, for I am Melchizedek," he declared.

"You couldn't be. Melchizedek wouldn't visit me," Etania retorted.

"I care about everyone, including you. Now, I need you to use your Neuma to save Tamnarae."

"Neuma? I don't have Neuma. Besides, Tamnarae doesn't need to be saved. We've been at peace for a hundred years."

"Everyone needs to be saved," Melchizedek asserted. He looked up at the bright blue sky and said, "It is time. Remember."

He lowered his head and gazed at Etania with such intensity that she felt she would faint.

"I have chosen you," he said.

Chapter Two

E tania's eyelids fluttered open, the image of Melchizedek fading like the dream she just experienced. Abruptly, she felt acute pain in her head.

"Melchizedek," she mumbled, as her vision came into focus."What do you mean?"

"Etania, are you all right?" Tala said, bending over Etania's prone body.

Etania groaned, sat up slowly, and replied, "I think so."

"You will be as long as you rest," someone said.

Etania looked to her right and saw a man she didn't recognize standing in the corner, writing something on a tablet of wood. By his blonde hair, Etania knew he was a Leici, a human with the Neuma of healing. He had healed her wounds, but she would still experience side effects.

"I feel sick," she complained.

"That too will pass," the healer explained. "You've suffered a concussion. If your mother hadn't found you when she did, you might have suffered permanent damage to your brain."

"What happened, Etania?" Tala asked.

"I'm not sure," Etania said slowly, trying to remember. "I think a Praytor attacked me..."

"That doesn't make any sense," Tala said. "When I found you, there was no one else there. I thought the books fell on you and hit your head. I was so worried about you...."

"There wasn't anyone there?" Etania's brow scrunched together, a shooting pain passing through her temples as she tried to piece together the images she remembered.

"Memory loss is a common side effect. Here, have her take this herbal tea twice a day until the headaches subside," the healer instructed. He handed her mother a small pouch of leaves. "I must see my other patients."

"Of course," her mother agreed, and dropped coins in the healer's hands. He left, walking past a large armoire. The armoire made Etania realize that they were in her room.

"Etania, are you sure you're all right?" her mother said.

Etania replied, "I'm fine. How long was I out?"

"At least six hours. It's almost sunset now," her mother answered. "I'll have Serena bring you some tea while I'm away."

"Away?" Etania repeated.

"Your father needs to know what happened."

Etania groaned. "Must he?"

Her mother nodded, kissed her cheek, and left to go find her father. When she left, the house felt empty, even with the clinking of glasses and the sound of Serena preparing tea. Etania sighed, adjusting the pillows so she could lean her head against something soft instead of the hard headrest.

What happened? Etania wondered, searching her memories. She saw flashes: searching the bookshelves, tugging out the scroll, feeling cold hands against her neck. Then, a bright light. She shivered. *Did I really just imagine someone attacking me?*

The only clear memory was her dream of Melchizedek. That seemed more real than any of the images in her mind. He had told her that she had Neuma, and this Neuma would somehow be used to save Tamnarae. *I don't have Neuma!* Etania protested. *I'm no one special. Even my father sees that; that's why he ignores me.*

A door creaked open and Serena, their maid, entered carrying a steaming tea cup and scones on a large, wooden tray.

"Your tea is ready," Serena said. "It's really hot, so be careful."

A ginger-scented steam rose from the liquid, so Etania asked, "Did you add sugar and cream?"

"Yes, but it still might be strong," Serena answered.

Etania nodded and carefully took a sip of the tea. The strong taste of ginger was hard to digest. She blew over the top of the liquid, grimaced, and drank as much as she could in one gulp. Her stomach protested, but she took another swig of the hot tea until it was gone. Then she grabbed the scones and stuffed them into her mouth, trying to rid her tongue of the taste.

"Thank you," Etania said. "If you don't mind, I'd like some water also to wash it down."

"Of course," Serena replied. Taking the tray carefully in her hands, she exited the room.

Suddenly, the room was illuminated by purple flames. Etania glared at the fire as her father appeared in the middle of the room and the flames dissipated. He rushed to Etania's side and put his hand on her head and cheeks.

"How are you feeling? Is everything okay? Can you make out what I'm saying? I..."

"I'm fine!" Etania retorted.

"Good, because I need every sane thought you have!" Jakin teased. "Tell me everything."

"I think it started when the Praytor bumped the scrolls," Etania explained. "He asked me questions about who I was ...and then he attacked me. His eyes were yellow, emotionless; his hands, like a snake's scales."

She shivered and looked at her father. His eyes were narrow, making them look like small, purple flames in the midst of a smooth face.

"A Soacronis!" Jakin hissed the word, as if saying it would bring the monster into the room. "I knew he was nearby!"

"So-a-crow-niss?" Etania repeated, "What's that?"

"A very nasty type of Skazic which once was a Draconian," Jakin said.

The Draconians were humans who rode dragons, a gift of Neuma given to them by Deo at creation. Yet, Etania couldn't even think about what their opposite would be, since she hadn't seen a Draconian before.

"A Skazic, disguised as a Praytor, attacked me?" Etania yelped.

Her father nodded.

"Yes, but why is it after you?" he mused, "It doesn't make any sense. Unless..."

"Unless what?" Etania wondered aloud.

"Unless you were targeted for being my daughter," Jakin replied.

"Well he did ask about that, I think," she said.

"He did?" Jakin repeated. "And you told him the truth?"

"What else was I supposed to do?" Etania questioned.

Jakin sighed.

"Well that still doesn't explain how you escaped," he pointed out.

"I fended him off," Etania said.

"Did you have the dagger I gave you?" he questioned.

"No," Etania felt sheepish.

"Then how did you defend yourself?"

"I remember a bright light, and he was knocked back," she admitted, her eyebrows furrowing.

"A bright light?" Jakin broke into a smile. "You have Neuma! I told you that you should be my second apprentice!"

"I don't have Neuma! Did Melchizedek talk to you too?" Etania said.

"Melchizedek?" Jakin said. "You've met him at last?"

Etania reddened, and then said, "Depends on what you mean by *meet*."

"In a dream," Jakin whispered, and folded his hands under his chin, "But not a dream."

"Yes."

"What did he say?" Jakin asked, leaning forward.

"He told me that my Neuma is vital to saving Tamnarae. But I didn't understand, so I denied everything, then he said..."

"Everyone needs to be saved," Jakin said softly. After a long pause, he stood, walking toward the door. "Get some rest, Etania."

"But my dream—"

"I know." Jakin told her.

"You do?" Etania wondered.

"I just have to investigate first, then we'll talk," Jakin answered mysteriously.

"But..." Etania began.

He winked at her and disappeared in a ball of purple flame. Etania's head began throbbing like the beating of a drum. *Why does he always overrule my opinion? Doesn't he see that I don't want anything to do with him? Just like he has never wanted anything to do with me.* Another pain shot through her temple, slightly dulled but still present. That wasn't the truth. She wanted, more than anything, to have her father's love and affection. Yet, until this moment, he hadn't paid attention to her. She sighed and tried to think of something better. She imagined working alongside her mother in the library, sorting through scrolls and meeting a handsome apprentice just like her.

They would get married and spend their days reading books....the thoughts lulled her to sleep.

When Etania woke the next day, the pain in her head had lessened yet not disappeared. She could walk without feeling dizzy, but she wasn't sure if she should return to her apprenticeship. However, at breakfast, her mother said, "I want you to return to work with me."

"Okay," Etania said, surprised. "Why?"

"The annual meeting of the lords and ladies is this week, and I have been assigned to record it. I would like you to come along," Tala explained.

"Me, at the meeting?" Etania repeated. "But I'm not qualified, I haven't even had more than a day of training, I—"

"I believe in you, Etania," Tala interrupted. "Besides, Priest Alfred said that you have great handwriting, which is all you need."

"Al-alright," Etania answered. "When is the first meeting?"

"Tomorrow morning. First, we need to get you some clothes appropriate for the meeting and for the dance."

"D-d-ance?"

"Yes. Now that you're a woman, I need you to meet as many eligible bachelors as possible," Tala declared, "The dance is the perfect place."

"Mom!" Etania protested. "I don't know if I'm ready for that sort of thing."

"Well, you have all week to get ready for the dance. In the meantime, we're going to get you some dresses!" Tala exclaimed.

She rose from the table and held out her hand to Etania. Etania hesitated before taking it, but once Etania's hand was in her own, Tala pulled her toward the door.

"Barick, please wash the dishes for us. Etania and I are going shopping!"

"Yes, milady," Barick replied.

Etania grabbed their cloaks and Tala retrieved some money from their chest. Etania also strapped the amethyst dagger in its sheath to a belt around her waist. She had learned her lesson, and despite her dislike of the gift, it was necessary. They strode out into Nova, the sounds of the village surrounding them.

Walking toward the bridge, they passed by various homes. Etania noted that the traffic of the previous day had lessened, so they were able to make it through the first tower on the bridge in much less time. Etania and Tala admired the stillness of the lake around them while they walked to the second tower. Once they passed underneath it and were on the island, they made their way uphill, passing first through the crafts' district before reaching the merchants' district.

Store owners set up their wares for the day, with colorful tents and flags designating the type of goods they sold. Her mother dragged Etania past the intoxicating aroma of fresh-baked goods and toward a series of seamstresses who sold bolts of cloth for custom dresses. Tala took Etania to a shop with a blue flag, run by a woman with a tan, wrinkled face, her white hair tied back in a bun. She stood behind a booth on the front porch.

"Tala!" the woman exclaimed when she saw them.

"Bethel," Tala greeted her and gave her a hug. "Are you ready for us?"

"I am and so is my apprentice," Bethel replied, gesturing toward her shop. "Follow me back to my measuring room."

She took them indoors, her feet shuffling against the floor of the studio where mannequins displayed the various dresses she could design. Before Etania could admire them, Grace flew at her, wrapping her arms around Etania.

"Oh, thank Melchizedek!" Grace cried out. "I feared the worst when I heard you were hurt."

"Is anything secret around here?" Etania wondered.

Her friend ignored her comment, lightly touching the scar the Leici's healing had left on her forehead.

"Should you be walking around?" Grace questioned.

"A Leici healed most of it," Etania replied. Backing out of her friend's hug, she added, "I doubt surprising me helped my balance."

"Oh, sorry!" Grace replied.

"Alright, enough fussing!" Bethel exclaimed. "Come on Grace. Your friend came for a fitting."

"Really? What's the occasion?" Grace wondered.

"The diplomatic meetings and the ball," Tala replied for Etania.

"Eek!" Grace squealed, taking her friend's hand. "Come with us."

The pair led them past Bethel's open studio into a hallway which split in two directions. Grace and Bethel turned left and entered a doorway which opened into a wide room with mirrors, strips of cloth lying on a table, overturned stools and dozens of bolts of fabric. Bethel bent down to grab one of the stools and turned it upright, beckoning Etania to stand on it in front of a mirror. Then she took out a long piece of fabric with marks for measurements, telling Etania to stretch out her arms or suck in her stomach for accurate dimensions. As she spoke, Grace recorded the measurements on a piece of paper.

"She is very attractive, Tala," Bethel complimented. "She has a great hourglass figure."

"I've always said so," Grace said, "but she never wears anything to emphasize it."

"Well, I think that should change," Tala said. "I want grandchildren before I am two hundred and fifty!"

Etania often forgot that her mother's prolonged age meant that she waited longer than most to have children, and was only granted one. Despite this impatience, Etania would not be pushed.

"Mom, I'm standing right here!" Etania protested.

"I know," Tala teased, and winked at her daughter. "But I can still compliment you, can't I?"

Etania looked away from her mother, blushing and crossing her arms.

"She has a strong will too, I see," Bethel added.

"You only know half of it," Grace snorted.

"Grace!" Etania exclaimed.

"It's the truth," she said, with a shrug.

"That's her father's will, I think. Greens, reds and blues would work best on her, as long as they're a darker shade," her mother said.

"Red probably would be best for the dance and gold for the meetings. How many dresses do you need?" Bethel asked.

"Two, I believe. One for each event," Tala instructed, "and two outfits for Jakin and I. We need to have matching outfits as well. Probably something purple, because it's his favorite color."

"How long do I have for the formal attire?" Bethel asked.

"You have until Friday afternoon. As for the diplomatic dress, I was hoping you had a dress you might be able to adjust to Etania's size since the meetings begin tomorrow."

"Tsk, Tsk," Bethel censured, "Giving me so little time."

"Oh, we can do it!" Grace said.

"You know we pay you well for your time," Tala added, dropping coins in Bethel's palm.

Bethel laughed, her wrinkled fingers grasping the coins.

"I'll see what we can do. Besides, you always ask me to do impossible tasks," Bethel teased.

Tala added, "We will give you more when you're done. Just send a pigeon to the house and Barick will pick up the clothing with our remaining payment."

Before Bethel could answer, a bell rang out.

"It seems I have another customer. If you'll excuse me, ladies?" Bethel began.

"I'll see you later, Etania," Grace added.

Tala and Etania went into her parlor while Grace stayed behind to finish her scrawling. In the middle of the studio, a handsome young man with short, blonde hair stood.

"What can I do for you, Leici?" Bethel asked.

"Actually," he replied, looking directly toward Etania with sharp, blue eyes, "I'm here to see her."

Chapter Three

Before Etania and his wife were awake, Jakin strode up the stairs of the library. He passed the librarians' assistants, who were descending the stairs with scrolls in their hands, before he found it: the area where Etania was attacked. He bent down, looking at the slightly pink stain still present on the stone floor. *What really happened here?* He wondered.

From the stain, it was clear that Etania's head had been hit multiple times. Jakin winced, and then glanced up at the shelves. There were a few scratches and indents from where Etania's head had connected with them. *I will not be happy when I find who did this to my little girl.* He thought, and then shook his head. *She's not my little girl anymore,* Jakin realized, *she's an adult.*

Why had she chosen to be a court librarian instead of his second apprentice? He knew daughters generally took after their mothers. However, his daughter's personality reflected his own, so he'd thought she would want to hunt Skazic. He sighed and returned his focus to the bookcase.

Examining the scene of the crime hadn't helped. He was about to turn away when he saw a glinting scale. Stooping down, he picked it up and examined it. The scale was green and hard, just like a Soacronis—which is what Jakin suspected from the beginning. Here was concrete evidence of his fears!

Melchizedek had said his daughter's Neuma was the key to saving Tamnarae. Neither Jakin nor Etania knew what that really meant, but Jakin realized it made his daughter an enemy of the Skazic. She would need to be protected. *I have tried so hard to eliminate the Skazic,* Jakin thought, *ever since HE betrayed me. Apparently, I haven't tried hard enough.* He observed the area was clear of witnesses, so now he could teleport without alerting anyone. He closed his eyes, feeling the heat of flames stir within his breast.

The warmth surrounded him and Jakin imagined the place he wanted to be: next to his wife. He arrived home moments later, and Tala looked up at him with a dazzling smile.

"Good morning," she said.

"Good morning," he replied, sitting down on the bed. "I need to talk to you."

Tala took a seat beside him, interlacing her fingers with his own. Then she said, "I was about to eat and head out with Etania. Can you tell me quickly?"

"Before you leave, you need to know something about Etania," Jakin answered.

"What is it? Is she okay? She's still sleeping, I think..." Tala began.

"Etania's fine, though I think she'll need a bodyguard," Jakin explained.

"What! Why?" Tala asked.

"I found evidence that a Skazic did attack our daughter," Jakin replied.

Tala squeezed Jakin's hand.

"So I was wrong," Tala admitted. With a trembling voice, she asked, "Are they targeting her?"

"I believe so, because she has Neuma, just like me," Jakin said. "I'm just not sure what it is."

"Why did this have to happen to her?" Tala said, sniffing and keeping back tears. "I wanted to keep her out of this battle against the Skazic! I wanted her to be safe."

"I hoped the same," Jakin said. "I wanted to eliminate the Skazic so no one would be in danger— our daughter least of all."

Jakin sighed, and his wife put a reassuring hand on his shoulder.

"I know that you've tried, but don't you remember what Melchizedek told us?" Tala reminded.

"Only by believing in his good can evil have less hold," Jakin recited.

"Yes," Tala said, taking a deep breath to steady her voice. "We must trust him now, believing that his gift to Etania is for a purpose beyond ourselves."

"Trust," Jakin reminded himself aloud. He lifted the scale from the library to the light and looked at it.

"What's that?" Tala asked.

"This is a scale from the Soacronis that attacked Etania," Jakin explained. "Like dragons, Soacronis' scales are harder than rock. This scale puzzles me, because Etania doesn't have the strength to defend herself against that."

"No, she doesn't. Thank Melchizedek she lived!" Tala said, and took another deep breath. "Can I see that?"

Jakin handed it to her, and Tala examined it closely.

"Jakin, do you remember Daas?" she questioned.

Jakin's eyes narrowed. Yes, he still remembered his old "friend." He still remembered how Daas had betrayed Melchizedek, turning him over to the enemy. So he replied, "How could I forget?"

"Do you also remember what happened to those Daas attacked with his Neuma?" Tala questioned.

His heart started pounding.

"You don't think that she's a—"

Tala put her hand on his arm and stopped him.

"I think you should do your research first. The only place that still holds knowledge of him is the Leici archives. Are you still on good terms with the librarian there?"

"Mostly," Jakin admitted. "I think she's still upset because of her son."

"Any mother would be. Talk to her, and see if she's willing to help you."

"Will do," Jakin said. He stood, ready to teleport again. "I will also send a bodyguard for our daughter."

Tala acknowledged his statement with a nod. Then she whispered, "Be careful."

Jakin kissed her softly and replied, "I will. I love you."

"I love you, too," Tala said, stepping back. With that, Jakin teleported away.

KEYEL JUMPED WHEN JAKIN appeared next to him, coming in a whirlwind of flames. Since Jakin had not reappeared as promised that morning, Keyel took it upon himself to clean and polish their weapons at the Lehrling's house in Khartome.

"Why do you always do that?" Keyel asked him.

"Because I enjoy it," Jakin replied, with a wink. "Do you have a minute?"

"Of course, Master," Keyel answered. He put down the weapons and faced him. "What do you need? Are we going to hunt more Skazic?"

"No," Jakin replied, waving away his words. "I have a more important mission for you."

Keyel gulped. *More important? What does he mean?*

"I need you to keep my daughter safe until I return," Jakin declared.

"Daughter?" Keyel repeated.

He didn't know about his master's family, let alone a daughter. Jakin must trust him extensively to allow Keyel to protect her. As far as Keyel knew, no other apprentice was allowed to know of Jakin's family.

"Her name is Etania. Here's a description of her and where to meet her," Jakin explained, sliding over a piece of paper to Keyel. Keyel arched an eyebrow at his Master.

"Why me?" Keyel wondered. "Why not a Praytor, or someone with Neuma?" *Or someone stronger?* He thought, hating to admit that he was the one Leici without any healing Neuma.

"I know your history, Keyel," Jakin said, "You are the only one I trust for this assignment." "If you know my history, then you know that is far from the truth," Keyel retorted.

"I know the truth, Keyel. I only wish you would accept it." Jakin countered and sighed. "I don't want to order you. Will you do this for me?"

Keyel considered his master's words. Jakin believed in him. *Isn't that why I begged to be the Lehrling's apprentice? To prove that I am better than my past.* He thought.

"I will protect your daughter," Keyel declared.

"Good," Jakin replied, turning to leave.

"Wait, M-master," Keyel stuttered. "Why does she need protection?"

"The Skazic are after her and I intend to find out why," Jakin replied.

Before Keyel could ask him to expound more, Jakin disappeared in a ball of flames. Keyel sighed and looked down at the instructions, trying to imagine the daughter of a Lehrling. By this description, she sounded like a beautiful woman, with brown hair and brown eyes. He crumpled the paper in his hand.

He wouldn't fail to protect a woman again.

JAKIN CONCENTRATED on his destination. The Leici library was not a simple teleport because it was so far away, so he needed to focus on the details. When he felt his mental image was clear, he allowed the heat of his Neuma to seep through his limbs, surround him, and carry him away.

He appeared in the library, scrolls flying upward as he landed. No one was there this time, but Jakin was sure the Leici librarian would be bothering him soon. He didn't want to speak with her, so he began searching for the records, flipping through various tomes, scrolls, and fliers.

"What are you doing here, Lehrling?" a female voice questioned.

"Shayna," Jakin replied with a smile, "so nice to see you again!"

"I wish I could say the same," Shayna said, crossing her arms over her chest.

"You know you like seeing me. Especially since I bring news of your son," Jakin declared with a wink.

"I don't when you mess up my records!" Shayna protested, "Whatever you're looking for, you could've asked me to find it instead of disorganizing all my work."

"But it's so much more fun to fluster you," Jakin said, with a laugh. Shayna sighed and threw up her hands.

"Well, do you have news of my son?" she asked.

"He's well, and doing all that he should," Jakin answered, once again sifting through the records. Shayna immediately stopped him and gathered what Jakin was looking through into her arms.

"That's not enough news for me to allow you to rifle through these," she declared, with a sniff.

"Aww, please. I really need to look at those records!" Jakin begged.

"I'm sure," Shayna said unsympathetically. "Tell me what you're looking for and I'll get it for you."

Jakin ran his hand through his hair. Although he didn't want the Leici to know, he had to give her some clue.

"I'm looking for a couple of manuscripts about Daas," Jakin explained.

"Fine," Shayna said, and began looking through the documents. She pulled out a scroll and handed it to Jakin.

"I want that back in pristine condition," Shayna instructed.

"Aye ma'am." Jakin saluted her and took the scroll from her hands. Shayna arched her eyebrow at him and left him, muttering something about how long it would take her to reorganize. Jakin scanned the scroll.

The twelve kings grew arrogant, just as the first parents did, and went to war with one another. Malstorm helped them, corrupting Neuma users so that their soldiers became Skazic: shadows of their former selves. The wars raged on, killing thousands and corrupting hundreds for many, many years...until one day.

Deo sent his son, Melchizedek, to stop the war. Melchizedek made peace wherever he went, and many followed him. Melchizedek appointed twelve men to be his peacemakers in the war. They were called Lehrlings.

Jakin paused. He knew this part of the scroll. He would have to read further down, where it described the individual's powers.

Jakin was once a Pyros, with flames as his weapons. To him, Melchizedek gave the ability to teleport across Tearah.

Cephas was once a Naymatua, with plants as his weapons. To him, Melchizedek gave the ability to shield others.

Daas was once a powerless human, with no weapons. To him, Melchizedek gave....

Jakin finished the text, collapsing into his chair. After reading the account, there could be no doubt. He teleported away once more, knowing he must tell his apprentice and his wife what he had discovered. Etania's safety could well depend on it.

Chapter Four

"Me?" Etania repeated, astonished. *This handsome Leici couldn't possibly be here for me,* she thought.

"Yes. My name is Keyel Evant, your father's apprentice," the man began.

"Apprentice?" Etania stuttered.

"Ah, it's nice to meet you at last. Jakin talks often of you," Tala said. Keyel arched his eyebrow at Tala.

"I'm guessing you're his wife?"

Tala nodded.

"He didn't mention me or Etania, did he?" she questioned. Keyel shook his head, and Tala sighed.

"Well, Etania, I think Keyel can explain what's going on and escort you home."

"What?" Etania exclaimed, looking toward her mother for help. Before she could complete her sentence, her mother waved goodbye and left the shop. *Why does she always take Father's side, even when he acts like this?* She thought, scowling.

"I apologize," Keyel said, taking Etania's hand and putting it to his forehead. "I thought your father talked to you about our arrangement."

Etania felt like her heart was beating in her cheeks as they heated. "What arrangement?"

"He assigned me to be your bodyguard."

"<u>My</u> bodyguard?" Etania repeated.

"In light of your recent..." Keyel began.

"I don't think it's a good idea to talk about it in public," Etania interrupted.

"A wise decision," Keyel agreed. "In light of the 'incident,' your father appointed me to be your bodyguard."

"Basically, you're saying he forced you," Etania stated, rolling her eyes. "Great."

Keyel's hand gripped the sword at his hip, his blue eyes narrowing as he said, "I volunteered. Your father gave me a choice."

"Why? I don't know you," Etania wondered.

"Let's just say I was unable to protect someone I care about," Keyel stated, "and I wouldn't want him to bear that burden."

As if my father loves me that much! Etania thought grumpily. *If he did, wouldn't he be here?* She sighed, and then wondered: *Who had Keyel failed to protect?*

"So you are the first apprentice," Etania said aloud.

"You say that like there is a second," Keyel said.

"He wanted me to be his second apprentice," Etania admitted.

"That would be different."

"Well, I'm surprised a Leici is his apprentice."

"Why is that so odd?"

Keyel offered his arm so that he could lead Etania home. Heart thumping, she put her hand on his arm as gracefully as possible.

"Most Leici choose to be healers rather than warriors, because of their Neuma," Etania explained.

"I can no longer heal," Keyel said, his voice even but his eyes dark. "So I left the Leici to be useful in another way. What about you? Why don't you want to be his Apprentice?"

"I want to be a librarian, like my mother," Etania replied.

"My mother is a librarian as well."

"And your father?"

"He's not important," Keyel said gruffly.

"Oh, I'm sorry, I didn't mean to offend you."

"Don't worry about it," Keyel said. "Let's just say my father and I don't see eye to eye."

"I can relate to that," Etania added, with a little laugh.

They reached her home, where Serena was hanging clothes outside to dry. Keyel said he would return in the morning to escort her to the diplomatic meetings, and bade her goodbye.

"How'd it go?" her mother asked as Etania walked inside the house.

"How do you think?" Etania asked.

"You know your father is just trying to protect you," Tala stated.

"If that's so, then why doesn't he protect me himself?" Etania questioned.

"He had to research something first. He'll be back later tonight," Tala told her. "Besides, he has other duties. He can't be guarding you every minute like Keyel."

"You mean like hunting Skazic?" Etania said.

"And advising the king, priests, lords, and ladies."

Etania sighed. The excuses for her father were always the same, and she was tired of trying to understand them. She turned and started to ascend the stairs to her room.

"You're not going to eat dinner?" Tala asked.

"I'm not hungry," Etania replied, and she increased her pace until she was inside her room. She changed into her nightgown, curling beneath the covers. The sun was barely setting but she felt like she hadn't slept in days. As soon as her head hit the pillow, she was asleep.

MELCHIZEDEK AND ETANIA were in a large, stone room, shaped like an octagon. Everywhere she looked were windows reflecting various images in a blurred haze. In the center of the room was a stand that held a stone bowl with clear water. When she took this scenery in, Etania looked over at Melchizedek.

He stood staring into the bowl, his elbow angled under his chin. Etania walked up to his side.

"What do you see?" she asked.

"Everything," he answered, and turned to her. "What do you see?"

"Images. A blur," she replied.

Melchizedek touched the water in the bowl and said, "How about now?"

Etania stared as the water rippled, revealing a series of images. The lords and ladies, squatting behind stone bars. A dark forest, breathtaking. Keyel and herself, holding hands and leaning close to one another. Her father, holding her mother, who looked pale—was that blood? And a silver gauntlet, shining so brightly it blinded her. Etania shuddered and looked away.

"What was that?" she whispered.

"Visions of truths yet to come," he said vaguely.

He tapped the water again. The images stopped. He turned his face toward Etania and asked, "What is your decision, Etania? Shall you save Tamnarae?"

"Save? I told you before, Tamnarae is fine the way it is!" she said.

"Is it?" Melchizedek said. He reached out to touch the small scar above her eyebrow from the Skazic.

"Mom thinks I fell."

"What do you think?" he questioned, his eyes dark.

Etania avoided his gaze.

"That's what I thought." Melchizedek began. "I know you don't want to save Tamnarae. You don't think you have any Neuma, and you don't think you're chosen."

Etania looked toward the window.

"But you do have Neuma," Melchizedek added, "and you will soon know what it is. When you see the gift I have given you, I hope that you will see the truth."

"I don't have any gifts," Etania whispered.

"You only believe that because of Jakin," Melchizedek replied. "My servant is flawed, but he does care about you. Just like me."

Etania was surprised at Melchizedek. He seemed to know her innermost thoughts.

"If he cares about me so much, why did he send Keyel instead of himself? Why is he <u>never</u> home when I need him?"

"You'll have to ask him," Melchizedek said. "That is for him to tell. But I know him, Etania, just like I know you."

Etania didn't believe Melchizedek's words. "If you know me, why do you still pester me about doing something I don't want?"

"Because," Melchizedek's tone changed. "I never give up helping my people and they shall soon be in danger. Then you will have to make a choice."

"Danger? Choice?" She repeated the words as if they were foreign phrases.

"Choose to serve me and save Tamnarae or choose to do nothing and let the storm destroy everything."

"What a great choice," she bit back sarcastically.

Melchizedek was unmoved as he answered, "I know you'll make the right one."

His voice was deep and powerful. His eyes were bright and penetrating. They were etched in her mind even as they slowly faded away.

ETANIA WOKE IN HER bed, back in Tamnarae. Despite her ominous dream, she felt energized. Serena came into her room to announce that she had poured a bath for Etania. She thanked the maid and then went to the secluded part of her room that had a standing bathtub. The tub was filled with steaming water, which she sank into with a sigh. She hoped soap and warm water would wash away her memory of Melchizedek, but that was fruitless. This was especially apparent when Etania looked at her appearance in the mirror, noting the pink scar left from the Skazic's attack.

Trying to ignore her sudden uneasiness, she slid on her undergarments. As soon as she was finished, her mother entered her room with her new dress. Etania gasped at the beautiful simplicity of the gown, which was gold with filigree lining the bell sleeves, round neckline, and skirt.

"It's gorgeous!" she exclaimed.

"I agree," her mother replied, with a smile. "Bethel and Grace do wonderful work, don't they? Now, let's see you in it."

Serena assisted Etania with lacing up the dress, and Tala braided her hair. She made it so that Etania's hair covered most of the scar, despite being tied back. Then Etania put on her belt, with the sheathed dagger from her father.

"You look beautiful," Tala complimented.

"Thanks Mom," Etania replied.

Now ready, they descended the stairs and entered the dining room, where Keyel and her father were already seated, waiting for them.

"You look great," Jakin said, and Keyel nodded his agreement.

Are they really telling the truth? Do I really look like I belong with the other lords and ladies? She wondered, taking a seat next to them around the table. Her father wore a long-sleeved purple tunic and black pants tucked into matching boots. Keyel wore a green tunic like her father's, with tan pants tucked into brown boots. *Keyel's clothing compliments my own,* she realized, a blush lining her cheeks. *It's only because he is my bodyguard,* she told herself, trying to calm her nerves.

Tala sat beside Etania while Serena brought in a platter of eggs, toast, and slices of bacon. Etania cleared her entire plate quickly and gulped down her tea. Her stomach loudly protested, clenching in knots.

"What a blessed man I am! Both my daughter and my wife get to accompany me to work today!" Jakin exclaimed, rising to his feet.

"That certainly doesn't happen every day," Tala agreed with a laugh, wrapping her arm around Jakin's.

Keyel stood and offered his arm to Etania, who took it upon standing. Leaving their plates behind, they walked out the door to the street, where a horse and wagon awaited them. Jakin and Keyel helped the ladies inside the wooden coach and then joined them before Barick flicked his reins, urging the horses forward. The bumpy drive to the castle was far different than walking.

Walking was pleasant and helped Etania take her mind off the day's events. A drive to the castle was rough, jerking Etania's already unsettled stomach. She was so nervous that she barely spoke to the rest of the party, despite their journey across the bridge, past the trade district, merchant district and to the top of the hill where the castle sat. Barick brought the carriage to a stop and they stepped out, dusting themselves off after their feet hit the ground. Jakin thanked the servant and they strode back to the castle.

Once again, the portcullis was raised, and Etania stifled a wave of nausea that threatened to bring back her breakfast. *Was it really four days ago that I was attacked by a Skazic?* She wondered. Her thoughts were pulled away as Keyel took her arm again and led her away from the library she loved toward the meeting hall. On their way, they passed a storeroom, kitchen, and stables, until they reached the building that functioned as both a chapel and place of gathering. Before they could enter, Etania stopped short because another diplomat was before her: the leader of the Leici.

She was beautiful, with a petite figure and long, silver hair that flowed to her waist. She wore a long-sleeved gown that matched her blue eyes. Yet, when her eyes glanced at Keyel, she sniffed, and turned her head away. By her reaction, Etania wondered how they knew each other.

Etania's parents followed the Lady inside, where they paused in a hallway enclosed by doors, which immediately split into two directions. They took the door to the right, which led to a meeting room. In the center of the room was a long, oval table, and most of the representatives from the territories were already seated around it, conversing. Even though Etania was hidden behind her parents, her palms were sweaty and she wanted to shrink behind Keyel. When they first entered the room, some of the lords and ladies looked up at them, probably making sure that they were not King Toren or Queen Jazel. She quickly took a seat next to her mother, near the head of the table, and Keyel stood behind her, joining the other guards and servants against the wall.

Etania heard a bark and a resounding hiss. Apparently, the Eritam's wolves had met the Draconian's baby dragons. Etania shifted in her seat and gulped. A trio of trumpets sounded, and the herald spoke.

"King Toren and Queen Jazel!"

The leaders immediately ceased talking and stood behind, Etania doing so as well. King Toren and his wife entered through double doors, striding arm and arm to their seats at the head of the table.

King Toren was young, probably a mere ten years older than Etania, and his wife was five years older. Queen Jazel's pregnant belly made the royal couple's walk slower than usual as they came to their seats. She had to squat slowly to take her seat, her blonde hair falling in her face from beneath her silver crown. King Toren sat automatically, his back erect against his chair; his hands folded in front of him on the table. His brown hair was smooth under his golden crown, and his eyes were dark even with the light streaming from the stained glass windows on the right side of the room. He motioned toward the leaders, who seated themselves.

"Let us begin," King Toren said.

One of the servants brought scrolls and ink for Tala and Etania.

"Please record the date and hour," King Toren commanded.

"Yes, your majesty," Tala replied, and immediately began her transcription. Etania copied her mother's writing.

"I will start with Alphas Kayne and Sarai." King Toren pointed to the Eritam man and woman sitting by Queen Jazel. "What issues plague your lands?"

Etania glanced over at the Eritam representatives, who were the only ones dressed in furs. Their wolf companions were seated behind them so that they could glare at anyone who looked at their masters disrespectfully. Their yellow eyes, matching those of their owners, gave Etania the chills.

"My lord, as a representative of the Alphas of Eritam," Kayne began, tucking his white hair behind his ears, "I would like to discuss how the Leici have been hunting our wildlife without our permission."

"Lady Maiya," King Toren shifted his brown eyes from the Eritam to the Leici, "What is your response?"

"We deny any illegal hunting on Eritam land," Lady Maiya replied, "and are offended that the Eritam would state such things, considering the longtime peace."

"How else do you explain the sudden disappearance of deer, and carcasses picked clean of meat but whose bones are left to rot?" Alpha Sarai questioned.

"I would explain it by asserting that not all in your pack are accounted for," the Leici countered. "You have told me yourself that many have disappeared, and it is hard to keep track of them all."

"None of my pack would leave the bones! We don't waste any part of the animals we kill," Kayne argued, "And those that disappeared are traitors. They have no place in the pack!"

The wolves barked in approval. Lady Maiya's blue eyes seemed like they were sending icicles across the room. Etania shifted nervously in her seat.

"Alright, calm down everyone!" King Toren exclaimed. "Jakin, will you investigate this?"

"Yes, my king," Jakin replied.

"Is this agreeable to the Eritam and Leici?" the King asked.

The four lords and ladies nodded, and Etania and Tala scrawled down notes about this arrangement.

"Now Zeremu and Larora of Naymatua, what is your grievance?" the King continued.

The two dark-skinned Naymatua whispered to each other for a moment before one of them spoke up.

"The trees are disappearing, and we believe the Kinzoku are using the trunks for their fires," Zeremu explained.

"And Calder..." the King began.

Calder, the Kinzoku leader, was large and muscular, with bright red hair and green eyes. His fist curled and slammed on to the table as he spoke.

"We are not using the trees!" the bearded Kinzoku leader exclaimed. "We only chop wood from our own lands. It's the Naymatua that are stealing our gems!"

"Why would we need gems, Calder?" Zeremu asked. "Trees are the most valued to us. It makes more sense for you to be stealing wood to melt down your precious metals!"

"Your trees are doing fine," a Ningyo leader said. "The Eriam river is drying up and who else would need water but the Naymatua with their precious trees?"

"Adrianna, that's ridiculous," Zeremu protested.

Adrianna, the tan-skinned Ningyo woman, was not pleased with Zeremu's reply. She rose quickly, her billowy clothes flowing around her as she protested Zeremu's words. Her protests were drowned out by the other lords and ladies.

The lords and ladies used their Neuma to show their anger. The entire room bristled as plants suddenly started creeping up the wall, the metal candlesticks began to bend, and water started to float upward from the goblets on the table. Etania gulped, and seeing that her mother did not react, tried to do likewise.

"Now wait!" the King roared, sweat beading on his forehead. "You'd better not fight. If you put my pregnant wife in danger, I'll throw you in jail!"

Queen Jazel, who seemed nonchalant about a potential battle ensuing, suddenly changed moods and put a pitiable look on her face. The water splashed to the ground, the plants retreated, and the candlesticks resumed their natural state.

"That's better." King Toren smiled slightly. "We always gather once a year to resolve these matters, not make them worse. Since it seems that there are many mysteries, I would like to propose sending my Praytor with Jakin to resolve these issues. Surely, that is agreeable to all?"

There were murmurs of assent. Suddenly, there was a commotion as a bald man dashed into the room.

"My king!" he cried. "King Toren!"

Toren's eyebrows furrowed and he spat, "What is it you want? As you can see, I am in the middle of a meeting."

"It is an emergency! I have news that could change everything!" The man reached the King's side, but gasped as he saw Etania.

"It...it's you!" his yellow, slit eyes met Etania's.

Chapter Five

E tania felt a chill rush down her spine as she looked at the man. *Do I know him?* She wondered.

"This is ridiculous," King Toren said, standing. "I apologize, but I apparently need to take care of a personal matter. We will have to continue this tomorrow."

"My liege, do you need my assistance?" Jakin asked.

King Toren shook his head. Shoving the crazed man forward, he strode out of the hall with Queen Jazel following. When the royal couple left, the entire crowd buzzed with conversation.

"Who was that, Etania? Did you recognize him?" Jakin asked.

"No, I don't think so," Etania replied. She winced as a trace headache ran across her temple.

"You saw him, Jakin, he's not in his right mind," Tala replied.

"Yes, but..." Jakin began.

"I recognize that man," one of the Draconian leaders said. "He resembles one of our own Captains, doesn't he, Jonida?"

"Yeah, he looks a bit like Damien, our previous Captain of the fourth platoon," Jonida, one of the Draconian leaders, agreed.

Etania eyed the Draconian representatives, whose bright green and blue hair was a contrast to everyone's in the room. The small patches of scales on their skin made Etania afraid to ask her question.

Finally, she managed: "What happened to Damien?"

The male Draconian shrugged and replied, "He joined the Praytor."

"The Praytor?" Etania repeated shakily.

"Yes, Saigon, but it's surely a mistake," Jonida said.

One of the Ningyo turned to Jakin and asked, "What do you think, Lehrling?"

Jakin's brow was furrowed.

"I'm not sure," he said, after a slight pause. The lords and ladies groaned.

"We'll have to see what we can discover during tomorrow's meeting," Tala said, "So let's finish for the day."

Everyone murmured agreement, and then departed from the room.

"You haven't seen him before, right Etania?" Jakin asked again. Etania winced as another headache arrived.

"I-I don't know," she stuttered.

"You don't think..." Tala said. Jakin turned his purple eyes to his wife.

"What is it?" Etania asked.

"There's one person capable of making these men disappear and turning them to Skazic. And there's only one person capable of turning them into hafif—powerless humans," Jakin declared.

"Okay, you're not making any sense." Etania said. "I thought Skazic chose to be evil, turning their backs on Melchizedek."

"Yes, they do choose. But often someone comes and helps them along," Tala explained. "His name is Malstorm."

Jakin nodded glumly, and added, "Melchizedek's opposite in every way."

"But you said that there is someone capable of turning the Skazic back to normal. Is that Melchizedek?" Etania wondered.

"Yes, and no," Jakin said. "Every once in a while, he chooses someone special and gives them the Neuma to reverse a Skazic's condition by removing all their powers. That person can't save their soul, but they can be a great weapon against the Skazic. We call the people who can do that Vexli."

Etania's heart quickened.

"That crazed man confirms it. You are a Vexli," Jakin declared.

"What! No I'm not," Etania protested.

"I have to admit this confirms my theory, Jakin," Tala said, her voice stiff. "If she was attacked by the Soacronis and she changed him to the man who rushed in here..."

"He would recognize her and be alarmed," Jakin continued. "That's what I went to research in the Leici territory. Now the only problems I have are that the King seemed to know the man, and this rumor about the Praytor. I wonder why..."

"Wait, wait!" Etania said. "You're saying I'm a Vexli because that man recognized me? That's insane."

Both Tala and Jakin didn't reply for a minute, and Jakin was the first to speak.

"Both of us know what a Vexli does," he said. "We met one during the War."

"What happened to her?" Etania questioned.

"Him. He betrayed Melchizedek and was killed." Jakin replied, his voice terse. "I appointed a bodyguard because I suspected this."

"If you suspected it, couldn't you have told me beforehand?" Etania demanded. "I had a right to know."

"We want to protect you," Tala said softly. "We don't want you to be in danger again."

"This is ridiculous!" Etania exclaimed. "All of this stuff about me being a Vexli is complete hogwash! I've never met that man before, and I doubt I'm in any danger."

"That Soacronis disguised itself as a Praytor and found you in the library. You're in more danger than ever," Jakin declared.

Etania's headache grew, hammering her temples. She clenched her hands at her side.

"I've never met that man before...I don't understand. I can't be a Vexli ...I don't want to save Tamnarae. I-I-"

Her voice broke. Her head pounded. She felt tears flowing down her cheeks.

Etania stood and, with a huff, left the room. She heard her father's protests and her mother's words in blurred murmurs. Keyel followed her, keeping his distance. Then she headed to the only place she felt like she could go: the library. She rushed out of the meeting hall and entered the library doors after showing her papers to the Praytor.

The library looked just like it had the day she was attacked. The circular room with shelves of scrolls and leather bound books was unaltered. The only difference was that the room was quiet, as all the librarians had returned home for the day. Etania walked to her left, scanning the placards above the shelves, running her fingers across the ends of the scrolls, the smooth wood making noises as she passed. Before she knew it, she had arrived.

The bookshelf had been replaced, and the scrolls had been reorganized. Everything looked similar to before she was attacked. Even the floor beneath her feet was scrubbed clean. Etania shuddered unconsciously. Keyel stood nearby, observing, but Etania didn't notice him.

Is it true? She wondered. *Am I really a Vexli?* She put a finger on one of the scrolls, trying to remember. She had been reaching to pick up scrolls when she was attacked—was she bending down? Was she standing? The memory had long been a blur.

All she could recall were his cold fingers around her neck, and the thought that she was going to die if nothing happened. Was there a glow? Maybe that had been a trigger for her Neuma....She quickly put the thought aside.

Etania knelt on the stone, trying to see if there were any traces of the attack on the surface. She moved aside a rug and found a small circle of pink. Blood, her blood, had stained the tile. Another salty tear found its way to her lip. She licked it away.

How could I be a Vexli? She forced herself to run her finger against the pink stain.

I have chosen you. Melchizedek had said.

Why would he choose me?

I am no one.

Not finding her answers there, she stood and walked out of the library, making her way back home on foot.

KEYEL TRIED TO KEEP up with Etania, practically jogging as she walked out of the tower and into the courtyard, beginning the long trek home from the castle gates. Did she not notice he was there at all? He groaned. She was as impulsive as his master.

Etania walked with hardly any regard for others, making her way through the merchant district, past the craftsmen district, and out to the bridge. Jakin and Etania's fight brought back memories of his own...disagreements...with his father. Keyel's heart sympathized with Etania, but his mind reminded him of his duty. He had to protect her, even if it meant overruling some of her feelings. He jogged so that he was by her side. Just as they were walking through the last tower on the bridge and toward Nova, Etania looked up at him.

"Oh, you followed? I'm sorry Keyel," she said.

Keyel's eyes widened and he repeated, "Sorry?"

"You shouldn't have to see that. You shouldn't even be here," Etania explained.

Her words stung. How often had others told him the same? A nothus didn't belong among the Leici. Keyel gulped these emotions down to the pit of his stomach.

"My duty is with you," Keyel replied.

"What if I could release you from that duty? Would you want that?" Etania questioned.

It didn't matter what he wanted. He would protect her as long as Jakin commanded it, maybe even longer. After all that had been revealed to him about Etania, her protection seemed not only for his master personally, but for Tamnarae as well.

"My wants are of no concern," Keyel said.

"They should be considered," Etania snorted, her head tilted upwards. "You shouldn't have to guard me. I'm not a Vexli."

He smiled slightly. Even though she would hate the comparison, he could see a bit of her father in that tilt.

"What are you smiling about?" Etania snapped.

Keyel forced his face into a neutral position and was about to answer when they reached her home. Etania stopped at the doorway, her eyes piercing. She lifted the knocker and looked up at Keyel.

"You can go home now," she said simply.

Home. Keyel almost laughed at the word. Instead, he bowed from the waist down, and turned his heel on Etania. He peeked over his shoulder to see that she was ushered inside by a servant, and then increased his pace to his Master's other house. The small hut in Khartome was the nearest he could call *home.* Yet, even as he ate a solitary dinner and went to bed, he felt hollow inside. *Home* wasn't anywhere.

Not for a nothus, anyway.

JAKIN SMILED AT HIS daughter as she walked through the door, his fingers tapping beside his plate. Tala had barely kept him from leaping up and taking off after his daughter when she left the meetings. He was also restrained because he saw Keyel go after Etania and knew she would be safe. Oh, why did she have to be so stubborn? He would show her who could be the most hard-hearted! He wouldn't speak until *she* did. The silence stretched between the family members, only filled with the scrape of silverware and the crunch of vegetables. Jakin's knee moved up and down underneath the table. How long would she make him wait? At last, Etania spoke.

"I don't believe I'm a Vexli."

Jakin opened his mouth to protest. He had done the research. He knew.

"But I accept that it is dangerous for me to continue to be at the castle," Etania continued. "As such, I will only venture out with Keyel."

"I'm glad you understand that much," Jakin replied.

"I do," Etania said.

"Good. I also want you to train each morning with me," Jakin declared. "The practice area of the Praytor should be available before the meetings."

"Why?" Etania asked.

"Even though you don't believe you have powers, I do," Jakin explained. "I will show you how to use them as my second Apprentice."

"I thought I told you I don't want to be your Apprentice!" Etania said, a slight bite to her words. "But if you're not going to listen to me, then fine, I'll train under you."

"That doesn't mean you can't learn about being a librarian, too!" Tala exclaimed. "I can take some of the scrolls home."

Etania nodded, but her eyes remained dark. Jakin wondered why she didn't believe him. Shouldn't she be excited to have Neuma like him? Why couldn't he convince her? Jakin tried to observe his daughter and determine the answer.

"You can also attend the ball at the end of the week," Tala said, looking over at him.

Jakin replied, "Of course! I want to have all my girls there, and you should be well protected."

"Then it's settled," Tala declared. "I can't wait to see you in your dress." Etania gave a brief smile and stood.

"I'm going to bed," she declared.

Jakin watched her leave, questions still swirling within him about his daughter. She should be rejoicing, but instead, she looked like this was the worst news she had heard in her life.

Tala went upstairs, probably to reassure Etania. Jakin barely looked up as she did these things, new thoughts preoccupying his mind. How did the king know the Soacronis? Were the king's Praytor to blame for the recent problems?

Jakin would have to be alert. Something wasn't right.

Chapter Six

King Toren dragged the man into his keep. The keep split into three sections, with the throne room directly in front of him and two large rooms to his left and right. He strode forward, past the watching Praytor and hustling servants, while his wife hurried behind him. Toren stopped at the wall behind the thrones and lifted up the large tapestry that covered the area behind the royal chairs. Beyond it was a solid oak door, and Toren took a key from around his neck and used that to open the door. He stomped inside, where he immediately had to walk downstairs to the keep's basement. He yanked the man down the stairs and into the circular room which functioned as a prison.

"Damien, you embarrassed me in front of the lords and ladies! What is so urgent that you felt the need to burst into the meeting?" Toren censured, his voice echoing because of the empty jail cells.

"Haven't you noticed, your majesty? What's different about me?" Damien questioned. Toren scanned his soldier.

"What happened to your Neuma?" he demanded.

"*She* happened!" Damien spat. "That girl. She did something to me!"

"The Lehrling's daughter?" Toren hissed. Damien nodded.

"I had her, my king! I was about to complete your orders when her hands started glowing. When I was transformed, I fled, hiding at home until I recovered. When I felt strong enough, I came to see you immediately. Her Neuma isn't like anything I've ever seen."

"I know of it." Jazel's voice swept over King Toren like a wave.

"You do?" Toren asked.

"Yes," Jazel said. "That woman is a Vexli and she is very, very dangerous to our cause."

Toren shivered and his hands trembled.

"Go home, Damien," he commanded.

"Yes, your majesty," Damien replied, with a bow.

As he was exiting, Toren said, "And Damien..."

"Yes?"

"Do not fail me again," Toren threatened.

Damien flinched, walking away as quickly as his feet would take him. His fear fed Toren's confidence. Perhaps he had more control than he thought. He turned to his wife.

"You said that Jakin's family needed to be destroyed," Toren began. "You said we should be able to do it without using *them*, but a little girl defeated one of my soldiers."

"I didn't lie, my husband. This just complicates our plan," Jazel said calmly.

"What should we do?" Toren wondered.

"Our plan for the last night is still in place. If we can't kill her then, I have one other solution," Jazel explained.

"What's that?" Toren asked.

"It's a surprise," Jazel replied, "I promise it will make the Vexli powerless."

"Really?" he said, with a smile.

"Yes," Jazel replied confidently. Toren wrapped his left arm around her waist, and touched her belly with his right.

"Then my son will ensure our future," Toren added, "and that of a new Tamnarae."

Jazel smiled back at him and said, "Indeed."

ETANIA LAY IN HER BED, staring at the ceiling. *Why do Melchizedek and my father think I am a Vexli? They have no real evidence that I am.* Yet, even as she thought that, the memory of the glow from her fingers contradicted her thoughts.

No longer would she be able to attend the meetings. No longer could she set foot in the library. Yes, her mother would strive to teach her, but it was hollow compared to learning like a normal apprentice. All was ruined because of that man.

Although Etania didn't recognize him, she felt a shiver run through her body anytime she thought about the man who had interrupted the meeting. He looked like he knew her, and when she saw his yellow, reptilian eyes, she wondered if he was the man who had attacked her. She shivered again, and a knock interrupted her thoughts.

"May I come in?" her mother asked, and Etania nodded.

Tala entered, sitting on her bed. Etania didn't say anything, waiting for her mother to speak.

"It's not the end, you know," Tala said.

Etania didn't reply. She didn't trust her words.

"Once the meetings are over, I'm sure you can continue your apprenticeship," Tala reassured.

"You know I can't," Etania said. "Nothing can go back to normal if I'm really a Vexli."

Tala sighed.

"You may be right," she admitted. "But whatever happens, Melchizedek has a plan for you. You must trust him."

"Trust him! I barely know him," Etania retorted.

"Of course you know him, dear. We've told you stories of Melchizedek since you were a child," Tala said.

"Stories are one thing. Reality is another. Isn't Melchizedek the reason that father is gone all the time?" Etania questioned.

"Melchizedek called your father, but he doesn't dictate your father's actions," Tala explained. "I have often reminded your father that his determination to eliminate the Skazic may be off course from what Melchizedek truly wants."

"What does Melchizedek truly want?" Etania wondered.

"He wants us to spread the truth so that evil will no longer take hold of people's hearts," Tala replied, "That's why I became a librarian. There, I could preserve his stories and try to spread his truth to other people."

She looked at her daughter and questioned, "Why did you decide to become a librarian?"

"Because I wanted to," Etania answered quickly.

Too quickly. Her mother's answer was noble and true, but Etania's answer was selfish. She mainly wanted to be a librarian because it was the exact opposite of what her father desired. She swallowed hard and looked away from her mother.

"I understand that you want to escape your father," Tala said, reading her mind. "But did you ever think about what Melchizedek wants? He will answer your questions, if you ask him."

Etania knew what Melchizedek wanted for her, but she didn't agree with him.

"What if Melchizedek wants something different than what I do?" Etania commented.

"He is Deo. His purpose is better than what we want," Tala said. "If I have not made that clear from my stories, I suppose I have failed."

"You haven't failed," Etania said. "I just don't know if I can believe Melchizedek."

"Why do you doubt? Melchizedek's death and new life demonstrate his love for us and that his purpose for our lives is good!" Tala countered. "I was there, daughter. You know that your father and I witnessed his death and resurrection and his love for each of us."

Etania couldn't argue with that, so instead she asked another question.

"If Melchizedek lives, why doesn't he just guide us in person instead of in dreams?"

"We asked him the same question. First, he told us that he must leave to prepare a place for us to live when we die," Tala said. "You've probably seen Safarast in your dreams."

"I have," Etania agreed. *I've never seen any of the dead there, though.*

Tala continued, "He also told us, that in a few days, we would be Marked by him. That Mark enables all the Lehrlings and their wives to live 300 years."

She pulled down her dress so that part of her chest below her shoulder showed an outline of light in the shape of a rose.

"This is evidence that He is still with us even when we are alone," Tala said. "The Marks are not just for us, but for anyone. Since you haven't followed him, you haven't been Marked, so he appears in your dreams to communicate with you."

"So you're saying that he can talk to you if you have his Mark?" Etania wondered.

"Yes, and the Mark also assures me of his love," Tala replied.

"Love?" Etania scoffed. "No wonder he hasn't Marked me. I'm no one. Even father didn't pay attention to me until I became a Vexli."

"Ah, sweetie..." Tala began.

"It's okay Mom," Etania reassured her. "Do you mind leaving me alone? I really need time to think about all of this."

"Of course, darling," Tala said. She bent down and kissed her daughter's forehead, "I love you, and I know your father does too."

"Love you too," Etania mumbled, ignoring her mother's statement about her father.

As Tala walked out of the room, closing the door behind her, Etania contemplated Melchizedek and her father. Melchizedek had always been a story to her—until now. Now that she knew he was real, she wondered about her mother's words. *Does Melchizedek really love me?* Etania could visualize him; remember seeing him as he revealed he had chosen her. *But how, when my own father doesn't seem to love me?* Melchizedek had come to Tearah to defeat evil, so maybe he wanted to use her to conquer Skazic? After all, that's what her father had always wanted: to defeat the Skazic. Yet, her mother said that Melchizedek wanted to defeat evil through other means. It didn't make any sense. Etania only hoped sleep would put all these worries to rest.

THE NEXT MORNING, ETANIA ate a quick breakfast with her mother and grabbed her cloak and dagger, ready to go meet her father. As soon as she stepped out of her house, Keyel greeted her.

"Good morning," he said.

"Good morning. Did you already eat breakfast?" Etania asked.

"I've already eaten, thank you," Keyel replied. "What would you like to do today?"

He must not know about my father's command! This presents a great opportunity for me. Etania thought.

"How about...horseback riding?" Etania asked.

"Horseback riding?" Keyel said, considering.

Etania had always liked horses and wanted to ride. Her father had told her he would teach her, yet he never did. At least his Apprentice could complete the work. Thinking about apprentices, Etania realized that one advantage of becoming her father's second apprentice was spending time with Keyel. She smiled at the thought.

"I'm guessing by your smile that you would like to go?" Keyel ventured, and Etania nodded.

"My father keeps a few horses here in Nova. I bet we could ride one of those," she suggested.

"I have ridden them, so I think that's perfect. Follow me," Keyel declared.

Etania walked behind Keyel as he navigated through Nova until they reached the local stable. The horses lived in large corrals during the day and were brought into their individual stalls at night. A farrier's shop was adjacent to the stable, and from there, stable boys and apprentices ran from horse to farrier.

Keyel got the attention of one of the boys, who brought them two horses. One was black, with a single, white star on its forehead. The other was orange-red, with two white socks on its legs. Etania was told she would ride the black female, or mare, named Starlight. Keyel's orange horse, a chestnut gelding, was called Sunset.

The stable boy offered to saddle both horses, but Keyel insisted that they do it themselves. The Leici wanted to teach Etania the basics. They got out the brushes and Keyel guided Etania's hand, showing her how to brush in the direction of the horse's fur. With his rough hand on hers, she felt self-conscious. She was grateful when he left her on her own to finish. Then he showed her how to put on the horse's bridle and saddle.

Keyel put his hands out so that Etania could be boosted into her saddle. Unlike the countries in the east, women rode astride, which meant Etania's skirts were divided across the saddle. Starlight stirred underneath her, but Etania had a firm grip on the reins. She felt exhilarated on the horse's back, able to see above the crowd. Keyel swung himself onto Sunset.

"Okay, to start moving, tap with your heels on your horse's sides," Keyel told her.

With a gentle tap from Etania's heels, Starlight surged forward, eager to be on the road. Keyel guided Sunset beside her, and they walked the path from the village toward the woods beyond. This path wound throughout all of the territories of Southern Tamnarae and was well worn by the wheels of merchants and troubadours' carts.

"Now, to get her to go to the right," Keyel instructed, "you will be using opposite signals. Pull your reins slightly to the right and use your left leg...there you go ...now use the opposite leg ..."

As Etania experimented with her hands and legs, she felt like she was maneuvering in circles, turning every direction.

"Once you get used to commanding her at a walk, we'll have you trot and then canter," Keyel said.

"I don't know if I'm ready for anything beyond this," Etania admitted. "Where are we headed?"

"We aren't going anywhere," Keyel replied. "This path is perfect for green riders."

"Do I look green?" Etania wondered. "I feel fine."

Keyel laughed, and Etania blushed.

"No, a green rider is an expression for someone who is new!" Keyel explained.

"I guess I'm very green, then," Etania said, embarrassed.

"Maybe not," Keyel answered, "if I can get you to trot with me."

Without looking her way, Keyel clucked at his horse and kicked the gelding's sides. Sunset began trotting away, and Etania urged her horse forward. Starlight eagerly started trotting, but Etania bounced in the saddle and felt like she was losing her grip. Keyel pulled Sunset to a stop and waited until Etania did the same. She was breathless.

"Don't do that again!" Etania exclaimed.

"Why not?" Keyel said mischievously, and once again urged Sunset to a trot.

Etania took a deep breath and followed Keyel's actions. After a series of stops and trots, with Keyel shouting commands, Etania slowly got used to riding the jerking pace. They made their way back to the stables in a loop, and Keyel declared their exercise finished for the day. As he helped her down, he praised her for her skill.

"You take to riding horses like a natural!" he said. "I'm sure in a few days, you'll be able to canter."

"I don't know about that," Etania said, her face reddening.

"Sure you will." Keyel patted her shoulder encouragingly, and Etania felt like electricity trailed down her back with his touch.

They took care of the horses, put them away, and headed home. Once they arrived at the house, Etania invited Keyel to lunch, which he accepted. They chatted amiably until Priest Alfred arrived with a bunch of scrolls in his arms. He shared that it was Tala's request that Etania copy them for her while she attended the diplomatic meetings. Barick cleared the table, and they were able to unroll the scrolls and read them while Alfred fetched ink, quills, and parchment.

The scrolls were about Melchizedek and his life. They detailed how he cared for the poor and the rich, how he taught truth in every town, and how he had called the Lehrlings to be his messengers and counselors across the nations. Keyel was very familiar with the passages and answered any questions Etania posed to him. Alfred returned with the supplies and then left again. With Keyel's help reading them aloud, Etania copied down the words in her neatest handwriting.

When they finished with the scrolls, Tala arrived. Keyel volunteered to take the scrolls back to the library since he was on his way back to Jakin's house in Khartome.

"Thank you, Keyel," Tala said.

Etania thanked him, adding, "I'll walk you out."

Once they were outside, Etania looked at her hands.

"Um...Keyel..." Etania began.

"Yes?" he said.

"Thanks for 'guarding' me today. You make me feel...safe...when you're around."

This time, it was Keyel's turn to redden.

"I'm just doing my duty," Keyel admitted.

"Of course," Etania said. Keyel looked away.

"Well, good evening."

"Good evening," Etania repeated, and Keyel departed swiftly. *Did I embarrass him? I didn't mean to...* She wondered, re-entering the house. Her mind was swirling with these thoughts when she saw purple flames appear in the dining area. Before Etania could bolt toward her room, she heard her father calling her name.

"Etania, can you come here for a moment?" Jakin asked tersely.

"Yes, father," Etania said. She went into the dining room, where she was asked to sit across from her parents.

"Your father tells me that you didn't show up at the practice area this morning," Tala began.

"I went horseback riding instead. Isn't that a skill you also want me to learn?" Etania countered.

"That's not as important as learning how to hone your Neuma," Jakin said. "Besides, you also inconvenienced one of my friends. He said he waited for a full hour before giving up on you."

"Friends?" Etania asked. "Didn't you say that you would train me yourself?" *Of course he would hand off responsibility to someone else.* she thought bitterly.

"That's not the point!" Jakin said. "I wanted you to train, and I thought you agreed. Did Keyel know about this?"

"No!" Etania replied. "He knew nothing about your training."

"Because if he did, he would've marched you straight here," Jakin growled.

"Yes, because he's an honorable man," Etania spat. "One who keeps his word, unlike someone I know."

"Etania, don't be disrespectful!" Tala interfered. "Your father will keep his word. After the meetings, he will train you personally. Won't you, sweetie?"

Jakin ran a hand through his hair and said, "Yes."

"There, that's a promise," Tala said, turning to Etania. "Satisfied?"

She wasn't, but Etania wouldn't tell her mother that, so she gave Tala a nod instead. Dinner was served shortly after, and they ate in silence.

As Etania lay in bed after dinner, she tried not to think about her father's accusations. Why should she bother fulfilling her word? He never fulfilled his! He even sent someone else to train her. Yes, he did have meetings, but why would he commit to training her personally if he didn't think he could get away? Her mother always hoped Jakin would come through, but he didn't. Etania sighed. Thinking about these disappointments didn't change anything. She decided to turn her thoughts to the blond Leici with crystal blue eyes. He might be quiet and serious, but at least he was there for her...

ETANIA WOKE THE NEXT day feeling refreshed. Keyel came shortly after breakfast and took her horseback riding again. They ate lunch together once more and continued to copy the scrolls. Keyel then went home, and Etania's parents ate dinner with her.

Thus began a series of days in like manner. Each day, Etania improved in her riding. She was soon able to canter slowly, with Keyel riding Sunset by her side. Keyel's patience and dependable nature made Etania feel like he was becoming a friend. Another proof of Keyel's character was how he answered every question she asked. She also enjoyed recording the tales of Melchizedek. For the first time, she was reading the text as if it had really happened. Yet, even as her knowledge of Melchizedek grew, her doubts continued. She read how Melchizedek empowered others to do His will, but felt that there was no way he would do the same for her. Then, the night before the dance, she dreamed of Him again.

"Etania."

She heard her name distinctly, the warm whisper of HIS voice washing over her.

"Etania."

She groaned.

"What?" Etania said.

She was in the octagonal room once again, the pictures on the windows moving quickly. In the center, the water rippled in its stone bowl, and for the first time, she wondered where the water came from.

"I am the source," Melchizedek answered, reading her mind.

"How can you be the source of water?" Etania asked.

"I am the living water," Melchizedek replied. "Anyone who drinks this water will never thirst again."

Etania rubbed her temples. Did he always speak in riddles?

"What do you want?" she said. Melchizedek sighed, and his eyes looked saddened by her tone.

"I wanted to see if you'd trust me before the loss," Melchizedek said.

"What loss?" she wondered.

"You shall see. When it happens Etania, promise me that you'll come here," Melchizedek said.

"I don't even know how I got here. Don't you bring me?" she questioned.

"Yes, these times I have," Melchizedek said. "But next time, you will come to me."

Chapter Seven

Etania shook her head, rising from her bed to see sunlight streaming from the window. She wondered what Melchizedek meant. What loss would she experience? Her heart beat rapidly, but she tried to forget it as her mother came into her room to prepare her for the dance. Getting ready for such a grand occasion was mercifully distracting!

First, they went to a bathhouse, where mother and daughter soaked in rose petals and perfumed themselves. After that, they combed and styled each other's hair. Once back home, Tala sent Serena to fetch their dresses while they ate a light lunch. When the dresses arrived, Etania tried hers on first. There was a long mirror in her parents' bedroom, so Etania could see how she looked.

Her appearance seemed *older* than her age. Etania's hair was expertly woven back so that only two strands framed her face, which was tanned from riding. Her red dress had bell sleeves and a v-neck that was lined with gold filigree. The dress emphasized her hips, flaring out from a golden lace belt. She couldn't help but wonder: *Is that woman really me?*

Her mother adjusted her own dress in the mirror and Etania helped her with Jakin's necklace. The necklace, with its amethyst stone, perfectly matched the deep purple dress with black filigree that Tala wore. When Etania and both stood side by side, they smiled at each other.

"Are you ready?" her father called from the door.

"Yes we are, love," her mother answered.

At that moment, her father entered the room, dressed in a long-sleeve purple tunic that perfectly matched Tala's gown. Keyel followed, dressed in a red tunic and gold pants, similar to hers.

"What—" Etania began.

"He's here as your escort, darling," Tala said, smiling wide. Keyel came and bowed slightly to her.

"You look very pretty," Keyel said. Etania blushed.

"Th-thank you," she replied. Keyel offered Etania his arm, and she looped hers around his, trying to breathe steadily. Tala kissed Jakin on the cheek, hooking arms with him before looking back at her daughter.

"Ready?" Jakin asked.

Etania nodded and followed her parents out to the carriage, which took them to Khartome castle. They arrived as the sun was descending in the sky, and strolled through a well-lit courtyard toward the castle keep. The oak doors of the keep were flung open. Inside was a gigantic room split into three sections. Directly in front of them were the thrones, set upon a dais about three meters from the back wall draped with flags.

Keyel pulled Etania into the dining section. She stared at the long table in the center of the space, with a runner of black and white that stretched across it. Candelabra sat upon the table runner, bringing ample light to plates and silverware. The table had more than enough chairs for the lords and ladies, who were talking among themselves.

This will be an interesting night. Etania thought as Keyel escorted her to the table.

At the head of the table sat King Toren with his pregnant wife, Queen Jazel, on his right. Her father took a seat to the King's left, her mother sitting beside him. Etania sat next to Queen Jazel and Keyel was on her right. They did not have to wait long before the first course was served.

"My dear, I didn't have a chance to ask...what is your name?" the Queen questioned Etania.

"Etania, my Queen," she answered, trying to eat slowly and purposefully.

"It is a beautiful name," Jazel said. "The name reminds me of my mother's name—Lillith."

Etania wasn't sure how the queen made that connection, but she nodded politely as Jazel continued.

"My mother knew matters of the heart, and she passed that to me."

"Who was your mother?" Etania asked.

"One of the women of the court. She passed away when I was a child," the Queen said somberly. She cleared her plate just as the servants arrived with the next course.

"Do you—" Etania hesitated, thinking about how she often missed her father when she was younger.

"Miss her?" the Queen filled in her thoughts. "Not really. I enjoy my freedom with Toren. He lets me do as I wish and I let him do as he wishes. Our marriage works well that way."

Etania wondered how a marriage like that could work. Her parents were of one mind, even to her detriment. Before she could speak of it, the servants brought in dessert.

"Ah, dessert! I am craving Cook Kant's apple pie!" Jazel exclaimed.

The Queen devoured her food, whereas Etania barely ate a couple bites of the pie. With the meal finished, the King stood and announced that everyone would move to the ballroom side for the dance. He led the way across the space, with Queen Jazel by his side, and Etania's parents followed. Keyel helped Etania to her feet and they walked behind Jakin and Tala.

Etania admired the decorations in the ballroom side of the keep. Banners with Tamnarae's seal hung from the walls: a white shield against a black background with two white swords crossed over it. At the back of the space was another throne with two seats, which were lavishly backed with golden cushions. In this room, she could see several spiral staircases that led upstairs to the servants' and the royal couple's rooms. Near the throne was a small platform where musicians played a slow and inviting melody on their violins, the cello and bass filling the sound with lower notes.

"Welcome everyone," King Toren declared, opening his arms wide, "to the main entertainment! As is tradition, the Queen and I shall pick partners to dance first, and then everyone else will pick partners as well. "

After this announcement, both Queen Jazel and King Toren walked around the room. To Etania's utter shock, King Toren stopped in front of her and bowed.

"May I have this dance?" he asked, offering his hand.

Etania curtsied and took his hand. He pulled her into a slow song that sounded like someone weeping. She struggled with his rough guidance, but her feet soon remembered the paces that her father had taught her. *Why choose me?* She wondered. She didn't know whether to be honored or nervous.

"I heard," he said, "that you were attacked."

"Yes, my liege," Etania replied, goosebumps rising on her skin.

"I wonder how a Skazic was able to slip past my guards," King Toren said.

"I don't know, milord," Etania admitted.

"Well," Toren accused, "I have a source that says *you* attacked *him,* just like your father has done to my wife."

Etania leaned out of his grip in surprise, but the King drew her closer.

"My father, your majesty? What has he done to your wife?"

"He took away her inheritance," King Toren hissed, "but that is beside the point. Do you recognize the man *you* attacked? He was the man who interrupted our meetings."

"The insane man? Surely you don't believe his words over one of your subjects," Etania countered, her heart pounding.

"He is also one of my subjects," the King retorted. "Once a trusted and capable commander: now, a frightened child."

"I'm sorry to hear that, my king," Etania lied.

"Are you? Especially if you made him that way?" the King hissed.

Etania's breath caught, and she stumbled. The King caught her just as the song ended and Etania curtsied.

"Thank you for the dance, King Toren," she said, with a gulp.

The King didn't reply, but bowed his head slightly, a smile tugging at the corners of his mouth. Then he reunited with his wife, and Etania walked toward one of the servants for a glass of water. She drank swiftly, leaning against the wall. *What did the King mean by all of that?* She wondered. *My parents think the crazed man was the Soacronis who attacked me. Now the King is accusing me of attacking him. Which is the truth? If only I could remember exactly what happened...*

"Are you alright?" Keyel asked, interrupting her internal dialogue. He must have rejoined her while she was lost in thought.

"Yes, I'm fine," Etania assured him. "I just need a breath."

Keyel nodded and leaned against the wall, waiting alongside her. Having him there was like a salve to her worries, so she took this moment of rest to observe the dancers. There were many colors of outfits, like the booths at the marketplace: blue, purple, red, orange, and green. They blurred together as each person danced to the melody of the strings. Every once in a while, Etania would spot someone she recognized. Her mother and father, one of the lords and ladies, or the Queen or King would distinguish themselves. Before she knew it, several songs had passed, her glass was empty, and Keyel was asking her to dance. He bowed as he did.

"Would you be willing to dance with me?"

She curtsied, trying to keep her heartbeat steady as she replied, "Of course."

Keyel took her hand and led her to the dance floor. The melody was romantic. The peaks and valleys of the music swept them along. Keyel stepped in tune to the song, his strides elegant. He didn't speak, which made Etania wonder if he was commanded to dance with her. The music ended, and he took her to a bench as a faster song started.

"So," Etania began, "did my father force you to accompany me?"

"Force? No." Keyel replied. "As your guard, I am supposed to be by your side."

"Right." Etania sighed. *Always doing his duty,* she told herself. *Part of me wishes he wants to be beside me for more reasons than duty.*

"I'm surprised my father didn't give you the evening to rest," Etania said aloud.

"My master is vigilant," Keyel explained. "He is concerned that the dance would be the perfect time for the Skazic to attack."

"I understand," Etania affirmed, for her conversation with King Toren made her agree with her father's concerns.

"Besides," Keyel said, looking at Etania with a slight smile,"When else could I see you in that dress?"

Etania's heart beat loudly in her ears. Did he really mean anything, or was he being friendly?

"We should probably dance again before the other men ask you," Keyel commented, breaking her thoughts.

"You're not going to let me dance with anyone else?" Etania asked.

"No," Keyel stated, his blue eyes sparkling. "For tonight, you are my partner alone."

Etania tried not to construe that statement as anything other than the protection that he offered, but her imagination was already dancing at the same pace as the music.

The evening came to a close about five songs later. Some songs, Keyel and Etania danced. During other songs, they stood to the side, resting and chatting easily. When King Toren told everyone the dance was ending, Etania wondered where the evening had disappeared. Everybody began walking toward the keep doors, filtering into the throne area of the room.

"It seems I must leave you," Keyel said with a gracious bow, lowering his head to her hand. Instead of kissing it, he placed his forehead on her hand like he had at their first meeting. "It was a pleasure 'guarding' you this evening."

"And it was a pleasure being your partner." Etania curtsied in reply. Keyel lifted his head, and their eyes met. She hesitated, caught in the gaze of his striking blue eyes, before releasing his hand.

"Goodnight," she said softly, and he echoed her response. Then he turned to leave.

"Well, well!" King Toren's voice brought everyone's eyes to the thrones. Queen Jazel and King Toren were seated upon them, looking like they were about to command the dancers to leave, rather than dismiss them as pleasant hosts.

"I have one more surprise for you before we end the evening!" King Toren declared.

He motioned with both of his hands, and that was when they heard marching. Row by row, Praytor in gleaming armor came into the room, circling around the lords and ladies and guests. Some took positions right by Toren, blocking him and his wife.

"I thought this dance was a great idea!" Toren snarled. "Not only is it fitting to celebrate the old ways one last time, but all of you are unarmed."

Keyel pushed Etania behind him and retorted, "Unarmed but not defenseless!"

King Toren motioned and the soldiers lowered their swords, forcing the group of lords, ladies, and guests to gather closer together.

"What are you doing?" a shrill voice asked, and Etania saw her mother walk toward the King.

"T-tala—" Jakin stuttered as he tried to stop her.

"I'm capturing all of you, of course!" Toren declared.

"Why?" Tala asked, surprised.

"Your husband knows why," King Toren answered, "and these lords and ladies are guilty by association with him. Now I will be more powerful than all of you, and create a new Tamnarae!"

"This is wrong, Toren," Jakin said. King Toren met the Lehrling's gaze.

"What is wrong? What is right?" he questioned. "For now, I will ask you to decide: surrender or die."

"We would rather die!" Kayne spat, and the Eritams' wolves growled with him.

"So would we!" Saigon the Draconian agreed.

Before anyone else could protest, Toren pointed toward the crowd of lords and ladies. The Praytor pounced. Chaos erupted as men and women scrambled to flee the attacks of the Praytor. Keyel gripped Etania's hand, pulling her toward the keep doors. She resisted him.

"My parents," she said. "They're—"

"They'll be fine! My Master will see to that," Keyel retorted. "My duty is to get you out of this room without being harmed."

"I don't care what your duty is! I'm not leaving until I know my parents are safe!" Etania protested, pulling away from him and pushing to the center of the room.

Purple fireballs flew over her head. The Naymatua caused trees to spring from the ground, bursting through the keep's stone floor. Vines also came with them, whipping around. Water from the Ningyo surrounded the Praytor, trapping them until they were unconscious from drowning. The Eritam's wolves growled, attacking the Praytor, while the Draconians' baby dragons bit at the legs of the soldiers. Calder, the Kinzoku leader, used his Neuma to bend some swords and shields, leaving a few Praytor unable to attack. Although unarmed, the Neuma of the lords and ladies was not to be underestimated.

Etania climbed over this root, dodged under that vine, and headed toward the glowing purple fire she knew belonged to her father.

At last, she reached her parents, who were in the middle of the room. Her dress was torn, and parts of her hair were singed. Yet, she was relatively unscathed. Her heart pounded loudly in her ears, and she let out a breath she didn't know she was holding. Keyel had followed her without her knowing, so he joined Etania and her parents. They made it! King Toren observed all from his throne, and as the lords and ladies put up more of a fight, he motioned again.

To the shock of the crowd, the Praytor transformed. Some started throwing black-and-green fire from their hands, which melted anything it touched. Some turned into wolves and some to lizards, ripping out of their armor as fur or scales grew. Others became rock or jewel golems, stone figures that shook the ground with each step. With these new powers, the lords and ladies were quickly suppressed. Maiya, Jonida, and Adrianna were injured and captured. Kayne, Sarai, and Zeremu were killed, and the leader of the Kinzoku, Calder, was on his own against three soldiers.

Saigon, Etania, Keyel, Tala, and Jakin attempted to rescue the ladies, but the soldiers prevented them. Soon, their backs were against the closed door of the keep. The Skazic growled and grunted, about to leap upon them, when King Toren spoke to his horde. He glared at Etania.

"Capture everyone else," he shouted, "but make sure you kill Etania!"

The Vexli was so alarmed by the King's words she didn't have time to ponder why he would target her. The Skazic attacked all at once, but they were stopped suddenly by a wall of purple fire. Etania looked over to see her father's entire body covered in violet flames.

"Etania," her mother hissed, "Take my hand!"

She obeyed, her hand trembling as she grasped her mother's.

"You idiots!" King Toren snapped. "Throw your weapons through the fire or shoot arrows at them!"

"Time's up!" Jakin said with a confident grin. "I'll need you all to link hands with me, please."

Keyel took Etania's hand and her father took her mother's hand. Saigon joined hands with Tala, and the flames shifted. Instead of purple flames blocking the Skazic, they whirled around like a tornado, lifting them up.

"Fire!" King Toren shouted.

Etania watched an arrow fly through the air, straight toward her chest.

"No!" her mother exclaimed, pulling Etania behind her like a whip.

The arrow hit her mother right before the storm of fire swept them away from Toren and the Skazic.

Chapter Eight

King Toren glared at the spot where Jakin and his family had disappeared from. He stood, seeing a candelabra near him. He threw it down on the ground in frustration, cursing aloud. He had no clue where Jakin could've teleported to, and he was frustrated that his prey had escaped. His horde of Skazic trembled beneath his gaze, but Jazel placed a hand upon his arm.

Her reassuring touch cleared his head, and he turned to the soldiers before him.

"Take the lords and ladies to prison, and clean up this mess!" he demanded.

The Skazic quickly obeyed, escorting Toren's new captives to the prison that was underneath the keep. They used the door behind the thrones to do so. Other Skazic dragged the bodies of the dead lords and ladies to be burned. One Skazic approached his throne, and Toren recognized him as Damien, the first Skazic the Vexli had changed.

"My liege," he said, kneeling.

"What is it?" Toren snapped.

"One of my brethren has informed me that his arrow struck true. At least one of the escapees will die," Damien explained.

Toren smiled. "Thank you, Damien, for being brave enough to give me this information. If one of them is hurt, then Jakin won't teleport far."

"This is good news," Jazel agreed.

"Yes," Toren said. He turned to the Skazic, who were now done with their tasks and awaiting orders. "Tear Khartome apart, and once you are done searching the city, go to the mainland. They won't escape my grasp!"

The Skazic howled, barked, and growled in response. Within moments, they dispersed, Damien joining them in the search for Jakin and his companions. The citizens of Khartome knew nothing, and King Toren planned on keeping it that way. He planned on telling them the following morning of the council's "betrayal" and how the lords and ladies tried to kill him. They would realize that their benevolent leader, King Toren, had sent his "Praytor" to apprehend the escaped prisoners. Very soon, the captive lords and ladies would be forced to send out letters asking for surrender to the territories. Then, Toren would have absolute power over Tamnarae.

He smiled at the thought.

JAKIN HELD HIS WIFE tightly in his arms, cradling her on their living room floor. Her body felt so fragile, the energy slowly fading from it. She gasped, trying for breath as the blood stained her dress. The wound from the arrow. If only he could pull it out, stop it from bleeding! He reached for it, but Tala's hand stopped him.

"I'm sorry," Tala said.

"What for?" Jakin asked, his hand smoothing the wisps of hair surrounding her face.

"For leaving you first," she replied.

Jakin couldn't answer that. He merely said, "Then don't."

She smiled weakly, the tips of her lips curling up. He wanted to kiss her, reassure himself that she wasn't dying—but he couldn't.

"Where's Etania?" she asked hoarsely.

"I'm here," Etania said, kneeling by her mother's side and holding her hand.

"You are loved, Etania." Tala whispered. "You'll see why Melchizedek chose you to be a Vexli soon."

"What do you mean?" Etania said, voice breaking. "You're not leaving, are you?"

"I go...to meet Melchizedek...I'm sorry..."

Tala's voice faltered, and she looked at Jakin first and then Etania, her lungs barely filling with air. Jakin's heart wrenched in his chest. Surely, this wasn't real, this couldn't be real. Didn't Melchizedek say she would be able to live for as long as he did? Weren't they supposed to spend their entire lives together? He didn't understand. He wouldn't accept it.

"I wanted—" Tala's eyes glazed, and she wheezed, "To spend more time with you two..."

She didn't say anything else. Her chest had stopped moving.

"Mom!" Etania shook her mother.

"Tala!" Jakin screamed.

Jakin and Etania sobbed, their cries unified.

KEYEL STOOD SILENTLY, watching the familial scene as if it was a dream instead of reality. Was Tala truly gone? The sobs of his friend and Master were evidence that she had died. Yet, his failure stabbed deeper than any sympathetic grief he had for them. For the one who *should* have died was him.

His duty was to die for Etania. His Master had asked him to protect her at all costs. Here he stood, living and breathing, while his friend's mother and Master's wife died from his mistake.

He wanted to curse himself, punch the air, or do anything to find a fitting punishment for the grief he was responsible for inflicting upon them. But he could only stand, watching silently as his friend and Master sobbed for the loss of someone so dear.

Logic broke Keyel's stillness. He could do nothing about her death, but he could do something about her burial. He dashed out of the house, his steps taking him toward the chapel where Priest Alfred resided.

"Come quickly," he told the Priest. "Tala is dead."

"Dead? How?" the Priest exclaimed.

"The King...he betrayed us..." Keyel stuttered. "He killed her...we must bury her..."

Keyel's words were barely coherent, but the Priest followed him back to Jakin and Etania's house.

When Keyel returned, he found his Master and Etania still in the same place. They were no longer crying, but whimpering, holding Tala's body with a cold grip. Saigon stood respectfully to the side, and Barick and Serena wept openly.

"Master," Keyel began softly, "We must surrender her to the priest."

"Priest?" Jakin repeated the words, his eyes clouded.

"I am here, Jakin," Priest Alfred said. "I can find someone to prepare her for burial."

"Alfred," Jakin said, "Why did Melchizedek allow this?"

"I don't know, friend." Alfred placed his hand on Jakin's shoulder. "But it is time."

"Yes, Master, you must let her go," Keyel explained. "Toren's forces will be scouring Khartome for us, and Nova is the next logical place."

"Oh," Jakin said.

He looked down at his wife's lifeless eyes and back up at Keyel. Two tears slid down his cheeks.

"You may take her," Jakin whispered.

Etania was harder to remove. Keyel pried her fingers slowly and gently from Tala's. Once released from her mother, she bent down and removed the necklace from Tala's neck. She gripped it with white knuckles, choking down a sob as Priest Alfred took the body to be prepared for burial.

Once he was completely gone, Etania collapsed into a chair in the living area, her father joining her in another seat. Barick and Serena, still sniffling, saw that Jakin and Etania's clothes were soiled, and said they would try to prepare baths. Saigon also found a chair, his head held in his hands. Keyel had almost forgotten about the Draconian.

"I imagine you can rest here," Keyel replied. "I plan to myself."

"How can I?" Saigon said, lifting his face so that his tears were evident. "My wife is imprisoned, half the lords and ladies are dead, and King Toren has an army of Skazic!"

Saigon's sudden outburst echoed in the small room. He winced at the sound.

"I'm sorry," Saigon said, "so sorry."

Keyel didn't know how to reply to that. The man's apologies echoed the sentiments in his own heart. Suddenly, Saigon stood, wiping away his tears.

"I have my dragons," he said. "I will take them and ride to my people. They will surely come to our aid and rescue my wife and the others."

"Wait," Keyel said, and the Draconian leader paused at the doorway. "I believe it would be best if you help us plant a rumor that we have travelled with you to Draconia instead of going to our next destination."

"How can I do that?" Saigon wondered.

"There are several wooden dummies that the locals use as target practice. Take them, and have them pretend to ride your dragons," Keyel said.

"I will. In fact, I shall make a show of it," Saigon said, and turning to Jakin, asked, "Why aren't you coming with me? It would be easier to be in Draconia than anywhere else."

"We must—" Jakin stumbled over his words. "The Draconians can't take the castle and King Toren's army alone. We must recruit other allies. When we reach your territory, we will hopefully have enough armed forces to march against the King."

Saigon's brow furrowed as he answered, "I understand. We will wait for you in Draconia, Lehrling." With that statement, he left the room.

"Master," Keyel said.

"Yes?" Jakin asked.

"I believe you two should rest briefly, attend a small funeral, and then leave. We probably have four hours at the most before the King decides to search Nova, even with Saigon's deception," Keyel replied.

Jakin nodded slowly, keeping back tears. "I will leave that in your hands."

"It will be done," Keyel agreed.

"Take the money that is in the chest at the foot of my bed and use it to buy supplies," Jakin added, "We will need horses, travel clothes, weapons, and food."

"Yes, Master," Keyel said, bowing slightly to him.

"Thank you, Keyel," Jakin replied. "You are a faithful and loyal apprentice."

Keyel's ears burned with the compliment. *I don't deserve such praise.* He thought. When Barick and Serena announced the baths were ready, Keyel took it as a cue to find the requested items. Jakin and Etania would need the time alone to digest what had happened and wash away the blood.

Blood that would never disappear from Keyel's heart.

ETANIA DIDN'T SAY A word as she changed out of her tattered clothes and washed the blood—her mother's blood—from her body. Tears mixed with the water in the tub until she was finished. She dried herself and then reached for the nightgown Serena fetched for her. Changing quickly, she collapsed on the bed, knowing she had only an hour of rest before they would be on the road.

She felt the coolness of the necklace against her hand before she put it on the nightstand. As the silver and purple mixed with the moonlight, Etania remembered her mother's delight at receiving the gift from Jakin. She would never see that smile again. She pulled the covers over her head, tears drying on her pillow as she cried herself to sleep.

Etania stood in Melchizedek's castle garden. The flowers stood in stone planters, and the floor beneath her was made of golden tiles. Inside the planters were white lilies, pink carnations, purple chrysanthemums, and crimson rose bushes. Her mother's favorite flowers.

"These are for your mother's death, and her new life," Melchizedek said, appearing by her side.

"New life?" Etania scoffed.

"You shall see," Melchizedek said.

"I'll see what?" Etania questioned. "You said I would suffer a loss but gave me no details. You seem to 'see' many things but refuse to share them with me. Why is that?"

"Some things are beyond your understanding," Melchizedek explained. "Other things are the result of evil."

"Like King Toren?" she asked.

"Yes. But I think you are really wondering: am I responsible for your mother's death?"

Etania averted her eyes from the penetrating glance of Melchizedek. Who did she blame for her mother's death? Who was really responsible?

Technically, the soldier who obeyed Toren's orders to kill was the one responsible for her mother's death. But her decision to reject her powers also prevented her from making the man powerless to kill. Then, there was Toren, whose evil intentions contributed to the order. The blame was never clear cut.

"Could you have stopped it?" Etania asked. "You are all-powerful, aren't you?"

"I am," Melchizedek said. "Yet, if I stopped evil and made everyone good, would that truly be good? Would not everyone be without choice, merely pawns of my will?"

Etania hadn't considered that.

"I have given everyone a choice to follow me, including King Toren," Melchizedek continued, "But just like you, they have rejected following me."

The words "just like you" slapped Etania's heart like a stinging barb.

"Can I...can they...still follow you?" she asked, her voice a small whimper.

Melchizedek lifted Etania's chin, forcing her to look into his deep, warm eyes.

"Of course," Melchizedek said. "Would you like to trust me? Trust in my purpose and will for you?"

"I—" Etania met his eyes, the warmth and love washing over her. Why did she still cling to a dead hope that life would be normal, that she was normal? Because she felt...unworthy... to be called a Vexli. If her father had never bothered to see her, why would Melchizedek?

"I can't—" she admitted, and she turned and fled from his presence.

Etania woke after Serena's hand on her shoulder gently roused her from a nap. She stretched, stiff, making her way to a basin of water that sat on her vanity. She rinsed her face and wiped away the tears with a towel. Then, she braided her hair, slipped out of her nightgown and into undergarments, put on her mother's necklace, and tucked the heart amulet under her shirt. From her wardrobe, she chose a black dress, especially designed for mourning. She rarely wore the silk dress and never thought she would be using it so soon to attend her mother's funeral. Serena laced up her dress and Etania descended the staircase, where Keyel and Jakin were waiting for her. They too were dressed in black, creating a melancholy air as they escorted her to the funeral.

The funeral was in the graveyard by the church, and only Grace, Priest Alfred, and his wife were in attendance. Yet, Etania felt like she was watching actors portray roles in a play. She heard Alfred's wife sing about loss, the melody not stirring her heart. She listened as Alfred and Grace expressed their sympathy. Yet, she felt nothing—not even when her father gave a speech on how her mother would be missed. Not even when he cried.

She just sat, stiffly, watching while everything whirled around her. She was so grateful for Keyel's presence by her side, his hand resting on her shoulder. He didn't speak and he didn't offer any sympathy. He was an actor, just like her, in the play that had no name but Grief.

They were going to nail her mother's casket shut. Etania looked one last time at the pale, lifeless face of her mother. Her brown hair framed her face beautifully. Seeing that look, perfectly preserved, broke the façade. Etania knelt and wept.

She felt warm arms around her shoulders—her father's arms. Jakin's purple eyes echoed her own. Wrapped in her own suffering, she hadn't seen that her father was suffering too. Etania leaned her head into her father's chest. This was the first time she felt the same emotions as her father.

They stayed that way as her mother's casket was lowered into the ground and the last of the dirt covered it entirely. A gravestone, already etched, read:

Here lies Tala Selali.
Encouraging Wife.
Loving Mother.
She will be missed.

The last four words, "she will be missed," echoed in Etania's mind while they walked home. When they arrived, Barick and Serena prepared food, but no one wanted to eat. Jakin was the first to speak.

"Did you get the supplies we need, Keyel?" Jakin asked.

"Yes Master," Keyel replied.

"Supplies?" Etania echoed. She could remember, vaguely, something about needing supplies. However, her heart had been so consumed by grief; she only understood that she could rest a little before they had to leave.

"Yes, we have a long journey ahead of us," Jakin said.

"Where are we going?" Etania wondered.

"Calques, the Leici capital," Jakin declared. "I believe they will be the most receptive to joining our rebellion."

"I thought you told me I didn't have to go back there," Keyel countered.

"You're right, I told you that you have a choice in the matter," Jakin agreed. "Would you like to travel to the Eritam, our next stop after Calques, on your own?"

Keyel looked down and admitted, "No, Master. I couldn't do that. I have a duty to protect your daughter."

"Protect me?" Etania repeated. "My mother protected me, and look what happened to her!" *And I don't want the same thing to happen to you,* Etania added in her head.

"That should've never happened." Keyel assured her. "I failed to protect you like she did."

"You aren't to blame for my wife's death. King Toren is, and I will see to it that he is punished!" Jakin said.

"How am I not to blame, when I am the one who should've died to protect Etania?" Keyel argued.

"The Skazic killed Tala, and they are controlled by King Toren." Jakin's eyes flashed, warning Keyel to not argue. Keyel looked away, and Etania felt like that wasn't the end of the discussion.

"Speaking of protection: although I will protect Etania and so will you, she needs to learn how to protect herself," Jakin said. "I believe that you should teach her to use the crossbow and the knife. Both are good weapons to learn for beginners."

"Yes, Master," Keyel said.

Etania felt a tremor run through her. *I will learn how to use real weapons? Weapons that could kill?*

"I will train her in using Neuma," Jakin added. Etania's stomach clenched at that statement.

"King Toren targeted you for a reason, Etania," Jakin explained. "He knows you're a Vexli, and he wants to make sure that your powers aren't used to turn the tide of the war."

As much as she hated to admit it, Etania agreed with her father. King Toren had chosen her as a dance partner when he could've chosen anyone else. So, he must believe that the bald man was the one Etania changed, even if Etania doubted she had that ability. A part of her still hoped that King Toren, her father, and Melchizedek were wrong about her Neuma, but a voice within contradicted her doubts.

"Do you understand?" Jakin asked.

"Yes," Etania agreed.

"Then it's settled. We ride now," Jakin replied.

Etania's stomach flipped. *So quickly?* She looked around the dining room, considering its simple furnishings. Soon, all of this would be gone, replaced by the open road and the great unknown.

Chapter Nine

Keyel handed Etania some clothes and a saddlebag. He told her to pick a few more items to pack. Etania lugged the clothing upstairs, only looking at it fully when she put the items on her bedspread. There was a mail hauberk that reminded Etania of the danger she was about to face. Then, there were two tunics, two leather riding pants, a gambeson, and a split skirt.

Etania considered the choices and looked in her wardrobe. Most of her dresses were for running errands, working, or studying. There was still her dress from her visit to the council of lords and ladies, but she doubted she would need that. She chose two of her brown work dresses and stuffed them into her bag.

She changed out of her black dress and considered the items on the bed. She first put on the riding pants and gambeson, a padded undershirt. Then, she lugged the mail hauberk over her head, suppressing a groan. The short-sleeved hauberk had to weigh at least twenty pounds, cut off at her waist. She pulled the tunic over the top of it. Then, she pulled on her riding pants and the split skirt over it. She strapped on her belt, putting the knife in its sheath so it was on her side. Lastly, she put on socks and laced up her boots.

A quick glance in the mirror made her uncomfortable. She looked like some kind of mercenary. She didn't know how to use her knife, and the mail weighed heavily upon her. She wasn't a warrior, let alone the Vexli her father and Melchizedek expected.

She couldn't help but wonder, however: *what if I embrace this image?* Maybe she could become what they expected. She could prove to Melchizedek, Keyel, her father, and herself that she could be a Vexli. She folded everything into her bag and shouldered it. Casting one last glance at her room, she turned away and descended the stairs.

Keyel and Jakin were waiting for her. Both of them wore a gambeson, mail and tunic over their chests. They also wore leather riding pants tucked into tall boots. Etania's father carried a hammer against his back and Keyel carried a shield against his, a sword sheathed at his hip. They both carried, rather than wore, their saddlebags.

Jakin and Keyel walked outside of the house, Etania barely had time to give a cursory glance to the place. So much of her life was changing in so short of a time...

"We'll take care of it, Lady Etania," Barick assured her as she hesitated in the doorway.

"Indeed we will," Serena agreed.

Etania nodded in acknowledgement and turned away, closing the door behind her. When she saw the horses they would be riding, she felt slightly better.

"Starlight!" she exclaimed, running up to the black mare and petting its forehead. The horse nickered in response and Keyel chuckled. He held the reins of Sunset.

"I figured you would want the horse you learned to ride on," Keyel said. Etania looked over at the Leici.

"Thank you," she said.

"You're welcome," he replied.

They paused a moment, eyes meeting, hearts pounding.

"Give me your saddlebag," Jakin commanded, breaking the moment.

Etania handed the bag to him and watched as he secured it and the other saddlebags to the fourth horse in their party. He also secured another weapon to the horse—a crossbow.

"Is that what I think it is?" Etania questioned.

"Yes, that is what I will be training you to use," Keyel explained. "It's an easy weapon to learn and effective for long-distance fighting."

"What about close fighting?" Etania wondered, trying to keep a tremble from her voice.

"That won't happen," Keyel replied, a slight edge to his tone. "I will keep the enemy from getting that far."

At Etania's look of uncertainty, Jakin spoke up.

"The dagger," he reminded.

Etania gave a brief nod, feeling like a snake had coiled in her stomach. She turned back to Starlight.

"Could you, uh, help me up?" she asked Keyel.

He agreed, folding his hands so she could use them as an extra stirrup to get on the tall mare. Jakin was already squeezing his horse and urging the pack horse forward, not waiting for the pair. Etania allowed herself to be hoisted into position.

"You know, you're different from my father," Etania said.

"How so?" Keyel asked.

"You're...dependable," Etania answered. Keyel chuckled.

"My master may be flighty, but when he is present, he is wise. Don't you agree?"

Etania shrugged and replied, "What good is wisdom if it is never shared? Everything I learned was from my mother." She bit her lip, trying not to cry at the mention of Tala.

"Your mother was a good woman," Keyel quickly said. "I never got a chance to say that I'm sorry she's gone."

"It's okay. I could feel that you were sympathetic. You took care of everything when my father and I were at a loss. Thank you." Keyel shifted uncomfortably.

"You're welcome," he mumbled, turning to get on his own horse.

He bade Etania to move forward so that Starlight was between her father's horse and Sunset. Etania did so, looking over her shoulder at her childhood home. She bit back tears once again and tapped her heels on the horse's sides.

Starlight followed her father's horse, both animals happily trotting along the well-kept path through Nova and into the forest beyond. They passed by cabins with small cleared areas, but as they ventured further into the forest, the cabins lessened. The path continuously moved upward as the trees thickened, closing their small party within dark branches. There were so many twists and turns on the road that Etania felt a bit woozy.

Etania was glad to slide out of the saddle at noon, feeling sore. They hobbled their horses and allowed them to graze nearby as they sat down to lunch. The trio was picnicking on a small peak, overlooking the valley of Nova and the forest they had just passed. The view gave Etania room to breathe, sweeping away prior dizziness. As she considered the panoramic landscape, she wondered at its beauty—the tall pine trees, the glittering lake in the distance.

My mother would've loved this, Etania thought, two tears sliding down her cheeks. She tried not to sob as they finished their lunch. Then they rode again, journeying farther and farther into the forest. When the sun began to set, they came to a stop. At that moment, they were approached by a group of Leici.

All of them had long, blonde hair that was tied back. They wore blue or green outfits, depending on their eye colors. At their hips, they carried long swords sheathed in leather scabbards. Yet, none of them compared to the man in the center. He had silver-blonde hair that was tucked underneath a crown woven of branches. The clothing he wore was more gold than green, whereas his eyes were a sharp blue. He didn't wear a sword, but stood with his hands behind his back. Just by looking at him, Etania knew he was the Lord of the Leici.

"Son, I am glad to see you," he said, looking straight at Keyel.

Etania tried not to gape at Keyel. *If he was related to the Lord, why wouldn't he sit by the Lady or speak to her at the meetings? Why would he become her father's apprentice?* These questions sped through her mind.

"Let us take care of your horses," Lord Thandor said. The trio dismounted, and the Leici took their horses into the darkness of the woods.

"I am not your son, Lord Thandor. I am Keyel Evant, son of Shayna Evant," Keyel said, and then bowed.

Lord Thandor let out a long sigh.

"Yes, of course," he said, and turned his piercing gaze to Jakin and Etania. His blue eyes looked like Keyel's, now that Etania thought about it.

"Lehrling Jakin, this is unexpected," Thandor said. "Who is this by your side?"

"I am Etania Selali, daughter of Jakin," Etania replied and curtsied.

"Welcome, Etania," Thandor said.

"Why are you near the gates, Lord?" Jakin questioned, "since the center of Calques is further away?"

"I wait for my wife to return," Thandor responded. "She was supposed to ride back here yesterday."

"Yes, about that..." Jakin began. Before he could say anything further, a woman's voice was heard.

"Keyel?" she said, making her way forward to them. Thandor paled and gave the woman a wide berth as she came and embraced Keyel. Keyel smiled as he hugged the petite woman, whose silver-blonde hair was tucked behind her ears.

"Hello, Mother," he said, smiling.

"Excuse us, Keyel," Jakin said. "I believe we need to tell the Lord why we are here first."

"Of course, Master," Keyel replied, giving Jakin a quick bow of his head and backing away.

Etania's head spun from all the facts she was receiving about Keyel. If she understood correctly, Lord Thandor and Shayna had an affair in the past, and Keyel was a result of their union. No wonder Keyel didn't associate with the Lady!

"Yes, what is this about my wife?" Lord Thandor asked, still keeping his distance from Shayna.

"She is well," Jakin told him. "But I believe it would be best to tell everything behind closed doors."

"Then I will take this opportunity to leave," Shayna said. "However, I would like to offer my home as shelter for the Lehrling and his daughter. Is that alright with you, Lord?"

Thandor didn't meet Shayna's gaze but nodded as he said, "I will send servants to bring the knapsacks to your house."

"Sounds good," Shayna agreed, and looking at Keyel, added, "You know where to find me." She curtsied to Thandor and walked to the east, heading to her home.

Chapter Ten

Lord Thandor led Jakin, Etania and Keyel onto a wide path surrounded by large trees. They were so tall that they crowded the sky. The only light came from the myriad of lanterns hanging from branches and they came to the first "house" after a few meters. Built on a platform, each Leici house surrounded the trunk of a single tree. Sometimes, the house would be in parts, with a single bedroom near the foot of the tree, a ladder winding its way up to another bedroom near the middle of the tree, and another ladder to the third bedroom near the top. There were large, swinging ladders between the trees that acted as bridges from one house to another.

Eventually, they came to a stop at a tree in the middle of other tree houses. It was wider than the other trees, and the house at the very top was large. Three ladders hung from the edge of the porch above.

"After you," Lord Thandor said.

I have to climb? Etania thought nervously. Keyel went first and Etania followed. The mail hauberk Etania wore made climbing slow and difficult. When she reached the top, Keyel put out his hand and hauled her onto the platform. There, they were able to stand side by side and look out at the forest. From this viewpoint, Etania could see the tree houses, lit by lanterns, for kilometers around them. The lights blinked like small stars in the forest glade.

"This is just a small part of Calques?" Etania wondered.

"Yes," Keyel replied, "but the farther you go, the closer you get to the center of Calques, where you'll find even more Leici."

"Wow," Etania said, "I had no idea the Leici lived like this!"

"You have much to learn, Etania," Jakin said, breaking their conversation. Etania looked down. *I know, but why do you remind me?*

"Now that everyone is here, let's go inside," Lord Thandor declared.

They followed Thandor into a round room with a circular table that surrounded the trunk of the tree that held the house. There were chairs made of wood lining the table and a young woman with brunette hair and blue eyes was seated at the table already. A Leici man stood behind her, his hand rested casually on his sword, a bored expression on his face. Thandor beckoned them to be seated.

Keyel's confident steps were stilled as he looked over at the young woman. Etania glanced between him and the woman, wondering what was going on. Jakin alone was unmoved.

"This is my daughter, Adeline. She is the future leader of the Leici after her mother," Thandor introduced.

Ah, Etania realized, *Adeline is Keyel's half-sister. But why does he seem so nervous, suddenly?*

"Good to see you again, my lady," Jakin said. "This is my daughter, Etania. You already know Keyel."

"Nice to meet you," Adeline said, inclining her head politely toward Etania. She turned to look at Keyel. "I'm glad to see you as well."

Keyel nodded stiffly and they took their seats around the table. Keyel, Etania noted, took a seat furthest away from his half-sister.

"What news is so grave, Lehrling, that we must be indoors?" the Lord asked.

"King Toren created an army of Skazic," Jakin began. "He captured your wife, as well as a dozen other lords and ladies."

"How do you know this?" Thandor asked.

"We were at the ball when it happened. We barely managed to escape with our lives. My wife..." Jakin choked on his words, unable to complete the sentence.

"I'm sorry for your loss," Adeline said, and Etania swallowed her tears at the woman's compassionate statement.

Thandor was more practical. "How large is this army?"

"I don't know," Jakin confessed. "We only saw a third of his soldiers, but it seems that most of the Praytor are actually Skazic."

Thandor groaned, slumping in his chair.

"What do you suggest we do?" he asked. "We are healers, not warriors. Only my guards know how to use a bow or sword."

"Then you need to train more soldiers," Jakin commanded. "We will go to the other territories and convince them to help."

"The other territories won't cooperate," Thandor said, with a shake of his head. "Our alliance with our nearest neighbor, the Eritam, is tenuous at best. I've heard rumors that the Ningyo, Kinzoku and Naymatua have been bickering as well. How do you expect us all to work together?"

Jakin shrugged, and with an easy smile said, "I'll convince them. But it would help if I had one leader in agreement with me."

The Lord ran a hand through his silver hair. Adeline reached over to place her hand over Thandor's own. Keyel bristled in his chair next to Etania.

"Do you really think we can get my wife back?" Thandor asked.

Jakin met Thandor's and Adeline's gazes steadily.

"Yes," he answered.

Lord Thandor sighed.

"I'll trust you, then. Just like I trusted you'd bring my son back to me."

"I'm not your son, and I'm not back!" Keyel snapped.

Adeline flinched in her chair, and Etania felt compassion for the woman. *What had happened that made Keyel ignore her?* Etania wondered.

"At least you're here long enough for me to see you," Lord Thandor said softly. "I understand why you don't want to associate with me, but I am your biological father, whether you like it or not."

Keyel didn't reply, but looked away. The Lord sighed again and Jakin glanced at Thandor and Adeline expectantly. Adeline nodded and Thandor spoke.

"I agree to support you with my men. I know the soldiers will put down their lives for the right cause, but I wish I had some hope to give them. Do you have a plan?"

"We will gather allies and meet near Khartome," Jakin said. Glancing over his shoulder at Etania, he added, "I also have a secret weapon."

Etania shuddered at the word "weapon," wondering if she could really embrace that role.

Thandor arched his eyebrow at Jakin.

"Whatever you say, Lehrling. Where should I send my men?" he questioned.

"To Nova, in five to six months," Jakin replied. "That should give us plenty of time to let the others know of our plan."

"And plenty of time for me to train more soldiers," Thandor said grimly.

"We will need healers as well as fighters, my lord," Jakin said, rising from his seat. "I thank you for your support."

"You're welcome. Until next time we meet," Thandor said, offering his hand to Jakin. Jakin took it, and they locked wrists and bowed slightly to one another. He did the same for Adeline, who responded in kind.

"Melchizedek bless you on your journey," Thandor said.

"May he watch over you as well," Jakin replied.

"Thank you for your time, Lehrling," Adeline added.

Jakin nodded in acknowledgement of the female Leici, and Etania and Keyel stood. The Leici guards began to escort them out of the room.

They were at the doorway when Thandor said, "May I speak to you for a few moments, Keyel?"

Keyel stiffened, but nodded. The guards started walking outside of the room, expecting them to follow.

"Come on, Etania," Jakin said. "Keyel will be able to find his way to us soon enough."

Even though Etania wanted to stay and hear the conversation, she knew her father would not allow it and Keyel would not appreciate her eavesdropping. She sighed and turned away, following her father and the guards as they walked away from Keyel and his father.

"SEE YOU LATER, KEYEL," Adeline said as she was escorted from the room by her guard.

Keyel dipped his head, not wanting to respond with words. Once she was gone, Thandor spoke.

"You have grown."

Keyel stifled a grunt.

"I know you may not understand me, but I have done what is best for everyone," Thandor explained.

Keyel had heard this story a thousand times. His mother was appointed as librarian so that she would be away from the center of Calques and away from Lord Thandor. This didn't stop the name-calling: words his father never sought to control.

"I just wish you shared your ambitions with Sh-Ms. Evant and me. You left without a word to us," Thandor said. Keyel had left shortly after the *incident*, never intending to return. "We only found out because Jakin told us. I would rather not have information about you conveyed through a third party. Would you at least do us the courtesy of sending letters?"

"Courtesy?" Keyel spat the word. He clenched his fist around his sword, and the tips of his ears felt hot.

"Yes. We would've liked to have letters of your life outside these walls," Thandor said.

Keyel stifled a retort. Since when had they become a "we?" They were not a family. They couldn't be.

"I admit that I should've kept in touch with my mother," Keyel replied, "but I have no obligation to write to you. My leader is Jakin, and my father is no one. That is what it means to be a nothus."

Thandor's eyes darkened. "They still call you that?"

Keyel didn't answer.

"I thought I put a stop to that with a decree," Thandor explained, and Keyel was surprised. Thandor wrote a decree to stop their harassment? Keyel's temper ebbed slightly.

"I'm sorry, Keyel," Thandor said.

"Sorry?" Keyel scoffed. "Sorry for having me? Or sorry for not stopping the name-calling?"

"Both," Thandor said.

That single word stabbed at Keyel's well-guarded heart. He was an unwanted byproduct of an illicit act. Secretly, he felt he deserved the title nothus, especially after what he'd done.

"Well, you no longer have to live with regret. I won't come to Calques," Keyel declared. "You wanted me to write you letters. Well, consider this my letter: Lord Thandor, I am no longer a Leici." Without waiting for a reply, Keyel turned on his heel and strode out of the room, not glancing back.

If he had, he would've seen a mirror of his anguish in Thandor.

ETANIA AND JAKIN FOLLOWED the Leici guards, crossing long, swinging bridges and platforms. They turned so many times that Etania felt like her sense of direction had disappeared into the trees. Eventually, they stopped by a well-lit house with flowers blooming in pots by the front door. By this time, Keyel rejoined Jakin and Etania. She wondered what he had talked about, but chose not to ask when she saw his brooding expression. Keyel knocked on the door and Shayna answered it, beckoning them inside.

When Etania entered, she noticed there were many candles lit, placed in either lanterns or windowsills, revealing a cozy living area with several large chairs and a huge bookshelf filled with books. Against a wall was a brick fireplace, with several metal containers standing nearby for cooking.

"I'm sorry for not greeting you earlier," Shayna said, looking directly at Etania. "I am Shayna Evant, Keyel's mother."

"It's nice to meet you, Ms. Evant," Etania said. Shayna smiled and Etania felt warm inside.

"Call me Shayna," she said. "You must be hungry. I have sandwiches in the kitchen if you would like some."

Etania nodded, following Shayna to a small kitchen that seemed precariously balanced on one of the limbs of the trees. She handed them sandwiches and then beckoned them back to the living room to sit.

"So, how long have you known Keyel, Etania?" Shayna asked.

"A week," Etania replied, between bites.

"Oh, so quick! I would have expected a bit longer until..." Shayna began.

"Mother, it's not like that!" Keyel protested. "I am Etania's bodyguard, and this is Etania's father, Jakin." Shayna turned her eyes to the Lehrling.

"You never mentioned a family," she said. Jakin shrugged.

"I never had a need," he said, with a smile.

"If there's a daughter, there must be a mother. Is she at home?" Shayna inquired.

"No," Etania said, trying not to tear up. "She passed recently."

"I'm sorry, I didn't mean to..." Shayna said.

"It's—alright," Etania lied.

Nothing was alright with her mother gone. Even talking to someone else's mother felt wrong, like Etania was betraying her own. They finished their sandwiches and Shayna rose to her feet.

"Let me lead you to your room, Etania. Keyel, will you set up a bed for Jakin in your old room?" Shayna asked.

"Of course," Keyel said, and he took a door to his right, Jakin following. Once they were gone, Shayna glanced at Etania with a sly smile.

"Good, it's just us girls now," Shayna teased.

"Y-yes it is," Etania said, feeling tongue-tied.

"Don't worry, I mean no harm," Shayna said.

"Yes, Ms. Evant," Etania replied.

"I thought I told you not to call me that," Shayna reminded.

She reached into a closet and took some blankets out, handing them to Etania. Etania gathered the blankets into her arms and followed Shayna as she took a door to her left. Beyond the door was an outer staircase that descended to another level. Etania and Shayna stood temporarily on a small platform, and then she followed the Leici down the stairs until they came to another door.

She entered and found herself in a small room with a bed, dresser and desk by a large window. Etania put the blankets on the bed and saw that her saddlebag was sitting in a corner, waiting for her.

"This is our...my...guest room," Shayna said. "You can sleep here. Let me know if you need anything and I'd be happy to get it for you."

"Thank you."

Shayna smiled. "Well, I will serve you as long as you stay. I hope you aren't leaving soon."

"I hope I'm not, too."

"Good, because I'd love to get to know you better," Shayna said.

Etania's heart fluttered.

"Anything else you may need?" Shayna asked.

"Actually, could you help me with this?" Etania asked, pulling out her mother's necklace. Shayna agreed, having Etania lift her hair so she could unbuckle it. She placed the delicate necklace on Etania's palm.

"This is beautiful. Where did you get it?"

"My father gave it to my mother before she..." Etania stopped herself.

"I didn't mean to stir up bad memories, now or before," Shayna said.

"It's okay," Etania said. "It's just...I lost her when King Toren killed most of the lords and ladies."

"King Toren did?" Shayna repeated. "Is Lady Maiya...?"

"She's alive, as far as we know. We're gathering allies to free her and the others imprisoned." Etania walked over to the dresser and put the necklace on top of the wooden surface.

"You have a hard task ahead of you."

"Yes, we do. I'm sure you're worried about your son, but I promise I'll protect him," Etania said.

"Isn't that supposed to be reversed?" Shayna questioned, from the doorway.

She didn't wait for a reply. With a goodnight, Shayna disappeared, and Etania was alone.

Etania tugged off her boots, belt and knife, lugged off her clothes and mail, and changed into her nightgown. She smoothed the blankets on the bed and sighed as she curled underneath the covers. The moonlight filtered through the window and cast its beams on her knife and the necklace. The necklace glinted, reminding Etania of when her mother showed her the Mark of Melchizedek. Who was she kidding? She couldn't protect Keyel, or anyone.

Etania turned away from the light. Warm tears streamed down her cheeks as she fell asleep.

JAKIN COULDN'T SLEEP. He tossed and turned in his bed, seeking Tala's presence next to him. But she was gone and he was alone. Keyel slept fitfully on the ground, giving his bed to his Master. Jakin jealously wished for the same sleep, but knew it was his sorrow, rather than the bed, that kept him awake. Even though he exuded self-assurance, the truth was that he had no confidence, only grief.

Why, Melchizedek? He asked, but there was no answer. He felt tears roll down his cheeks once more as he echoed his previous cry: *Why?*

His Mark, an outline of a hammer, glowed in the moonlight. It was a reminder of when Melchizedek claimed him. Even though Melchizedek wasn't physically with Jakin anymore, Jakin sensed his presence, trying to comfort him in his grief.

Jakin retreated from that feeling, flipping on his stomach and squashing the light. His heart felt a different kind of fire. A fire that stirred as he realized Toren was the man behind the Skazic. He was so focused on killing Skazic that he hadn't noticed King Toren's growing evil. He would have to double his efforts to wipe out this new threat. Jakin would build an army that would ensure that none could ever kill again. On his wife's dying breaths, he swore his vengeance.

The fire of that promise kindled in his breast until he fell asleep at last.

Chapter Eleven

A slight rapping noise roused Etania from her slumber.
"Breakfast is almost ready, Etania. Your father and Keyel are
dressed and ready to head out, so you might want to get dressed yourself."

Etania grunted in reply to Shayna and stretched. She was sore from
riding and her whole body ached. She quickly rummaged through her pack
and brought out another riding outfit like the one she had worn the day
before. She quickly tugged on her layers of clothing, buckled on her knife,
pulled on her boots, and headed upstairs.

When Etania walked inside the living area, Jakin and Keyel were sitting
in oversized chairs, sipping tea from mugs. Shayna stood by the fire, picking
up the lid of a small pot and stirring its contents. The aroma of blueberries
and sugar wafted through the living area and Etania's stomach grumbled.

"Do you want some tea?" Shayna asked, putting the lid back on the pot
and moving over to the kettle.

Etania nodded. Spotting a metal rack holding mugs, she snagged one for
herself. Shayna carefully poured the liquid into Etania's waiting cup, and the
warm scent filled her nostrils, making her smile. She took a seat on a wooden
rocking chair.

"So what are we going to do today?" Etania asked.

"We are going to practice," Keyel and Jakin said in unison.

Keyel dipped his head in deference to his master and Jakin continued.

"Keyel will teach you to use the crossbow and I will help you hone your
Neuma. Then we will continue on our journey toward Eritam territory. Keyel
tells me that there are several unused areas called Tenah that are for the Leici.
We can go there."

"O-okay," Etania said, her tea feeling sour in her stomach.

"You're leaving already?" Shayna stated.

"Of course," Keyel replied. "We have a long journey ahead of us."

"Well, if you're going, I'll follow you to the border. I'm sure Jakin wouldn't mind, would he?" Shayna added, winking at Etania's father. "Especially if he wants to see my library again."

"Maybe," Jakin said, turning his head away in mock disinterest.

"Wouldn't Lord Thandor be upset that his head librarian is leaving?" Keyel asked.

"Since when have you cared about your father?" Shayna asked, her eyebrow arched at her son. Keyel looked away, a slight redness on his cheeks.

"Besides, I can leave my assistant in charge for a week. He's always wanted to be promoted," Shayna declared, dishing out the blueberry cobbler to the three of them. "I'm going to tell him now what I intend. Don't you dare leave without me."

With that statement, she walked outside to inform her assistant. Even though Etania wanted to see the library, Shayna was gone before she could ask her. Keyel let out a large sigh, but Etania stifled a laugh.

"What's so funny?" Keyel asked.

"I thought I was the only one whose parent overran her will," Etania said. "I guess not."

"I don't overrun your will," Jakin said with a sniff. "I merely point you in the right direction."

Keyel and Etania glanced at each other and chuckled. Jakin crossed his arms over his chest and stared at his food. They had just finished their berry cobbler when Shayna arrived. She had changed into a travelling outfit and was carrying a saddlebag.

"Well, I'm ready to go. I even told the horsemen to bring your horses to the nearest Tenah," Shayna said.

"We just finished eating, mother, and we have to put out the fire and wash the dishes...." Keyel began. Shayna waved his excuses away.

"Leave that to me," she said. "You can all grab your gear and meet me outside."

"Yes ma'am," Jakin said, with a mock salute.

Shayna glared at him and Etania stifled another smile. This would be an interesting trip to the border.

Etania went upstairs and grabbed her saddlebag. By the time she descended the stairs with her gear, the others were waiting on the porch. Etania joined them, looking around in awe at the bustling city. Crisscrossing bridges linked tree house to tree house, and Leici walked across them everywhere she looked. They carried packages, glass jars with unusual liquids, or scrolls of paper. Sometimes they worked in pairs, speaking to one another. Other times they rushed by each other, calling out to priests dressed in robes. Etania guessed there were thousands of Leici because the tree homes and bridges never seemed to end.

Etania didn't have a long time to look as the others began walking away. Keyel gently pulled her forward, and they crossed a bridge. The four travelers came to the porch of another treehouse and turned right, walking over a longer bridge that went past a house with more windows than walls. Inside, Etania saw many Leici surrounding the sick. Their hands glowed as they healed their patients. Keyel pulled her forward again and they crossed another bridge, heading farther north.

Despite the activity around them, whenever Keyel or Shayna came onto a bridge with another Leici on it, the Leici would pass them with his or her face turned away. They would never greet them and if they could, they would pass onto another bridge instead. Eventually, Etania was so irritated she spoke to Shayna.

"Why are they doing that?"

"Because he is a nothus," Shayna replied.

"Does that mean what I think it means?" Etania wondered.

"Yes," Keyel said, increasing his pace. "It means illegitimate son."

Shayna sighed and whispered to Etania, "I've always regretted my foolishness, but I've mostly regretted it because of the effect it has on Keyel. As much as I love him and don't regret having him, I wonder what I could've done to protect him from my shame."

"Why didn't you move?" Etania wondered.

"Because I wanted him to be near his father. Boys need their fathers, just as girls need their mothers," Shayna said. "I didn't predict that this would be a problem for Keyel, too."

Girls need their mothers. Etania's heart sank. She needed her mom, now more than ever. She stifled her grief and looked away from Shayna. A comforting arm draped around her shoulders, and Etania patted Shayna's hand in gratefulness.

"Are you coming?" Jakin called, and Etania realized they were lagging behind. She jogged to catch up, coming alongside Keyel. His eyebrows were furrowed, his blue eyes dark.

"Does it matter to you that I am a nothus?" he asked, his voice barely above a whisper.

"Of course not," Etania said.

"I'm glad," Keyel whispered. He smiled slightly and looked at Etania sideways.

"Your father and you judge me based on who I am, not on my birth," Keyel added. "I appreciate that."

"You're welcome," Etania said. "But don't compare me to my father."

"We're here," Shayna announced, stopping on a platform that looked just like the rest. Jakin went down the rope ladder first, slinging his pack onto his back and descending with ease. Shayna followed, and Keyel beckoned Etania to go after his mother. Etania took a deep breath, tugged her pack on, and descended the rope ladder, only looking at the rungs. She was glad when her feet hit solid ground.

They were in an area cleared of debris, making the dirt smooth. Lord Thandor stood nearby, flanked by two of his guards. Etania noticed their horses were tied to trees and eating from feed bags, which tied around their ears.

"What are you doing here?" Keyel asked.

"It's not what you think," Lord Thandor said. "Adeline wanted to see you."

"Yes, I came to see Keyel before you leave," Adeline called.

Etania finally got a good look at Keyel's half-sister. She was a small woman resting in a wooden chair that had wheels on either side of it. The same guard pushed the seated cart forward. She wondered why the woman sat in the chair, but was more curious as to what Keyel would do. He stiffened and didn't reply with words but a dip of his head. Etania sighed. *Why doesn't he say anything?* she wondered inwardly.

"Well, you won't have to say goodbyes just yet," Jakin said. "We intend to train ourselves in this area before we leave."

Etania gulped. *I'll have to practice in front of Keyel's half-sister? I don't even know how to use my Neuma!* Her stomach twisted at the thought.

"Great! We get to see how your training works," Thandor said.

You won't see that great of an effort from me, she thought bitterly.

"Okay! Let's focus on the crossbow first," Jakin commanded.

They went over to an area specifically used for archery, where there were several trees marked at various lengths, with targets carved into them. Keyel fetched the crossbow from the pack horse's saddle bags and handed it and the bolts to Etania.

"A crossbow is simple to use," Keyel said. "Step into the stirrup with your foot, and using your hands, pull back the bowstring until it clicks into place. Then align the bolt along the stock, put the tiller against your shoulder, and push the trigger upwards."

Keyel demonstrated the technique using Etania's crossbow, the small bolt flying through the air and landing with a loud thunk into the tree nearest to them.

"Now you try," Keyel instructed.

Etania took the crossbow and finagled her foot into the stirrup, pulling the bowstring into position and placing the bolt in as instructed. Keyel checked her stance and helped her align her arms correctly so she would get an accurate shot. Despite his checks, when Etania shot, the bolt flew wide.

"That's alright. Try again," Keyel encouraged.

Etania followed his directions, once again missing her target. They repeated the exercise several times, and Etania missed almost every single shot. By the end, they were both growing frustrated and terse with one another.

"I think that's enough for now," Jakin said. "Etania should practice using her powers. We'll work on fighting with knives tomorrow before we keep travelling."

Averting her gaze from Keyel and Jakin, Etania wondered if she would do much better at using her Neuma. Jakin gave her directions and she began what felt like an impossible practice. Etania glanced at Keyel whose brow wrinkled as her practice continued to decline. She wondered if he was as disappointed as she felt.

"Etania, are you listening to me?" Jakin asked.

"Um, maybe," Etania replied.

Jakin sighed and repeated his instruction.

"I want you to close your eyes and imagine your Neuma as a flame, holding your hands in front of you to cradle it."

Etania obeyed, trying not to be distracted by the sound of chatter around her.

"I didn't know your friend has Neuma," Shayna said to Keyel.

"I knew, but I've never seen it," Keyel said.

"Then how do you know it is really true? Aren't humans like her without powers?" Shayna questioned. Keyel didn't answer, and Etania tried not to let Shayna's doubts reflect her own.

"What color is your Neuma?" Jakin asked.

Etania knew the answer, based on what she remembered from the incident with the Skazic, but it still felt strange to admit it.

"White," she said, her brow furrowed.

Once she acknowledged this, she felt like warmth was seeping from her heart down into her arms. She tried to cradle it in her hands and she heard Keyel, Adeline, Shayna, and Thandor gasp. Etania didn't open her eyes, afraid to see what she might have created.

"Good," Jakin said. "Now, I want you to throw that ball of flame to me."

Jakin's command meant that Etania would have to open her eyes. She nervously did, and gasped. White flames were sitting contentedly over her hands, playing over her fingers, and bathing her with warm light! Her heart beat wildly, and the flames went out. That glimpse confirmed that she was, indeed, a Vexli.

Before she could wrestle with this fact, Jakin commanded, "Do the same exercise again."

Etania obeyed. This time, she concentrated when she saw the flames. Following his command, she tossed the white ball of flame toward Jakin as if throwing a rock across a pond.

The flame sped over the field and slammed into Jakin's chest, pushing him back. Etania exclaimed, and immediately, the flame died. She rushed over to her father's side.

"Are you alright?" she asked.

Jakin rubbed his chest.

"That's my girl!" he declared. Keyel came and helped his master to his feet.

"Maybe it's a good idea for you to practice elsewhere, Lehrling. Your daughter's Neuma is too dangerous for my daughter," Lord Thandor said.

"There's no danger," Adeline spoke up. "Besides, I thought it was beautiful."

Etania blushed. Her Neuma—beautiful? She never thought of it that way. Instead, she felt afraid of its power; especially after her father was knocked back by the flames.

"I agree with your assessment, my lord, and yours, my lady ," Jakin said. "We should eat lunch and be on our way."

Lord Thandor agreed. He ordered a few of his guards to bring a lunch out to them, so they rested in the shade while they waited. Once they returned, her guard put down a blanket and lifted Adeline from the chair, placing her on it. Lord Thandor, seeing everyone situated with food, decided to leave them. Etania knew it was because Shayna was with the group. As Etania turned her gaze back to the others, she noticed something for the first time.

Adeline had no legs beyond her knees.

Chapter Twelve

Jakin rubbed his chest with his hand. He hadn't expected his daughter's Neuma to be so powerful. He quickly realized Etania had disabled his Neuma. So, she was different from Daas!

Daas: the man who started Jakin's journey toward vengeance. The man that Jakin once called a friend. He had never been able to affect both Skazic and regular Neuma users. He had only disabled Skazic...until he'd become one.

Now, another man Jakin trusted had turned to evil. Why hadn't he seen that Toren was falling prey to darkness? Was it because of his wife, Jazel? He should've never spared her, all those years ago. Yet, judging a person based on their parentage was wrong—Keyel being a prime example—so he had let her live.

"Lehrling Jakin." Adeline's voice interrupted Jakin's thoughts. "You haven't touched your food. Are you alright?"

"Yes, of course," Jakin answered, now purposely eating.

"Good. Can I ask you a question, before you leave?" Adeline asked.

"Of course," Jakin replied. "I'm just surprised you chose me over your brother."

Adeline's gaze flitted from Jakin to Keyel, who was currently engaging Etania in conversation.

"I will talk to him," Adeline said. "In the meantime, I need to think about what I need to do as the leader in my mother's place."

"My lady, I'm not sure you..."

"You believe that this disability hinders me, don't you?" Adeline said. Jakin didn't reply.

"It doesn't, no matter what Keyel thinks. With Rhys' assistance, I am able to move freely," Adeline declared, giving her bodyguard a nod of respect.

"Can you prepare for war, my lady?" Jakin questioned.

Adeline blushed at his question, but Jakin was serious. If Adeline couldn't ride a horse alongside her men, they would never respect her. She had to learn to dictate and make decisions that her mother would ordinarily make in her place. Thandor couldn't do it for her, because the matriarchy the Leici prefered had to be preserved.

Adeline didn't flinch as she answered, "I can."

"You'll do fine then," Jakin said and smiled.

A laugh brought his focus back to Keyel and Etania. Etania's laugh reminded him painfully of Tala, and he pushed aside the last image of his dying wife.

"No matter what he says, Jakin, he did all he could for me," Adeline said.

"I know," Jakin replied.

"He doesn't believe that, does he?" Adeline asked.

Jakin didn't answer; he merely stood.

"Come on, Etania! Shayna!" Jakin announced, "We should get the horses ready and allow the Lady to say her good-bye."

When Jakin looked back at Adeline, she mouthed "thank you." He nodded in reply and walked toward the horses.

KEYEL WATCHED ETANIA, his mother, and Jakin depart, unable to bring himself to face Adeline. Even though they were not alone, with her bodyguard, Rhys, near them, he felt sick. Adeline laughed, and Keyel turned to glare at her, then caught himself.

"You look so silly when you're being serious. I like your smile much better," Adeline said.

"The last time I smiled was when I teased you," Keyel retorted, "which I'm not sure you enjoyed."

Adeline pouted slightly, tossing her head.

"Maybe I did, maybe I didn't," she said. "It's been a long time since you teased me."

Yes, it has been a very long time, Keyel realized, *but for good reasons.*

"Are you able to heal again?" Adeline began.

Keyel shook his head, his heart pained.

"I wouldn't be alive if not for you," Adeline said.

"But you would have both your legs," Keyel countered.

"Legs? Who needs them?" Adeline joked, but Keyel wasn't laughing.

"Melchizedek allowed this, Keyel. Have you talked to him about why that might be?" Adeline wondered.

Keyel hadn't spoken to Melchizedek since the day he failed to protect Adeline from the Skazic. He was certain that Melchizedek would be angry at him, or regret Marking him. His incandescent Mark was of a shield, a symbol of protection. He had failed to live up to it with Adeline and he wasn't doing so well with Etania.

"I think I know why," Adeline continued. "He decided to use this to grow me. I used to be so headstrong, you remember?"

"You're not anymore?" Keyel blurted, and bit his lip at his impudence. Adeline laughed again. *She seems freer with those laughs*, Keyel noted.

"He humbled me with these," Adeline said, moving her legs up to show them briefly to Keyel. He shuddered, not wanting to remember.

"Sorry," Adeline replied. "The point is, I know this happened for a reason, and I feel blessed to be a part of Melchizedek's plan."

"Whatever you say," Keyel remarked.

"I wish I could make you believe, yet I have a feeling it might not happen until this rebellion is over," Adeline said with a sigh. "I like Etania, by the way."

"You've known her for an hour," Keyel pointed out.

"Yes, but I have a feeling we will be good friends," Adeline countered. She looked up at Rhys, her bodyguard, who nodded in reply and went to get the chair. Keyel stood, and when Rhys brought it, Keyel cradled Adeline in his arms, lifting her into the chair.

"Thank you, Brother," Adeline said, her blue eyes flickering with sincerity.

"It's the least I can do," Keyel replied. Straightening, he looked at Rhys. "You take care of her, understand?"

"I already have been," Rhys declared, and Keyel nodded in agreement.

"Goodbye, Keyel," Adeline said.

"Goodbye, Adeline," Keyel replied.

He bowed and put her hand to his forehead, then released it. He turned on his heel and didn't look back. The past was in the past, even if it haunted his future with Etania.

THE HORSES WERE SADDLED once Keyel rejoined Etania and the others, so they were on the road again in moments. As they rode back to the path that would lead them out of Leici territory, Etania wondered if she would be able to discover what exactly had happened to Keyel. She pulled her horse back so it was walking alongside Shayna's mount.

"Why is Adeline's hair brunette?" Etania asked.

"That's the question on your mind?" Shayna replied. "I thought you would ask something else."

"No," Etania said, with a blush. "I think *he* should tell me."

"A respectful decision, and something I would've said anyway," Shayna agreed. "As for your question, only the female leaders of the Leici are brunettes. They are said to be marked that way for succession."

"What if they have more than one daughter? Wouldn't that be a problem?" Etania wondered.

"No," Shayna said. "Melchizedek has willed it so that the Leici leaders have only one daughter. However, they often have multiple sons, though most of my lady's sons didn't live to term."

"Wow, so that means..." Etania began.

"Yes. Keyel is the Lord's only son," Shayna said. "Thus, Lady Maiya doesn't like me for two reasons: the affair, and my birth to a living son."

"I see," Etania said, sneaking a glance at Keyel.

Keyel didn't acknowledge her. He was merely riding and looking actively around them, as if a Skazic would jump from the trees. Etania sighed and turned back to Shayna.

"Why didn't you marry?" Etania asked. "That would've dispelled any rumors or hard feelings, right?"

"Not really," Shayna said. "I would've just drawn resentment from the Lady for 'covering' my deeds."

"I understand that," Etania agreed.

"Besides, I'm actually quite happy single," Shayna said. "I am free to do as I please, managing a library."

"Speaking of your library; if I am ever able to return, I would love to see it. I was actually apprenticing to become a librarian before—" Etania faltered and took a deep breath to steady her nerves. "Before everything at the ball, I was learning under my mother's tutelage. She was teaching me about preserving texts and copying them."

"Sounds like your mother was a good teacher," Shayna said.

"She was," Etania replied, with a slight smile.

"If you would like, I could show you what I know," Shayna added. "I brought a few books with me and they would give you examples."

"I-I would like that," Etania stuttered. Shayna nodded and Etania's heart fluttered. *I just wish my mother would have taught me instead.* She thought.

The travelers stopped for the evening in northeast Calques. They were welcomed stiffly into the home of one of the officials of Lord Thandor. With five levels of rooms, the house was large enough for all of them. The hosts also made themselves scarce during dinner, leaving food on a table for them to eat. Etania sighed. Apparently, the prejudice against Shayna and Keyel extended here as well.

Saying their goodnights, Shayna and Etania departed to their own room, where there were two beds inside. A single, low dresser stood between the beds, a mirror and a bowl of water sitting on its surface. There were fresh towels but no nightstands. They both rinsed their faces, and Etania unbraided her hair. She stood in front of the mirror and tried to comb out the knots in her hair.

"Here, let me help," Shayna volunteered.

Etania handed her comb to the Leici, who began working on Etania's curls. Relaxing, Etania tried not to feel guilty that she was enjoying having another "mother" present to fix her hair. Once Shayna was done, Etania helped the Leici with her own silver-gold locks.

After this, they went to their beds and Shayna blew out the candle. This time, Etania didn't ask Shayna to remove her mother's necklace, instead fingering the amulet between her fingers.

Is it okay, Mom? To like someone like you?

She couldn't answer as she closed her eyes and fell asleep.

AFTER BREAKFAST THE next morning, the travelers packed and rode out to another Tenah, which was as deserted as the first. Jakin had Etania practice her Neuma first this time. She was able to maintain the flame, but still had difficulties reining in the intensity. Even though her father told her to relax, Etania always felt nervous, her palms slick with sweat that had nothing to do with the heat of the flames. After practicing a few times, they moved on to knife practice.

"Before we begin, I should explain that a knife will not protect against anyone with a sword," Keyel said. "If you are attacked by someone with something that long, you should try to get far enough away to shoot at them with your crossbow or use a shield. A knife should be used for defending yourself against people similarly armed or without a weapon at all. Don't try to throw your knife, either. Throwing knives takes years to master, and I've only seen the Eritam successfully do it. Instead, you need to grip your knife like so..."

Keyel put his fist around the knife so that the edge was facing outward and he could use his thumb for leverage. Then he swiped in several directions, arcing across his body.

"You should aim for parts of the body that will do the most damage. The artery near the neck, for example," Keyel explained.

As Etania mentally took notes, Keyel told her to practice slicing the air. So Etania used her knife until she was covered in sweat, and Keyel only had a few pointers.

When they finished, they rode out, her sweat drying as a cool breeze swept through the group. She shuddered. The knife practice, the crossbow training, honing her Neuma...all of it was a reminder that her life would never be the same. She wished her mother was there to help her deal with her feelings! A tear slipped down her cheek. *Why has Melchizedek chosen me? Why did Melchizedek allow my mother to die?* she wondered. She never wanted to be a warrior, but King Toren's betrayal had made that decision for them both.

Chapter Thirteen

King Toren woke in a cold sweat in his bedroom. Queen Jazel slept next to him, her snoring loud as her time came sooner to completion. He blinked as he tried to reorient himself. Standing, he stumbled out of his lavish four-poster bed and flung open the window shutters to let in the night air. The breeze soothed him, calming his beating heart. He gazed out at the moon, which lit his room slightly, revealing two large wardrobes and a standing mirror.

He hadn't had *that* dream for a while.

In it, he was a child wandering the castle hallways and looking for his father. Just when he was about to give up hope, his father would leap out from the curtains, dragging him inside.

"Did you hear that?" his father asked.

"Hear what?" Toren wondered.

"The assassins. They're in the castle now, looking for us. I saw them kill your mother," his father said.

"Mom is fine," Toren insisted. "She's the one who sent me."

"No, she's not real, none of them are!" his father insisted.

They'd argue until Toren woke, covered in sweat like he was now. He vowed on his mother's deathbed that he'd never become the paranoid king. Yet, the thought of Jakin and Etania on the loose stirred his old memories. He hated the fact that his Skazic were unable to find them in Khartome or Nova before they escaped.

The day after they escaped, he had felt hopeless, uncertain of what to do next. But then, Jazel gave him an idea. He would send the toothbreakers after Jakin and Etania. Surely, those wolves would be able to track down Jakin and Etania.

He shook his head to clear his mind. The citizens of Khartome had been informed of his propaganda, and many believed him. He had an army of Skazic and most of the leaders imprisoned. He had sent out toothbreakers to search for Jakin and his companions. He also sent emissaries to the different tribes, stating his demand for surrender. He had done all he could do. Toren found comfort in these thoughts.

"Come back to bed, darling," Jazel called.

Toren turned and ventured into bed, cuddling next to his wife, his hand on her stomach. Yes, his future was secure.

JAKIN REINED IN HIS horse. They had travelled for almost seven days, and would reach the end of Leici territory soon. With each passing day, his daughter slowly improved in using the crossbow, knife, and her Neuma. Yet, her progress made Jakin wonder why he hadn't forced her to learn self-defense before she was attacked.

Because I thought I had the Skazic under control. Jakin realized. He had been so focused on wiping out the Skazic, believing he didn't need to train another generation to defeat evil. Keyel would be his last Apprentice, he had believed.

Tala had often warned him of this foolishness. She'd reminded him that Melchizedek hadn't tasked them with wiping out evil completely, for Deo would do that himself one day. Instead, he had asked the Lehrlings and other Melchizedek-followers to spread his words. Tala had focused on this task. Jakin hadn't, and it cost him his wife.

He still couldn't bring himself to give up the hunt for the Skazic. Especially not now, with a rebellion looming on the horizon. Glancing at his daughter, he sighed. He understood why she grumbled and complained about her aches and sores. Yet, she must become his weapon if they were ever to win.

Jakin was grateful that Shayna accompanied them because the woman acted like a mother to Etania, reminding Jakin painfully of his wife. She even took up his wife's mantle of training Etania to be a librarian during their breaks. Shayna also made Keyel laugh...a feat that Jakin couldn't accomplish, even with his jokes! Soon, they would be departing from the Leici lands and Jakin wondered if Shayna would consider accompanying them. She could help Etania and Keyel so that Jakin wouldn't have to worry about them. The evening before their last day in Leici territory, Jakin cornered Shayna after dinner.

"I know what you're going to say, and the answer is no," Shayna said.

"Are you sure you don't want to come with us?" Jakin questioned.

Shayna shook her head.

"I can't. Keyel must go through this trial on his own. I only came to spend some time with him," she replied.

"But we need you," Jakin said. "Your healing skills would be valuable in the days ahead."

"I'm sure," Shayna countered, "but Keyel is a skilled healer. His powers are just inhibited right now. With your encouragement, he will find a way to start healing again."

"I don't know about that," Jakin said. "I can't charm him with my good looks and wit like I can you."

"I'm sure you say that to all ladies, and don't mean a single word because you are—were—married," Shayna teased.

Jakin ignored her comment.

"Please," he pleaded, "Come with us."

"I can't come." Shayna shook her head firmly. "If anything, the Leici needs me now more than ever. The library contains many texts from the old wars on how to be a combat healer. I owe that much to my Lord."

"Even if he is partially responsible for your shame?" Jakin remarked.

"The people must have someone to blame," Shayna replied. "To them, a leader must be above reproach. I am willing to be that person until they can forgive us."

"What if they never forgive you?" Jakin asked. "Wouldn't it be worth it to make your own future with us?"

"They will forgive, just as you will one day," Shayna said.

Jakin clenched his jaw and looked away from the Leici. *How has she read my mind?*

"Goodbye, Lehrling. I will see you again when we march on Khartome," Shayna rose and gave Jakin a brief kiss on the cheek. Then, she walked away from him, joining his daughter in their room. Her kiss, the coolness of it, lay on his cheek as he settled into bed that night, thinking, *oh, how I miss my wife.*

KEYEL REALIZED THAT he would have to say goodbye to his mother after the last round of practice in the Tenah. He hadn't understood how much he missed her until she was with them every day. She was solid and strong, whereas he felt weak and like a failure. She was everything he strived to be and more, and his heart hurt at the thought of leaving her once again.

Their good-byes would be different this time. Last time, he had left without telling her once he knew Adeline was fine. He was angry and depressed, determined to start over. He still felt at fault for failing to protect Adeline. Yet, Adeline never blamed him, so why did he continue to condemn himself?

He didn't know. All he knew was that they finally arrived at the border between Eritam and Leici territory and he had to say goodbye. Etania and Jakin gave their words of parting to Shayna, so now it was his turn. Mother and son stood across from each other, ready to ride out in opposite directions, and all Keyel could do was look at his feet.

"I love you, Keyel," Shayna said.

"I know," he replied.

She raised his chin to look at him.

"You can't protect Etania from everything, you know," she said.

Her words stung. He knew he was a failure. Why did she have to say it?

"Melchizedek can. You only have to talk to him and surrender your fears," Shayna advised.

"Easier said than done," Keyel muttered.

"I know," she replied, and enveloped Keyel in her arms. He squeezed her tightly and felt tears slide down his cheeks. He wiped them away, turning from his mother in shame.

"Goodbye, Mom," Keyel said.

"Goodbye, Keyel," Shayna replied.

Keyel nodded, put his boot in his stirrup, and swung himself onto his horse. He looked back only once. When he did, he saw a lone woman with golden-silver hair flowing with the breeze, a sad smile on her face.

He mouthed, "I love you too," and looked back at the path ahead.

THE FOREST DARKENED and the trees closed in around them, making the path so narrow that only one horse could walk at a time. Etania's father took the lead, putting Etania in the middle and Keyel at the end. Etania noticed that birds fluttered from one branch to another, calling out, but their voices seemed hushed. The horses' hooves crunched over the leaf-strewn path.

They stopped only once, eating quietly and quickly before mounting their horses again. Jakin thought that they would wait until the Eritam found them, winding their way through the forest for days before the wolf-tamers arrived. Etania hoped that the Eritam would come sooner rather than later because she didn't want to sleep on the forest floor.

Suddenly, she heard a loud and long howl, piercing the night with its mournful sound. She shivered, hoping that howl belonged to an ally. Another howl echoed through the night, sounding like a threatening growl, deep and equally long. Starlight moved uneasily beneath her, and Etania felt her pulse quicken.

"Master—" Keyel began.
"I know. Etania, load your crossbow!"

Etania dropped her horse's reins and pulled out her crossbow from the pack, grateful her father insisted she carry it in her saddlebags. She nervously put the bolt along the stock and lined it up as best she could. Despite a week's worth of practice, her hands were shaking.

"Master, what's..." Keyel said.

Before he could finish, Etania saw yellow and green eyes staring at her in the distance. Their horses trotted without command, and she heard the yips and barks of wolves coming from their rear. The wolves were closing in, loping and howling as they drew closer to their prey. The horses whinnied and reared, and all three of the travelers bailed lest they be stomped underfoot. Their mounts fled to the west, galloping away with their supplies before anyone could stand. Etania had no time to grieve the loss of her favorite horse, but instead focused on standing and arming herself.

Luckily, their weapons had come down with them. Keyel was on his feet first, sword drawn and shield ready. Jakin was next, lighting the dark forest with purple fire in one hand and a hammer in the other. Etania tried to keep her legs from wobbling as she peered into the darkness over the stock of her crossbow. They stood in a triangle, twirling around to see their opponents. All was silent.

Out of the darkness, a wolf leapt from the side. Etania instinctively shot it straight in the chest. It yelped and died, but Etania had no time to react as more jumped from the darkness. Keyel killed them with swift and efficient strokes. Her father burned them or whacked them with his hammer as he defended Etania, who struggled to load another bolt into her crossbow. These wolves took multiple hits to kill. Etania had been blessed with her first shot. She needed to hit the wolves coming from a distance so they wouldn't be overwhelmed. Her heart was pounding and her palms were sweaty, but she took a deep breath. *Concentrate. You have to help them!*

She felt the coolness of the wood stock, the taut lever beneath her fingers, and fired.

She missed. Etania cursed, fumbling for another bolt. Keyel cried out, and Etania saw that his sword arm now bore bloody scratches. Making matters worse, her father's flames seemed like they were fading. She had to do something, anything, to help them.

Her Neuma—of course! But how could she project her Neuma in such a way that it wouldn't hurt her companions?

She looked at the bolt on her crossbow and smiled. Etania concentrated, trying to ignore the noise around her. She created a small flame of Neuma with her hands, lighting the bolt on the crossbow. She took a deep breath, trying to recall what Keyel had taught her. Feet apart, breath even, she aimed the crossbow and fired.

The bolt soared through the air, landing in a werewolf's shoulder. Etania watched in shock as her Neuma transformed the werewolf, a cry of agony rising from the Skazic as its fur flew from its body. Suddenly, it was no longer a werewolf, but a man covered in fur! The other wolves shrank back from his abrupt transformation, and Keyel and Jakin took advantage of the situation, killing the rest of the pack.

When the battle ended, Etania looked for the man, and she couldn't find him.

"Where is he?" Etania questioned.

"I don't know," a deep voice answered, "but I will find him and kill him."

Chapter Fourteen

E tania shivered, looking over to the source of the voice. It was a man with white hair and green eyes, who had appeared from the forest. Next to him was a white wolf that stood as tall as his waist. The wolf growled at them, making Etania step back. It then stopped and sniffed, as if intimidation was all it meant to do.

"Why kill him?" Etania wondered, secretly thinking, *Is this all I am, a weapon?*

"He is a toothbreaker," the man replied, as if that explained everything.

"Vartok, I don't think my apprentice or daughter know what you mean," Jakin said, walking up to join them. Behind Jakin, Etania could see the bodies of wolves strewn across the path. She gagged, turning away from the sight.

"A toothbreaker is a wolf who turned against his pack," Vartok explained to Etania and Keyel. "I'm sorry we couldn't come earlier. We were fifty meters hence and it took all of our speed to reach you."

Vartok whistled. Suddenly, other men and women with shades of white and silver hair surrounded them, their wolves by their sides.

"We will take care of the bodies," Vartok said. "Come with me, Lehrling."

Etania followed the man as best she could in the dark. The Eritam and their wolf companions carried no lights and followed no discernable path. The only thing keeping her from stumbling over rocks and brush was the small flame her father lit from his palm.

Just as she was about to ask if she could sit, they arrived at the mouth of a cave. Etania was delighted to see the cave well-lit, with a bearskin rug in the center and several chairs around its edges. They entered and took a seat.

"As you know, Lehrling, we prefer the open sky," Vartok said. "However, we do use caves occasionally, such as for the birth of our children. This is one such cave, unused since it isn't the season."

"Thank you," Jakin said. "We welcome the shelter."

Vartok nodded, looking over them with a cursory glance which stopped at Keyel's wound. Etania looked at the scratches on Keyel's arm and flinched. Was it her fault he was hurt? Her hesitation could've cost him more than a flesh wound.

"Can you heal that on your own?" Vartok asked.

"Yes, I can take care of it," Keyel said.

"Keyel, are you sure?" Etania began, but the Leici silenced her with a glare.

Vartok stood, his wolf following the motion.

"I'll leave you to rest," he said. "You know where you will find us in the morning, Lehrling."

"I do, Vartok. May Melchizedek's moon shine brightly on you."

"And may he bless you with sharp teeth!" the Eritam replied, and exited the room.

Etania let out a breath she didn't know she had been holding.

"Keyel, are you sure that you can treat that? It looks really bad," Etania wondered.

"I should be fine as long as I can find some bandages and alcohol," Keyel replied.

"There will be plenty in the caves," Jakin said. "Come on."

Jakin led the way as they walked past the sitting area to one of the tunnels on the left, where Etania could see lit torches revealing several different dens. She assumed that one of the Eritam had lit the torches and set up the rooms for them. The dens were filled with furs, animal bones, and a stench Etania preferred not to name. She was glad when they finally reached the back, where four rooms with normal beds were present.

Jakin found a dress made entirely of animal fur for Etania, as well as two fur pants and shirts for Keyel and himself. Keyel also found some bandages and alcohol.

"Do you need help with that?" Etania asked, guilt motivating her words.

"Yes, but I think you should get changed first," Keyel said, giving her a cursory glance.

Etania looked down and was horrified to realize she was covered in mud. She reddened, taking the dress Jakin offered, and went into another room.

As there was no door, Etania undressed quickly. There was a bowl of water sitting upon a dresser in the room and she used it to wash all the dirt from her body. She did the same for her hair, which she wrung dry. Then, she attempted to wash the blood from her weapons and belt, piling the useless split skirt and tunic in a corner next to the relatively clean gambeson and riding pants. Last, she surveyed the dress Jakin had given her to wear, which was made of fur and sleeveless. She wasn't used to showing her arms, but it would have to suffice. She changed into the dress and headed for Keyel and Jakin's room, pausing to the right of the doorway.

Etania called out, "Can I come in?"

"There's no need," Keyel replied. "Master helped me with my wound."

Etania felt a stab of disappointment at Keyel's words. Why wouldn't he wait? Did he believe she was not worthy of helping him, since she had failed to use her Neuma sooner? Then again, he probably was in pain and just needed help. She shouldn't be so self-conscious.

"Get some rest, Etania." Jakin said. "We have an early morning meeting with Vartok."

"Alright," Etania agreed, turning back to her room and finding the bed. Sleep did not come, however, for nightmares began as soon as she was asleep.

Werewolves came with red gums and white teeth, opening their mouths to eat her. Tala was crying out, her blood red against a white dress. Other voices cried and screeched. So many dead. They were all dead.

"Etania!"

Melchizedek's voice silenced the nightmares.

"It's all right Etania, I'm here."

His warm voice destroyed the fear.

"I'm here."

Etania woke, breathless. Wet tears stung her cheeks. *Everything keeps falling apart. My mother is dead. My precious horse is probably dead. Our supplies are gone. I want to run to the library and hide among the books and scrolls!* Even as that thought entered her mind, she pushed it aside. Why had Melchizedek silenced her nightmare? She didn't deserve his favor—especially after she ran from him.

She shook her head and went to where her clothes were piled. Her gambeson and riding pants were still usable, but her split leather skirt and tunic were too covered in mud. She couldn't wear the pants, gambeson and mail by itself, so she was stuck with the dress. She pulled on her knife belt and stepped into her boots. Deciding to leave the muddy clothing, she gathered her other gear and crossbow into her arms and exited the room.

Keyel and Jakin were waiting for her in the cave entrance, each wearing fur shirts as well as fur pants, and carrying their gambesons and mail. Etania stifled a grin as she took in the sight. Their fur pants and shirts suffocated, rather than complemented, the two men's body types.

"I know, I look dashing," her father said sarcastically.

Etania laughed, and even Keyel was smiling. The Leici handed Etania a fur knapsack for her items. Etania stuffed the clothing inside and put her crossbow and bolts on top so that the wood stock was sticking out of the bag. Then, she shouldered the pack and they headed out, following Jakin.

The forest was less oppressive by the light of day. Even though the trees were clustered together, the normal elements of a forest—brush, pinecones, and stray branches—were present. There was light filtering from the tree tops, giving illumination to their surroundings. The only odd thing remaining was the hushed animal noises, but Etania supposed the animals knew predators were nearby.

They made their way uphill through brush and twigs, taking the unorthodox path from the night before. Etania was glad when they halted at the top of a small hill, a plateau that overlooked the rest of the forest glade. Many wolves and their owners slept peacefully, curled up with one another. Vartok seemed to be the only one awake, sitting comfortably on a stump overlooking the forest. His wolf rested by his side, but its ear turned to the visitors.

Etania noticed that, as they walked toward Vartok, the other wolves turned their ears toward the trio, watching quietly. Only when they approached, and Vartok made a signal, did the wolves flick their ears back and close their eyes completely.

"Alpha Vartok." Jakin sat at the man's feet, beckoning Etania and Keyel to do the same. Vartok turned to face them, his bright green eyes flashing.

"I am Alpha, not Beta?" Vartok asked.

Etania recalled that, unlike the Leici, the Eritam were not a united people governed by a noblewoman. They were clans, or packs, at peace with each other, each with a social hierarchy similar to a wolf pack. The "Alpha" was the Lord—or noble—for each pack.

"Yes," Jakin replied, "You are Alpha now that Kayne and Sarai have perished."

"The other Alphas will not be pleased," Vartok said. "They were the ones who sent Kayne and Sarai as our representatives. Tell me, who should I kill to avenge their deaths?"

"King Toren," Jakin declared.

Vartok bared his teeth and snarled at them, just like his wolf.

"I knew that hafif couldn't be trusted!" he said.

"Hafif?" Etania repeated.

"A Neuma-less human or a person of mixed race," Jakin explained, and then turned back to Vartok.

"So you'll help us?" he questioned. Vartok gave a brief nod.

"I should be able to convince the other Alphas to rebel against King Toren once they hear the circumstances of Kayne and Sarai's deaths—and of the toothbreakers haunting our land."

"Speaking of the toothbreakers," Jakin said, "Have you found the one that escaped?"

"No," Vartok spat, "But I will! Any toothbreaker deserves death."

"I couldn't agree more," Jakin said.

Etania's stomach clenched at the coldness of the two men. She understood that Skazic deserved to be punished, but if their powers were removed and they surrendered, should they really be slaughtered on sight? Even though nightmares of werewolves were still on her mind, she felt compelled to speak for the one she had changed.

"Will you please offer him a chance to surrender?" Etania asked.

Vartok showed his canines and growled, "Why would I?"

"Yeah, why should he?" Jakin agreed.

"Well, I just feel...responsible for him. If he is Neuma-less, and like a hafif now, isn't he harmless? It just doesn't sit well with me."

"Please!" Jakin snorted. "He would probably slit your throat if you let him."

Etania glared at her father. He was being so unreasonable! Even though the first man she'd changed still sought her life, that didn't mean all of them would. Vartok sniffed.

"If the toothbreaker is peaceful and surrenders, I will consider it," he said.

"Thank you," Etania said.

Now it was her father's turn to glare, but when Etania ignored it, he turned back to Vartok.

"Would you be able to provide us with food and blankets? Our horses fled when we were attacked," he explained.

"Certainly," Vartok replied. "There is a cave a kilometer east of here that acts as our storeroom. Let Kappa Jaydon know that I sent you."

"Thank you," Jakin said, standing to his feet. "If you can convince your Alphas, tell them to meet us at Nova."

"I will," Vartok agreed. "I will also have a few of our wolves monitor your activity until you reach our borders."

Jakin dipped his head in thankfulness, rising to his feet. Etania and Keyel followed suit.

"May Melchizedek's moon shine brightly on you," Jakin said.

"And may he bless you with sharp teeth," the Eritam replied.

They took that as a cue to leave and walked by the sleeping pack, toward the east, where the storeroom was located. They found it easily enough, waking the napping Kappa so that he could retrieve their supplies. With two new knapsacks full of supplies, Keyel and Jakin moved their weapons from their backs to their sides.

Thus began a new day of travel for Etania and her companions, this time on foot. As they followed an almost indiscernible path westward through the forest, Etania could feel, but not see, their Eritam companions. Their next destination was the land of the Naymatua, for they bordered the Eritam territory. She tried to ignore the Eritam when they decided to stop for the day.

"Father, why do you want to kill the toothbreaker so much?" she questioned.

"He's a Skazic," Jakin replied. "He'll always be a Skazic."

"Even if he wanted to change?" she wondered.

"Please," Jakin snorted. "Skazic don't change. They sold their souls to Malstorm, remember?"

"I don't think that's true," Keyel piped up. "They may have pledged their loyalty to Malstorm, but I don't think anyone can truly sell their soul."

"Yes, isn't Melchizedek in charge of souls?" Etania questioned, smiling at Keyel to show her gratefulness for his support.

"Fine, I'll give you that," Jakin relented. "But I still won't believe a Skazic can change until I see it. They're too far gone."

With those words, Jakin said he had to forage for firewood, leaving the pair alone. They took a seat on a fallen log, removing their heavy knapsacks to rest. Etania turned to Keyel.

"I don't understand him," she said, "You've spent a lot more time with him than I have. Do you know why he hates the Skazic so much?"

Keyel shook his head.

"I've always thought my Master was passionate about his pursuit," Keyel admitted, "but I've never seen such vitriol from him."

"So, do you agree with me about the toothbreaker?" she wondered. Keyel rubbed his chin thoughtfully before he answered.

"I think we should give him a chance to prove himself," Keyel said. At that, Etania grinned.

"I'm glad I have someone on my side for once," she said. Keyel reddened and cleared his throat; a look that Etania thought was rather cute.

"Speaking of someone on your side," Keyel began. "I heard from my mother that you didn't press her regarding my past. I wanted to thank you for respecting my privacy."

"It's no problem," Etania replied, digging in her bag and pulling out some dried berries. "I figured you would tell me when you felt ready."

She popped some berries into her mouth and offered a few to Keyel.

Changing the subject, he asked, "How long does it take to find firewood?"

"Probably a *log* time," Etania replied, shrugging.

The tips of Keyel's lips turned up at her pun, so she pressed forward to create a genuine smile.

"I bet he *wood* take a while to find something dry."

Keyel's lips twitched at her remark.

"But by the time he gets back, the *tree* of us will have to go!"

Keyel began to chuckle and Etania joined in so that the pair of them were laughing by the time Jakin returned with the firewood. When he asked what they were laughing about, they burst into more giggles until Jakin scowled at them.

The laughter lightened Etania's mood. By the time they settled down for the night, she completely forgot about her father's hatred of the Skazic. But Melchizedek didn't, and almost as soon as her eyes closed, she dreamed of him.

Etania was in the octagonal room once again, the images on the windows flashing by at an incomprehensible speed. The basin of water was in the center and Melchizedek was standing over it. She felt suddenly embarrassed. He had comforted her in the werewolf nightmare, and now she felt ashamed. She was so weak to need his help—totally unworthy of the title he bestowed upon her.

"It's okay to be weak," Melchizedek said, "For I will give you strength."

"Why have you called me here?" Etania asked.

"I wanted to reassure you. You are not wrong to feel compassion for the ones you Changed. Even now, I am working to heal the toothbreaker that fled."

She let out a breath. Somehow, it felt right to hear him say that.

"Will you keep him safe?" Etania wondered and Melchizedek nodded.

"I plan on visiting him soon," he replied.

"From Safarast?" Etania asked.

"Perhaps," Melchizedek replied.

"Safarast, the land where the dead live again— or so my mother said. I don't see any dead here," Etania remarked.

"They are here, but not visible to one living in the world," he said. "But I have not called you here for that. I have called you here to ask you to visit me in Safarast."

"Why?" she asked.

"I will equip you with what you need to fight King Toren," he replied. "Until then, stay safe, Etania."

"Ha! Surely you've seen how I've been faring in my practice!" she retorted.

"Remember, Etania, you can always call on me for help," Melchizedek said.

"Call on you? But—" Etania's words failed her. Why would he want to help?

"It is time," Melchizedek said. *"Come see me in Safarast."*

"Where is Safarast?" she remembered to ask.

"Your father will know," Melchizedek replied, *and the dream began to fade.*

When Etania woke, she wondered how Melchizedek could be with her and present at Safarast at the same time.

Chapter Fifteen

Etania told Jakin during breakfast that Melchizedek had instructed them to visit Safarast.

"Safarast?" Keyel repeated. "I thought that was a legend."

"Oh, it's very real," Jakin replied, running his hand through his hair. "The visit to Safarast will delay us."

"Where is it?" Etania wondered.

"It changes locations," Jakin answered. "Some believe it's a floating island, travelling between stars. Others believe it is an entirely different universe, perhaps one parallel to our own."

"If that's the case, how can we reach it?" Etania questioned.

"I'm getting to that," Jakin said. "There's a portal the Draconians guard that leads to Safarast."

"We will reach the Draconians last," Keyel said.

"Yes," Jakin replied. "I know Saigon is on our side, so I was hoping we could fly to Nova immediately."

"We will still be able to," Etania pointed out.

"Yes, but several days later," Jakin said. "Time passes differently in Safarast. It would not surprise me if a week passes here and to us, it seemed like hours."

Etania shrugged. She was curious to see Safarast, regardless of the delay. Besides, she wanted to know more about Melchizedek's purpose for her Neuma.

"Melchizedek beckons, so who are we to argue?" Keyel said, standing to his feet and shouldering his pack.

"That doesn't mean I can't complain about it," Jakin teased,, standing as well. "Now, on to instruction."

He then explained that Etania would still practice using her Neuma or defending herself with weapons, but Keyel and he would take turns every other day. This time, it was Keyel's turn to teach her. They found a meadow nearby and practiced using the crossbow and knife. Since Keyel's arm was still healing, Etania had to practice with the Leici coaching her step by step. Even though Etania slowly got used to both, she still missed most of her shots. *Will I ever be proficient with weapons?* She wondered inwardly.

After this, they ate a quick breakfast and headed to the road. Etania's limbs ached, but she pushed through the pain, concentrating on her surroundings. As they walked, she observed birds singing, deer grazing by a river, and even a few wild hogs. The river had plenty of fish, which both Keyel and Jakin caught for dinner. Sometimes, Etania would see yellow or green eyes in the distance, or hear the howls of wolves. Jakin assured her that it was the sound of their Eritam allies.

Their days of travel became a monotonous pattern once again. They would train, eat breakfast, hike, eat lunch, hike some more, eat dinner, and sleep. During that time, they would all converse, but Etania's friendship with Keyel grew exponentially. She enjoyed talking to him, feeling like she could share anything with him. Also, unlike her father, he was compassionate toward the toothbreaker, and more understanding of her desire to rehabilitate the Changed. From that point on, she felt a connection to Keyel that wasn't quite friendship. She only wished her mother were there to tell her the definition of that feeling.

EVENTUALLY, THE TRAVELERS reached the last of the Eritam lands and entered the Naymatua territory. Here, the trees changed, growing taller and wider, with branches full of leaves and flowers. Colorful birds flew from branch to branch, singing songs. The air was wetter, and the path was wide and simple to navigate. Keyel's arm was finally healed, and Jakin was itching to find the Naymatua to talk to them. On the fourth day of their travel in the Naymatua lands, a group of men approached them. Dark skinned, bare-chested men wearing dark green pants greeted them. In each of their hands, they held staffs intricately carved with various designs. Each man's staff was unique, and Etania wondered what the different designs meant while her father talked to them.

"And this is my daughter, Etania," Jakin said.

Etania realized it was probably rude to stare and tried to focus on the man Jakin addressed.

"I am Suliman, second to chief Zeremu. We welcome you to the land of the Naymatua in honor of his name," Suliman said.

"He was a good man," Jakin said.

"Was?" Suliman questioned, leaning on his staff.

"Zeremu was killed when King Toren attempted to capture the lords and ladies," Jakin explained.

"I heard, but I didn't think it possible," Suliman said, rubbing his fingers over the ridges of his staff.

"His wife Larora is still alive, though imprisoned. Still, I believe succession of power is through the male line, which makes you chief, Suliman," Jakin declared.

The men around Suliman began to speak amongst themselves so quickly that Etania didn't understand them.

"Enough!" Suliman said, and the men were silenced. The new chief turned to Jakin. "Since we confirmed Zeremu is dead, we must mourn for his passing in Naymatua tradition. You are welcome to join us."

"Thank you, Chief." Jakin bowed.

Etania and Keyel followed his action. Suliman nodded in reply and turned away from the path toward the trees. To Etania's shock, the trees got out of the way for the procession, moving their branches or uprooting with loud creaks to make room for the group. As soon as the company passed them, the trees moved back in place. That was when Etania noticed that the Naymatua leading them were parting the trees, using their hands or staffs to order the trees to move with their Neuma.

They walked like this for a while, until the trees naturally stopped and they arrived at Ligasha, the capital of Naymatua territory. Unlike the homes of the Leici, which were in a tree's branches, the homes of the Naymatua existed in the trees' roots. The trees seemed to stand on the tips of their roots, enveloping a home.

Women in bright dresses washed clothes in the Timane River or picked fruit. Children ran around them, screaming and playing with delight. Here or there, Etania would see their playing develop into battles or bets to see who could grow trees or plants the fastest. Old men and women would watch them in rocking chairs made and moved by their own Neuma in a gentle rhythm. The villagers greeted the men who returned, and openly stared at Etania. Suliman pressed on until he reached a raised platform that Etania swore was not there before.

"My fellow Naymatua, I have grave news. King Toren killed our tribe leader Zeremu and imprisoned his wife, Larora," Suliman said. An outcry rose among the women and men who were listening. They began to speak urgently among themselves. Suliman interrupted, causing the conversations to dwindle.

"As such, I will be appointed as chief of the tribe in his place."

More whispers took place, with some wondering whether Suliman, who was young, could handle this responsibility. Others cried over the loss of chief Zeremu, unable to accept his death.

"Before I become chief, we will grieve Zeremu's death," Suliman stated, "As his body is not with us, we will be unable to lower it in the roots of a tree. Instead, we will grow a tree here in his honor. Asher, begin this ceremony for us."

Suliman stepped off the platform and, as Etania suspected, the platform disappeared, all of the roots that created it retracting. Asher, a young man who looked about Etania's age, brought out a large drum. He drummed softly, the beating growing and growing in intensity until a chorus of voices joined him.

> *Praise to Melchizedek, the giver of life*
> *Praise to Melchizedek, who provides a place for the dead*
> *All things were created by him*
> *The small seed grows by his will*
> *The tall oak enjoys his sunshine*
> *Flowers cover his meadow*
> *Their scent fills our nostrils*
> *The scent of new life*
> *The new life of this seed,*

The seed planted to grow
So we may remember the lost
Praise to Melchizedek, the giver of life
Praise to Melchizedek, who provides a place for the dead
All things were created by him

THE NAYMATUA SANG THE song three times. While they did so, a drum continued beating in the background. The people parted while Suliman brought forth a large seed, carried on a wooden pallet. He strode forth, two guards flanking him, and placed the seed on top of the dirt. Then, a group of men came and shoveled the dirt around the seed, leaving it exposed.

"Why do they do that, when a seed must be underground to grow roots?" Etania asked Jakin.

"To honor Melchizedek. They will not grow this seed, but instead allow Melchizedek to show his power by giving it roots and strength despite its position above ground," Jakin explained.

Etania stared at the motionless seed as the sound of the drum receded and the voices dimmed. The song was complete at sunset, and people began to return to their homes. Suliman approached them.

"My guests, follow me. We will provide you accommodations," Suliman said.

"Thank you," Jakin replied, with a slight bow of his head.

Suliman acknowledged the gesture and led them away from the center of Ligasha until they reached the outskirts of the capital. Here, they were shown into a two-bedroom root home. Suliman bid them goodnight, letting them know he would meet them the following morning. After eating dinner with her father and Keyel, Etania headed into her room.

Alone, the song of the Naymatua still ringing in her ears, Etania thought about her father when he would sing songs over her as a child. She wanted that man back in her life, rather than the one who resented the Skazic. *Like that will ever happen!* She realized, pushing aside the wishful thoughts.

Fingering her mother's amulet between her fingers, she thought about Tala, *I miss you so much, Mom...*

WHEN SHE WOKE THE NEXT morning, the dawn light was beginning to peek through the trees. Suliman's men had provided new clothing for all of them, which Etania was grateful for, and they changed into the light fabric. Although the bright colors didn't suit them, it was nice to change out of the fur dress to one that covered her arms. Etania, Jakin, and Keyel returned to the center of Ligasha, where a large table presented them with a bounty of fruits, vegetables, and nuts to consume for breakfast. Afterwards, everyone left and the wooden table shrank in size because of Neuma. With only Etania, Jakin, Keyel, Suliman, and some of his guard remaining, they now sat around a significantly smaller table. Jakin cleared his throat to ask Suliman for his help, but the Naymatua leader spoke first.

"Lehrling, I'm grateful for your patience," he began, "but I know what you are asking. And I must admit I'm hesitant to commit any of my men."

"How *do* you know?" Jakin replied.

"Let us say that the 'trees' talk," Suliman said.

"I see," Jakin remarked. "Why are you hesitating then? Your own chief's wife is imprisoned."

"I am the chief now," Suliman countered. "However, King Toren issued a decree that could change her status."

"How and when?" Jakin questioned eagerly, standing.

Suliman put up his hand and said, "The messenger is long gone. Don't fret; I didn't reveal your cause."

"I'm grateful, but why see Toren's men at all?" Jakin wondered.

"I want to find out who has the upper hand before I join the battle," Suliman explained. "His decree promised Larora won't be harmed as long as we don't join you."

"You know that's a lie," Jakin retorted. Suliman shrugged.

"Maybe, maybe not. Until one side proves I can trust them, I'm going to remain neutral."

Jakin's face reddened with rage, but Etania could understand the leader's logic. They were a ragtag group, with only the Eritam and Leici committed to their cause.

"My Master can be trusted," Keyel asserted.

"Can he?" Suliman said, motioning to the trees. "I heard there is a dangerous weapon he plans to use against the King."

Etania shivered, realizing the Naymatua was speaking of her.

"Etania is a Vexli, but she is not dangerous to us," Jakin explained, "Only to the Skazic."

Suliman stared at Etania, who avoided his gaze.

"This—girl—is the weapon! She has Neuma which can make someone powerless?" Suliman questioned. "She certainly doesn't appear strong."

Etania wanted to protest his words. Yet, her dismal performance with the crossbow and knife silenced her.

"Etania possesses an inner strength which is far superior to any physical skills," Keyel said. "You shouldn't underestimate her."

Etania brightened after hearing the compliment.

"Ach!" Suliman said. "Even if Etania is a Vexli, I don't think you could win against the King's men, who are trained and united. Do you really believe your little rebellion will succeed? We barely know how to work together, and they have trained together for years! For this reason alone, I would wait."

"While you wait, innocent people will die!" Jakin countered.

"We don't know that," Suliman said. "He could be right and you could be wrong. Then you wouldn't be so innocent."

Jakin clenched his teeth.

"Is that your final answer?" Jakin asked.

"Yes. As the new chief, I refuse to get involved until I see results," Suliman declared.

"Fine," Jakin said, rising. "Etania, I think it's time for us to leave." She nodded and stood, Keyel following.

"Before you leave, I want you to know we found horses that must be yours," Suliman said. "They will be at the guest house, waiting for you with new supplies. May Melchizedek straighten your paths."

Jakin didn't reply. Etania was almost certain that her father's flames were seeping out of his clothing and along his skin. Seeing her father's rudeness, she said, "Thank you."

Then, she looked away, and the first thing her gaze rested on was the seed which had been isolated in honor of Zeremu's death. She wasn't sure, but she thought she saw a small sprout emerging from the shell. Despite Suliman's refusal to help, the sprout made Etania smile.

Once they were back at the guest house, gathering together their supplies, they saw their horses. They checked their saddlebags, which were still on the horses' backs, now filled with plenty of fruit and vegetables. Etania was excited to see that not only her horse was well, but their saddlebags, with their regular clothing, were still on the pack horse.

"Hi Starlight! How are you, girl?" Etania greeted her horse, giving her a piece of fruit from the bag. The mare nickered in response as Etania happily pet her forehead.

"I think she missed us," Etania told Keyel.

"I'm glad someone did,'" Jakin grumbled. "Let's change into our normal clothes before we leave."

They split in different directions, and Etania dutifully wore her gambeson and mail, pulling on one of her tunics and split skirts. Once finished, they all met outside.

"I hope the Ningyo are more receptive," Keyel said, as they swung into their saddles.

"We shall see," Jakin replied, kicking his horse's sides and trotting away.

The wide path and constant bird song should have made Etania glad to be riding. However, her heart wasn't in the ride. She wondered if there was anything she could have done to convince Suliman to join them. Melchizedek said she would save Tamnarae, but so far, she hadn't done anything so grand. She wondered once again if Melchizedek had picked the wrong woman. *I guess I'll find out,* she thought grumpily.

KING TOREN PACED THE halls of Castle Khartome. As his wife's time drew closer, he withdrew into isolation. Ever since *that* day, he didn't like being around women near labor. Without Jazel's steady presence, Toren felt agitated and gruff. It didn't help matters when his spy informed him the wolves had failed to kill the Vexli.

He had to have another plan. Maybe visiting the jail would clear his head. Toren walked downstairs into the castle's basement, where the jail was located. There were several guards at the entryway, but they paid him no heed as he walked inside.

Each cell held only one person, in the stone prison. Behind the metal bars were stone beds, with buckets for a privy. Blankets, food, and water were provided so that the lords and ladies were uncomfortable but alive. They were valuable trophies after all—guarantees that the other territories would cooperate with his grand plan.

Toren looked at the first prisoner, a Naymatua woman. Vines grew all over her cell walls, seeking to erode the stone. But she couldn't get out, because the stone was a shield against someone with Neuma. Jazel had cast a spell over it using Malstorm's power, and the fact it worked on the prison itself pleased Toren. Yet, the enchantment didn't work on weapons. Seeing the leaders trapped made him happier. He walked past the other cells, counting his trophies. He possessed six lords and ladies out of twelve, and he intended to collect a few more.

Feeling better, King Toren decided to visit the courtyard where his men trained. There, the Skazic fought each other within full view of the castle servants. They no longer needed to hide their true nature, and anyone who protested was killed. An aura of fear had settled on most of the servants who stayed, and Toren relished in it. In the yard, Soacronis tested each other's wills with clawed fingers and loud hisses. Toothbreakers growled, biting and slashing at one another. Stone ground against stone as golems wrestled. Vortexes of water swirled from the fingers of pale-skinned Ningyo covered in scales. King Toren walked past them all and came to the target of his search.

This part of the yard was dark because of the castle wall—a perfect place for these Skazic to grow. These trees grew without light, in twisted shapes of bark and leaves. A dark face appeared in the middle of a trunk when King Toren stepped forward.

"What do you want, Darkness?" the tree asked, sounding like a cold breeze. Before King Toren could answer, the breeze continued along the row of trees.

"Whisperer of evil," another tree echoed.

"Servant of Malstorm!" a third tree confirmed.

"Tempter," a fourth tree declared.

"I only gave you what you wanted!" King Toren retorted.

"Power," the first tree said.

"Strength," the second tree added.

"Identity," the third tree cried.

"Unity," the fourth tree creaked.

"Yes, all of those things. Now you serve me in return," King Toren reminded.

"Agreed!" the four trees said in unison, sounding like creaking branches.

"I need you to send a message to your brethren," King Toren ordered. "I know your roots run deep, and you can reach them from here."

"What shall we tell them?"

King Toren smiled as he said, "Strangle the hafif woman with dark hair and white Neuma."

Chapter Sixteen

E tania tucked her brown hair behind her ear and clucked to her horse to
trot. Midday on the seventh day of their journey, they couldn't see the
sky. Forest branches blotted out the sun. They were almost out of Naymatua
territory, but it felt like they had just arrived. The trees were taller and wider,
with black bark that looked like fire had swept through the area. Their leaves
were pale imitations of green—nothing like the emerald they'd found at the
heart of Ligasha. Every once in a while, Etania heard snapping and creaking,
like when the Naymatua used their Neuma to move the trees, but there were
no Naymatua.

A breeze blew through the branches and trees, carrying with it a chill
that made Etania shiver. *When did the insects stop chirping and the birds cease
singing?* She wondered. Etania squeezed Starlight, whose trot quickened,
joining the rest of the group. She looked over at Keyel. His hand was on
his sword hilt and his eyes were sweeping over the darkness. Her father
lit a small, purple fire in one hand and held the reins in another hand to
illuminate their path. None of them spoke, but all of them sensed something
wasn't right.

An eerie creaking noise filled the shadowy wood. When Etania looked in
the direction of the sound, she saw a face in the tree trunk! Before she could
react, branches suddenly whipped out, striking them from their saddles so
that they slammed onto the ground. With a loud neigh, the horses took off.
As the travelers were stumbling to their feet, branches lashed forward again,
trying to reach them.

Jakin encircled the trio with fire, but as soon as the flames ignited, a
branch sped through, then another. Keyel hacked at the trees with his sword,
the flaming tree limbs falling to the ground. A branch distracted Keyel while
another sought to take his sword. Etania tried using her dagger to keep

the branches at bay, hacking away at them piece by piece. Still, the wooden tentacles reached for her, trying to wrap around her wrists as she fought them off.

"This way!" Jakin abruptly called out.

Using his flames, he cleared a small opening in the trees for them to escape. Etania followed Keyel at a sprint, the branches whipping against her cheeks and her shoulders. Once they were free of the circle of trees, they ran for the edge of the woods. Etania heard another snap and looked over her shoulder to see the black trees with faces in their trunks following her, running on their roots! With no time to contemplate the spectacle, she added speed to her steps. They were almost free of the forest, running to the beating of Etania's heart.

Before she could comprehend it, a branch flew and locked itself around her waist. She tried to cut it off, but more branches grew, faster and faster. She cried and kicked uselessly against the wood. Trapping her in a web of branches, the trees tightened around her wrists, legs, chest, and mouth. She looked around, trying to find the others, but they were nowhere to be seen. They must have escaped!

Etania tried to conjure a flame, but it flickered dully and went out. She panicked, realizing she could die as the vines constricted her. She couldn't breathe or concentrate. Air—Etania was losing air! Why couldn't she light her Neuma? She didn't know what hurt more: the branches, or realizing all of her training meant nothing.

Melchizedek, Etania cried, *help me!*

Her head spinning, her vision fading, she swore she saw someone approaching. Was it Melchizedek? Was he coming to take her to her mother?

"Etania!" the voice yelled.

It sounded familiar.

Air! She needed it so desperately! If she had air, she could recognize the voice. The pressure around her ribs and arms was unbearable. Were her bones going to break? Time seemed to pass slowly, but why would it be slow if she was dead?

"Etania!"

She felt a sudden release of pressure and she choked, unable to do anything but gasp as the musty air filled her lungs. Someone's strong arms were around her, and she cried out in pain.

He didn't pay attention to her cry. He kept running until the darkness turned into light and Etania breathed clean air again.

She blinked against the sunlight and saw the color of the man's hair. *Keyel.*

AS SOON AS KEYEL KNEW Etania was gone, he bolted, determined to rescue her. He screamed her name as he hacked his way forward, the branches retracting from the bite of his sword. When he saw her, wrapped in a web of wood, he felt renewed energy. He destroyed every branch and leaf with his sword, ripping Etania away and sprinting out of the forest. Placing her on the ground, he realized for the first time that he was shaking. He clenched his fists to steady them.

"Are you alright?" Jakin asked Etania, holding the reins of one of the horses. Keyel quickly realized that Jakin had somehow caught the horses on the outside of the forest. Etania had a few large scrapes and was catching her breath.

"Yes," Etania replied weakly, "but I think I've hurt something. My ribs..." Keyel knelt beside her.

"May I?" he asked, indicating them. She nodded, and he placed pressure slightly on them. Etania winced.

"A few of them are bruised, possibly broken," Keyel said. "We'll have to wrap them."

"I'll get the bandages," Jakin said, digging around in the pack and pulling them out. After Jakin handed him the bandages, he put a hand on Keyel's shoulder.

"Thank you," he said, empathetically.

"It's not that great a feat," Keyel replied, shrugging away Jakin's hand.

He didn't deserve praise when he couldn't heal her injuries or make up for the fact he'd let her be captured in the first place. Keyel wrapped the bandages around her waist and over her clothes; a makeshift brace, since they needed to ride. Jakin soothed the horses, which were still looking anxiously at the forest.

"I should give my thanks, too," Etania said hoarsely. "I thought you were Melchizedek coming to take me to the dead."

Keyel's heart skipped a beat. Dead—how close had she been to death? He looked at his Master, whose expression of fear matched his own.

"Turns out you were his messenger, rescuing me from trouble," Etania replied, but her eyes darkened. "I'm still so helpless. If I could use my Neuma properly, you wouldn't need to do that..."

If I could use my Neuma, you wouldn't be in so much pain, Keyel thought. He put the finishing touches on the brace of bandages.

"That should do it," he said. "You'll have to ride with someone for a while so we don't damage your ribs further. I'm sure Master and I can take turns."

Etania nodded and carefully stood, wincing as she did so. Keyel steadied her.

"Why don't you ride with me first?" Keyel asked.

"Okay," she agreed.

It's the least I can do, Keyel thought, as he helped Etania into the saddle, mounting his horse behind her. With the reins in his hands, he looked over at his Master.

Jakin nodded and said, "I don't know about you, but I'm ready to put those evil trees behind us!"

Keyel agreed, and they took off. Jakin led the pack horse. Starlight's reins were tied around Sunset's saddle horn so that Keyel could support Etania fully. She winced, leaning back against him as they rode. The smell of her hair reminded him of wildflowers and pine trees, soothing his heart. When she had almost died, he panicked. Now, all he felt was gratefulness that someone so precious to him was alive and well.

Precious. Somehow, Etania had snagged a place in his heart. He just wasn't sure how.

JAKIN WAS SURPRISED at his Apprentice. Keyel had always been one to take his duty seriously, but his impulsive rush to save Etania was unlike him. He had let his emotions rule him, and Jakin couldn't find fault with that when it meant his daughter was alive.

After a few hours of riding with Keyel, Etania switched from Keyel's horse to Jakin's horse. With his daughter firmly secured in front of him, Jakin brought up a subject that he had meant to tell her for weeks.

"Etania, I wanted to let you know that both your mother's necklace and your dagger have amethyst stones in them with just enough Neuma to be like a beacon. Wherever you are, I can find you," Jakin said.

"What! Why didn't you tell me before now?" Etania protested.

Jakin shrugged. "I've had a lot on my mind."

Etania glared at Jakin from the corner of her eye. "That would've been useful information to know, especially when I was captured by those trees."

Jakin's brow furrowed and his heart felt pained at Etania's suggestion. "I know I wasn't always there for you or Tala, but I did try to keep you both safe. If you're ever in trouble, you could use this amethyst to signal me."

"How?"

"Since you are related to me by blood, you can slightly use the stone. The stone may not be as effective as it would be with me, but you can give it enough Neuma to make it like a bright light in the sky."

"Okay," Etania said. She huffed and looked back at the road. *She is still mad at me for not coming after her,* Jakin thought.

Jakin tightened his grip around his reins. If he could, he would keep his daughter safe at all costs, even with his own life. He couldn't lose another woman he loved. Emotions welled inside of him. He'd been the first to run—the first to flee—he hadn't even realized the others weren't behind him. He was so used to hunting alone or with a partner that could fend for himself. He didn't consider others. This had built habits in him that had nearly cost him his daughter. Jakin swallowed hard to keep the tears from his eyes.

Tala, Jakin thought, *I really wish you hadn't left me alone...*

Chapter Seventeen

E tania dismounted, her ribs throbbing and her breathing tight. Limping toward a solitary tree that didn't look like it would kill her, Etania leaned against it, trying to take a deep breath. Every time she breathed, she panicked. She could remember the feel of the wood scraping against her throat as it tightened. She shook away the memory. A better question was why she couldn't use her Neuma. She looked down at her palms, unable to answer. Closing her eyes, she leaned against the tree and sighed heavily. Right now, all she wanted was rest.

"Are you feeling alright?" Keyel asked, once they finished setting up camp. Etania opened her eyes, snapping out of her reverie. She saw her father in the distance, hobbling the horses.

"I think 'alright' is the perfect way to describe my feelings," she joked.

Keyel blinked at her, unsure if she was serious.

"I'm fine," Etania clarified.

"I'm thankful," Keyel said. "I worried you were going to die."

"You're not the one who did nothing," Etania said, glaring at her father.

"He knew I could keep you in one piece. If I hadn't, he would've come after you," Keyel reassured.

"Yeah, because I'm his weapon," Etania snorted, "and a pathetic one at that!"

"Do you really believe he only thinks of you as a weapon?" Keyel questioned.

"Before I was a Vexli, did he ever mention me?" Etania retorted.

"He didn't tell me about his family," Keyel admitted. Etania waved at him as if to say he proved her point.

"Did I ever tell you how I met Jakin?" Keyel asked, and Etania shook her head.

"Well, I was at a Tenah, practicing swordplay, when I heard rustling bushes," Keyel said. "When I investigated, I found your father. Knowing he was a Lehrling, I asked to be his apprentice."

"I'm not sure what the point of this story is..." Etania said.

"I'm getting there. Anyway, I convinced Jakin to let me train with him even though I was thirteen."

"Thirteen. How long have you been his apprentice?" Etania asked, trying to figure out his age.

"Seven years," Keyel replied.

He's only three years older than me. She tucked away that information in her mind.

"Two more years and you'll be a journeyman," Etania realized. Keyel shrugged.

"There isn't a way to be a Lehrling's journeyman," Keyel said. "Besides, I never imagined doing anything other than hunting Skazic with your father."

"What about now?" Etania wondered. "Do you want to do anything else?"

A blush crossed Keyel's cheeks.

"Perhaps, if I ever have a family, I would take up a plough instead of a sword," Keyel said. The way his eyes met hers caused Etania's heart to beat erratically. Keyel cleared his throat.

"Anyway," he said, "the point of my story is that your father took in a boy who barely knew how to wield a sword to train as his apprentice. He saw more to me than met the eye, and I imagine he does the same for you."

"I hope so," Etania admitted, adding, "What about your father?"

Keyel's lip curled up.

"He's different!" he spat.

Etania suppressed a smile. The Leici didn't realize the irony of his statement, though his attempts to comfort were charming. Jakin came into the center of camp, putting an end to their conversation, and signaling preparations for bed.

The next morning, Jakin insisted Etania practice using her Neuma, despite Etania wondering if their practice did any good. Nevertheless, she wanted to improve, so she trained with him again. Would she ever be able to use her Neuma outside of training?

They continued their journey on horseback, and Etania rode with her father this time. With her hands free, she was able to observe their surroundings. The trees were gone, replaced by a grassy and muddy landscape. The horses walked through the muck slowly, so little progress was made. Bugs became a nuisance, from pesky mosquitoes and flies to chirping grasshoppers. Resting was a pain, with both her ribs and the wet ground creating discomfort. In this environment, her father struggled with lighting their fire every night.

A week passed before they saw Milapo in the distance by a long, winding river. The city had houses that were made of wood, sitting on platforms held together by various pegs. Children played in puddles, splashing happily, their hands making the water move according to their will. Women in long skirts watched them, scaling fish over clay pots or sewing together large nets for fishing. Before their group could come any closer to the village, tan men with seashell necklaces around their throats approached them, spears in hand.

"Why have you come here?" the one in the center asked.

"We have come to speak to your leader. Is he here?" Jakin replied, looking around the men.

"*She* is here, but you can't speak to her," the man snapped, pointing his spear at them.

"Rafael, who's there?" A gray-haired man approached.

"They're strangers and not to be trusted, Grandpa Andre," Rafael said.

"Let Isabella be the judge of that," Andre replied. "You two, care for their mounts. Are you hungry?"

Two of the men held the reins of the horses while they dismounted. Keyel kept himself between Etania and the spears even as the men led the horses away.

"Yes," Jakin said.

"Isabella will be where there is food," Andre said, beckoning them with his hand to follow him.

They trailed after Andre, Rafael and his men surrounding them. Rafael glared back at them as they walked, and Etania kept her face placid and unreadable. However, she was pretty sure that Keyel was meeting Rafael's gaze with an equally cold glare.

Walking past many of the standing houses, their boots sloshing through the mud, Etania tried not to cry out as the trek jarred her ribs. The women and children stared at them as they passed, even exclaiming "Leici" or "Lehrling." She thought one of them would say "Vexli" at any moment, but no child did, and Etania wasn't sure if she was happy about that or not. Andre stopped when they came to the largest house, standing on a wide platform. Keyel helped her climb on top of the porch. Two of Rafael's men went ahead of them and pushed open the double doors.

They entered, their eyes adjusting to the dim light provided by glowing seaweed in glass jars. At ten long tables arranged in rows, villagers ate their food. By a single table perpendicular to the room, a beautiful woman sat. Etania assumed she was Isabella. Her hair was a straight black that flowed to her waist, complimenting her tanned skin and deep, brown eyes. She wore a blue skirt and white linen shirt with a large seashell necklace hanging below her collarbone. Upon seeing Jakin and his party, she beckoned them forward.

"Greetings," Isabella said, her voice sounding like music. "What can I do for you, Lehrling?"

Jakin bowed slightly and the others followed suit, Etania taking a small curtsy.

"We have come, Isabella, to ask for your hospitality and for your assistance," the Lehrling stated.

"You are welcome at my table," Isabella said, "but I do not discuss politics until I've eaten."

"Of course," Jakin agreed. "This is my daughter, Etania, and my apprentice, Keyel."

"Greetings," Isabella replied, beckoning them to take a seat.

Rafael and his group moved behind the table, spears in hand, as if to guard both their leader and the newcomers. Jakin sat on Isabella's right and Keyel sat on her left, so Etania was next to Keyel. The Leici was as stiff as the wooden chair he occupied, but Etania was relaxed. Perhaps it was the soothing sound of the water beneath them, but she didn't fear the men behind her. Several men and women came and served them grilled fish and salad.

There was no conversation while they ate, but it wasn't silent. A steady stream of people entered the hall to eat, and then departed to return to their work. Finally, the food was finished, and Isabella motioned for them to follow her. They sauntered to a door that was in the back of the hall and were swept into another room, guarded by sentries. Inside, the same light from glowing seaweed lit the room, revealing a round table and chairs made of wood. In the center of the table was a large bowl of seashells, and the windows were covered with blue glass.

As they were seated once again, Jakin attempted to speak. Instead, Isabella motioned for silence and a servant came in, giving them each a wooden goblet and filling it with a dark liquid. Isabella lifted the goblet, all of them followed suit, and they tried their drinks.

Etania sipped the drink and tried not to spit it out again. The bitter drink had to be alcoholic: Jakin and Keyel also drank only a few sips of the mixture. Isabella drained her glass in one gulp. For the first time, her eyes opened fully, as if the bitter beverage lifted her spirits.

"Now, what can I do for you, Lehrling?" Isabella asked.

"As you may have heard, King Toren betrayed the council. He killed your father and imprisoned your mother," Jakin said.

"Oh, I've heard," Isabella said. "King Toren sent us a message and threatened repercussions if we don't obey."

"Do you plan on obeying?" Jakin asked. "Or joining us in a rebellion?"

"I don't know. Our water is low, and I doubt we are a match for him," Isabella admitted.

"Not even if we work together?" Jakin wondered. "We have enough strength to challenge King Toren's armies."

Etania bit back a choke. If she calculated correctly, they *didn't* have enough to challenge King Toren. Was her father that desperate to get an army that he would resort to lying or being overly confident?

Isabella shook her head.

"The lower part of the Eriam river is a source of power for my people. The mere fact that you walked on dry land instead of coming by boat is evidence of how weak we are."

"The *river* is the source of your Neuma, or Melchizedek?" Jakin asked pointedly. "*He* is the one who gave us Neuma. He is the one who will give you strength to stand against King Toren."

"Melchizedek abandoned us," Isabella said coldly.

"I know it looks that way, but..." Jakin attempted.

"Where is your wife?" Isabella questioned, cutting off his defense. Etania's pulse quickened.

"She was killed," Jakin replied.

"By whom?"

Jakin didn't answer, but his purple eyes darkened.

"That's what I thought," Isabella said. "If Melchizedek cared so much, why is she dead? Why is any of this happening?"

"We don't know why," Jakin said.

"Exactly," Isabella replied. "Melchizedek abandoned us."

"No he hasn't," Etania asserted.

Isabella's dark eyes turned to Etania. "How so?"

"He sent me to 'save' Tamnarae," Etania replied.

"You?" Isabella scoffed. "You're just a girl."

I'm a woman! Etania wanted to retort, but Isabella's words confirmed her own insecurities.

"She's also a Vexli," Jakin countered. "This means she can disable hundreds, if not thousands, of King Toren's Skazic. Her Neuma will defeat King Toren."

Isabella looked from Jakin to Etania to Keyel, confirming Jakin's word.

"You're serious," Isabella said.

Yes, Etania thought, *but I don't think I'm as great as my father would like her to believe.*

"We are," Jakin said. "Will you join us?"

"No," Isabella replied. "I will provide you with lodging, supplies, and boats to get to the next territory. However, I will not go against King Toren. Regardless of what you think *this girl* can do, you are no match for him."

"But—" Jakin began.

"That's enough," Isabella cut him off. "My people will provide for you, and then you will leave."

With those words, Isabella walked out of the room, boots clacking and skirt swishing on the wood floor. Jakin looked thoughtful, staring at the blue window. Keyel's fist tightened on the table and his mouth was a thin line.

From what Etania could see, they had merely a few thousand troops to join them—not nearly enough to defeat King Toren. They needed Isabella's men. But how could Etania blame Isabella for turning her back on Melchizedek and them? She was a failure of a Vexli.

A knock interrupted their cloud of gloom. Etania opened the door and a man and woman greeted her.

"We are here to lead you to your guest quarters and assist you," they said.

Etania nodded and motioned for the others to follow. They obeyed, and the pair led them back through the village, which was quiet now that it was growing dark. At a certain point, the man turned away and Etania was beckoned to follow the woman alone. She led Etania to a small house and told her she would come back in the morning.

Etania pushed open the door of the guest house and stepped inside. The room was large and comfy, with a sink and a stone fireplace on her left. In the center of the room was a small bed with light linens on a solid, wood frame. All of this Etania took in within seconds, but her eyes were drawn to the back of the bed, where a gigantic shell functioned as a headboard. Glowing moss sitting in its base revealed a myriad of colors: blue, purple, and pink. It was breathtaking.

At the foot of the bed was a trunk full of clothes like Isabella's—long, sweeping skirts and loose, long-sleeved tops. She promised herself she would wear those after her bath the next morning. She went to bed, her ribs aching despite the bandages Keyel wrapped around her waist.

Keyel. He seemed so distraught at the thought of losing her, but was that distress merely from friendship or something else? During their travels, they hadn't addressed the look Etania saw from time to time, or how her heart beat quickly sometimes around him. How could they speak of her confused feelings with so much happening around them?

She rubbed her mother's necklace between her fingers. She missed her now more than ever. Pushing away the thought, she settled into bed and fell asleep.

"MASTER!" A VOICE CALLED King Toren, rousing him from slumber.

The king groaned and staggered out of bed, walking over to the red orb from where the voice originated. This orb, a jewel put under a spell by Jazel, was how he stayed in contact with his Skazic. He blinked and peered into the red stone, which revealed a murky face.

"What do you want?" King Toren asked tersely. Nightmares about his father still plagued his dreams, so sleep was precious.

"The girl is here. I heard that she can wipe out thousands of Skazic," the voice replied.

"This I know already," King Toren replied.

"Well, I don't believe it!" the voice huffed. "This girl is weak."

"Really?" King Toren said, with a yawn.

"Yes. I'm going to prove it to you, Master, if you'll let me. I'd like to use my new powers on the girl," the voice replied.

King Toren considered it. His newest Skazic was untrained and alone in the field. He wasn't sure how well the Skazic would perform, especially since the others had failed him. Then, he would lose his spy in the area and he would be forced to hunt the Vexli himself. He rubbed his beard. But if the new one succeeded....

"Agreed," King Toren said. "Be careful though, for the Vexli already succeeded in turning one of my men, and her protectors are not to be underestimated. Understood?"

The face in the murky red orb nodded, and the image faded.

"Back to sleep it is, then," King Toren declared, stumbling toward his bed. A loud knock kept him from sleep again.

"Your Majesty, it's time," the servant declared at the door.

King Toren swallowed.

"Lead the way," he said grimly.

Chapter Eighteen

Etania woke to the sound of roaring water. Alarmed, she abandoned her mail and gambeson, quickly getting dressed in the clothes at the foot of her bed, and stepped outside. A large flood of water swept over the landscape, thundering by the guest house. A woman walked through the water, carrying Jakin and Keyel on a wave. Etania gasped when she realized the woman was Isabella, but not an Isabella she recognized.

Her black hair looked as oily as seaweed and her face and arms were covered with scales. Her black skirt clung to her body and her feet were like fins. When Isabella saw Etania, she strode right toward her, the water swirling around Jakin and Keyel in a vise-like grip. Water pinned their wrists, tied their legs together, and blocked their mouths. Etania was horrified and shocked at Isabella's sudden transformation. Her heart raced, and she wondered what she should do next.

A crowd of people fled from their leader, looks of horror on their faces. A few tried to fight Isabella, but she pushed them away with unnatural strength. That's when Etania realized that only she could stop the Skazic-Isabella.

"Stop!" Etania cried, the warmth in her heart trickling down her arms and lighting flames on her palms.

"Let's see if your father was right and you're powerful enough to take down an army of Skazic!" Isabella taunted.

With a flick of her wrist, Isabella created warriors made completely of water and they came toward Etania. She flung her flames at them so that the fire dissipated in a steam, obscuring Etania's view of Isabella.

"That's what I thought!" Isabella goaded. "You don't have enough in you to stop any Skazic, let alone me."

To emphasize her point, she brought Keyel forward and started surrounding him with water so that he was drowning.

"No!" Etania yelled. She willed herself to grow hotter, until she felt like her flames were covering her entire body. She would show Isabella! She would show her father. She was the weapon they wanted: a weapon worthy of saving Tamnarae.

Etania stepped off the platform of the house, and the flames evaporated the water so quickly she walked on dry land. As she went, her Neuma consumed all of the water near her, including the water around Keyel— releasing steam. The steam hit her like a hot fog, but still Etania charged forward.

Isabella cried in pain, as if boiling away the water had hurt her. Etania didn't care; she would free her loved ones and stop Isabella no matter what! She kept going, venturing toward her father next.

"What are you doing?" Isabella hissed. "You're weak! You can't do anything."

Etania wasn't weak. Finally, she could be the person who saved Tamnarae! She could prove to them she could control her Neuma. Her flames licked up the water holding Jakin. Isabella's water was weaker now, swirling slower around her. Her eyes were wide with fear, and she backed away from Etania.

"No!" Isabella cried.

She conjured a wave as tall as a tree and sent it toward Etania, but the Vexli countered with an even bigger wave of flames. It swallowed up the wave of water. Etania and the fire were one being, and there was no stopping either now. She felt so hot, so blazing, that it might consume her—but she pushed on. She would show the Skazic who they stood against! She imagined a spear of flame in her hand and it appeared. With a roar, she thrust it toward Isabella with all her might.

"Etania, *no*!" Jakin cried out, and he jumped to intercept the flame.

The spear wasn't meant for him. It sailed through him and into Isabella, who screamed in pain. The water dissipated. Isabella fell to her knees as the scales fell from her body, leaving her a Ningyo woman once again.

Etania stumbled toward her father. Why would he intercept her spear? Hadn't she done what he wanted? Didn't she prove with it that she was the weapon to save Tamnarae? She felt so cold. The flames were gone—not even flickering in her chest—and she shivered. Her ribs were throbbing, the thrill of the battle unable to disguise the pain any longer. She fell to the ground, unable to rise.

KEYEL STOOD AS SOON as he was released, trying to rush toward Etania despite choking on steam. He wasn't sure if he was going to help her or stop her as the flames around her grew in strength. She was living fire—something Keyel had never seen in all of her training. Before, her Neuma was controlled and contained; now, it burned a destructive path without restraint. He tried to get closer to Etania, but the flames burned him, too. He wouldn't be able to reach her, and she looked like she might *kill* Isabella. Keyel's heart thumped painfully in his chest.

Jakin rushed past Keyel, and he watched in astonishment as the Lehrling was unaffected by the flames or steam. Keyel couldn't see anything in the fog, but he heard Etania's roar and pushed forward. The steam and fire dissipated, and all he could see were three collapsed bodies: Etania, Jakin and Isabella. He rushed toward Etania.

Keyel gathered her carefully in his arms. She was breathing shallowly, and her eyes rolled back into her head as she lost consciousness. She was alive, but what had happened? Jakin was coughing, rising to a sitting position. From the black mark on his chest, Keyel knew that Jakin had intercepted one of Etania's flames. To leave a mark, it must have been bad. Keyel carried Etania to his Master, placing her by Jakin. He only wished he could heal them both.

Isabella stirred, and Keyel looked over at the Ningyo. He was grateful she was alive and Etania hadn't succeeded in her plan. Suddenly, a red, glass orb floated above Isabella's chest. The glass surface revealed King Toren's face as if it were a mirror.

"I see my servant failed," King Toren said.

"She did, you wretch!" Jakin shouted.

"Yes, but unlike some servants, she was useful," King Toren declared.

"Was? She's still alive," Jakin said.

"Not for long. I'm afraid this little communique spells her death," King Toren explained. "I'm only here because I want you to receive a message."

"You don't have to kill her!" Keyel cried.

"She's fulfilled her duty. Besides, you and I both know there are consequences to our actions," King Toren replied. Keyel shuddered. How much did this man know?

"The message is this, Jakin," King Toren declared. "I will come for your daughter, and I will have her Neuma as mine. Then, you will know who to fear!"

"Over my dead body!" Jakin replied.

"And mine," Keyel echoed.

"That is easily accomplished," King Toren said, and they heard crying in the background.

The cry of a newborn baby. Jazel had given birth.

The image disappeared, and the orb morphed into a red dagger, plunging toward Isabella's chest faster than Keyel or Jakin could react. They rushed to her side as she choked out her last words.

"I'm sorry," she said, her gaze toward the sky. "Will you forgive me?"

Keyel and Jakin didn't reply. Isabella closed her eyes and drew her final breath. Keyel shook, trying to steady his emotions. To his shock, Jakin cried.

"We will bury her," Andre spoke, interrupting them. "You must take care of your own."

He motioned toward Etania. Keyel walked over to her, brushing her hair out of her eyes; the tendrils crisp from the flames. Even though she was breathing, she mumbled incoherently in her sleep. He had failed to protect her once again, but how could he protect her from herself?

"Let's get her away from this place," Jakin said, standing slowly.

Keyel agreed, wrapping his arms around Etania and carrying her gently to avoid hurting her ribs. Andre and his men carried away Isabella.

ETANIA BURNED.

She hurt everywhere.

Etania couldn't breathe.

She could see faces: her mother, her father, Keyel, even Isabella.
Etania cried out, unanswered.
She rocked back and forth, her only comfort coming in the pain.
Days or weeks later, Etania felt Him coming.
He was clothed in white, and his face shone like the flames around her, but his voice and eyes were gentle as he said, "Enough, Etania. It is time."

ETANIA WOKE AND LOOKED around her. It was early evening. She was on a large raft gently riding down the river. At the helm was a Ningyo man she didn't recognize. In the center, Keyel and Jakin ate dinner.

"Where am I?" she whispered.

The others didn't hear her. She tried again.

"Where am I?" she hissed, and they turned toward her. Keyel was the first to move. He ran, practically tipping their craft, sliding to kneel beside her.

"You're on a raft. We're on our way up the lower half of the Eriam River to see the Kinzoku," he said, squeezing her hand gently. "The horses are safe with the Ningyo. Thank Melchizedek your fever finally broke."

His touch felt electric. Etania blushed, and Keyel removed his hand. He cleared his throat to say, "Are you alright?"

"I think so," Etania replied. "What happened and how long was I out?"

"Three days. And you lost control," Jakin said.

He pulled up his shirt and showed her a black mark on his tan skin. A mark from where the spear of flames had sailed through him. Etania gasped.

"Isabella?" she asked.

"Dead," Jakin replied, and at her look, reassured her. "King Toren ended her life. You merely weakened her body. But if I hadn't interfered—"

"I would have killed her," Etania completed, and she shuddered.

By becoming the weapon she thought was worthy of saving Tamnarae, her Neuma had consumed her.

"I don't understand," Etania whispered. "I didn't think my Neuma could kill anyone."

"It doesn't normally," Jakin explained. "Do you remember when I told you that I knew another Vexli before you?"

"Yes. He died," Etania said, a cold pit forming in her stomach.

"He did, but it was his own doing. Daas was his name, and he was—" Jakin hesitated for a moment and then continued. "He was one of my closest friends."

"What happened?" Etania questioned.

"He never trusted Melchizedek's plan completely," Jakin said. "He always questioned why Melchizedek wanted to help the Skazic instead of killing them. He and I were similar in that way—focused on eliminating the problem. You have to remember that back then, we were in a war that spanned the entire world. The war that never seemed to end."

Jakin's eyes darkened as he continued.

"Daas was the only one of us without Neuma. So Melchizedek blessed him with the same Neuma as you, saying that with this Neuma, he would do great things. Daas grew impatient, and behind my back, he sold information about our location to Malstorm. Then he joined their side, destroying everyone and everything with his flames. The flames that were meant to transform, not kill."

Just like me. Etania thought, and shuddered.

"But worst of all, Melchizedek died because of Daas' betrayal," Jakin finished.

"Died?" Etania repeated. "Because of Daas..."

"Yes. Melchizedek said Daas' betrayal was part of his plan," Jakin explained, "but that doesn't excuse Daas' actions."

"Or mine," Etania admitted.

"It's okay, Etania," Keyel said. "You didn't realize what you were doing."

"No! I knew," Etania retorted. "I fought against Isabella with everything because I want to prove I was a good weapon. Turns out, I'm just as weak as a Skazic, willing to do anything for power."

"No, you're not," Keyel countered.

"Yes, I am. Even my father doesn't want to admit it. That's why he's silent!" Etania accused.

"I'm silent because I was wrong," Jakin said. "I was wrong about Daas and I'm wrong about you. I thought the way to counter a Skazic was to turn you into a weapon. Instead, you became an explosive. All because I wanted to wipe out the Skazic, to keep them from ever surfacing again..."

He trailed off, and looked at the river that was passing by at a rapid speed.

"That flame you had roaring around you is like mine inside. But once I saw you about to kill Isabella—" Jakin hesitated. "I knew it was wrong. I fed your flame, Etania. So I am to blame, in the end."

Etania wanted to accept this, to throw the blame back at his feet. After all, hadn't she blamed him for never being there for her when she was a child? Hadn't she blamed him for never paying attention to her? Yet, she couldn't accept it—not when her flames created a black mark on his skin.

"Have you always felt this way?" Etania asked. "Your hatred for the Skazic?"

Jakin nodded.

"It's the reason I wasn't there for you, Etania," Jakin explained. "I'm sorry for not being there, then or now."

The explanation hit her heart. Maybe, just maybe, her father did love her, and his hatred for the Skazic kept him from showing it!

"Just because you have that hatred doesn't mean it could pass to me," Etania said. "The truth is that I lost control and almost killed two people. If you don't think training can help me control it, then I don't know what will."

"Melchizedek," their Ningyo guide spoke up, and they realized he was listening. "He can help you. Just call on him."

Etania blushed. How could she go to him, after all this? But Jakin and Keyel nodded at her in encouragement, so she closed her eyes and prayed.

Etania stood in the octagonal room, waiting for Melchizedek. The basin of water in the center gurgled, and images flashed incoherently across the windows of the tower. She walked up to one of the images.

To her horror, it showed her attacking Isabella and how the flames had consumed her. She turned away, ashamed, and saw Melchizedek approach.

"Destructive, isn't it?" Melchizedek said, his eyes never wavering from the images.

Etania couldn't look up.

"You were consumed by your own desire to prove your worth as a weapon," Melchizedek explained.

"I know this," she said, still avoiding his gaze.

"As do I," Melchizedek replied. "Look at me, Etania."

She lifted her head, and her brown eyes met Melchizedek's.

"I saw the flames of your nightmares. I see the flames in your heart. Some of them are my gift—some of them are your pain," Melchizedek said.

Etania could feel it; his penetrating gaze stripping away her defenses. She felt naked, even though she was fully clothed. But even when everything was laid bare, she sensed something else too.

"You still love me?" Etania said. It was a statement more than a question.

"Yes. Nothing will stop me from loving you," Melchizedek declared.

"B-but how?" Etania stuttered, flabbergasted. "I am worthless."

She'd done everything wrong and had almost killed someone. How could he love her?

"Yes, you are, apart from me." His words pierced her heart, but he wasn't finished. "When I died, I put to death that evil. The evil that would cause you to burn away everyone and everything. But when I lived, I gave everyone the opportunity to put to death the evil in their hearts."

"So you're saying even people like Isabella could be yours?" Etania questioned.

"Even her, and she has been saved by fire, so to speak. So will you be mine, too?"

Etania's heart quaked. If he could accept Isabella, it made sense, he could accept her, flaws and all. Melchizedek's love was warm and inviting. Just like in her nightmares, all her fears dissipated in his gaze. Etania's shortcomings could be covered by his everlasting love.

"I will," she declared.

Etania felt searing warmth on her shoulder and, after looking down, noticed the incandescent glow of Melchizedek's mark. The shape of a rose—just like her mother's Mark.

"This Mark will give you control of your Neuma," Melchizedek said, "and it will be a daily reminder of me."

"Thank you," Etania cried. "I don't deserve it."

"No one does," Melchizedek declared. "Remember, Etania; this is just the beginning. You will face great trials, but I will always be with you. This Mark is evidence of me. Cry out, and I will come."

"I will," she agreed. "Goodbye, Melchizedek."

"Not goodbye, for I am always with you," Melchizedek corrected, smiling. His words caused the rose to glow as the image of his kind face faded.

Chapter Nineteen

Etania opened her eyes. Keyel was by her arm, and Jakin was standing a few feet away.

"Well?" Jakin asked.

She smiled wide, and the rose Mark glowed in response.

"You're Marked!" Jakin also smiled. "That means you're officially part of Melchizedek's family."

"He told me he would help me control my powers!" Etania exclaimed.

"I told you," the Ningyo guide replied, "And just in time, too."

"What do you mean, Gabriel?" Keyel asked.

"We are getting close to the Khartome lake," Gabriel answered.

"What's so dangerous about that?" Etania asked.

"I can't control the water around Toren's island," Gabriel said.

"Why not?" Etania questioned.

Gabriel shrugged. "I don't know."

"The Skazic," Jakin said. "King Toren must have his Skazic controlling the water around the castle and the island."

"What should we do then?" Keyel asked.

"I'm not sure," Jakin said.

"Can we carry the boat to water that Gabriel controls?" Etania suggested, looking at the others.

"Will you be able to tell which water you can control?" Jakin inquired of Gabriel.

"Yes, by touch. However, you do know that we will have to carry the raft for about three days until we reach the Timane River, right?" Gabriel said.

"I realize that, but it is the only plan we have to evade the creatures living in Lake Khartome," Jakin explained.

"I guess we'll get to stretch our arm muscles then," Keyel said.

"And try to pass by Lake Khartome undetected," Gabriel added.

"Easy," Jakin said sarcastically.

The statement did nothing to soothe Etania. Her heart was skipping like a stone across the water.

QUEEN JAZEL CUDDLED her newborn. The baby girl was wrapped tightly in blankets so that when her father came to check on her, he would not be able to see that his son was a daughter. Jazel knew that would keep them both safe—for now.

With her child in the world, she could now focus on assisting Toren. Her husband had tried to take the Vexli's life and all his attempts failed to do so. It was past time for her to interfere and hand him the one weapon that would disable the Vexli forever.

"Jazel!" Toren called out. "Jazel, I want to see my son!"

Toren burst into her room and Jazel gently handed the fussy baby to him.

"Oh, is he hungry?" Toren stroked the small amount of fuzz that was growing on the baby's head.

"Yes, I was about to nurse him," Jazel said.

"Are you sure you don't want a nursemaid for the baby?" Toren said.

Jazel shook her head. She wanted her baby to bond to her so completely that she would follow in her footsteps, just like Jazel was following her mentor's steps. The mentor who had taught her to take vengeance on the person responsible for her mother's death. Toren handed Jazel the baby and Jazel prepared to nurse her daughter.

"Now that our son is born, I wanted to tell you what is happening with the Lehrling and Vexli. I believe they are heading toward the Kinzoku territory next because it's the most logical area after the Ningyo."

"How many races have they recruited?" Jazel asked.

"Only the Leici and Eritam committed soldiers. The Naymatua still hesitate and so do the Ningyo, though I lost my servant there," Toren explained.

"Oh, Isabella? I had great hopes for her," Jazel replied.

"So did I." Toren sighed deeply. "I think that I need to take care of this myself."

"I agree, and I have just the weapon to take care of the Vexli once and for all." Jazel pointed to the chest at the foot of her bed. "Open it."

Toren walked over and thrust the wooden lid open.

"Grab the black box," Jazel commanded.

Obediently, Toren pulled out a long wooden box that was painted black. His eyes widened.

"Is this what I think it is?" Toren asked. Jazel nodded.

"Go on, look," she encouraged.

Toren slid the lid off the box and pulled out the objects within. When he held them up, the candlelight glinted off the silver surfaces.

"The gauntlets of Daas. He used them to change his Neuma, and now you will use them to control the Vexli. She will be your personal slave," Jazel said, with a wide smile.

Toren held the two gauntlets up in triumph.

"Yes, she will!" he declared, walking over to Jazel and kissing her cheek. "I will be back for you and my son, carrying the Vexli as a trophy when I return."

"I know you will," Jazel replied.

Toren walked out of the room and Jazel encouraged the child to nurse.

"See," she whispered in the child's ear, "It's not hard to get someone to do what you want."

THE NIGHT WAS TOO STILL for Keyel's liking. There were hardly any noises from bugs, and he only spotted a bird or deer occasionally. He wanted to grab Etania's hand, pull her close, and guard her with his arms—just like his Mark of a shield. This feeling had blossomed from the moment Keyel saved Etania from the tree Skazic and was interfering with his duties. He wondered if it was the true reason he had failed to protect Etania from Isabella.

Sweat dripped down the inside of his shirt as they carted the raft through the woods for the last time. Every day, for three days, they'd hiked through the woods, carrying the raft during the day and hiding the raft in brush during the night. Each day, his arms felt heavier and heavier until this day, when he knew the hiking would end. Always skirting Khartome lake, they were careful to stay far enough from the shore to evade any Skazic.

At last, they reached the northern part of the lake and Gabriel knelt down to touch the water. He nodded at them, indicating it was safe. They placed the raft down on the flowing water and Gabriel beckoned the waters to turn the opposite direction. Their boat would have been going upstream, but now, it created its own current. Keyel appreciated the Ningyo's Neuma.

Arms sore and beyond tired, Keyel prepared for sleep with the others on the raft. As he settled into his blankets, he saw the island castle, an outline of darkness against the moon. The stone towers stared at him, as if they were watching him like King Toren, waiting to strike.

He shook off the foreboding feeling by looking over at Etania, who was gazing serenely at the lake. Ever since her return from Melchizedek, she laughed and smiled more, and it added greatly to her beauty. Keyel shook away the thought.

"Anything wrong, Keyel?" Etania asked.

"No, I'm just glad we'll be putting that castle behind us," Keyel said.

Etania glanced at the shadowy outline.

"Only for now," Jakin said. "Next time, we will be back with an army."

A battle. Something neither Etania nor he was prepared for. Keyel had fought in plenty of skirmishes with the Skazic, but nothing compared to a battle of so many armies. Etania was also inexperienced. She could defend herself with a crossbow and a knife, but that was about it. He wasn't sure how she would react or how he would protect her against hundreds of Skazic.

As if reading his mind, Etania said, "We'll be fine, Keyel."

Keyel nodded and pulled the blankets over him. Inwardly, he wrestled once again with the fact that he couldn't protect Etania from everything, as much as his heart longed to do so.

THEY TRAVELLED FOR three more days on the river. Etania's ribs continued to heal as they sailed up the Timane river to the Kinzoku territory. As each day passed, Etania felt her heart grow lighter, flying like the birds that followed them through their journey. They were leaving behind the dark castle and rafting toward the mountains. The Timane river stopped flowing right at Azeeka, the city that marked the beginning of Kinzoku territory.

"Thank you for taking us this far, Gabriel," Jakin said.

"You're welcome! Despite what happened, I know that you care about the Ningyo. I only hope my people will be able to see it that way," Gabriel replied.

"So do I," Jakin said, shaking the Ningyo's hand before the man got back into his raft and floated away. Etania waved goodbye and then shouldered her knapsack, looking over at her father.

"Where to next?"

"We'll stay at Azeeka and then head up into the mountains, where the Kinzoku leader lives," Jakin said. "Stay close. I don't like this wind,"

Etania wondered what he meant, until she saw the gathering clouds and felt the penetrating, cold wind. She was grateful when they spent the night with the Kinzoku living in Azeeka. These men and women were very different from the other races. With mostly red or black hair, they were very blunt, expressing their grumpiness about taking in a Lehrling and his party. However, their anti-Toren sentiments made Etania hopeful about garnering the support of the leader of the Kinzoku.

The next day, the three of them traded their lighter gear for weather appropriate clothing. Thin cloaks were exchanged for fur-lined ones, and wool undergarments were purchased for each person. This finished, the trio faced the trail again, starting their hike from the bottom of the mountain. The wind increased as they continued, the pine trees offering little resistance as they ascended in elevation. They stopped briefly for lunch, shivering together as they ate. Then they were back on the trail, continuing their long journey until the sun descended in the sky.

"How long this time, father?" Etania asked, as they shivered around a small fire.

"We should reach the Kinzoku leaders in a few days, and hopefully before the first snow falls," Jakin replied.

"I hope they have fires there," Etania said, her teeth chattering. Jakin chuckled.

"They have big ones," he told her. Etania scooted closer to Keyel for warmth.

"We must get some sleep while we can," Jakin said. "Keyel, take first watch and wake us if it begins to snow."

"Yes, Master," Keyel replied, and walked over to one of the rocks and sat.

Without her companion's body heat, Etania decided to slip into bed early and snuggle beneath the blankets. She looked up at the clouds in the sky and recalled the first time she had experienced snow.

Mother woke me early to see the snow falling like twirling, white dancers in the morning light. She remembered. *Then, when the snow stopped falling, we built a snowman, adding a scarf my father never wore to its neck. We laughed and then ran inside to a roaring fire and a great bowl of soup that Serena made.*

Etania fiddled with the heart amulet of her mother's necklace as she reflected on the memory somberly. She was far from home and its familiar faces. Were Serena, Grace, Barick, Alfred, and the others okay? So much suffering had occurred since King Toren betrayed them: her mother's death, the Skazic's corruption, and Isabella's murder. She wondered if King Toren hunted her now. She shivered, pushing those thoughts to the back of her consciousness as she fell asleep.

"FATHER! FATHER!" TOREN stumbled through the castle halls, looking.

"Mom's having another baby!" he called out, searching, constantly searching. Jakin stopped him, his eyes a dark purple.

"Come," he said.

He followed the Lehrling, winding through the halls until they came to his mother's bedroom.

This didn't make sense. His father wouldn't be in there, would he?

He pushed through the doorway, and the servants were weeping. At his entrance, they stopped. The room was dark and it stank. He looked over at his mom, but she was still, so very still. He went to her side and shook her.

"Mother? Mother?" Toren repeated.

"She's dead, and so is your sister," Jakin pronounced. "I'm sorry."

"No!" He exclaimed. "Where is my father? There has to be something we could do."

"My prince, we have been unable to find your father. I'm afraid...he's finally lost it," one of the servants said.

"I know this is the last thing you want to hear right now," Jakin said, "But it looks like you're King."

Toren woke in a sweat, trying to shake away the memory of how helpless he had felt seeing his mother dead. He was in a tent in Naymatua territory, and he guessed the dreams had returned because Jazel was not by his side. Walking over to a basin of water, King Toren dipped his washcloth in the liquid and patted his face with a cool cloth.

Trying to remember happier times, he recalled how he first met Jazel at a ball in Northern Tamnarae and their immediate connection as a couple. After a quick courtship, they were married. Then, when Jazel shared what Jakin had done to her mother, Toren agreed to her plans, eager to please his wife. Besides, he also held a grudge against the Lehrling who was supposed to be like a father to him, but instead abandoned him as soon as he turned eighteen.

Yet, the nightmare-memory shook him. They had travelled for about a week now, making their way north through the lands of the Naymatua, and the journey was wearing on him. That must be another reason, he rationalized, shaking off the fear.

"My liege, we have news of the Lehrling and Vexli," Damien said, emerging into his tent. Toren smiled at the Skazic who was first changed by the Vexli.

"Where are they?" Toren asked.

"Near the Kinzoku fortress. Apparently the Ningyo dropped them off and was returning home when our soldiers captured him," Damien replied.

"Well, I'm glad he gave us the information," Toren said, with a smirk.

"The Ningyo didn't give us the information willingly, Sire," Damien said.

Toren shrugged as he questioned, "Is the information legitimate?"

"Of course, my king," Damien replied.

"Good. We are a few weeks away from the Kinzoku, but we will get them. I'm sure of it."

"If you would like, the other Soacronis and I would be willing to fly ahead and see if we could capture them."

Toren arched an eyebrow and stroked his beard, asking, "You would lead them, I expect?"

"Yes," Damien replied. "Arie said he would be able to carry me and fly."

"Great!" Toren slapped Damien on the back, but squeezed his shoulder tightly.

"I'd rather see you dead than come back to me without the girl, you hear me?" Toren warned.

Damien paled and said, "Yes, your Majesty!"

Damien shuffled out of the tent just as Toren was putting on his cloak. Ruling by fear was a benefit of Jazel's plan—one that made him feel better every time he lashed out. With the gauntlets and his army, the Vexli would soon be as obedient as Damien.

Chapter Twenty

Jakin, Etania, and Keyel travelled for two days in the bitter cold, making their way farther up the mountain, to the tree line, and the entrance of the Kinzoku fortress. Each day became cloudier, and Jakin found himself on high alert during the night watch. Yet, when he could sleep, the bitter cold made it difficult.

Jakin hated being in the mountains at the beginning of spring. Because of the elevation, this area was almost always cold, even when spring was trying to show its face. As someone who originally hailed from the desert, this weather was not his preference. He would much rather face heat.

Sighing and shivering at the same time, Jakin rose to his feet and peered out into the darkness. Snow was beginning to fall, and he might have to wake the others. He sneezed, and suddenly he could see it: a single, flickering flame.

Was that a fire? Who would be making a fire at this time of night? He thought. He quickly realized what it could be. *The Skazic. King Toren sent more after us!*

Brandishing his hammer, Jakin thought briefly about waking Keyel to help him. He pushed that thought aside. The Leici needed rest, and Jakin could handle a few Skazic on his own. He wasn't called a Lehrling for nothing. He trudged forward, even as the snow began to swirl around him.

Today, vengeance will be mine! Jakin thought, grim determination seeping through him.

IN KEYEL'S HALF-CONSCIOUS mind, he wrestled with his new feelings. He knew his emotions weren't good and would impair his abilities to protect Etania. Yet, he couldn't help feeling a thrill as he helped Etania practice with her crossbow or shared a blanket with her around the fire. If he was to court her, would her father no longer be his master? Would he be—

Keyel startled awake. Something cold hit his shoulder, and Keyel swatted at it as he stretched. Something wet dropped on his nose, and he looked up.

"It's snowing!" He said, and immediately went to wake Etania.

"Where's my father?" Etania asked, once she rubbed the sleep from her eyes.

Keyel looked around, even kicking the growing snow to see if he was underneath.

"I don't see him."

"We better look for him. He could freeze to death out here," Etania said.

"So could you," Keyel said. "It would be better to find the Kinzoku. We're probably a few kilometers from the entrance."

"I don't care, I'm going!" Etania retorted.

"Don't you—" Keyel began, but Etania started off in the snow.

He followed her, silently frustrated. *Why did she have to be so stubborn?* The snow was falling steadily now, growing around them, packing around their feet. Soon, they would be overwhelmed by it.

"Do you know where you're going?" Keyel shouted.

Etania didn't reply. The snow was falling so swiftly that Keyel could barely see her back.

"We should turn back! I'm sorry, but there's no way of finding him in this storm!" Keyel yelled again.

This time Etania paused, and Keyel hastened to reach her. At her feet was a light-purple glow from his Master's amulet. They immediately began working together to unbury the Lehrling.

"He's alive. Barely," Keyel said, flinging Jakin over his shoulder. "Let's go."

"Go where?" Etania said. "The snow covered our path."

Keyel cursed himself. He should have been keeping track of where they were going! Maybe if they just started hiking in one direction, they could make it to safety. As he moved forward, he checked to make sure Etania followed by holding her hand with one arm and steadying his Master on his shoulder with his other. He blinked away snow, his fingers numb despite the warmth from Etania's hands. He wrapped his scarf around his mouth, but the wind and snow still felt like it froze his lips. Even his breath didn't feel warm as it escaped in labored huffs. His nose felt ice form over it, and his bones seemed as stiff as the snow around them.

Time stretched exponentially before Etania brought them to a stop.

"You have no idea where we're going, do you?" She said, her voice soft. Keyel didn't reply, but tried to tug her forward again. She resisted.

"Stop, Keyel. It's too late. There's no way we can find our way in this storm!"

"Then what do you suggest we do?" Keyel snapped.

"I don't know, dig a shelter?"

Etania was right. They couldn't keep hiking forward. But her idea to dig a shelter took too much time. Keyel saw a cluster of trees and headed toward it, dragging Etania to a sitting position by the trees. Jakin's still body was on his left and Etania was cuddled next to him on the right.

"I think this is the best we can do," Keyel said.

"So do I," Etania agreed, shivering and drawing closer to him.

They sat, side by side, hearts beating in unison as the snow continued to fall, growing steadily around them.

"Why did Melchizedek choose me to save Tamnarae, if just to die out here?" Etania asked.

Die? They couldn't die. He didn't want them to die. He wanted to...

"I'm sorry Etania," Keyel said.

"Sorry, for what?" Etania wondered.

"For getting us lost. I should've watched where we were going," Keyel replied.

"I should've gone to the Kinzoku like you said," Etania admitted, biting her lip. "What was my father doing out in this storm, anyway?"

"I don't know," Keyel admitted. "It's weird for him to be out on his own, unless he saw a Skazic."

Etania groaned.

"I could see that."

"He can be stubborn sometimes," Keyel said. He wanted to add *Just like you* but felt that wouldn't be appropriate. Etania shivered, and Keyel drew her closer to his chest.

"I'm sorry too," Etania said. "It's just...when I thought of my father dying out there...losing another parent..."

Her voice broke, and he tightened his hold around her.

"That's why I like you, Etania. You have a kind heart," Keyel said.

"Like me?" Etania's eyes widened. "Do you mean—?"

"No, forget it," Keyel retracted.

"Keyel, we're about to die. If there's anything that should be said, it should be said now!" Etania said firmly.

Keyel hesitated. She was right. More than likely they would die out in the snow. What did it matter what he said? Drawing her close, he kissed her forehead.

"I love you, Etania," he whispered.

"What?" Etania asked, because at that moment, the snow swept upon them like a blizzard, roaring out the noise.

Keyel laughed desperately. His confession, blown away by the wind, would only be known in Safarast, where it no longer mattered. He closed his eyes as she snuggled into his chest.

At least they would die together.

ETANIA REMEMBERED HEARING and seeing other people arrive just as she was losing consciousness. She was lifted and slung over someone's shoulder and saw that Keyel and Jakin were taken away too. Only then did she allow herself to sleep.

When Etania woke, an unknown woman's face was in her field of vision. Her bright red hair matched the flames burning to her right. Etania felt like stinging needles were covering her body as her skin thawed. She was lying on a cushioned mattress, but there were no blankets on her. Rock walls without windows comprised the room. She must have been brought into the underground Kinzoku fortress.

"How are you feeling?" the woman asked.

"I'm fine. Keyel...my father..." Etania began.

"They're both thawing in another room, but they're all right," the woman said. "My name's Bayanna, by the way."

"Thank you, Bayanna, for rescuing us. How did you find us?" Etania wondered. "All I remember is—"

She hesitated when she realized that she was about to say she remembered Keyel confessing something, but it being swept away by the wind. She blushed as she thought about what he was going to say.

"We captured some Soacronis patrolling the snow and found the three of you shivering like squirrels," Bayanna replied. "What were you doing out there? It's freezing!"

Etania looked down. How could she tell Bayanna that it was a mistake? That they were stupid?

"Etania!" her father exclaimed from the doorway, running inside and throwing his arms around his daughter. Keyel hovered behind him, shyly looking over his Master's shoulder. Etania blushed. Had he forgotten his confession? Changed his mind?

"Thank Melchizedek the Kinzoku found us!" Jakin said. "I thought I would investigate the fire and return."

"Were you looking for the Soacronis?" Bayanna asked.

"I wasn't sure what I was looking for, only that I spotted a fire in the distance and thought it would be worth checking out. The snow surrounded me before I could reach them," Jakin said. "Did you capture a Soacronis?"

Bayanna nodded. "Two of them. The rest froze to death or escaped, I don't know."

"Show me where they are," Jakin said. "I need to question them."

"If the acting Vizeheir will agree to that," Bayanna said, rising from her seat by Etania's bed.

"I'm sure he will when the heir asks, right?" Jakin questioned, elbowing Bayanna.

Etania looked over from Bayanna to her father in confusion. What did he mean by that?

"My father is Calder," Bayanna explained, "the true Vizeheir."

Why the heir to the Kinzoku lordship was tending to Etania was beyond her, but Bayanna was whisked away before Etania could question her, leaving Etania with Keyel. Keyel's face showed relief, but his river-blue eyes never met Etania's.

"I'm glad you're okay," Keyel said softly.

"Thanks to you," Etania replied.

"I didn't do anything." Keyel swallowed. "You could have died."

"We both could have," Etania countered, "and you kept me warm. We probably would have frostbite if you hadn't kept me close."

At the word *close*, Keyel reddened. *So he did remember*, Etania thought.

"I'm really sorry, Etania," Keyel said.

"Don't be," Etania replied, wondering if he was sorry for confessing.

"No, really," Keyel said. He sighed, running his hand through his hair. "I know I've never told you, but I think it's important you know."

"Know what?" Etania asked, breath catching.

"Just like I've failed to protect you, I failed to protect my half-sister."

Etania let out the breath she didn't realize she was holding.

"What is it?" Keyel asked. "Do you already know the tale?"

"No," Etania admitted. "I just thought you were going to say something else."

"Oh," Keyel said. "No, I just wanted to explain why I have failed you."

"You haven't," Etania retorted.

"Just let me explain," Keyel said. He sat down at the end of her bed and looked at the burning fire. "My sister Adeline was eleven years old and I was twelve, almost thirteen, when it happened. We knew we were siblings, even though we weren't allowed to play with each other or talk to each other. One night, she sneaked out to horseback ride alone, and I was practicing in the woods with my sword. She asked me to train her to use the blade. I wanted to bond with the sister I never knew, so I agreed. We met every night for six months, to train together, and slowly became friends. Then, one night, we decided to race one another."

Keyel paused and glanced at Etania sideways before continuing his story.

"We ran when werewolves suddenly attacked us," he said. "I fended them off as best as I could, but they knocked me out with one paw and took away Adeline's legs. I thought we were going to die, but Jakin saved us. I crawled over to my sister. There was blood everywhere...I tried to heal her, but I couldn't do it...the damage was so extensive...Rhys, who was following us, fetched my father. It took three healers to help my sister live, and I wasn't allowed to see her or talk to her. Eventually, she called me to her bedside, against Lady Maiya's wishes. She told me she didn't blame me, that I was her hero— but I couldn't accept it. When I saw your father to thank him for saving us, I was grateful to leave my past behind and try to make up for my wrongs. I thought, by protecting you, that I could do that. I was wrong."

He paused, meeting Etania's gaze.

"I can't protect you, Etania. I'm sorry. If you want me to stop being your guard, say the word, and I will let my Master know of my failure."

Etania wanted to protest, but she couldn't find the words. His gaze, so sorrowful and apologetic, pierced her heart. After a period of silence, Keyel spoke.

"There are some clothes for you to wear in the trunk at the foot of your bed. Bayanna said she would fetch you for breakfast in a little bit."

"Alright," Etania replied.

Keyel stood, about to exit the room.

"And Keyel," Etania managed.

"Yes?" he asked, pausing at the door.

"I still want you to be my guard."

He nodded, his eyes solemn, and stepped outside. Once he was gone, Etania pondered Keyel's words as she headed toward the trunk at the foot of her bed.

Keyel's story made his motivations so much clearer to Etania. All this time, he carried the guilt of the past with him, wondering whether he would finally be able to protect someone. Even though Etania thought of Keyel as a wonderful protector, she could see how he perceived the dangers they faced as strikes against him. She only wished she knew a way to let him know that he was a competent protector and a good man.

Etania lifted the wooden lid of the trunk and pulled out a blue dress with a tan vest that laced over the front. She pulled on the clothing and socks, and started lacing up her boots. Someone rapped on the door.

"Come in," Etania said.

Bayanna swiftly entered and Etania surveyed her clothing. Bayanna wore a long, brown skirt and long-sleeved, green shirt that accented her hair and eyes.

"Well, are you going to stare at me all day or come to dinner?" she asked, hand on her hip.

"Is this alright to wear to dinner?" Etania questioned, noting the difference between their clothing.

"That's fine, you'll probably get food on it anyway," Bayanna replied.

"What—why?"

"Is it alright to come in?" Jakin called from the door.

"Yes!" Bayanna and Etania said in chorus.

Jakin entered, and Etania noted that he had found his signature colors: a purple tunic and black trousers.

"You look just like your mother," Jakin said, a catch to his voice.

"Thank you," Etania replied, fingering her necklace.

"Stop gawking, silly birds, let's get going! I'm starving," Bayanna said, pushing past the pair to take the lead.

"Did she call us birds?" her father asked.

"I don't know about me, but you wear the colors of a peacock," Etania teased.

"I guess I shouldn't complain about the comparison, since the peacock is a proud creature," her father said, feigning a few struts.

"Exactly." Etania agreed.

Jakin laughed and Etania smiled. Then, together, they followed Bayanna through a tunnel. Metal lanterns lit their path, and Etania could see stalactites hanging from the ceiling. The tunnels turned and twisted so many times that Etania couldn't keep track. There were also hundreds of doors like the one she'd emerged from, so she wasn't sure if they were rooms or doors leading someplace. Eventually, the tunnel widened and they came to metal doors that were so large Etania wondered if they were in the center of the mountain.

Two guards stood by the gates, and when they saw Bayanna, they nodded. With their hands glowing with Neuma, they waved over the gates. The gates creaked open, the metal contorting itself to let the three of them enter. Once they had, the gates moved back into place with a loud clang.

Etania gaped at the huge cavern that they entered. The cave was at least thirty feet high and the cavern floor stretched at least one hundred feet. Everywhere Etania looked were long, metal tables with metal chairs where the Kinzoku ate and drank. On her left was a huge kitchen with roaring fires where cooks roasted what looked like goat and chopped some sort of root vegetables. The Kinzoku would line up to receive their food and return to their tables to eat. Lanterns lit the room, and long spires of stalagmite spun upward between tables and chairs. Bayanna led them to the line to receive food, they got their dinner, and they walked to a table where Keyel was waiting.

Jakin took the seat by Keyel before Etania had a chance, and she ended up sitting by Bayanna instead. As they dined, Etania noticed how loud and rambunctious the male Kinzoku ate: spilling water on the table, elbowing each other, tossing bones to the ground to be eaten by dogs, wiping grease from their beards and belching without shame. She had not been exposed to this behavior at Azeeka, so it was a shock to her.

Leaning over to Bayanna, she asked in a whisper, "Are your men always this impolite?"

Bayanna laughed loudly before answering, "Impolite? They're always like this. Is there any other kind of man?"

Etania didn't answer, but instead motioned with her hand toward Keyel, who was carefully taking small bites of his leg of goat.

"Nah, sissies don't count," Bayanna said, taking a large swig of her own beer.

"I wouldn't call Keyel a sissy," Etania retorted. "He's kept me alive more than once."

"Have a crush on him, do ya?" Bayanna stated.

Etania blushed. Did she have a crush on him?

"Understandable," Bayanna added. "He's a pretty thing."

Etania tried to change the subject, "So which do you prefer, one of these men or one like Keyel?"

"My own, of course!" Bayanna declared, and the men around her cheered. Then she lowered her voice and said to Etania, "These men may be considered "impolite" but they are good at heart and work hard to provide for their families."

"I'm sure they are," Etania said. "Speaking of that, why are you serving us, when you're the heir of the Kinzoku?"

"Heir?" Bayanna choked on her drink. "Ha! I guess I am, but I never thought of my class as making me above serving others. I volunteered because I wanted to see for myself if the rebellion leaders really can free my father."

"I'm sure finding us in the middle of a snowstorm didn't help," Etania admitted.

"I wouldn't be so sure. I heard you risked your life to rescue your father," Bayanna told her.

"Well yeah, but—" Etania began.

"Regardless, your act shows great character, and I think my uncle will see that as well when he tests you," Bayanna said.

"Uncle? Test?" Etania repeated.

"My uncle is the acting Vizeheir, or Lord," Bayanna said, with a wide smile. "And yes, test. You had better eat up, you'll need the energy."

Etania started gulping down her food, wondering what the Lord's test would entail. Her stomach lurched at the thought.

Chapter Twenty-One

Bayanna guided Etania and the others to their meeting with the acting Vizeheir. They made their way back through more tunnels with hundreds of doors. This journey seemed shorter than the first one, ending at another wide doorway with two metal doors covering it. Once again, the guards allowed them entry by bending back the solid metal with their own Neuma.

Once inside, Etania noticed that this was a large cave but not quite as large as the dining hall. This cave was also covered in stalactites, the glint and gleam of them reflecting off the lanterns around them.

A spring of water was against the wall, gushing down behind the thrones of two individuals whom Etania assumed were the temporary Vizeheir and his wife. Bayanna's uncle didn't have her bright hair. Instead, he had black hair, with bright green eyes that matched Bayanna's. His wife was a redhead with brown eyes and her apparel was very similar to Etania's. However, both the acting Lord and his wife wore sheepskin bolero jackets over their shoulders.

"Welcome, Lehrling Jakin, Vexli Etania, and Leici Keyel," the Vizeheir said, his voice booming against the cave walls. Etania, Jakin, and Keyel bowed. Bayanna didn't, but took her place standing by her uncle's side.

"I see you know us," Jakin said. "However, I was unable to introduce myself to you earlier before questioning the Soacroni."

"I am Ramar. We know much about you, because the King's messengers warned us not to ally ourselves with his enemies," the acting Vizeheir declared.

Etania gulped. Were they already enemies in Ramar's eyes, too?

"Yet, you welcomed us into your halls and assisted us with your medical aid. So which is it, rebellion or compliance?" Jakin inquired.

"Rebellion!" Ramar said, clenching his fist around the stone arm of the throne. "That cursed man thinks he can usurp us? We shall show him the might of the Kinzoku!"

"Great! How many men will you commit?" Jakin asked, with a smile.

"That depends on your ability to pass my tests," Ramar challenged, his eyes glinting as he stroked his beard,

"Tests, milord?" Jakin repeated.

"Indeed. Each of you will have to pass a test before I permit you to leave and before I commit any troops. You must prove to us that you can crush King Toren with whatever men we choose to lend you."

"I see," Jakin said, unphased.

Etania felt her stomach churning. Did Ramar just say *each* of them?

"I have heard that you were a blacksmith before you were a Lehrling. We, the Kinzoku, prize a blacksmith," Ramar said to Jakin. "The challenge I give you is to create a shield which I cannot bend with my Neuma."

"I agree," her father replied.

Is he insane? Etania wondered. *There is no metal that won't bend to the Kinzoku's Neuma!*

"To you, Leici, I heard you were a skilled healer, even saving your half-sister from the brink of death," Ramar declared. "One of my commanders recently suffered a wound from a boar and it is said he will not live. You are to heal him."

"Milord, I—" Keyel began.

"He will be pleased to complete that assignment," Jakin finished.

Keyel bowed his head in response, clenching his fists by his sides. Etania's father had completely lost his mind! Keyel didn't have any Neuma, and with his traumatic episode, she wondered if he would ever be able to regain it.

"Vexli, I heard you can make anyone powerless with your Neuma. You will fight the Soacronis we found, alone, in our arena," Ramar instructed.

"She can't! Etania doesn't—" Keyel began.

"I will," Etania interrupted. She had no idea why she felt confident enough to agree. Was it because of Melchizedek's mark? Or was her father's enthusiasm infecting her?

"When would you like us to complete our tests?" Jakin asked Ramar.

"In three days," Ramar declared heartily. "You will present your shield to me, my commander will come to the arena to be healed by the Leici and then we will end with your daughter's battle. It will be a night to remember!"

His wife's smile widened as she added, "Yes, and I will order the cooks to make the greatest feast ever to be seen!"

"Then we will really know whether they can handle running the rebellion," Bayanna agreed.

"It's settled," Ramar said. "Bayanna, show Jakin and his companions where they will train for their upcoming tests."

Etania definitely didn't think *anything* was settled, but Bayanna dragged them away before anyone could protest. Once again, their path twisted and turned down different tunnels until they came to the area where Jakin would work. It was marked by significant heat. Etania began sweating long before they approached it—a contrast from the cold cave and snowstorm outside.

There was no metal door at the entrance of this blacksmith's shop. Instead, there was a roaring fire in a large hearth that was against the wall of a medium-sized cave. There were several stumps with anvils sitting on top of them. The Kinzoku would stick raw metal into the fire so that it was malleable. The swordsmith would then use their Neuma to refine the metal to a proper shape. A few of the other Kinzoku dipped finished blades into a bucket of water before using their Neuma to sharpen the metal's sides to a razor-sharp edge.

"I just have to make a shield Ramar won't be able to break! Do I get any well wishes from my daughter?" Jakin asked, his purple eyes begging. Etania sighed.

"You can do it," Etania managed, patting her father's back.

How he would manage, Etania didn't know.

"So can you," Jakin replied.

Etania reddened. Her father never gave her compliments. Ever since the incident with Isabella, things seemed different between them. She only hoped it lasted.

"You two are an interesting pair, aren't you?" Bayanna said. "Well, I won't keep the awkwardness alive any longer. Let's move on to the Leici's assignment."

Etania said goodbye to her father and continued with Bayanna, sneaking a glance at Keyel. They walked side by side now, and Etania figured that he didn't want to talk about his feelings in mixed company—romantic or otherwise. She wasn't as concerned about romance now as knowing whether Keyel would be able to heal Ramar's commander. How did he feel about it? Was he nervous?

His face was indecipherable, and Etania hoped he would be up to the task.

They arrived at another medium-sized cavern with no door. This area stank of herbs and incense, and patients lay on slabs of stone, coughing or groaning. Healers walked from person to person, caring for their needs. One healer was a young woman with black hair and bright, blue eyes. She smiled at Bayanna and winked at Keyel.

"So is this my new recruit?" she asked Bayanna.

"Yes, Reselda, this is Keyel," Bayanna introduced.

"Thank you for hosting me," Keyel said, picking up Reselda's hand and placing his forehead upon it.

Etania felt her stomach clench. She knew this motion was a traditional greeting, but the way Reselda looked at Keyel…. When had she started becoming so jealous? Was this what it meant to like someone?

"You're welcome!" Reselda replied with a giggle. "Let's get started, shall we?"

Keyel nodded, and as Reselda trotted off, he turned to Etania.

"Be safe," he said, lifting her hand and kissing it gently.

Etania's heart rate skyrocketed while he walked away, leaving her flustered and confused. Bayanna cocked her head to the side, smiled, and gave her a knowing wink.

They continued their journey through the tunnels. This time, Etania tried to count: two rights, one left, three rights. She eventually stopped as they came to a halt in front of a room with two metal gates and two guards on either side. Once again, the metal was moved out of the way to permit them entrance, then clanked shut behind them.

Etania tried to ignore her growing nervousness as she looked around to see Kinzoku training. Her ribs were still healing—how did the acting Lord expect her to beat the Soacronis?! Men with huge muscles were lifting metal bars with gigantic stones hanging from them. Other men were fighting with axes, knocking against each other's shields and shouting. Women were practicing archery with deadly accuracy, their short bows sending arrows toward a target with loud thunks. Bayanna led her to one of the metal dummies that was unused.

"Show me what you've got!" Bayanna said.

"Um, don't I get a trainer or something first?" Etania wondered.

"I am your trainer," Bayanna replied.

"Volunteering again?" Etania wondered.

"You got it. But just because I don't practice as often as our guard here doesn't mean I don't know how to defend myself," Bayanna asserted. Something in the glint of Bayanna's green eyes made Etania gulp.

"Great, let's get started," Bayanna continued. "You have a knife around your waist, so why don't you use it on this dummy?"

"Well, um, here's the thing...I'm not great at close combat or using my knife," Etania explained. "If my opponent gets close to me, I won't be able to use my Neuma. That's, uh, generally why I work with Keyel."

Bayanna groaned. "Seriously?"

Etania nodded.

"Okay, fine. You need to keep people away so you can use your Neuma, right?" Bayanna repeated.

"Yes," Etania said.

"Okay." Bayanna grabbed a tower shield, and her hands started glowing with Neuma. The metal reshaped itself to a small, round shield. Bayanna gave her the shield. She then grabbed a sword and lunged for Etania. Etania dodged, surprised.

"Were you trying to kill me?" she asked.

"Maybe," Bayanna answered, with a laugh. "But seriously, block with your shield and aim with your Neuma. Come on!"

"I don't want to hurt you," Etania said.

"You can't hurt me if you can't hit me," Bayanna taunted, and she thrust once again toward Etania.

This time, Etania blocked with her shield and tried to light her Neuma in her palm.

"I saw the way you were eyeing Reselda earlier. Let's see if we can get that murderous look back on your face again!" Bayanna said, leaping toward Etania with an arcing sword.

Etania gritted her teeth and blocked, this time throwing a flame toward Bayanna as she retreated. She missed, but Bayanna was smiling.

"There we go!" Bayanna said. "If you keep attacking like that, those Soacronis will definitely back off."

At the word 'Soacronis,' Etania suppressed a shudder. Bayanna attacked again, and Etania felt like the dirt beneath her was slippery sand.

Etania. She felt Melchizedek's voice, warming her whole body from the rose mark she now bore. *Lean on me.*

Etania nodded unconsciously, and it was as if her entire body stopped reacting defensively and started moving instinctively. Everything Keyel had taught her, with self-defense and knife lessons and archery, kicked into place. She didn't even feel the pain in her ribs anymore. Now, instead of thrusts and blocks, Bayanna and Etania were dancing a duel of death. Back and forth they went, swaying to the beat of an unknown music. Bayanna called them to a halt when both were covered in sweat and breathing hard.

"I don't know what happened, but you definitely improved from your prior hesitancy. Where did you learn skills like that?"

"Keyel taught me, but I never really caught on until now. When I heard Melchizedek's voice, it suddenly became clear," Etania said.

"You heard from Melchizedek?" Bayanna repeated, mouth open.

"Yes. Why is that strange?" Etania wondered.

"I've never heard that Melchizedek talks to people," Bayanna said.

"I didn't think he did," Etania said, "But then, my best friend back home, Grace, said she could talk to Melchizedek."

"Really? Hmmm..." Bayanna paused for a minute and then shrugged. "I don't know how that could be, but I have figured out one thing."

"What's that?" Etania asked.

"I think I have competition for the title of best friend," Bayanna replied, with a wink and a smile. Before Etania could react, the Kinzoku pulled her back toward the entrance of the cave.

"Come on, we have to check on the others," she said.

"Yeah, I wonder what happened to Keyel and my father?" Etania mused.

JAKIN SURVEYED THE metal he had to choose. The shape and type mattered, so he needed to select a piece carefully because he was supposed to create a shield the Vizeheir couldn't bend with his Neuma. He knew it was an impossible task, and if he could find wood, he would build the shield out of that. Yet, even as he considered scrambling out of the mountain and searching for usable wood pieces, he dismissed the thought. Using wood seemed like cheating, so he decided to work with metal instead.

After choosing the pieces he wanted, he went to the fire and began melting them with a long pair of tongs. He would straighten the convoluted result by hammering away at the unformed shape. As he worked, he recalled that a blacksmith's shop was where he had first met Tala. His mind flashed back.

"Can you create a necklace from this?" she asked.

She handed him a piece of silver and told him to create it for her. So he did, even inscribing a dedication in the amulet. That dedication had gotten them into more trouble than he could have imagined, but it also had brought them together in ways only Deo could conceive. He supposed that the new necklace he'd given her a few months ago was a completion of their relationship—a necklace his daughter now wore.

How could King Toren, whom Jakin had mentored since he was a teenager, betray him like this? When Jakin laid his hands on the King, he would...

You would what?

Melchizedek's voice startled him. Jakin hadn't heard from his Master lately. Then again, he was ignoring Melchizedek's call. Jakin told him again. The Skazic didn't deserve mercy or compassion.

Isabella didn't deserve mercy?

The look on the woman's face as she died reminded Jakin too painfully of his wife. She was so young, and how she had called out to Melchizedek...

I recall a certain blacksmith being that way before I came.

Jakin shrugged away the feeling. *Go away! I don't want to talk about this.*

You cannot be separated from my presence, Jakin. You know this. But I will cease talking to you, if that is what you wish.

Jakin didn't answer. Instead, he turned back to his project and continued to hammer, using the heat to form the shape of a shield.

Chapter Twenty-Two

Keyel followed Reselda to the back of the clinic. There were aprons, towels, bandages, and buckets on a shelf. Reselda gave him an apron, which he donned obediently, and handed him some towels and bandages.

"Follow me," she commanded.

Keyel didn't reply. He simply walked forward until they came to one of the patients that had his own, curtained area.

"Commander, the Leici is here," Reselda called.

"Let him in," the man grunted.

Reselda pulled back the curtain and allowed Keyel inside. Immediately, the stench of herbs and blood assailed Keyel's nose. A small lamp, sitting on a metal table, barely illuminated his patient.

He was a pudgy man with a wide scar across his stomach. The stitches were clearly infected, red, and inflamed. He wore no shirt, but was covered with herbs to treat the smelly injury. His face bore a gray beard and his long, gray hair was tied back. He had a book in his hand which he read slowly, flipping the pages and adjusting his elbow with a grunt. When Keyel entered, he barely looked up.

"Commander Ivan, this is Keyel. He is going to heal you," Reselda explained.

Ivan looked up, his green eyes meeting Keyel's. Keyel dropped his gaze and shifted his feet. She had no idea how wrong her words felt.

"Yeah, right," Ivan snorted.

His dismissal poured salt on Keyel's confidence. Why did this man have to remind him of what he already knew?

"Well, he has to, on the order of Lord Ramar," Reselda said. "In the meantime, he will treat your wounds and serve you during the day."

"Fine," Ivan agreed.

Reselda offered Keyel a small smile.

"Let me know if you need anything, sweetie." She winked and then disappeared, leaving them alone in the curtained area.

"So—uh—do you need anything?" Keyel began.

"Need anything?" Ivan snorted. "How about the ability to read without being in pain?"

"Well, I'm sure they have some sort of medicine that will help with the pain..." Keyel said.

"I'm being sarcastic," Ivan grunted. "Don't they have sarcasm in Calques?"

"Yes, I think, I mean—," Keyel stuttered.

Ivan laughed, and the movement caused him to wince in pain.

"What's your name? Key...? Kay...?"

"Keyel," he replied.

"Do you have a woman in your life, Keyel?" Ivan asked.

Keyel felt heat rise to his cheeks. He loved Etania, but he knew he wasn't worthy of her affections. Why had he confessed in the snowstorm? It was such a reckless thing to do!

"I'll take that as a yes," Ivan answered. He sighed, leaning back against his headboard. "I had a wife once. She rode alongside me every hunt, wielding an axe that no man could master. She was a vicious woman."

"Sounds *interesting*," Keyel said, unable to decide if "vicious" was an attribute he should look for in a woman.

"Aw, yes, she was," Ivan said. "What an amazing woman! Even her cooking was delicious."

"How did she, uh—" Keyel began.

"She died in a hunt a few years ago," Ivan replied, his face darkening.

Keyel's heart pounded in his ears. What if the same thing happened to Etania? What if, like the snowstorm, he wasn't able to protect her? *Just like my sister...*

"It's funny," Ivan said. "Of all the things to get me killed, it had to be the same as my wife."

"You're not dead yet," Keyel attempted to comfort.

"I will be, soon. Now, leave me alone. I want to sleep."

Keyel began to leave, but Ivan had one more thing to say.

"If you love her, you should tell her. I didn't say goodbye to my wife. I've regretted that ever since."

Ivan's words haunted Keyel. How could he court Etania when he couldn't keep her safe? Just days from now, she would face a Soacronis by herself. She was undoubtedly training right now, and Keyel doubted his instruction would help her in a one-on-one battle with two Soacroni. Why would she ever respect a man who couldn't heal or help? He was a failure, and no one could love a failure—a nothus.

When Etania and Bayanna came to fetch him later, he wasn't able to meet their gazes.

"How was your time with the healers?" Etania asked.

"It was fine," Keyel replied.

"Did you meet the man you're supposed to heal?" she added.

"Yes."

"What's he like?" Etania questioned.

"He's interesting," Keyel managed.

Etania's brow furrowed, and Keyel figured she would give up soon.

"What's his name?" Etania said.

"Ivan."

"Do you feel like you could..." Etania began.

Before she could ask, they arrived at Jakin's blacksmith shop. He was covered in sweat but still cornered his daughter with a hug. Keyel breathed a sigh of relief, hoping his Master's distraction would be enough to keep him away from Etania's pestering questions. They headed toward the dining hall again.

"I'm not really hungry," Keyel said.

"Really?" Bayanna groaned. "No wonder you're so skinny..."

"Go on, Bayanna. I'm sure I can find the dining hall from here if you want to lead him back to his rooms," Jakin said.

"But Father..." Etania began.

Jakin winked at him.

"I will see you later, Keyel," Jakin said, and teleported in a fiery cloud of purple, dragging Etania with him. Bayanna gaped.

"Does he always do that?" she asked.

"Yes, but it expends a lot of energy, so he doesn't do it often. I'm surprised he had enough in him to teleport to the dining hall," Keyel explained.

"So am I," Bayanna said warily. "Come on, then."

She led him back through various tunnels until he came to his room. Once inside, Keyel was grateful for the silence. Bayanna talked about every topic under the sun while she walked, not once asking him a question. He supposed he was grateful for that in Etania. She was only asking him questions because she cared.

Why would she care about someone like him? Someone who continuously failed to protect her? Someone who would never be a good partner?

He shouldn't have accepted the position as her bodyguard. His master expected too much of him. Even the Interim Vizeheir expected him to heal Ivan, and Keyel was helpless. He took off his shirt and tugged off his boots. He was ready for sleep to take away his worries. The lamp was still lit and as Keyel went to blow out its flame, he noticed the glow of his shield. It was the mark Melchizedek gave him when Keyel first followed him as a child.

Keyel snuffed the flame and tugged the covers over his chest. Even Melchizedek expected more than he could ever offer.

HER STOMACH FULL FROM dinner, Etania lay on her bed and counted the rocks in the ceiling. She hadn't noticed until now the beautiful, geometric pattern—a combination of blues, purples, and greens—clustered together in circles and squares. Counting the rocks was just a distraction from the real problem on Etania's mind, though. What should she say in response to Keyel's story and his confession? She was almost entirely certain that Keyel was going to confess he loved her, and she still hadn't formulated a proper response to his story about Adeline.

Etania couldn't understand why he would love someone like her. She was a failure as a warrior and librarian, and could only control her Neuma with Melchizedek's help. She doubted she was that attractive, with plain brown hair and eyes. How could he love her?

Still, hadn't she felt the same about Melchizedek's love? Yet, he freely gave her a love that was beyond any human being's. If Melchizedek could love her, maybe Keyel really could, too.

No, that's impossible, She told herself. *Keyel didn't want to confess. He only protected me because he wanted to make up for almost losing his sister. He admitted as much today, and my inability to reassure him shows I'm not even a good friend.*

The thought wasn't comforting; rather, it felt like an arrow pierced her heart. She wasn't entirely sure why Keyel not confessing was so painful. *Could I be...* No, she cut off the thought, burying it inside the gash the emotional arrow had opened within her heart.

Besides, she had more pressing things to concern her. She would face the Soacroni in the next few days. Even though her skills were improving, she still struggled to defend herself against Bayanna. If that happened with the Soacroni, she would end up injured like Ivan, whom Keyel was tasked to heal.

Maybe she could go over the moves she had done earlier in her head until she fell asleep? Etania imagined wielding the shield and blocking the sword arcing toward her. She thought of her paces, how her feet were moving, and how the Neuma shot from her hands. These repetitive thoughts helped her fall asleep.

When Etania woke, she certainly didn't feel more confident than the night before. Instead, her stomach clenched into a tight knot. Bayanna came to her room to pick her up and teased Etania about her pale face.

"It's only the second day and you're white with fear?" she said. "That's not going to look good for the acting Vizeheir."

"I'll, uh, manage," Etania stuttered.

"Right," Bayanna said, slapping her back, "because you've got me as a trainer! Now come on, the boys are waiting for us."

Etania smiled. She couldn't understand Bayanna's enthusiasm, but it cheered her considerably.

When they reached the dining hall, Keyel and Jakin were already eating. Etania took a seat across from Keyel, who avoided her gaze.

THE SELALIS AND LEICI finished their food, and Bayanna led them back to their individual work areas. Keyel was not looking forward to seeing Ivan again. His inability to heal the Kinzoku was depressing, and Ivan's encouragement to confess to Etania again just made him feel guilty. He should never have said those words before proving that he could protect Etania. He was grateful the wind had blown away his foolish declaration.

He sighed and followed Reselda back to where Ivan waited for him. The older man was reading again, this time with pillows propped between his infected wound and arms.

"Ah, the Leici. You're back," Ivan said. "Maybe you can read to me. I'm having the hardest time getting this to work."

"Sure," Keyel replied.

That was at least one thing he could do for the man. He flipped open the book, which looked like a copy of Melchizedek's teachings, and began reading.

"Come to me, all who labor and carry heavy burdens, and I will give you rest. Learn from me, for I am gentle and have a humble heart, and you will find rest."

"Sounds good, doesn't it?" Ivan said, after Keyel finished that sentence.

"Yes," Keyel agreed, "but how do you give your burden to Melchizedek when he is in Safarast?"

"He isn't in Safarast alone, son. He dwells within us if we have his Mark." Ivan showed his arm, which revealed the incandescent glow of a hammer. Keyel thought of his own mark, the shield he failed to be for others, and winced.

"I can see you take some convincing," Ivan said. "I understand that. I asked Melchizedek to heal me and he said to be still and wait. Ha! What choice do I have?"

Had Melchizedek sent him to heal Ivan? Keyel realized that he would fail at that, too.

"Keep on reading, over here now," Ivan told him.

Keyel did as he was asked until he was dismissed from Ivan's presence. The rest of the passage didn't impact his soul as much as the words he first read. Would Melchizedek truly take his responsibility from him? Would he really help Keyel, who failed him often?

His thoughts made dinner, even with Etania, silent and sullen. Etania tried multiple times to solicit more than a one-word response from him, but Keyel didn't feel up to talking. Instead, after dinner, he went straight to bed. As he laid underneath the covers, he wondered, *Melchizedek, I am a nothus. Why have you told me to do the impossible?*

This thought brought him into Melchizedek's kingdom.

They were standing on the wall of Safarast's castle, overlooking the great meadow and the blue sky. The wind whistled by them; warmth that Keyel had not felt since they left the Leici. Here, it was always spring— the perfect weather existing eternally.

"It's beautiful, isn't it?" *Melchizedek said.*

"Yes, it is," *Keyel admitted.*

"Makes everything seem a little less daunting, doesn't it?" *Melchizedek added.*

"It doesn't take away my concerns, if that's what you're wondering," *Keyel said.* "Why have you brought me here?"

"You asked me a question. I am always willing to answer, even if my children aren't willing to listen."

"So what's the answer then? Why have you asked me to protect Etania and to heal Ivan, which I cannot do?"

"Who says *you* have *to do anything?" Melchizedek replied.*

"What do you mean?"

"You have read the ancient texts. 'I can do all things through him who strengthens me,' and today's passage, 'Come to Me.' Who do you suppose is 'Him' and 'Me'?"

"You, of course. But Melchizedek, I don't see—"

"No, you don't *believe," Melchizedek replied.* "You don't trust."

"How can I, when you left me without my Neuma? When you let my sister lose her legs?" *Keyel asked.*

"I allow my children to experience many things, and I bring good from them. But I am not the one who took away your Neuma, nor am I the one who took away your sister's legs. Let me ask you, does Adeline see no good from her injury?"

Keyel looked away, gazing at the peaceful blue sky.

"She sees good," *he whispered.*

"*Then why do you continue to blame yourself? Why do you carry your burden alone? Give me your sorrows and your burdens. Believe in me, and allow me to work. Only then will your Neuma work again.*"

Could he? Would he? Keyel glanced back at Melchizedek, meeting his gaze for the first time. Melchizedek's spirit flooded him—a spirit of strength and love, honor and beauty. Keyel felt it pour into him until he fell to his knees, overwhelmed.

"*Yes, Lord. I will trust in you.*"

Chapter Twenty-Three

When Keyel woke, he sensed a peace within his heart that he hadn't experienced for a long time. His mark of a shield glowed, and he felt the warmth of Melchizedek's presence even when waking. Stretching, he was confident that he would heal Ivan during today's ceremony. He also knew that with Melchizedek on his side, he could open himself up to a possibility he had previously rejected. So before he ate, he went looking for his Master, following his instincts for guidance through the tunnels. After a short search, Keyel found Jakin grinding and polishing a small shield.

"Are you finished?" Keyel asked.

Jakin looked up at him and smiled. "Yes."

"Do you think the Vizeheir will be able to bend it with his Neuma?" Keyel wondered.

"Most likely," Jakin laughed. "But that's not why I think he asked me to create it. He wanted us to prove ourselves, remember? How about you, do you think you'll be able to heal Ivan?"

"Yes, I do," Keyel replied.

"Oh, did something change?" Jakin asked, arching an eyebrow.

"I spoke to Melchizedek," Keyel said. "About that, Master, I, uh..."

Keyel felt confident enough to heal Ivan, but speaking to Jakin about Etania was like trying to swallow fire.

"Yes?" Jakin said, a small smile tugging at his lips.

"I l-l-ove your daughter," Keyel managed, "and I wondered if I could court her."

Jakin's smile disappeared, and Keyel gulped.

"Permission denied," he said.

Jakin's outright refusal stabbed at Keyel's heart. Just when he was beginning to feel like he could protect Etania, his own Master doubted his abilities?

"Don't question yourself," Jakin replied. "I am not denying you because you can't protect my daughter. I'm denying you because now is not the time."

"I see," Keyel said, mentally kicking himself for jumping to conclusions.

"This rebellion will consume us, and there is no room for courtship until it is all over. Even then, you and I can't be sure if any of us will make it through the upcoming battle," Jakin explained.

Keyel understood that completely, but then thought of what Ivan had told him about his wife.

"I know," Keyel agreed, "but don't you think I could tell her my feelings? If I don't, and one of us dies, we will die without knowing the truth."

Jakin looked pained, his eyes darkening.

"I hate to bring this up, Master, but what if you had never told your wife you loved her before you died? Wouldn't you regret that?" Keyel argued. "I understand now is not the time for courtship, but could I at least make my feelings known to her?"

Jakin huffed and then let out a long sigh. "I will give you permission to do that. However, you understand that my daughter must return your feelings, don't you?" he said, "If she doesn't, I will deny permission to court her again."

Keyel nodded. He hadn't even thought about that possibility when he went to his Master.

"Let's get some breakfast. We'll need it before the ceremony," Jakin said, rising and carrying his new shield with him.

Together, they walked toward the dining hall. Keyel considered what he had just committed to doing. Before talking to Melchizedek, he had kicked himself for confessing to Etania. Now, he wanted to tell her the truth and had permission to do just that. However, he'd never even considered that Etania might reject him! What would he do if that happened?

His nervousness was now two-fold. One: that he might not be able to heal Ivan despite what Melchizedek said. Two: that Etania might not return his affection. He forced himself to eat breakfast and barely made eye contact with Etania. This day would be a turning point for both of them, and eating seemed like a secondary concern.

ETANIA SWALLOWED HER breakfast mechanically. Bayanna informed her that the Kinzoku intended to thrust all three of them into the arena right after breakfast. If they were victorious, her people would enjoy the rest of the day. Etania simply hoped she would live long enough to make it. She couldn't tell if her father and Keyel, seated nearby, were just as nervous.

"Eat up, warrior," Bayanna said, with a wink.

Yesterday, Etania had barely managed to make Bayanna step back. Today, the Kinzoku acted like Etania had beaten her soundly. Etania managed to swallow her bread and eggs, but she had to physically force the food into her mouth. The squeezing she felt in her abdomen indicated her body didn't like that very much. When they finished, Bayanna eyed them each carefully.

"Ready?" she asked.

Jakin nodded, clutching his shield to his chest. Keyel nodded as well, but Etania trembled. Her ribs were almost healed, and she wondered if she would be hindered by them in the upcoming battle. They stood and followed Bayanna as she led them away. As they walked, everyone in the cavern followed them.

That's when she heard the people chanting.

Etania wasn't sure what they were saying because it was so loud, but the shouts echoed against the cavern walls. Etania shuddered as they were paraded forward, through multiple tunnels, until they reached two tall doors. With the Neuma of the Kinzoku, the metal doors slid back into slits within the stone, revealing a large, round arena. Surrounding the dirt area were seats at different levels. As the trio walked forward, the crowd behind them took seats in the audience. The trio was surrounded.

There was a large platform with thrones on it directly ahead of Etania. The acting Vizeheir, Ramar, and his wife, were sitting on the thrones, overlooking the field below. On the field itself were two cages, each containing a Soacronis. They hissed, clanging against the metal, and Etania shuddered again.

Bayanna disappeared, leaving Etania, Keyel, and Jakin standing before Ramar. He raised his hammer to silence the crowd. Even the Soacroni hushed before his authority.

"Today we have come to see if these three are worthy of leading the rebellion against King Toren!" the acting Vizeheir announced. "We have assigned them three different tasks, as suited to their abilities. First, Lehrling Jakin, we asked you to create a shield which could not be bent by our Neuma."

"It is here, milord," Jakin replied, presenting the elegantly-engraved shield to the man. Ramar smiled and ran his hand across the metal surface.

"This is beautiful craftsmanship," the Vizeheir said. "I can see why you were a great blacksmith in your previous life. However, you know that this shield will be bent by my Neuma, yet you didn't choose a different material. Why is that?"

"Because I'm aware you only wanted to test my patience and will, sire. I hoped this would prove them both to you," Jakin answered.

"You are very wise, Lehrling." Ramar smiled. With his hand, he used his Neuma to shrink the shield.

"Come forward, Vexli," the Regent added.

Etania obeyed, and he handed her the shield. Now that it was smaller, it fit Etania perfectly.

"My niece told me that you have practiced with a shield, so this will be perfect for your upcoming match," Ramar explained.

Etania nodded and thanked him, backing away with the shield. There were cheers in the crowd.

"Bring forward Ivan, my commander!" the Regent said.

Four Kinzoku obeyed, carrying Ivan on a mat that was balanced between four rods. They brought him within the arena and then placed him on the ground before the acting Vizeheir.

"Heal him," the Vizeheir said.

"Heal him! Heal him! Heal him!" the audience shouted continuously.

Etania hoped they wouldn't shout during her battle with the Soacronis, but she figured they would despite her desires. Saying a quick prayer for Keyel, she wondered if the Leici would be able to accomplish the task. He had been avoiding her lately, so she had no idea what was on his mind.

Keyel bowed his head, and Etania could see his lips moving and his eyelids closed. When he opened them, he extended his hand toward Ivan. A light glow flowed from his fingers, and the Neuma slowly stitched the wound together.

Etania wanted to squeal with delight or jump and embrace the Leici. She contained herself to a smile as he stepped back and Ivan stood straight for the first time. The Kinzoku erupted in a roar of pleasure, and Ivan was paraded around by the four who carried him. Keyel smiled at Etania, and she felt her heart flutter. She looked away.

He's just being friendly, she reminded herself.

"Next, the main event! Etania Selali, step forward please!" Ramar commanded. Etania obeyed, and Ramar added, "Jakin and Keyel, join me on my platform."

"My lord, if I may, I would like to heal Etania's ribs before she battles. They were injured a few weeks ago, and I want her to be able to fight at her best," Keyel requested.

"I would like to witness the Vexli's best prowess as well. You may do as you asked," Ramar agreed.

Etania was so relieved as Keyel healed her ribs. The warmth of his Neuma filling her with strength was just what she needed.

"While the Leici heals, I need the guards to carry Ivan out of the arena," Ramar further directed.

The guards obeyed and Keyel quickly finished healing Etania. Jakin and Keyel mounted the platform, both of them shooting meaningful glances at Etania. She gulped. Her heart fluttered like a stampede of horses in her chest.

"Guards, open the cages," the Vizeheir said.

There was a metal clang as the guards used their Neuma to release the Soacronis from their cages.

"Melchizedek be with you, Vexli!" Ramar said.

That was when Etania knew she was really, completely *alone*.

She looked at each approaching Soacronis: one blue, one red. They were covered in scales and their eyes were narrow and yellow like a serpent's. They had burly arms ending in hands with long, sharp nails, and two feet that were large claws. Bat-like wings were attached to their bodies, but the wings were sliced vertically so that they could not fly. They each wore leather pants, but no other armor, for their scales would be as hard as a dragon's. She was grateful that the Kinzoku had removed their armor and clipped their wings to make the fight more fair. Etania shuddered at the memory of the cold, scaly grip of the Soacronis that had attacked her in Khartome and sent a prayer to Melchizedek.

Melchizedek, help me, she pleaded inwardly.

Always, child.

His vote of confidence surged through Etania, and she threw a fireball of white Neuma toward the first Soacronis on her right. He dodged while the other Soacronis attacked her—an attack which she blocked with her new shield. His sharp nails didn't even scratch the shield. The other Soacronis recovered and was heading straight toward her.

Etania backed away, turned, and ran. The Soacroni chased her. This was something Bayanna had failed to cover: trying to hit a moving target. Etania tripped, falling backwards. A Soacronis leaped on top of her and she screamed, hiding underneath her shield as he tried to get at her face. She was panicking. The crowd was silent with worry.

Peace, child. She heard Melchizedek's voice. *Think!*

Etania took a deep breath and concentrated. A new idea came to her and she channeled her Neuma through her arm to the shield so that the white fire burned the Soacronis. He leaped back, screeching in terror. The scales fell from his body as he transformed into a Draconian again, so Etania focused on the second Skazic.

He was waiting for her now— cautious after seeing his friend disabled. Etania knew this was a perfect opportunity, so she put her shield down and filled both of her hands with Neuma. The white flames danced in her palms and she threw them, rapid fire, toward the Soacronis. He ran, but Etania's flames were faster. At last, she hit his arm. She moved the fire so it consumed him and he cried out as the scales shed from his skin. The Soacroni were now two Draconian men in shorts. They shivered, looking around, while Etania went back and fetched her shield. The Kinzoku men took them away.

For the first time, Etania heard the crowd cheering and chanting. Her breaths were coming out in what felt like hundreds of huffs, but she had done it! She had defeated two Soacroni with her Neuma because of Melchizedek.

Thank you, Melchizedek, she prayed. She could feel his smile of approval.

"Well done, Vexli!" The acting Vizeheir boomed. "You three have passed all of my tests. As a result, we will commit troops to your cause. But first, we must celebrate!"

He clapped his hands, and servants brought forth large trays of food. Musicians followed, singing and playing large horns. The Kinzoku began to eat, drink, and dance all around them. Keyel made his way through the crowd and embraced Etania enthusiastically. She felt her heart quicken.

"I'm proud of you!" Keyel complimented, stepping back.

Etania blushed, and she saw that Keyel was blushing, too. Before she could wonder at what it meant, Bayanna tackled her and gave her a hug as well.

"Good job! I thought you wouldn't make it there when the Soacronis had you pinned. But I should know better. My pupil wouldn't let me down," Bayanna said, with a smile.

"Yes, you did great at making that Skazic extra crispy!" Jakin told her with a laugh. Etania glared at him playfully.

"Will the new champion consider a dance with me?" Keyel asked.

Etania nodded and gave her shield to her father. As soon as she started to dance with Keyel, her exhaustion was temporarily forgotten.

KEYEL WALKED BESIDE Etania toward the women's bath, where she would enjoy a soak after her battle. The only reason Keyel volunteered to escort Etania there was because he wished to talk with her alone. But his stomach clenched at the thought, halting his words. She had agreed to dance with him and walk with him, but did that mean she liked him? He wouldn't know until he confessed, and as awkward as it was, he decided now was the best time.

"Um, Etania?" Keyel began.

"Yes?" she said, barely pausing.

Keyel gently stopped her with his arm.

"I need to tell you something," Keyel said.

Etania looked up at him. She blushed, and Keyel felt his heart beating faster. She looked so beautiful when the slight pink came to her cheeks.

"I know, Keyel," Etania said. Her statement confused him.

"What do you know?" Keyel wondered.

"That you want to be friends. That's what you were really saying at the mountain, right? That you didn't want us to be any more than friends?" Etania said.

Did that mean *she* wanted only to be friends? Keyel's heart felt like it was crushed before beginning. Yet, he knew he had to tell her, despite the cost. Ivan was right. The cost was greater if she died without knowing.

"No," Keyel managed. "I said I love you, Etania. The wind carried away the words, but I wanted to tell you: I love you."

Etania blinked.

Did that mean she didn't return his feelings? Keyel thought he should say something to assure her.

"I know I will probably still fail to protect you, but I'm beginning to accept that. Melchizedek showed me that I can trust him with my worries about your safety. Your father said we couldn't court now because of the rebellion, but he would approve when it ends. I couldn't wait until the battle was over because I wanted you to know— in case anything happens to us. It's fine if you don't return my feelings. I mean you could take time to consider it..."

At Etania's wrinkled brow, Keyel decided to close his mouth.

"I think...I do need time to think about your feelings and really consider mine," Etania admitted.

Keyel's heart sank.

"I admire you, Keyel, I really do," Etania continued. "But does admiration mean love? I'm not sure. I will say this though: I have always considered you an amazing protector."

Keyel's heart surged. Maybe he was wrong to doubt himself.

"Because I'm not sure about my own feelings, I was wondering if you would wait for me to give you a proper reply. Will you?"

Keyel nodded. How could he say no? Besides, admiration could lead to love, right? He was hopeful, even if he wasn't sure he would enjoy the answer.

They came to the doorway of the public bath and went separate ways. Once alone in his room, another thought came to him. If Etania said she didn't love him, would he be able to let her go? He hoped he would, but it would be the hardest thing he'd do in his life.

Chapter Twenty-Four

Damien sniffled and sneezed. He and ten of King Toren's Soacroni had been in an abandoned cave for at least a week, waiting for the Lehrling and his daughter to emerge from the Kinzoku's fortress on the other side of the mountain. Damien didn't know how his force had managed to survive so far. They had lost two men from trying to breach it and at least three from attempting to fly over the fortress in the blizzard. He only hoped they would be rewarded soon, for Damien dared not to leave without his prize.

He doubted King Toren would be pleased with him. They had been gone too long, and without achieving their goals. Yet, he shuddered to think what the King might do to him if he returned without the girl or her father. He scooted closer to the fire, shivering. He hated the fact that he was back to being a regular human; his only defense the pitiful armor he wore. At least the other Soacronis had scales and sharp nails.

"Well, well, well," a voice called out from the cave entrance. Damien and his men stood straight, their hands on their hilts, waiting for the unknown person to approach.

The man was without any weapons, but dressed head to toe in fur and leather well-suited for the cold. His dark skin and bright, green eyes were unusual, but Damien guessed he was a Naymatua. With no trees or branches in the terrible cold, Damien knew the man was helpless.

He smiled, pleased he could take his frustration out on an unwilling victim.

"What can I do for you, Naymatua?" Damien asked.

"You can get out of my cave," he answered. "This is my cold storage, and I try very hard to keep it stocked."

Damien and his men laughed. One of the Soacronis even kicked an empty crate toward the Naymatua.

"Too bad, tree hugger! We ate all of your stock," his man laughed.

"I can see that," the Naymatua answered. "I'll tell you what: leave now, and I will call it even."

"Sorry, old man," Damien declared, "We aren't going anywhere."

"You're calling me old?" the Naymatua said. "Well, I guess being two hundred or so is old."

"Two hundred?" Damien repeated, brow furrowed. "Wait a minute, does that make you—?"

"A Lehrling? That's right!" the Naymatua said. "My name's Cephas, and you better leave now before I change my mind about letting you live!"

Damien's men froze, looking to him for advice. He had no choice. He couldn't go to King Toren without someone in his hands, and what better person to bring in but another Lehrling?

ETANIA FELT HER STOMACH clenching as she entered the bathing pool. *Keyel, like me? How could that be?* she thought, as she slipped into the waters. After all the convincing she gave herself to think otherwise, Keyel blew her assumptions away. He loved her even when she couldn't love herself. She could barely formulate a response to that.

She was telling the truth when she said she admired him. He was handsome, strong, and patient with her failings. For weeks she had wrestled with an unrecognizable feeling within her for Keyel. Was that love? She supposed it could be, but Etania wished she could ask a woman for advice. A woman like her mother.

Etania's heart twisted in her chest at the thought. When would the loss of her mother ever go away? She clutched the necklace still hanging around her neck and stepped out of the bath, glad to erase the filth and sweat. She slipped on a nightgown and dressing gown, tucking her old clothes under her arm as she walked toward her room. Despite the numerous tunnels and turns, she managed to find it. On her door was a note, tacked on the wall and sealed with a purple insignia. She snatched it from the metal surface and stepped inside to read it by candlelight.

She broke the seal with her dagger and then scanned the contents.

Dearest Etania,

Keyel stole you away before I could tell you how proud I am of you. You have shown yourself to be remarkably skilled in wielding your Neuma and I want to compliment you on that. I know Keyel probably confessed his feelings to you; if not, I hope I don't ruin the surprise. He loves you, daughter, that much is clear. However, if you do not return his feelings, give me the word, and I will keep you away from my eager Apprentice. If you do return his feelings, then Melchizedek help me to bear it, for if it leads to marriage—ah! But I go too far. The task before us is grave, so such thoughts must wait. Now, to the point of my letter! You must pack your things, for we will be leaving for the Draconians in the morning. Then, you will meet Melchizedek in person, and he will hopefully give us more than just your Neuma to win the upcoming battle.

I love you.

Your father first,

Jakin Selali

After she finished the letter, Etania pressed it against her bosom and flopped onto the bed. *I can't believe Father told me he loves me!* She thought, lifting up the letter to read it again. *And that he's proud of me.* Ever since Isabella's death, her father had been opening up little by little, showing his emotions more to her. She accepted that Melchizedek's love might be all that she received, but tonight she was blessed with not just one, but two confessions of affection. *Melchizedek, do you have a hand in this?* Her Mark glowed in response, and she smiled.

Even if they were leaving in the morning, at least she felt like she was leaving with more confidence than when she had arrived. Etania packed all of her clothing into her knapsack, laying out her riding pants, split skirt, gambeson, tunic, and mail. She found a cloak in the trunk and added it to the clothing. By the time she was done with everything, she was too tired to consider Keyel's confession anymore, and went to sleep.

The next morning, Ramar, Bayanna, and Ivan stood by the exit to say their goodbyes. With the layers of clothing, and a bolero jacket Bayanna gave her in addition to the cloak, Etania knew she wouldn't be cold in the mountains. Etania curtsied to Ramar, shook hands with Ivan, and then turned to Bayanna.

"The next time I see you will be after you make a name for yourself," Bayanna said.

Etania smiled weakly at the thought of this.

"Oh, come on, you'll do great! You were amazing out there, beating those Soacroni and using your Neuma like a pro," Bayanna encouraged.

"I think Melchizedek helped with that," Etania said.

"Well, whatever the reason, if you are that way on the battlefield, you'll be fine. Besides," Bayanna leaned in and whispered in Etania's ear, "You have a handsome bodyguard to keep you safe out there, too."

Etania blushed and her heart quickened. She had temporarily forgotten Keyel's confession, but Bayanna's teasing words brought it back again.

"Right," Etania said, unable to think of anything else. She hated saying goodbye, especially to someone who had been her constant female companion the last few days. Bayanna brought her into a close embrace.

"Don't worry. Once a friend, always a friend," she said, letting her go.

Etania felt a genuine smile tugging at the corners of her mouth.

"Agreed," she said.

Etania bid her new friend goodbye and headed out into the open air behind her father.

KEYEL SURVEYED IVAN, surprised to see him standing in leather pants, with a blue tunic and silver bolero that matched his hair.

"You're looking well," Keyel said. "I didn't think my healing was so effective that you could stand one day afterwards!'

"You didn't think you could heal me at all," Ivan reminded gruffly.

His off-hand comment made Keyel wince, but it didn't reach his heart like it would've before.

"You didn't believe in me, either," Keyel pointed out.

"And I have never been so glad to be wrong," Ivan slapped Keyel's arm. "I guess Melchizedek was right. I just had to be still and wait."

"Yeah," Keyel said, "he's right about a lot of things."

"He is indeed, lad." Ivan leaned in and whispered, "By the way, is that your lady over there?"

He gestured to Etania and Keyel reddened. He nodded.

"Great pick!" Ivan complimented. "I saw her in the arena. She's ferocious!"

Keyel chuckled. Even though he didn't love her because she was a warrior, he had to admit Etania's prowess in the arena made him proud.

"Did you tell her?" Ivan questioned, waggling his eyebrows at Keyel.

"I did," Keyel replied, wishing this conversation was a bit farther away from Etania. However, Etania seemed caught up in her own goodbye.

"What did she say?" Ivan wondered.

"Well—uh—I don't know if I should say," Keyel stumbled upon his words. "After all, matters of courtship are private."

"Of course, of course!" Ivan slapped Keyel on the arm again. "Good job, Keyel. May Melchizedek be with you on your journey."

"Thank you," Keyel replied. "May he be with you as well."

"Apprentice, we're heading out!" Jakin called.

Keyel nodded, gave a salute to Ivan, and followed Jakin out to the path. He swore they were only a few yards away when Ivan shouted.

"Apprentice? He deserves to be a journeyman by now, Lehrling!"

Keyel wasn't sure if his Master heard Ivan's ravings, but his ears burned.

THE VIEW SPREADING before Etania and her companions was spectacular as they emerged from the base of the mountain. The entire valley before them was green, with pockets of snow gathered at the base of a few trees. The sky was sunny and cloudless, but there was a cool wind blowing.

"Be careful," her father warned. "There could be ice."

Etania nodded and watched her steps, making her way behind her father. Keyel followed her, sometimes reaching to steady her if she slipped on the icy ground. His touch, soft and strong, continued to rattle her emotions. She tried not to think about it while they hiked. As the sun set, they found an empty cave for shelter. The cave contained many crates and, based on the ashes, Etania assumed that someone had camped there but was currently gone.

As if reading her mind, Jakin said, "Keyel, you will take first watch after dinner."

Keyel nodded. After putting his pack down, he went outside to find firewood. Etania helped roll out all of their blankets. When Keyel brought in the wood, her father lit a fire with his Neuma.

They brought out some goat meat and roasted it over the fire. The delicious scent of the meat filled the cavern. After it was cooked, they split it among themselves. Each person was eating ravenously when they heard a booming voice from the entrance.

"Well, well! I get rid of some rats only to find more!" a distinctly male voice exclaimed.

Etania jumped, Keyel drew his sword, and Jakin flourished his hammer. A dark-skinned man came into the circle of firelight, his hands glowing with green flames.

"Cephas?" Jakin said.

"Jakin?" Cephas replied.

They laughed, put out their Neuma, and sheathed their weapons before embracing one another in a hearty hug.

"I haven't seen you in months, old friend!" Cephas said.

"I've been busy. King Toren..." Jakin began. Seeing his daughter's gaping mouth, he started over. "First, let me introduce you to my daughter, Etania, and my apprentice, Keyel."

Cephas stuck out his hand, and Etania took it. He grasped her wrist, and she followed suit in the traditional Naymatua greeting.

"I kept telling Jakin he should bring his wife and daughter on one of his trips, but he never listened to me!"

"Nice to meet you," Etania said, wracking her brain to figure out why his name sounded so familiar. Cephas repeated the greeting to Keyel.

"Oh!" Etania realized suddenly. "You're a Lehrling that was once a Naymatua! You and my father were closest to Melchizedek when he was alive."

"I don't know about closest," Cephas said. "Melchizedek trusted us, that's for sure. I'm sorry for my earlier behavior. I had to take care of some Soacroni who were occupying this space before you, and I thought you were them."

"Soacroni?" Etania repeated.

"Yes, I took most of them out, except for the leader. He fled before I could question him," Cephas explained.

"What did this leader look like?" Jakin asked.

"That was the weird thing," Cephas said. "He looked human, which is odd for a Skazic."

Etania wobbled, and Keyel steadied her until she took a seat on one of the overturned crates and smiled at him gratefully.

"It's not strange once I explain what has been happening in Southern Tamnarae," Jakin said.

"What's happening?" Cephas asked.

"First, join us by the fire. Unless you want us to get out of your cave?" Jakin teased.

"Yes, I want you to get out of this cave!" Cephas teased.

Jakin chuckled and both of them took a seat.

"You're welcome to rest here," Cephas said. "Tomorrow, we can hike to my house, where you can spend the night with my wife and son."

"Sounds like a plan," Jakin agreed.

"I'll still keep watch," Keyel said, and Jakin nodded.

As they gathered around the fire, Etania warmed her hands and listened to her father recall their journey. When her father went over her mother's death, she felt her grief afresh. Tears streamed down her cheeks. She hid her face and calmed herself while her father continued telling Cephas their story.

When he finished, Cephas said, "This is grave news indeed."

"Yes. King Toren is well-fortified in his castle and it will be difficult to overthrow him, even with the support of the other leaders' armies," Jakin admitted.

"I will definitely lend my support," Cephas agreed. "I'm not sure two Lehrlings will be enough if he has amassed a Skazic army over time, but I will stand with you no matter what."

"Well, I have another person who will tip the odds in our favor," Jakin said, motioning to Etania. She shifted uncomfortably. Even if she was more confident using her Neuma, she still didn't like the idea of being the one person that would guarantee victory.

"Your daughter? Why?" Cephas wondered.

"She's a Vexli," Jakin said.

"What? I thought after Daas..." Cephas began.

"I know," Jakin replied, "but Melchizedek blessed her with the powers of a Vexli for this time. Who knew the Skazic would grow to such a size?"

"Agreed," Cephas said grimly.

"Anyway, we were on our way to the Draconians, then we plan on going to Safarast," Jakin explained.

"But to get to Safarast, you have to—" Cephas began.

"I know. That's why I'm glad you're here, Cephas. You can help me reach them without burning myself," Jakin said.

"*You* reach them, Father? Aren't we coming with you?" Etania wondered.

"You can't," Cephas said. "The dragons live between two semi-active volcanoes, subject to a constant flow of rocky, jagged lava."

"But it won't be dangerous for you two?" Etania questioned.

"I can shield us," Cephas explained. Opening his palm, he made a small bubble of green flame appear. "This is my Neuma, my gift from Melchizedek."

"Wow, it's impressive," Etania agreed. "However, if you can expand that over the two of you, then why not all of us?"

"Like your father's gift, mine is limited. I can only shield a few people at a time, and shielding both of us while travelling will be hard enough," Cephas said. "I'm sorry, but you'll have to stay with my wife while we go to theDraconians."

"Oh yeah, how is Alondra?" Jakin asked.

"She's great! Our son is now six months old. Can you believe it?" Cephas declared proudly.

"Wow! I'm definitely looking forward to seeing him!" Jakin admitted.

"Well, you've been busy and so have I." Cephas yawned. "I think it's time to sleep. We have a long day of travel tomorrow."

"Yes," Jakin agreed.

Etania went to her blankets and pulled them over her head while Keyel took first watch. Cephas prepared his own bed and then laid down in it. Even though Cephas and her father started snoring after they went to bed, Etania was wide awake. How could she sleep with the news she'd just received?

Her father and Cephas, the most powerful among them, were going to leave them defenseless. Her previous fear of her inability to fight grew in her stomach while her heart beat wildly in her ears. She wasn't sure how long she lay there, trying to calm herself, trying to pray, until Keyel came. His soft blue eyes gently locked onto her own, and she felt an immediate calm. Did this feeling mean she loved him?

"Did you get some sleep?" Keyel said.

"Not really," Etania admitted, "but it's okay, I'll take the next watch."

"Are you sure?" Keyel asked.

Etania nodded, rising from her blankets and coming to her feet.

"Is there something wrong?" Keyel said.

"I was just worried about my father and Cephas leaving us. I still don't feel confident in protecting myself."

"Etania." Keyel brushed her hair out of her eyes. "I will protect you, but more than that, *Melchizedek* will protect *us*."

His closeness caused Etania to blush and withdraw, but his words were sweetly reassuring. She felt her heart beating closely to her rib cage. This feeling wasn't going away, and she hoped that maybe, just maybe, Cephas's wife would be able to tell her what it meant.

"I'll take the watch," Etania said, quickly striding toward the mouth of the cave.

She found a rock and looked out at the wilderness. There were clumps of trees and wild grass and flowers, but what drew Etania's eye was the sky. Thousands of white lights glittered against the dark background, and a full moon shone white like the fire that came from her fingers.

Melchizedek, I feel like a fish trying to swim in foreign waters. Are you sure you picked the right person to wield your Neuma? Even though I defeated those Soacronis with your help, I still struggle with believing that you really chose me for this task. The mere thought of my father and Cephas leaving is enough to make me panic. I wish my mother was here. I miss her. Melchizedek, is she happy in Safarast with you? Is it selfish for me to want her back?

Etania's conversation continued until she heard Melchizedek's whisper within her chest.

Trust me.

His words, echoing within her, caused her Mark of a rose to glow like the night sky. Melchizedek's peace flooded her until the watch was over and she was able to sleep.

WHEN KEYEL WOKE THE next morning, his mind was on Etania. She had withdrawn when he comforted her, and it increased the worry within the pit of his stomach. Did she think he couldn't protect her? Was that why she rejected his affection? Did she see him as a failure and, therefore, didn't return his love? These questions kept him from speaking more than a few words to Etania as they ate breakfast.

They hiked slowly along the windy road after breakfast, making their way through the valley. The sun continued to shine on them, warming Keyel's body for the first time since they came to the Kinzoku. Darkness was just beginning to fall when they reached a meadow.

"We're here," Cephas announced.

"Here?" Keyel questioned. "There's nothing."

Jakin smiled at him and looked over at Cephas.

"May I?" He asked.

"Could I ever stop you?" Cephas joked.

Jakin laughed and put his hand forward in the air. He must have touched something, because Keyel saw a green ripple of fire retract from his hand, revealing a small, two-story cabin in the midst of an orchard and garden.

"Welcome!" Cephas said. "What you just witnessed is my own invention, which I will have to show you later."

A blonde woman with green eyes opened the door of the cabin, carrying a baby on her hip, who had tan skin and light hair.

"Cephas, you're home!" The woman said, with a wide smile. "And Jakin, is that you? I haven't seen you in forever!"

"Alondra!" Jakin said, enveloping both woman and baby in a brief hug.

"Excuse me, husband coming in," Cephas interrupted, sweeping Jakin aside and bringing Alondra close for a kiss. Keyel, although slightly uncomfortable at the display of affection, also felt a pang of jealousy. Would he be able to have that kind of relationship with Etania?

"Who are your guests, Cephas?" Alondra asked.

"This is Etania, Jakin's daughter, and Keyel, his daughter's protector," Cephas said.

"Nice to meet you all!" Alondra said. "Come inside! I will have to make extra for dinner."

"Is there anything I can do to help you?" Etania asked.

"Do you mind looking after Garel?" Alondra handed the baby to Etania before she could reply.

As Etania held the boy, Keyel observed that he looked up at her with wide, green eyes. Etania gripped him protectively, supporting him as she ducked inside. Keyel followed. Once in Cephas's cabin, they stood within a small sitting room with a fireplace in the corner. A steep staircase led to the bedrooms on the second floor. To Keyel's left were a table and chairs, which meant the room functioned both as a living and dining area. There was an opening in the wall which Keyel assumed led to the kitchen, because Alondra quickly made her way there.

Etania found a rocking chair to sit on with Garel, while Keyel sat on the floor next to the fire. Jakin and Cephas began talking amiably amongst themselves. Etania held Garel closely to her chest as she rocked back and forth. The motion must have been soothing, because the child fought to keep his eyes open.

"Look at him," Etania said, with a smile. "Not a care in the world."

"Envious, are we?" Keyel commented.

"A little," Etania admitted. "I wish that I didn't have to worry about anything."

Keyel felt the same—a whimsical wish that they were at peace. Yet, he knew the time ahead of them would be fraught with dangers.

"Maybe someday you will not have to worry. We can live together in peace," Keyel said. Etania looked up at him, her brown eyes soft.

"We?" she repeated.

Keyel's breath caught. He blushed and coughed. Had he really just said that aloud? Fortunately, Alondra emerged with a tray of steaming cups.

"Here's some tea while you wait," she said. "I had to put more meat on the spit, so there may be some time left before you can enjoy what I've cooked."

"Anything you've cooked will be fine, Alondra. We understand that we arrived unannounced," Jakin said.

"When don't you arrive unannounced?" Alondra questioned, and Cephas laughed.

Jakin looked sheepish in response, but Keyel wasn't surprised that his Master's behavior was consistent across the territories. Alondra placed the tray on the coffee table and walked back into the kitchen. Keyel fetched two teacups from the tray, handing one to Etania.

"Thank you," she replied, sipping carefully with one hand while rocking Garel to sleep with the other. Keyel decided he should change the subject and asked what had been on his mind since the night before.

"Did you manage to get some sleep last night?" Keyel questioned.

Etania blew the steam from her cup and took another sip before answering, "Yes."

"That's good," Keyel managed. He wondered if he should say anything else, but Etania spoke again.

"With Cephas and my father leaving tomorrow, I feel vulnerable," Etania said.

He knew it. She still thought he couldn't protect her. He bit his lip as he spoke.

"The shield around this place should be more than enough to defend us," Keyel said. "If that fails, you know I am by your side."

"I know," Etania said, and a slight blush crept upon her cheeks, "but will that be enough?"

Keyel tried not to get angry. How much more reassurance did she need? Was he really an awful guard?

"I will personally make sure you are safe," Keyel declared.

"Safe? Of course you'll be safe, what do you need to fear?" Alondra exclaimed as she emerged from the kitchen, taking a seat next to her husband.

"I'll explain later," Cephas said.

"We have time, why don't you explain now?" Alondra questioned.

Cephas sighed and then agreed with a grunt. He recounted everything that had occurred to their guests. Keyel put a reassuring hand lightly on Etania's shoulder as Cephas told Alondra that Tala had died.

"She will be greatly missed," Alondra said. "She is a woman who could relate to me about being a Lehrling's wife. I had wondered why her letters stopped after all these months..."

Alondra sniffed, and Cephas hung his arm around her shoulders and continued. When he reached the end, Alondra looked at each of them.

"You have been through so much, in so short a period of time! I wish I could hug you all," Alondra said.

"Because of this, I have to leave with Jakin to reach Draconia," Cephas said. "We will need the dragons and their riders in the fight."

"I understand," Alondra said. "When do you leave?"

"Tomorrow morning," Jakin said.

Alondra sighed. Resting her fierce, green eyes on Jakin, she said, "Jakin, you promise me. Promise me you'll bring Cephas home in one piece."

"Of course," Jakin agreed, "as long as you protect Etania and Keyel."

Alondra laughed.

"I think my husband's machine will have to protect us all. You know I have no Neuma, just like your wife."

"I knew that,"

"Machine?" Keyel asked.

"I will show it to you after dinner," Cephas said. Alondra rose.

"I guess that's my signal to start cutting the roast," she declared. She went back into the kitchen. After a few minutes, she came out with a tray of sliced meat, roasted potatoes, and a salad. She instructed Cephas to distribute the plates and asked Etania to put Garel in his crib, to sleep. Soon, everyone was seated around the table, with Cephas at one end and Alondra at another.

"Deo," Cephas prayed, "we come before you during a dire time. The King you placed on the throne has gone against your sacred commands and betrayed you and us. We are grieved and ask that you protect us from his evil reach and guide our rebellion against him. Help us to seek the alliance of the Dragons and find you in Safarast. Bless the food that Alondra has prepared this evening. In your son Melchizedek's name we pray, may it be so."

Once he was finished, they began to eat. Keyel listened as the two Lehrlings exchanged stories about their times with Melchizedek, laughing often. All too soon, their conversation came to an end and Cephas stood.

"Well, do you want to see the machine?" he asked.

Keyel nodded. He definitely wanted to know what was supposedly so powerful that it could protect them as equally as two Lehrlings. Jakin, Etania, and Keyel followed Cephas out of the door, but Alondra stayed with Garel.

Cephas led them to the barn next to his house. He climbed up the ladder and the others followed him until they were standing in the loft. Inside was a large, round, metal chest, sitting on a stand. In the center of the chest was a concave surface, covered with emeralds. The light from a skylight reflected from the emeralds, which glittered like green rain drops. Only Cephas was able to approach the machine. With his hands glowing, he poured more Neuma into the emeralds, which seemed to absorb it. Sparks of green floated upward in response.

"So, what do you think?" Cephas asked.

"How does it work?" Keyel wondered.

"Well, you probably didn't notice, but your Master's Neuma can be contained with a jewel—specifically, an amethyst," Cephas explained. "Mine can as well, but within an emerald. I planted emeralds around the border of my property and then used this device to continuously feed them power."

"That's why you have to keep it full of Neuma?" Keyel asked.

Cephas nodded.

"Yes, and the only way for this shield to be broken is if you break the emeralds. So you see, Etania, there is very little to fear."

"Thank you," Etania said, and Keyel echoed her.

As they descended the ladder and headed back to the house, Keyel had to admit that the machine relieved some of his anxiety. He only wished that Etania trusted him enough to keep her safe. He tried not to let this fact bother him as he shared a room with Jakin, pushing aside his negative thoughts as he lay in bed and fell asleep.

JAKIN ROSE WHEN THE peak of dawn was showing through the curtains of the shared room. He wanted to leave early before the others woke, hoping to avoid saying his goodbyes. He had never been good with them—that's why Tala had always taken care of that.

Jakin carefully went to Cephas' bedroom and knocked lightly. The Lehrling answered, his black hair plastered against his face. Jakin bit back a laugh.

"Seriously, you want to leave now?" Cephas said in a whisper. Jakin nodded.

"You don't want to say goodbye, do you?" Cephas said. Jakin shook his head."Ugh, fine. But I'm saying goodbye to my wife. I will meet you in the kitchen in a few minutes."

Jakin descended the stairs carefully, trying not to wake Etania, who slept in the sitting room because of the limited space. He tip-toed across the floor and entered the kitchen, where he began packing food into his knapsack.

"What are you doing?" Etania's voice, slightly tired and irritated, came from the doorway. Jakin sighed.

"I'm packing," he said.

"Leaving before dawn?" Etania said. "Why am I not surprised?"

"I wanted to get an early start," Jakin replied.

"No, you wanted to avoid us. You used to do that to mom and me, remember? I know all your tricks."

Jakin shrugged, continuing to pack.

"Father," Etania began, and Jakin turned toward her. Was she going to accuse him? Shout? "How did you know you were in love with Mother?"

Jakin bit his lip. *Tala, how did I end up having this conversation?*

"I just realized I wanted to be with her, and that no matter what we went through, I would choose to love her," Jakin said aloud.

"*Choose* to love her?" Etania repeated.

"That's right. The feelings of love—stomach aches, blushing, heart beats—those are temporary. True love chooses to continue loving and forgiving even when it's hard."

Etania's brow scrunched together. She opened her mouth to ask another question, but Cephas entered the room.

"Ready to go?" Cephas asked, "or did I interrupt something?"

"No, you didn't," Jakin said, grateful his friend had arrived in the middle of their awkward conversation. "Goodbye, Etania. Stay safe."

"You too," Etania said, pulling him into a hug.

Jakin nodded, stepping away. He turned his back on his daughter, walking out of the door without turning back.

"Didn't want to say goodbye, huh?" Cephas needled.

"Oh, shush," Jakin grumbled.

Cephas laughed, and Jakin peeked over his shoulder to see Etania standing in the doorway.

Even if Tala isn't alive, I'm glad I still have a piece of her with me, Jakin thought, turning back to the road ahead.

Chapter Twenty-Five

Damien stumbled through the snow, knowing he would have to make it to the meeting place where King Toren's camp was located or freeze to death. Even if King Toren wasn't happy with him, at least it would be warm.

He tripped and fell, his wounded arm breaking his fall. He cursed. If only that Naymatua hadn't come into their cave, his mission would be complete! Instead, the irritating Lehrling had killed the rest of his men and sent him fleeing, injured. Yet, more than the Lehrling, Damien hated the Vexli for what she had done to him by making him a weakling once again. When he got a hold of that girl, she would pay, piece by piece. If King Toren gave him permission, of course.

He scoffed as he rose to his feet. King Toren wouldn't let him harm the girl when he wanted to use those gauntlets to control her. Damien didn't know exactly what it was, but every time he came near the trunk that carried the gauntlets, he shivered. Those items had wicked power, and he didn't want any part of it. He caught sight of the King's flags in the distance and called out to the guards.

"It's me, Damien! I need to speak to the King immediately," he said.

"Where's the Vexli?" the toothbreaker Skazic growled.

"Not here, but close," Damien said. "I'm not saying anything until I see the King."

The toothbreaker raised his lip to show his white fangs.

"Fine!" he snarled, and allowed Damien to pass. Damien stumbled forward, heading toward the King's tent. He called out to let the King know he was coming, and Toren beckoned him inside. Immediately, Damien was surrounded by warmth. He shivered as feeling began seeping into his fingers, including his wounded arm.

"I believe I told you to return with the Vexli," King Toren threatened.

Damien suppressed a shudder from the King's cold voice.

"I know," Damien replied. "I'm sorry, but several of my men died from the cold, then we were attacked by another Lehrling."

"Cephas is here?" King Toren spat. "I hoped to keep him out of this small squabble."

"Yes, he is," Damien said. "He lives in a house close by. After he killed most of my men, I fled and waited in hiding. The Lehrling, the Vexli, and the Leici arrived, joining with Cephas and heading out. I followed them until I saw where the second Lehrling's house is."

"Why didn't you follow them farther?" King Toren questioned. "Surely you can do that much."

"I would've my liege, but they have a shield around the house. I couldn't get close."

"A shield?" King Toren repeated, rubbing his beard. "This does cause concern."

"Your Grace, I would be pleased to lead you to the house if I could get some food and treatment for my arm...."

King Toren whirled on him, eyes wide. He slapped Damien across the face.

"You demand food and treatment when you couldn't bring me the girl before she entered this fortress?" King Toren scoffed.

"I'm sorry, your majesty," Damien apologized, bowing as low as he was able. King Toren sniffed.

"That's better," he said. "I suppose we will need you healthy to lead us to her, even if you failed me."

Damien said nothing. He knew it was better to wait than provoke Toren's wrath again.

"You may leave," Toren declared, "but keep this in mind, Damien—your information better be good, or you will die."

Damien nodded, giving a quick bow before exiting the tent. He was confident his directions would earn the King's favor once more. After all, he had seen the Vexli with his own eyes.

ETANIA REALIZED SHE wouldn't get any more sleep as she thought about her father's parting words. He'd told her that the symptoms of love were only feelings, but that true love was a choice. When Etania considered that explanation, she was even more confused. She knew the symptoms her father had mentioned were all ones that she felt whenever Keyel was present. So she had to be in love, right? But then he had added the choice part....

A creak from the stairs broke Etania's thoughts. Alondra was at the foot of the steps, a cloth sling holding Garel close to her chest.

"Good morning, Etania," she said. "Did you wake when Jakin and Cephas left, too?"

Etania nodded.

"Yeah, Jakin is ridiculous, leaving before everyone is awake." Alondra sighed. "Garel needed to nurse, so I guess I can't complain too much." Etania smiled at the infant, who snuggled against his mother's chest.

"Alondra," Etania managed. "Do you mind if I ask you a question?"

"Sure, just come into the kitchen. I might as well get started on breakfast since I'm up."

Etania followed her into the cozy space, where Alondra began making bread. As she mixed the dough, Etania asked her question.

"Um...how did you know you were in love with Cephas?"

Alondra laughed, beginning to knead the dough with her hands.

"I didn't. My parents gave me as a gift to him," Alondra said. Etania balked.

"But then how...I mean, you seem so in love now..." she stuttered.

"That love developed over time," Alondra explained. "Cephas never pressured me and took his time to learn who I am. He even told me that if I wanted to leave, he would understand, since our marriage was one of convenience."

"But you chose to stay?" Etania asked.

"Yes," Alondra said. "I realized how great a man he is and how I really felt. I decided I would continue to love him from that point forward—especially after my conversation with Melchizedek."

"Did you speak to Melchizedek when he walked Tearah?"

"Yes. Melchizedek had more followers than just men, you know. When I spoke to him, he reminded me that love comes from him, and that it is all right if I feel like an inadequate wife. He would give me all the love I needed to be a good wife to Cephas."

"Love comes from Melchizedek. Does that mean if I chose to love someone despite their flaws, I am loving like Melchizedek?" Etania reworded.

"Yes," Alondra replied. "Melchizedek is the source of all kinds of love: familial, friendship, and romantic. But the love he has for us is unique, surpassing all those types of love. That is why it is important to keep your relationship with him a priority, even if you are married. Did you have someone particular in mind?"

"Maybe."

"The Leici?"

Etania blushed, looking down at her feet.

"Maybe," she repeated.

"Well, whoever you like, you better tell him. Now is not the time to leave things unsaid."

"Yes, I know," Etania agreed. After all, how many things she wanted to tell her mother, which would remain unsaid?

A slight knocking on the wall caused both women to look up and see Keyel standing in the doorway.

"How's breakfast coming along?" Keyel asked.

"It will be ready soon. Set the table, will you?" Alondra said.

Etania blushed, her thoughts racing. Had Keyel overheard their conversation?

"Don't worry," Alondra reassured. "Now, do you know how to fry an egg?"

Etania nodded and turned to the fire, cracking eggs and seasoning them as Alondra instructed. She also helped slice fresh fruit and bread loaf that had baked most of the day before. When they were finished, the bread, fruit, and eggs made a hearty meal. Breakfast complete, Alondra assigned them different tasks.

"Keyel, I need you to feed the animals, clean their stalls, and milk the cows. Our farm lad, Sorrel, will be here shortly to show you how it's done. Etania and I will be picking fruit and vegetables and we'll meet back here when we're done," Alondra said.

Keyel agreed, and they split off in different directions, each to their own task. Etania held the basket while Alondra carried Garel to the garden. The rows with tall, green plants were neat and the long vines were well-kept. Etania spent the time with Alondra weeding, watering, and picking the ripe vegetables. They were just about to reach the fruit trees when Alondra called a stop for a midday meal. She sent Etania over to call Keyel back for lunch.

When Etania arrived, Keyel and Sorrel were finishing milking the cows. Sorrel carried the buckets of milk toward the house with Etania.

"Put those over there." Alondra pointed toward a corner where there was a washbasin and a churn. "Please wash your hands. I don't want Garel getting sick."

Etania handed Keyel a basin of water and a washcloth after using it herself. Sorrel followed in cleaning his hands and face. Soon, they were clean enough for lunch. They ate cheese, bread, and leftover roast for lunch and then Alondra assigned new tasks.

"I have a whole bunch of dead branches that need chopping," Alondra said. "Any wood you chop, place on the side of the house for easy access. Etania and I will gather fruit and join you for dinner."

"Wow, you sure know how to work someone!" Keyel whistled.

"Of course!" Alondra said with a smile. "You've got to earn your keep."

"Miss Alondra says she has been working on a farm since she was a little girl, and now it is time for the young people to work," Sorrel added.

"Oh does she?" Keyel chuckled.

"Now that you understand, there's no more time to rest, let's get back to work!" Alondra commanded.

"Yes ma'am!" Etania said, with a slight salute.

Alondra slapped her playfully and they split up once again. With so much to do, Etania put aside any thoughts of romance and enjoyed the peaceful rhythm of farm life.

JAKIN WAS VERY GRATEFUL for the presence of Cephas. The rocky lava plain was jagged and uneven, making it difficult to trek on. Cephas protected their feet with his Neuma, making them look like they were walking with bubbles for shoes. Jakin bit back a laugh at the thought.

Finding a place to rest where there weren't sharp volcanic rocks was almost impossible. They usually slept on a rocky slope, able to get snippets of sleep instead of full hours. If it wasn't for the fact that the Draconians didn't like surprises, Jakin would have transported them there in a heartbeat. He normally didn't care about surprising people, but when dragons were involved, he would rather not risk it.

The Draconians were humans who mastered the art of riding dragons. Their Neuma was the ability to tame the ferocious beasts, and once they were bonded to a dragon, they changed in appearance. Their hair color and eyes would match that of their dragon. For example, if a dragon was purple with green, reptilian eyes, the man or woman's hair and eyes would change to match them. Jakin could remember the first time he met a Draconian of that description, and how odd he thought it was. At least the human's skin didn't become reptilian, and they were just as vulnerable to attack as any other man. The dragons, on the other hand, had skin as tough as nails, and most weapons could not harm it. Only a catapult or a stationary crossbow could pierce the skin of a dragon. Jakin found that out the hard way during the Long War.

The two Lehrlings were cautious even though there were no signs of Skazic, taking turns watching and sleeping. Jakin just wished he could have a chance to fight. His fingers were itching to grip his hammer and swing it until he could stop the pain—the pain that Tala had left behind.

On the morning of the third day, when both men were ready to snap at each other over their lack of sleep, they spotted two peaks. The Draconian people lived in a crater that used to be a volcano; two jagged edges acting as sentinels to the entrance. The edge of the crater was as sharp as the volcanic slopes surrounding them, making entrance only possible by air. So Jakin and Cephas stood at the bottom of the mountain and waited, knowing it was only a matter of time before the Draconians noticed the pair.

Three dragons appeared almost on cue, their large wings stirring the trees and grass around Jakin and Cephas. They descended with bat-like wings, floating into a landing on four feet. When they did land, Jakin tried not to gulp. He had forgotten how big the dragons were. They were taller than most horses at the shoulder, with long necks that reached to the top of trees. There were riders on the back of each.

A man with red hair that matched the color of his dragon's scales, and yellow eyes that reflected their reptilian glance, dismounted. He approached Jakin and Cephas.

"Lehrlings!" he practically shouted. "What are you doing here?"

"We're here to see you," Jakin replied. "What else would we trek out here for?"

"No, I mean, *what* are you doing *here* when your home is being attacked?" the man asked.

"My home?" Cephas exclaimed. "Alondra!"

"Yes," the man said. "My men and I just spotted the smoke during our daily patrol. We were coming here to get reinforcements. I've never seen so many Golems."

"Golems?" Cephas replied, glancing at Jakin, his green eyes wide.

Jakin's heart thudded in his chest. He hadn't seen Golems since the war. What had King Toren done now?

"Well, are you going to stand there or come with me?" the man questioned. "You, tell Lord Saigon that we need reinforcements. The rest of you, come with me! And someone with a less tired dragon, please take the Lehrlings."

"Who do I have to thank for this warning?" Cephas asked.

"My name is Tevan," the man said, and patting his dragon's neck, added, "and this is Flamir."

"Thank you," Cephas said, and Tevan guided them to step-stools that would allow them access to the dragon's backs.

Etania, please be safe, Jakin thought, as he climbed aboard one of the dragons.

THE SUN SHONE BRIGHTLY on the third day since Jakin and Cephas had been gone. Etania took the sunshine and the birds singing as a good sign for what she had decided. During the last few days, they had enjoyed the peace and quiet of the countryside. It gave Etania time to think, and those thoughts led to a simple conclusion.

If love is a choice, then I choose Keyel.

Keyel was always by her side as her protector, confidante, and friend. He was strong and quiet, thoughtful and gentle, and she knew she could depend on him more than anyone else. She also knew that she wanted him by her side from this point onward. Melchizedek made Keyel especially for her—a man who could be a lifetime companion.

She just had to tell him. They were rarely alone, but maybe Melchizedek would afford them a moment to connect. Alondra must have sensed her desire as they prepared the morning meal together, for she spoke up.

"Go to him," Alondra said.

Etania gave the woman a hug before she rushed out to the stables. Keyel was just finishing feeding the animals and was about to start mucking out their stalls when she entered. Sorrel was gone for the day, receiving a day off since Keyel now knew how to help Alondra around the farm.

"Good morning, Etania," he said. "To what do I owe the pleasure?"

With him standing there, his blonde hair swept back from his face, his blue eyes shining, Etania felt her throat closing. *How could this amazing man love someone like me?* She shook away her doubts and swallowed.

"I wanted to tell you something," she began, "something important."

"What is it?" Keyel asked. "Not that I mind being interrupted from work, but the heat of the day is coming. I'm still shocked over how hot it gets here compared to the Kinzoku mountains..."

"It'll be quick," Etania replied. "It's just that..."

"My, my, it seems I'm interrupting!" a voice called from the stable doors.

Etania and Keyel turned to look at the source and saw King Toren standing next to a bald man with yellow eyes.

"How did you get in here?" Keyel questioned. "The shield should've stopped you."

Sweeping Etania behind him, he drew his sword.

"I had a little help," King Toren bragged, moving temporarily aside.

They could see golems that were made of rock or jewels behind the King. The golems looked like large humans, with huge arms and legs. However, instead of a head, they had a rock with two eye-sockets that showed normal eyes. This is because they were once Kinzoku who had sold their souls to Malstorm to become these golems. They also had stumps for feet, but their hands were formed out of rock, looking like they could crush someone just with their grip. There must have been a hundred of them, standing as still as statues in the daylight. They probably found the emeralds planted around the property that powered the shield and crushed them with their bare hands.

"Now, are you going to come quietly or do I need to use force?" King Toren questioned.

"Remember me? I'm Damien, and I'm happy to use force," the bald man hissed.

For the first time, Etania looked at the man fully. That was when she recognized him...the man who had attacked her at the library and stumbled into the meetings! The first man she had transformed with her Neuma. Based on the vitriol he was sending her with his eyes, this change was not a welcome one.

"I won't let you have her!" Keyel declared, flourishing his sword and pointing it toward the King.

Etania let the heat of her Neuma flow from within her to the palms of her hands, making small fires. They were about to advance, even outnumbered, when King Toren flicked his wrist. The golems parted, and two Skazic dragged Alondra forward. She was clutching Garel to her chest.

"I wouldn't do that if I were you," King Toren threatened.

Etania and Keyel hesitated, and Alondra spoke.

"I would rather die than be used as a pawn!"

Keyel shook his head and sheathed his sword. Etania extinguished her flames. They couldn't attack, with Alondra and Garel's lives in danger. More Kinzoku-Skazic stepped forward, pulling Etania and Keyel's arms behind their backs. They pushed the two of them out of the stables and into the yard.

"Bring out the gauntlets!" King Toren commanded.

Once again the golems parted—this time for two soldiers carrying a large case. They opened the lid, revealing a pair of gleaming gauntlets.

Covered in silver and black markings, the gauntlets pulsed with a dark energy which reached toward Etania with black tendrils of smoke. Etania flinched, trying to pull away. Toren put one gauntlet on his hand and it enveloped his fingers, coming down halfway to his elbow. The guards yanked Etania's arm forward, and Toren forced the gauntlet over her hand.

The cool metal slipped easily over her fingers, but as soon as it was secure, it became hot, digging into her skin like needles. Etania cried out in agony as the gauntlet stung. Keyel struggled against the guards.

"What is that thing?" he asked. "What have you done?"

"This is Malstorm's gauntlet," Toren said, "and it will make me invincible!"

He raised his arm with the gauntlet and motioned for the guards to step back from Etania.

Etania watched in horror as her hand rose up without her volition. She felt the heat from the gauntlet course down her arm, pour into her heart, and steal the heat of her Neuma. That stolen flame appeared on the palm of the hated gauntlet.

King Toren laughed, moving his hand around in synchronization with Etania. She shuddered, feeling a dark presence creeping over her.

"Let's test this," Toren said, and one of the guards pushed Keyel forward. Etania balked.

"What are you doing?" she demanded. "The flames won't hurt him."

"That's what you think," Toren replied.

His tone chilled her, right before Etania felt a searing pain in her wrist. Her white flames suddenly turned a sickly gray. Toren forced her hand up and she was about to fling the flame toward Keyel when she heard a roar. Looking skyward, Etania cried in relief. Five dragons, commanded by their human riders, roared and blew a huge rush of flames, causing the golems to scatter. The flames were so hot that they could melt the golems into piles of ash, and some of the golems were unable to escape the power of the dragon's flames. Etania and her company were surrounded by green bubbles; protected by Cephas' shields from the devastation. Toren screamed in frustration and agony as his men rushed him away from the flames of the dragons. He barely managed to escape the flames without a scratch, his golem army protecting him. Damien also escaped by hiding behind golems, who turned into rubble.

"This isn't over, Jakin!" Toren screamed. "I have your daughter, no matter where you go!"

Etania was shoved on the back of one of the dragons and they flew away. As she looked at the gauntlet, she wondered if the King was right. For even now, she felt like the gauntlet was writhing around on her arm...

Chapter Twenty-Six

Despite the wind in her hair and the clear, blue sky, Etania couldn't enjoy the dragon ride. All she could think about was how King Toren had taken control of her Neuma. She had worked so hard to master it, but now, her Neuma was out of her control once again. When Toren tried forcing her to kill Keyel, she had fought against his every movement. Nothing she'd done worked, and it had felt so frustrating and frightening.

Tears slipped down her cheeks as she tugged at the gauntlet hopelessly. Instead of it slipping off, the gauntlet felt tighter on her arm. How could that be? How could something seemingly made of metal move and adjust itself when Etania tried to take it off? All her questions were unanswered as the dragon and its riders flew through the air.

Etania looked down at the small dots of trees speeding by below her. Even though she should be scared, she wasn't. Instead, she wondered whether the gauntlet would remain attached to her arm even if she died. Would it always be a part of her? A metal device that restrained her for the remainder of her life? If so, she would be useless in the upcoming battle. Everything that her father had hoped for her would turn into ashes.

Melchizedek, why? Etania cried inwardly, no answer coming to her.

HALF AN HOUR LATER, the dragons landed in the middle of a crater, in which rested the Draconian capital city. The city was made of two-story stone houses that were very similar to those in Nova. One level contained a living area and kitchen, and the second level was for bedrooms. The sturdy houses made sense to Keyel. What didn't make sense to him were the dragons that were everywhere—sleeping on rooftops, watching over children playing, or wrestling one another. Bright-haired Draconian women and children barely blinked an eye as dragons of all sizes played, slept, or ran. Keyel saw all of this in a moment as he dismounted, surprised at how the normalcy of the Draconian people was a direct contrast to his definition of normal. He was used to hafif alone walking around alone, not accompanied by medium-sized dragons!

Keyel had no time to reflect before the six of them were ushered into a large, stone meeting hall. Only then did Keyel mull over what had happened to them at Cephas's house. His heart felt as heavy as the rocks around him. Even when he sat down in a stone chair beside Etania, all he could do was stare at the thing which had infected her arm.

"Why do I always fail to protect her, Melchizedek?"

"To show you who really protects," he answered.

Melchizedek's warm reply was comforting, though it didn't remove the doubt within his heart. Keyel knew it was not a coincidence that the dragons had arrived when they did, or that he was alive because of their divine timing.

"What happened?" Jakin asked, examining Etania's gauntlet.

"King Toren's golems broke the shield," Keyel explained. "One of the Soacronis led them to the farm."

"They broke my shield?" Cephas replied. "I didn't think that was possible!"

"Neither did I," Alondra agreed, cuddling their infant close.

"How did a Soacronis know where to find us?" Jakin wondered. Cephas stroked his chin.

"I bet one of the men escaped that cave," he replied. "I'm surprised I didn't notice..."

"I think I know him," Keyel said. "He's the man who Etania changed with her Neuma."

Etania nodded solemnly, and Jakin spat.

"This is what happens when we let Skazic slip through our fingers!" he growled.

"Regardless," Cephas said, looking at the gauntlet, "what are we going to do about *that?*"

Keyel put a hand on Etania's shoulder to reassure her.

"King Toren said the gauntlets belonged to Malstorm during the War. And when he used his, Etania had no control over her Neuma," Keyel said.

"I was so scared I would lose you, Keyel," she whispered. "I couldn't believe what he was doing with my Neuma..."

Her voice was so soft, so frail. Keyel wanted to envelop her in a hug and hold her until the evils of the world disappeared. He pushed the thought aside.

"So, is it Malstorm's gauntlet?" Cephas questioned.

Jakin examined it, carefully lifting Etania's arm.

"I'm afraid so," Jakin said heavily. "I recognize it as the one Daas wore during the war."

"Is it true what Toren said," Etania piped up, "that I could kill with it?"

Jakin nodded grimly.

"Can we get it off?" Keyel wondered.

"Not that I know of," Jakin admitted. "I hope that Melchizedek will be able to remove it."

Etania shuddered again and Keyel squeezed her shoulder.

A man coughed, and their group turned to look at him. Keyel hardly recognized the man who had survived the attack on the council. He was dressed in clean clothes and looked like he'd lost a bit of weight. His sharp, yellow eyes and bright green hair hadn't changed, though.

"Lord Saigon," Jakin acknowledged, bowing to the man. Keyel and the others followed suit.

"I'm sorry for being so rude," Jakin said. "I wanted to make sure my daughter was safe."

"And I, my wife," Cephas added.

"I understand," Saigon answered. "With my wife Jonida imprisoned, it has taken all of my patience to wait for you, Jakin."

"And I am glad you did," Jakin affirmed, "but I'm afraid I will need you to wait a little longer."

"Why?" Saigon questioned. "With King Toren's attack on you, I would think you are also eager for a fight."

"Melchizedek commanded them to meet him at Safarast first," Cephas explained. "Neither my wife nor I will be joining them."

"There is a portal to Safarast here," Saigon disclosed. "The entrance to this portal has been guarded by our families for hundreds of years; ever since Melchizedek stepped through it when he left Tearah."

"Have you gone inside yourself?" Keyel asked.

Saigon shook his head. "No one can enter but those whom Melchizedek allows. I heard that my grandfather stepped through once, but none have since. Any who try entering without his permission are severely injured."

"Severely injured?" Keyel repeated, instinctively placing his hand on his sword hilt.

"We'll be fine," Jakin said, with a bold smile. Keyel's gut clenched, but Etania put her hand on his arm.

"Keyel, it will be okay. He told me to come," she said softly.

He relaxed slightly, but the thought of possible harm coming to them made him nervous. Keyel had never thought visiting Safarast would be dangerous.

"I will show you the portal later," Saigon said. "For now, I think you should get some food at my house."

Jakin agreed, and they stood. Saigon led them out of the stone meeting hall and outside, where the sun was high in the sky. *How much time has passed since this morning's attack?* Keyel didn't have a moment to reflect on this before they were ushered to Saigon's house for lunch.

SAIGON'S HOUSE WAS one of the largest in the Draconian city, and his dining room reflected his position as the leader of Draconia. There was a long table in the center of the room, and Saigon's children were eating there when Etania and her companions arrived. They greeted their father and his guests with smiles that brightened their orange, blue, and purple hair. Next to them, or on the table, were small dragons that matched their hair colors. Etania hadn't realized that Saigon was a father, and her heart hurt at the realization that these children probably missed their mother just as much as she missed her own. Several servants came and served food to Etania and her party as they took their seats around the table.

Etania picked at her food, barely eating it. Although the meal consisted of meat pies, bread and fruit, she wasn't that hungry. *How can I eat with this cursed arm?* She thought. She couldn't grip the stone fork or knife properly and it still burned with every movement. To her embarrassment, Keyel had to cut the food into smaller pieces so she could eat it. She couldn't believe that she was going to confess she loved him just this morning. Why did life seem to change so quickly? One moment, she was a librarian. The next, a Vexli. Now, she wondered if she would be able to embrace that title with the gauntlet gleaming menacingly around her wrist.

"What's wrong?" Keyel asked.

Where do I begin? Etania wanted to say, but she shrugged instead.

"It will be alright," Keyel assured. "Melchizedek will remove the gauntlet."

"I hope so," Etania admitted, but inwardly, she wondered if he would. She had failed once again to live up to being a "Vexli." Keyel tried to give her a sympathetic look, but his attention was divided when one of the children's dragons stole his portion of meat pie.

After lunch, Saigon led them to the entrance of the portal, taking them outside of the stone city to an entrance on the side of the crater. From there, they entered a long tunnel, which opened up into a small cavern. Here, a gateway made of stone was set, and etched upon the top were the words "To Deo be all power and glory." On the sides was a warning, "Let all who enter here call upon the name of Melchizedek." Yet, the most interesting part of the portal was the entrance itself.

There were blurry images flashing across the surface of a mirror-like gate—images Etania had seen before in Melchizedek's fountain. Flashes of places Etania could not even name ran quickly by. She saw a horseless cart with four wheels, a ship of the air instead of the sea, and a crowd of people in foreign clothing all looking down at square boxes which flashed lights as they touched it. Yet, as she and her companions approached, the images stilled. The castle which she had only seen portions of in dreams was revealed. They took this as a cue to enter, Etania swallowing her fear as she stepped forward, expecting a solid surface.

Instead, the three of them passed through the portal easily and into Safarast unharmed. They were standing in a large, open meadow filled with wildflowers, and a single tower stood nearby with heptagonal windows. The tower, Etania assumed, was where Melchizedek had met her in some of her dreams. They walked on a narrow path, following the meadow until they reached the castle itself. The limestone walls of the castle glinted in the sun as they approached. There was no gate, and they walked through the castle archway into the courtyard.

The courtyard was stunning. Etania recognized this area as the manicured garden where she had met Melchizedek after her mother's death. The flowerbeds and stone planters had changed and were now containing tulips, sunflowers, and poppies. There were several tables, benches, and chairs throughout the garden, though Etania could not understand why. No one was present. Another feature of the courtyard that Etania hadn't seen in her dreams were the colonnades all around them. Underneath the colonnades were hundreds of doors. Where they led, Etania didn't know. At the end of the courtyard was a huge keep. As they approached it, the large oak doors swung open.

Melchizedek strode forward. He was dressed in a billowy, long-sleeved, white shirt and pants tucked into boots. He had shoulder-length brown hair that matched his full beard, practically blending into his tan skin. Yet, his eyes were what drew Etania's gaze—though brown, they were ageless and contained a mixture of emotions Etania couldn't name.

"Welcome, my friends, to Safarast!" Melchizedek exclaimed.

"Master!" Jakin cried out, immediately kneeling. Etania and Keyel followed suit. Melchizedek smiled.

"My child," he said. "Raise your heads, for you are my guests and this is your place of rest."

"Rest?" Jakin repeated. "Master, as much as I would love to rest, we aren't here to rest. I hoped to receive help for the war against the Skazic."

"You have all the help you need," Melchizedek replied. "Have I not told you, Jakin? My Mark of Neuma is all you require."

Jakin snorted. Etania looked at her gauntlet and it tightened, the needlelike pain shooting through her arm. Melchizedek glanced at her, and she felt ashamed under his loving gaze.

"Do not be afraid," he told them. "Rise and find the door with your name: Etania, Keyel, and Jakin. There, you will find the answers you seek."

With that, Melchizedek returned to the keep. The double doors closed behind him, and the trio rose to their feet.

"I guess we do as he says," Keyel stated, and the others nodded their agreement.

Etania and Keyel went to the right colonnade and Jakin went to the left one. Keyel must have found his door early, because she heard him open one and step inside. Etania kept scanning the names on the doors. When she came near, she saw one name that intrigued her:

Tala Selali. Her mother.

She tried the door, tugging at its handle, but it didn't budge. She sighed deeply, realizing that only her door would open for her. She went to the left colonnade and saw her father find his door and disappeared within. At last, when she was about to give up, she found her door.

She gripped the knob. As soon as she reached for it, the gauntlet reacted, searing her with heat. She cried out, twisting the knob quickly and stepping inside to escape the pain.

She was standing within her room in Nova and nothing had changed. The clothes were still tossed on her bed from when she had packed to leave. The candlesticks were still half melted from frequent use. The view of a garden outside was the same. The only difference in the room was the absence of a second door, so she could not go out to the remainder of the house. The only door was the one that led back to Safarast.

Despite this, she heard the squeak of a door opening and closing, and her mother stepped inside. Etania wondered if she was seeing a spirit.

"Etania, what are you doing here?" Tala questioned.

Emotions overwhelmed Etania. She cried out and embraced her, finding herself weeping on her mother's shoulder.

"What's wrong?" Tala said.

Etania blinked, stepping back from her mother's embrace.

"You...you don't remember?" Etania questioned.

"Remember what? And why are you wearing your riding clothes and that horrid gauntlet? Where is Keyel? He was supposed to be with you at all times..." Tala babbled.

"Oh, I see," Etania said.

She had travelled back in time. Her real self was probably taking horseback riding lessons with Keyel. She imagined she only had a few minutes to speak.

"He's fetching something for me," Etania lied. "He showed me how to ride a horse today and said I should get used to wearing armor, so he gave me this gauntlet."

"I see," Tala said. "Then why were you crying?"

Etania choked on her words, trying to say them without crying.

"It's nothing. I just missed you is all," Etania said. "So much has happened. I worry about you—that I will lose you one day."

"Lose me?" Tala snorted. "What ridiculous nonsense. I'm right here, silly!"

"No, I'm serious! Be careful Mom, or you might die," Etania warned, even though she believed it wouldn't make a difference.

Tala arched her eyebrow at her daughter and beckoned Etania to sit next to her on the bed. Etania did, putting her head underneath her mother's arm and breathing in her scent.

"Haven't I told you before? If I ever die, I go to Safarast, where I will live in perfect peace and joy with Melchizedek. He is building me, you, and everyone a place where we can live forever after death. Then, when you die, you will be able to meet me there," Tala said.

"Not until I die, huh?" Etania repeated.

"Yes. You wouldn't be able to join me until you died and came to new life in Safarast," Tala said. "Does that make you feel better?"

"A little," Etania admitted, thinking of her mother's door and how she couldn't enter it.

"Good." Tala rose. "Now, go see if Keyel is back. I imagine that Leici is probably rushing here as soon as he can to make sure you're safe."

"Wait, Mom! About Keyel—" Etania began.

"Oh, don't worry, I won't start teasing you about marriage just yet," Tala said with a laugh. "But I wouldn't mind it if it came to be."

Etania blushed, and Tala began to leave the room.

"Mom," Etania said again. "I love you."

"I love you too," Tala repeated. "See you!"

"See you," Etania whispered.

Tala left the room and Etania wept.

JAKIN ENTERED HIS ROOM, and the door closed behind him. All around him, men and women fought each other. He retreated, but ran into the door from Safarast. Wood scraped against his back, not giving way, and the handle was gone. Weapons clanged and boots squished through mud, blood, and bone. He could hear the roars of both sides—the Skazic and the warriors of Deo. He knew this scene. It was from the Long War.

"Is this what you want?" a voice asked.

Jakin turned to see the source and recognized Daas, the man who betrayed Melchizedek. He wanted to attack the man, but he realized they were without weapons. What he was seeing was a vision from the past, anyway

"A war that never ends?" Daas repeated.

"That's the reality we live in, Daas," Jakin found himself saying. "The Skazic will never die. They will never stop."

"But what if we could put an end to the war? Would you want that?" Daas asked.

"I don't know," Jakin said, seemingly not in control of his words.

"An end to constant death. A place where our children could live in relative peace?" Daas questioned.

"Our children will never know peace. There will always be war," Jakin said.

"I think our children can know peace if we follow the man who will bring it," Daas replied.

As Jakin felt his mouth open again to answer, he remembered. This conversation was all wrong because in this memory, their roles were reversed. He had said what Daas was saying now. He had told Daas the war could be over with Melchizedek's help. He'd convinced Daas to stop fighting, and all of his answers in this vision were ones Daas voiced. The image of Daas faded, and Melchizedek took his place.

"What happened, Jakin?" Melchizedek asked. "When did you decide to stop following me, the Prince of Peace?"

"But Master..." Jakin protested.

Melchizedek put up a hand.

"I see your heart, Jakin, and I am not pleased," Melchizedek said. "Your heart is filled with the fire that threatened to consume your daughter."

Jakin felt the sting of Melchizedek's words and looked away.

"I understand this pain. It is not wrong to feel righteous anger against those who have done evil," Melchizedek explained. "It is wrong not to allow me to deal justice."

"But am I not your hand of justice?" Jakin asked.

"Since when are you my hand?" Melchizedek exclaimed, and the Neuma coming from him was as hot as Jakin's flames. "Who are you to determine punishments? Is not my Father Deo responsible for this? And did I not sacrifice my own life so that justice might be fulfilled with repentance? How could you declare yourself the arbiter?"

With every word, Jakin felt himself growing smaller and smaller. He fell down, drawing his knees to his chest and looking away from his Master. With this contrite position, Melchizedek changed his tone. He walked over to Jakin and put his hand on his shoulder.

"My son, allow me to take your hatred and replace it with my love," Melchizedek said. "Allow my truth to be firm in your mind, but do not forget to also offer a hand to those in need. Will you allow it?"

Jakin felt Melchizedek's emotions course through him. Melchizedek's love was more powerful than any hatred he felt. All of his anger disappeared as he surrendered to Melchizedek, crying tears of repentance. At last, his heart was finally at peace.

KEYEL FOUND HIMSELF standing in the middle of Cephas' farm. He felt immediate peace there, and everything was undisturbed, as if someone had wound back time to before the attack. Somehow, he knew such evils would not disturb this place, this vision. He found an axe and began chopping wood. Why, he didn't know. He needed something to do, someone to be, just for a moment. Maybe, if he chopped enough wood, he could rid himself of the thoughts that he couldn't protect Etania. That he would never be able to love her properly and have a home with her just like this one. That all the doubts about himself would be chopped into pieces, just like the wood, until they were burned in the fire.

"Keyel." He heard his name and turned his gaze toward a man he didn't expect to see: his father.

"How did I get here? What's going on?" Thandor asked.

Keyel blinked and reoriented himself.

"I think it's Melchizedek. He brought us here," Keyel explained. "I am at Safarast."

"You're dead?" Thandor questioned.

Keyel laughed.

"No, I'm not dead. Melchizedek asked us to step through the doors in his castle. He told us it would give us the answers we seek. Though I'm not sure why he thinks you have the answers," Keyel said, turning back to the wood pile.

Thandor didn't reply to the verbal jab, but simply said, "Can I help?"

Keyel nodded and Thandor found another axe, beginning to chip away at the wood pile, which seemed to grow bigger rather than diminish in size.

"Maybe I don't have the answers because I don't even know the questions," Thandor said.

Keyel huffed, biting back another retort. He sighed and thought it was worth a try to ask his father.

"You remember the woman I am in charge of protecting?" Keyel said.

Thandor nodded. "Etania the Vexli, right?"

"Yes," Keyel said. "She is in constant danger. I can never protect her from it, even when I try. Melchizedek told me to trust him with her life, and I do, but...."

"You love her, don't you?" Thandor said.

Keyel huffed. "What does that have to do with anything?"

"It has everything to do with your feelings," Thandor replied. "You protected her because of duty at first, but then found you protected her out of love. Those same feelings accompany me with Lady Maiya."

Keyel didn't want to hear about his stepmother, a woman who shunned him at every opportunity, but something in him tolerated Thandor's example.

"She is always in danger because she is the leader of our people. There are times where I don't want her to go on diplomatic missions to the other territories because I am afraid she will not return. Most of the time, my fears aren't justified. But this time, when she came to King Toren, they were. I can't tell you how panicked I felt when I heard the news," Thandor said.

"You seemed so calm," Keyel replied.

"That's because I have to be," Thandor said, "and because I know that no matter what, Melchizedek will take care of her."

"I know that too!" Keyel exclaimed.

"Yes, but have you believed it?" Thandor asked. "I have to believe that either Melchizedek will preserve her life, or he will take care of her in Safarast. Ultimately, her fate is not mine to decide."

"That sounds really grim," Keyel said.

"Is it?" Thandor said. "I will see her either way. When I believe that completely, I feel Melchizedek's peace."

Keyel digested his father's words as he put away the wood in his arms. When he turned around, the pile of wood was gone.

"I guess that's my signal to leave," Thandor said. "Though I'm not sure how."

"You probably just start walking," Keyel said, "but I do have one more question."

"What is it?" Thandor asked.

"Why did you cheat on Lady Maiya with my mother if you loved her?" Keyel wondered.

"Because I didn't truly love her at the time," Thandor said. "I've regretted that decision ever since. So has Shayna."

"I know," Keyel said, feeling the same hurt from before.

"One thing I have never regretted is you," Thandor said, placing a hand on Keyel's shoulder. "I hope you can believe that."

"I think—" Keyel began. "I can believe it now."

Thandor nodded his head, patted his son's shoulder, and turned away. He disappeared into the forest, and Keyel was left alone to accept his father's wisdom and his renewed faith.

ETANIA STAYED IN HER old room until she felt the tears disappear and resignation take their place. She had never been able to say goodbye to her mother fully until now. As she stepped through her door into the courtyard, she knew firmly that her mother was enjoying a peaceful life here in Safarast. Etania still grieved the loss of her mother so early in life, but she also felt hope for the first time that she'd see her mother again.

When she returned to the manicured garden, she noticed that neither Keyel nor her father were in sight. Instead, Melchizedek sat at one of the tables, a platter of scones and hot tea before him. He beckoned her to sit, and Etania's stomach grumbled in response. As he poured her tea, Etania felt the gauntlet react to his presence, tightening once again around her wrist. Heat rose to her cheeks. He should not be serving her; *she* should be serving *him*.

Before she knew it, he was finished. She could drink the tea and partake of the scones, which were the best she had ever consumed—perfectly flaky and sweet.

"The gauntlet of Malstorm," Melchizedek said, as Etania wiped the crumbs from her mouth. "May I see it?"

Etania nodded and lifted her arm to Melchizedek. He took it gently in his hands, but Etania cried out in pain as the gauntlet reacted once again with sharp heat.

"Remove it," Melchizedek said to her.

"It won't move," Etania replied. "I've tried everything."

"Have you really?" Melchizedek said, his eyes flashing.

To prove it to him, she tugged at the gauntlet, trying to force it off of her skin. It simply tightened around her wrist, refusing to budge.

"See?" she said.

"Yes, I do," Melchizedek replied, "but you do not."

"What does that mean?" Etania asked.

"I am Deo's Son and the embodiment of Deo himself. You contain my Neuma, which is part of me living within you," Melchizedek said. "Yet, you still doubt my love for you, despite having it beside you."

Etania looked away.

"I doubt because I failed again at being a Vexli."

"When I marked you, did I say anything about being perfect?" Melchizedek asked. "Instead, I asked whether you would let me love you. I ask that question again, but in a new context: will you allow me to remove the gauntlet? Will you trust in my love for you?"

Etania looked at Melchizedek, feeling his love wash over her again. She sighed deeply. How could she have forgotten? Hadn't he helped her with the Soacronis? Was it not he who enabled Keyel to protect her? She had been blind to his constant help once again, only concerned about her own failings.

"Yes, Lord," she said. This time, she felt the conviction of that statement seep into her heart.

The gauntlet, which had once seemed so tight around her wrist, clanked to the top of the table. Tears of joy streamed down her cheeks.

"This gauntlet that King Toren intended for evil, I will recreate for good," Melchizedek said, picking it up. He squeezed it, wrapping his fingers around the metal; light emanating from his fist. The light was so blinding Etania had to look away. When it faded, she saw a new object before her eyes.

The gauntlet had transformed from a glove to a bracer. Etched on its surface was the phrase on the gate to Safarast: To Deo be all power and glory.

"There," he said, "now it can be used for a different purpose."

"What is that?" Etania wondered aloud.

"To win a battle with very little loss of life," Melchizedek said.

"How is that even possible?" Etania said.

"To answer that question, I will ask one of my own. Why did I give you your Neuma?"

"My father says that my Neuma is meant to be a weapon: something that removes the Neuma of the enemy so they may be killed faster. I have always thought this was wrong without knowing why."

"You are correct in doubting your father. I did not give you Neuma to make killing easier, but to bring others into my family."

"You mean the Skazic? You want them to be part of your family?" Etania was astonished.

"Isn't Isabella a part of my family?"

"Yes, but what about the Soacronis?" Etania wondered.

Melchizedek's eyes darkened.

"Damien has chosen to reject me, despite your gift. Some will still choose to reject me, but that is not for you to concern yourself with. Instead, you are my hand of humbling, removing the Neuma of those who have fallen away from the truth, in the hope that this will bring them back to me. Just like Isabella."

"That's a lot of responsibility," Etania said.

Melchizedek smiled.

"You are to use this new gauntlet to amplify your Neuma, and change the armies of the Skazic, thousands at a time."

"Th-thousands?" Etania gulped.

"Yes," Melchizedek affirmed. "You will only be able to use it once, my child, and then you will be vulnerable to your enemies. Thus, you must be cautious."

Etania nodded, but her knees wobbled and her heart beat loudly in her ears.

"I understand."

"Do not worry," Melchizedek said. "I will be with you, remember? Call on me when the time comes."

He stood and was about to leave when Etania stopped him with a final question.

"What should I do when all of them are changed?" Etania asked. "They won't have anywhere to go."

"Keep them safe until my leader arrives."

"But how?"

"You will find a way," Melchizedek answered.

With those words, he once again left. The doors of the keep opened and closed behind him. Moments after he disappeared, Keyel and Jakin emerged from their own doors, stepping into the courtyard.

"I guess that means our time here is done," Jakin said. "Come, let us go back through the portal."

Etania wondered what her father had experienced in Safarast. Had he received the same peace that enveloped her heart? By looking at his face, and Keyel's, she had a feeling they did.

Even though Etania didn't want to leave, she knew it was time. Together, they walked back through the courtyard, the meadow, past the tower, until they reached the glowing portal from Draconia. They stepped through as one. Safarast faded, and the cave of the Draconians took its place.

Chapter Twenty-Seven

There weren't any Draconians in sight until they made their way back through the tunnel, where two Draconian guards were waiting, their dragons sitting lazily by their sides.

"We're glad you made it out," one of them said.

"Yeah, the whole city was making bets on whether you would be alive," the other joked.

"How long were we gone?" Jakin asked.

"Three days," the first said.

Etania tried to keep her mouth from unhinging from her jaw.

"How can that be? I just had lunch a minute ago," Etania said.

"Time acts differently in Safarast," Jakin replied.

"Apparently," Keyel agreed. "I was just with my father for a few minutes, maybe an hour."

"Your father?" Etania repeated.

"You can debrief later," one of the Draconians said. "Saigon is expecting you."

He led them away from the cave entrance and back toward the Draconian camp. The light was fading from the sky. It was evening, despite the three of them feeling like it was the middle of the day just moments before. Most of the women and children were inside, though a few peered at them from the windows of their stone homes. The dragons looked at them also, blinking warily with their reptilian eyes. The two men led them back into the stone hall where they had met previously and said they would fetch Saigon.

As the travelers took their seats, each shared what had happened in their visions: Keyel first, Jakin second, Etania third.

"You were right, Etania," Jakin admitted. "I just didn't see that your Neuma was meant to establish peace rather than dominance."

"It's alright, Father. I know that you have been a bit obsessed for a long time," Etania said.

"But that obsession kept me from noticing you." Jakin put his arm around Etania's shoulders. "For that, I'm sorry."

At his apology, the anger and resentment she felt for her father slipped away. She now understood why Jakin had been out of her life so often, and that her father did care about her. All of this made it easy for Etania to speak.

"I forgive you," she said.

Jakin smiled and squeezed her hand, while Keyel patted her on the back.

"I'm glad you feel closer to your father, Keyel," Etania added.

"Yeah, I'm not sure how our relationship will be from now on," Keyel admitted. "But I'm willing to give it a chance, and that's what matters."

"Yeah, it does," Etania agreed. *Speaking of relationships....*

"I hope I'm not interrupting anything," Saigon said, entering the room alongside Cephas. "I left a good dinner in the hopes of hearing some good news."

Etania sighed. She would have to wait until later to confess her feelings.

"Yes, milord, we have good but unexpected news," Jakin said, "and we will definitely need your dragons to accomplish it."

"How so?" Saigon asked.

"We need you to fly us to Nova to join the battle. Yet, more than this, we need you to pick one of your men for a very special mission," Jakin said.

"I'm listening," Saigon replied.

Jakin then put forth the entire plan. Saigon and Cephas nodded occasionally and made astonished comments from time to time. Etania felt hope surging in her chest. Maybe, with her new bracer and this plan, they could win the battle.

"Well, I can't wait until the rest of the races hear that!" Cephas said. "They're sure to be as fired up as I feel right now!"

"I agree," Jakin said. "Now, if you don't mind getting someone to share their meal, my group and I are famished. We would love to enjoy a hot dinner before bed."

"Of course," Saigon said, walking toward the door.

"Indeed," Cephas agreed. "To Deo & Melchizedek!"

"To him be all glory and power!" the trio echoed.

Cephas and Saigon left the hall. A short time later, a maiden arrived with some soup and dished it out to Jakin, Keyel, and Etania, giving them a piece of bread as well. They thanked her and gulped down their food. When they finished, they handed the dishware to the guards and asked where they could stay for the evening. The guards led them to separate quarters, and Etania was once again alone in a bedroom.

In a few days, I will see my room in Nova again. I wonder what that will be like? So much has changed since then. She pulled the covers over her and fell asleep.

BEING ON A DRAGON AGAIN was both an exhilarating and frightening experience for Keyel. He was paired with Tevan, one of the men who had flown Cephas and Jakin to their aid. Tevan's bright red dragon matched his personality, for the man hardly ceased dipping with the wind currents or spinning to show off Flamir's speed. By the time they reached lunch, Keyel's legs were wobbling beneath him and he felt like throwing up all of his breakfast. Seeing this, Tevan agreed to keep the tricks to a minimum for the rest of their journey.

Once Keyel managed to eat a small bit, they were back off the ground, flying over the Kinzoku mountains and following the river Eriam. With Tevan reining in his dragon, Keyel was able to enjoy the feeling of floating in the air through the clouds. He was also far too able to consider whether or not Etania returned his feelings.

They had yet to have a moment alone together. He hoped that Etania would affirm his affections if they did. Based on how she smiled at him, even as they flew on opposite dragons, he possessed some confidence that his feelings were returned. He didn't even let the thought of rejection come to mind, instead swiping it aside to concentrate on the upcoming battle.

Jakin's plan of attack was very bold and would require Keyel allowing Etania to be in danger. He knew Thandor was right to say that he had to let Melchizedek be in charge of his beloved's fate. That didn't keep him from being nervous, though. *Whatever happens is yours, Melchizedek.* he said in a quick prayer, and the feeling slowly dissipated.

The journey to Nova lasted five days. Each day, they traversed a hundred kilometers on dragon, only stopping to eat lunch or to rest at night. Everywhere they rested, word spread of how the Lehrling was gathering his army to resist the evil King. Many of the territories that were ready set out for Nova, mobilizing as Jakin suggested. Throughout the land there was silence regarding King Toren's movements. Some would claim that they saw his armies retreating back to the castle, and Keyel had no doubt that was true. Yet, he knew the stillness was merely the calm before the storm—a peaceful moment before they were swept away.

At last, they touched down in Nova. Keyel bid adieu to Tevan and Flamir and headed toward the town's meeting hall. Standing around a table were Priest Alfred and several townspeople Keyel didn't recognize. Next to them were Vartok and his wolf—the Eritam standing with his arms over his chest. Vartok also had an Eritam companion with him that Keyel didn't know. Ramar, the acting Vizeheir, was just as imposing as Vartok and covered in armor. His hand rested on his belt loop, which held a battle hammer. By Ramar's side was Ivan, who gave a nod of respect to Keyel. Keyel nodded in return, but dipped his head low when he saw his father and sister. Thandor and Adeline smiled at him reassuringly, and Keyel had a feeling that Adeline knew exactly what had happened in their visit to Safarast. Next to Adeline was her faithful guard, and beside Rhys, to everyone's surprise, was Andre, the Ningyo.

"You came!" Etania exclaimed. "I thought for sure..."

"We decided to come," Andre said, "after Gabriel was killed by King Toren, we could not excuse the King's spilling of innocent blood."

"Gabriel died?" Etania repeated, and Andre nodded. Keyel's fists clenched around his sword hilt. Another life he failed to protect. Andre put a hand upon Keyel's in reassurance.

"Gabriel knew the risks," Andre said, "but now is the time for us to avenge his death."

"Actually, about that..." Jakin said. "We have a plan that may be less vengeful but just as effective as putting an end to bloodshed."

"But bloodshed is part of the reason I agreed to join this rebellion!" Ramar scoffed. "I want to put Toren in his place."

"You shall," Cephas agreed, "but not in the way you may expect. I don't believe we desire to lose any more brothers and sisters than are necessary. I think my fellow Naymatua would agree, don't you? Wait, where are they?"

Jakin hung his head.

"Chief Suliman said he wanted to see who was more powerful before he participated. I'm afraid we will not be having the force of the Naymatua with us."

"That's alright," Saigon said confidently. "My dragons can burn away any trees that come against us."

"And our axes can take care of the rest," Ramar agreed. Keyel smiled at them.

"I'm glad you're so confident," Jakin said, "because tomorrow is when we enact the plan."

"You have a plan, *Lehrling* Jakin?" Priest Alfred asked.

Jakin chuckled, and Keyel realized that everyone in Nova now knew the true identity of his Master.

"I do indeed," Jakin said, launching into the details of his plan. When he finished, the leaders agreed to it.

"I think my wolves are ready for their part in this," Vartok said.

"I'm just glad there's a plan for the Skazic," Priest Alfred spoke up. "I wasn't very comfortable with so much death, but I know we're ready to defend our homes."

"Speaking of defense, how large is our army?" Jakin asked.

"About 5,000 strong," the priest said, "but Toren's castle contains at least 6,000 defenders from all over Tamnarae. We saw many Skazic marching in."

"They reveal themselves at last," Jakin said grimly.

"But we have a way to defeat them, and that's what matters most," Cephas added. The other leaders nodded in agreement.

"If that's settled, let's rest and march on Khartome in the morning." Jakin dismissed. The leaders began to disperse, but Adeline was wheeled up to Keyel.

"Brother," Adeline said, as Keyel leaned down to give her a hug. "I am so glad to hear that your Neuma has returned."

"How did you know that? I didn't even tell Thandor," Keyel asked.

"Melchizedek told me," she said with a smile, and motioned to her guard. Rhys brought out a round shield.

"I wanted to give this to you. It is meant to be passed down from the ruling Lady to her son. As acting leader, I think it is fine for me to give it to you."

Keyel admired the intricate scrollwork—especially the herbs in the middle, which were symbols of the Leici healers.

"I really shouldn't accept this," Keyel said. "You should give it to your son one day."

"Maybe I will," Adeline replied. "Until then, you can use it to protect Etania, on whom our hopes reside for a less bloody battle."

Keyel glanced at the Vexli, who was hanging back to wait for him.

"I will protect her, with Melchizedek's help," Keyel declared.

At those words, Adeline smiled. They hugged again before she departed, and Keyel walked up to Etania.

"Accompany me home?" Etania asked.

"Of course," Keyel replied, offering his arm.

ETANIA WRAPPED HER arm around Keyel's, taking her time to walk back to her house in Nova. The last time she was home, she had seen her mother alive. The time before that, she had witnessed Tala's final breaths. Neither were memories she wanted to revisit, so she enjoyed the peaceful walk home with Keyel instead.

"It seems so long ago that we walked together here," Etania said.

"It has been some time—around four to six months. I've lost track in all the travelling we've done since then," Keyel said.

"I wonder how things could've been different for us if I wasn't a Vexli," Etania said. "I don't think I would've learned combat training."

"Or seen the things we've seen. The homes of the Leici, the wildness of the Eritam, the tree ceremony of the Naymatua, the rivers of the Ningyo, or the caves of the Kinzoku."

"Don't forget about the dragons!" Etania added. "They're the reason we were able to return so quickly, and they will be the key to tomorrow's plan."

"I didn't forget, I just chose not to remember," Keyel said. "I'm not sure I could handle any more aerial dives." Etania chuckled.

"If I hadn't been attacked," she said softly, "I would have never met you."

"And I would never have gotten my Neuma back," Keyel agreed in a whisper. They walked in silence after that, stopping at the archway of her mother's garden—of her home.

"Do you think we would have fallen in love?" Etania asked.

"We?" Keyel repeated, turning toward her. They switched from linking arms to linking hands. Etania blushed, feeling the warmth of his palms more acutely than before.

"Yes," Etania said. "I love you, Keyel."

Keyel squeezed her hands, but Etania embraced him. At first, he stiffened in surprise, and then gradually relaxed, allowing himself to wrap his arms around her waist. Then he brought his hand up to her cheek.

"You return my feelings!" Keyel said.

"Yes!" Etania laughed. "What else do you think I mean by 'I love you?'"

He smiled. Etania felt her cheeks grow warmer as she gazed into his blue eyes and considered how much a smile suited him. He stroked her cheek gently, and a thrill ran through her.

"Excuse me, young man, but I believe such gestures of affection are best expressed in courtship!" Barick exclaimed, from the doorway of Etania's house.

Etania stepped out of Keyel's embrace, slightly embarrassed, and ran to throw her arms around the old butler.

"It is wonderful to see you again!" she exclaimed.

Barick, slightly surprised, patted her gently on the back. Etania stepped back. Serena also came up to them, and Etania gave her a brief hug.

"Barick and Serena, Keyel has obtained Jakin's permission to court me," she said.

"Is that so?" Barick asked.

"Yes, sir, but I agree with you," Keyel said. "I will wait until the proper time of courtship arrives. In the meantime, is it alright to escort my lady—under proper surveillance—to her quarters?"

"I think that's my job," another voice said from within, and Grace strode forward.

"Grace!" Etania exclaimed, embracing her friend.

"So your bodyguard turned into a beau," Grace said. "Why am I not surprised?"

"Hey!" Etania protested with a smile. "You act as if I lure men like bees to honey."

"Well, if I recall correctly, you *were* the one attracting the most attention during the adulthood ceremony," Grace retorted.

"Keyel, I do think Miss Stegel is correct. We should probably leave the ladies to themselves," Barick said. "I also recommend you take a bath before dinner."

"Oh yes," Etania realized. "Do you want to stay for dinner?"

Keyel smiled at her, and she felt her heart pounding in her chest.

"Of course," he said.

Etania returned his grin. She and her friend climbed the stairs to her room. She was surprised to find it clean, with a bed made and all the clothing returned to her wardrobe.

"I took the liberty of cleaning while you were away," Grace said. "I felt it was only right that the adventurer have a clean place to return to."

"And proper clothes to wear," Etania said, thumbing through the dresses in her wardrobe.

"Yes, I must admit I didn't recognize you, wearing mail and boots. With your hair braided, a crossbow on your back and a knife on your side, you look so different!"

"I don't think I recognize myself," Etania admitted, placing the weapons aside and taking off her boots. She bounced to a sitting position beside her friend and tried not to think of the last time she had sat on this bed, next to her mother. She fingered Tala's necklace in remembrance.

"Well, you have to tell me about your adventures," Grace said. "Besides a new beau, I know absolutely nothing."

"Are you sure you want to hear it all? There's quite a bit."

"Sure, but like Keyel, you need a bath." Grace said. "I helped Barick lug up the hot water."

"Oh, thank you Grace!" Etania moved to the curtained part of the room. A large tub of steaming water with soap waited. She stripped down and sank into the suds.

"How is it?" Grace asked, from the other side of the curtain.

"Perfect," Etania said. "Why don't you tell me about what you've been doing while I bathe?"

"Good idea," Grace agreed and she started explaining that after Etania's departure, she had banded together with every seamstress who supported the rebellion. They worked to make chainmail instead of clothes, fulfilling Melchizedek's mysterious prophecy to Grace at the adulthood ceremony. Most of the ladies would sew their normal projects by day so King Toren wouldn't be suspicious, and link together the metal chain by night. Next, they created tabards with a purple flame in the center so that all the men would be identified as following Jakin rather than the King. Eventually, they had enough uniforms for the entire town. But as the rebels began to arrive, they had to be even more inventive with material. Soon, there was an entire trade blossoming between the territories, with men and merchants fetching all the supplies they needed. They hid most of the growing army in the forests, making sure to stay off of the main roads so that Toren wouldn't know the numbers of the forces against him. Since he was focused on hunting Etania and her party, this had been relatively easy for Grace and the other villagers until recently.

"And that's about it," Grace said. "Are you presentable enough to tell your story?"

Etania nodded, stepping out from behind the curtain wearing one of her blue dresses, which matched the color of Keyel's eyes. For the first time, she let her hair down in waves, so that it fell past her shoulders.

"How do I look?" she asked, wanting Keyel to see her as a lady, rather than a traveler.

"Beautiful," Grace complimented. "So tell me, was it as scary as the gossip of the town? I've heard so much from the people of the other territories, but I don't know what parts are true. Did you really get attacked by werewolves?"

"Yes, and haunted trees, and golems, and we were almost buried in snow..." Etania began.

"Woah, whoa, back up! You were almost buried in the snow?" Grace repeated.

"Yes, but that wasn't until later. First, we visited the Leici..." Etania began.

She went on to describe most of their adventures, keeping some facts out so that she didn't scare her friend—up until Safarast, at least. She had finished describing all of Melchizedek's words to her and their battle plans right as Barick was calling them to dinner.

"Well, I'm glad you have finally been marked by Melchizedek," Grace said. "But do you really have to do *that* tomorrow?" Etania nodded.

"Yes, but I know Keyel will protect me and Melchizedek is with me. Even if I'm scared, I know I can call on Him."

"Goodness." Grace pulled her friend into an embrace. "You've faced so much that my problems feel like little ones, compared to yours."

"Nonsense," Etania said, returning the hug and then standing. "Everyone has done their part, exactly as Melchizedek asked."

"That's for sure!" Grace said.

Etania and Grace left the bedroom. Etania shut the door of her room and descended the stairs to the dining room with her friend. How good it was to be home again!

"JAKIN," CEPHAS SAID, as the council was filtering out of the meeting hall.

"Yes?" Jakin asked. "I gave you a chance to say goodbye to Alondra this time, so..."

Cephas waved his hand dismissively.

"No, it's not about that," he said. "I need your help. I want you to teleport me to the Naymatua."

"You know I can't teleport you without going myself," Jakin reminded. "Besides, they've already made their choice. How in the world do you expect to get them here quickly, even if they change their minds?"

"Let me worry about that. Plus, I know how to have you teleport me without you needing to leave."

"Really?" Jakin asked.

"Yes, but we'll need a private area," Cephas replied.

"Fine," Jakin said, leading Cephas away from camp to a more deserted area he always used for practice.

"Do you have any amethyst stones with you?" Cephas asked.

"Only my amulet." Jakin removed the necklace, placing the amethyst-encrusted amulet in his friend's palm.

"Perfect." Cephas drew out a gauntlet that looked similar to Etania's old one. Jakin stepped back.

"Woah, what are you doing?"

"Don't worry; it's just a normal gauntlet," Cephas explained. "I asked one of the Draconians if I could have it, then modified it to carry a jewel."

He popped out the green emerald that was in the center of the gauntlet and put Jakin's amethyst in its place.

"You pour your Neuma into this stone, right?" Cephas asked, and Jakin nodded. "Then it should work. Think of the Naymatua, and act like you will be transporting me there with you."

Although skeptical, Jakin did as Cephas commanded, closing his eyes. He visualized the Naymatua realm and pretended he was taking Cephas with him, even feeling as if the flames of his Neuma were leaving him and wrapping themselves around Cephas. When he opened his eyes, Cephas was gone, and there were markings from his purple flames in the grass.

"I hate it when you're smarter than me," Jakin said with a smile, shaking his head as he walked away. "I just hope you are successful."

Jakin knew he was running late to dinner in Nova but should still bathe before attending. Consequently, he teleported to his bedroom to get a new pair of clothes. He noticed a pile of Keyel's clothes in the corner, so the Leici had probably used the bath himself to clean up for dinner.

Grief washed over him as he looked around. The room was neatly organized, with everything in its place. Even the bed was made— a bed he would no longer share. His wife's wardrobe stood next to his own, filled with dresses that would not be worn. Then it hit him how much he would miss about Tala. He would no longer see his wife combing her hair by the vanity or glaring at him when he came in the middle of the night.

She was gone, and the part of him that had hated her killer was gone too, leaving only grief. He allowed himself to feel that, to allow the grief of losing her wash over him completely. He sobbed fully for the first time, knowing now that all of his anger was just a disguise for the raw pain he felt inside.

Only when he could no longer shed any tears did Jakin decide to teleport to the public baths. He found a secluded area away from the other men and washed away the dirt and mud—everything that would give evidence he had been on an adventure. Then, he donned black clothing, which he felt was appropriate. He also resolved that he would ask Keyel to stay the night, since the Leici didn't have a place to sleep. They would share a room once again, and Jakin wouldn't have to be alone. He walked back home instead of teleporting, striding inside just as Barick was placing the flatware and plates on the table for dinner.

"Master!" Barick said. "It is wonderful to see you again. I wasn't sure if you would attend."

"Of course, Barick, I didn't want to disappoint," Jakin said.

"You never do, Master."

"Oh, I think I often did, but I appreciate your patience," Jakin countered. "What have you prepared tonight?"

"Roasted quail with vegetables from the garden," Barick said. "I bought the quail from one of the boys, since it is so rare to catch these days."

"Sounds delicious." Jakin took his seat at the head of the table. Looking down its length, he felt—rather than saw—the empty seat at the other end.

"Where is my daughter?" Jakin asked.

"Right here, Father," Etania replied, emerging from the backyard with Keyel. "I was just saying goodbye to Grace."

Jakin tried to contain a smile at his daughter's appearance. She looked so much like her mother in that blue dress, with her wavy brown hair glowing in the candlelight just like Tala's. Yet her face was oval, similar to Jakin's. He was pretty certain her nose matched his as well. She was a perfect combination of them both—a blessing neither of them had expected, but had always longed for.

"You look amazing," Jakin said.

"I agree," Keyel added, coming up to Etania and giving her a hug.

Etania blushed furiously and piped out, "Thank you."

"Oh, I see you both talked," Jakin said.

"Yes," Etania replied, with a smile.

"And I talked to them about having a chaperone," Barick added, with a glare at Keyel. Keyel took his seat with a slight grin on his face, and Jakin admired his apprentice's slightly rebellious attitude in courtship. *At least I have accomplished that much,* Jakin thought. *Though it is truly my daughter who has gotten him to smile.*

"They will not officially start courting until after the battle," Jakin said, teasingly glaring at them. "Then we will decide about chaperones."

"Of course, Master," Keyel said, the thought of war making him serious.

"Humph, well, I prefer that you eat more and express affection less," Barick said with a sniff. Jakin took that as his cue to pray.

"Melchizedek, please bless this evening of rest and food that Barick and Serena have so graciously prepared. Equip us with your strength tomorrow and enable us to win a decisive victory in your name. May it be so," Jakin finished.

"May it be so," the others echoed, and they began to eat.

As Keyel and Etania engaged in conversation regarding what had happened while they were away, Jakin wondered if his plan was really as solid as he hoped. A lot of it hung on his daughter's shoulders, and it bothered him to place that load on her. Yet, she had agreed fully.

Melchizedek, Jakin prayed silently. *Keep my daughter safe. I don't know if I could lose someone else I love.*

"I will," Melchizedek replied.

Jakin's mark of a hammer glowed slightly; enough for him to see, but for the others to think it was candlelight. Only then did Jakin feel a semblance of peace.

JAZEL WELCOMED HER husband home with an extravagant dinner, relaxing bath, and a massage to soothe his frayed nerves. Yet he still seemed as strung as a ball of yarn, constantly berating servants and soldiers alike. Jazel, despite having the help of multiple servants with her child, could feel his strain wear upon her exhausted nerves. She also had to disguise her growing daughter so that none in the castle, not even Toren himself, would know the truth. She was genuinely tired of it all, and glad for the final battle the following day. Maybe then all her plans of vengeance would be over. She could just visualize it: Jakin and Etania's heads on stakes, standing like guards to the castle and as a warning to all who passed by. *Do not cross the King and Queen of Southern Tamnarae*, the sign would read.

She sighed as the reverie passed, her daughter crying to be nursed. She came to the child and lovingly embraced her as the girl suckled. She still had not named the child. Tradition dictated that mothers not name their children until the infants reached a year of age. She imagined her mother had done the same with her.

Her mother. The reason why she took this path of vengeance on Jakin and his family. Ever since her mother was executed for killing the King and Queen of the Pyros, Jazel had plotted vengeance alongside her mentor. When Jakin was appointed the Lehrling of Southern Tamnarae, and Cephas the north, Jazel and her mentor knew it was the perfect time to strike. Too bad her mentor had been unreasonable and perished. The woman had missed how convenient it would be to use a love-struck and foolish King.

The small part of Jazel's conscience still alive, despite her attempts to destroy it, felt bad for the King. She had never loved him, and all he really wanted was someone to assuage his fears and comfort him. That made him a perfect victim and a perfect pawn. Her moment of pity passed when Toren came stomping into her room, and she had to cover her baby with a blanket. Toren searched through the covers on her bed, fingered over the dresses in her wardrobe, and stomped through her bedroom.

"Where is it?" he asked.

"Where is what, my dear?" Jazel said.

"The gauntlet, where is it? I had the servants clean it, and..."

"Here it is," Jazel said, lifting it off of her dresser and placing it in his hand. "The servants couldn't find you, so they asked me to present it to you."

"Oh, really?" he asked, taking the gauntlet and coddling it like an infant.

"Yes," Jazel said. "Now, will you come to bed? You must rest before the battle tomorrow."

"I'm not sure I can. I heard from our spies that their numbers almost match ours."

"Their numbers may match ours, but we are well fortified! The dragons are our only fear, and they will be busy with the Soacronis, so it will all work out."

"But—" The old whine was returning to Toren's voice.

"Shush," Jazel said, taking the baby from her breast and placing it back into the cradle so she could comfort her husband. She beckoned him to sit beside her on the bed. Then she placed his head on her chest and stroked his hair until he closed his eyes.

"Rest is just as important as a battle," she said. "Especially one we have been planning for so long."

"Yes," he agreed.

"It is finally time to take vengeance for all the wrongs Jakin has done to both of us," Jazel purred.

"Yes," Toren said, his eyes slowly closing.

"We will destroy them all, and with your gauntlet, control the Vexli."

"Yes."

"Sleep, my king, and know that you are victorious." Jazel moved his nodding head from her chest to a pillow.

"Victorious," he mumbled.

"Exactly," Jazel said, covering him just as he began to snore.

With both baby and husband asleep and fed, Jazel had only one more task to complete. Everything was going according to her plan.

Chapter Twenty-Eight

Etania woke the next morning, surprised to feel refreshed and prepared for the day ahead. She knew that she was going to battle, but the reality of it had not taken hold of her spirit. She tried to keep this in mind while she dressed in undergarments that would act as additional padding for her chain mail. She pulled the chain mail shirt over her head, making sure to tuck Tala's necklace underneath the padding so her mother's memory remained close to her chest. Then, she pulled on a tunic to cover it. She also donned a light helmet and tugged on her worn, leather boots. Lastly, she fastened the gauntlet, now a harmless bracer, around her right wrist. She balanced it with a plain bracer on her left wrist, grabbed her gloves, and walked downstairs.

When she reached the bottom step, she noticed that both Keyel and Jakin were dressed in their chainmail, about to partake of their meals. They were also wearing the tunics that Grace had made—a black surcoat with a purple flame in the center. Against the wall were the other pieces of their armor: a breastplate, helmet, and greaves.

"Will you need help getting into all of that?" Etania asked, feeling very blessed that she didn't have to wear so much armor. At the same time, looking at the armor made her very nervous about her beau and father's wellbeing.

"I think Barick will help me with mine, and I will help Keyel with his, but I appreciate the offer," Jakin said.

Etania took a seat at the table next to Keyel, and she reached over to hold his hand. Serena came and placed a plate of eggs and bacon in front of Etania.

"Thank you," Etania said.

"You'll need it," Serena commented.

Barick nodded, and both disappeared into the kitchen while Etania started to eat. The idea of a battle, just moments away, still hadn't sunk in—despite growing nervousness. She cleared her plate, giving it to Serena.

Etania watched as her father and beau prepared for battle. As suspected, Barick helped Jakin into his armor, and Jakin helped Keyel. Etania was able to assist with a few of the pieces that needed more hands but, in the end, each man was covered in metal. They looked like walking, metal statues. Jakin, Keyel, and Etania grabbed their weapons before stepping out into Nova.

Etania gasped as she saw the armies of nations they had visited passing by her. Most wore boots like hers or leather ones with hand-stitched chainmail overlaying them. Some soldiers had only chainmail armor, with no helmets or breastplates. Others were as covered as Keyel, with their helmets barely revealing their eyes. Even the animals were protected. The Eritams' wolves wore fitted pieces of armor over their underbellies, while the horses of her fellow hafif had metal plating over their heads. One of the dragons roared, and Etania glanced up to see his underside covered in metal.

Only after witnessing people marching to battle did Etania feel the weight of the task she was about to complete. All of these people could die if she was not successful. Her heart started pounding in her ears. She felt dizzy, and her vision blurred. Keyel steadied her with his hand, and she felt like it was Melchizedek working through him to calm her frayed nerves.

Give me strength, she prayed, and Melchizedek's Mark glowed in response. This comforted her as she walked to the front lines with her father and her beau. When they reached the front, the leaders of each race were waiting for them.

"Are you ready to enact the plan?" Jakin asked them.

"My wolves are ready," Vartok agreed.

"The Leici are on standby for the wounded," Lady Adeline said, "and the archers have prepared their bows."

"Our axes are sharp, and we've distributed enough extra metal to deal with the golems!" Ramar added.

"We're prepared for our mission," Andre said, looking directly at Jakin.

"And I am ready to fly," Saigon put in, patting his dragon's neck. Etania glanced at the formidable dragon, which was the largest in the current fleet. She only hoped he would be successful in reaching the second tower on Khartome's bridge, with them sitting on his back.

"Alright then," Jakin said, "We're ready!"

"Don't forget about us!" Priest Alfred added, hurrying up to meet them.

"Just in time, Alfred," Jakin replied. "Will you pray for us?"

"Certainly," Alfred agreed. "Lord Melchizedek and Deo, the ones who have given us our Marks: we pray your blessings on this battle. May we be successful in freeing the prisoners and disarming our enemies. Please give us the strength and fortitude we will need to face the darkness of King Toren. In your holy name, we pray."

"May it be so," Etania echoed, and she felt the glow of her mark affirm her words. She went up to her father and embraced him.

"Stay safe," she said.

"You as well," he agreed, giving her a tight hug and then walking away.

Keyel pulled Etania into an embrace, giving her a light kiss on the forehead. The kiss made her head spin just as much as the thought of walking into battle, but she ignored it.

"I love you," he said. "Be safe."

"I will," she said, "and I love you, too."

Keyel watched as Saigon helped Etania climb onto his dragon. The deadly spikes on the dragon's neck were bare, looking like they had been sharpened for the battle. His flight upwards was thus slower than the three dragons that accompanied them, giving Etania time to listen as the rest of the army marched through the forest to the shores of Lake Khartome.

She heard the stomping of boots and clanging of armor as thousands of men surged forward to meet the armies of King Toren, which waited on the bridge. Then, she heard the unsheathing of weapons—blades ringing out as they were drawn. She listened to the responding hisses and growls from the Skazic, and the howls and roars from the dragons and wolves. Somewhere, far away, she heard King Toren call out his command to attack. The multitude of noises merged into a single din. Etania ceased listening and focused.

She was suddenly grateful she was not in the midst of the battle. As they soared through the air high above, she prayed their armies would be successful.

KEYEL HATED WATCHING Etania and Saigon fly away. This part of the plan had been the hardest to accept, yet Keyel knew Etania must go to the second tower of the bridge to the city of Khartome. Their plans hinged on that bridge. He hoped Etania would land safely so that she could flank the hordes of Skazic that would be facing their army. Keyel was assigned to join the Eritam, who would be the foot soldiers waiting in the forest. He could've joined the Leici but, knowing their prejudice, decided to go with the Eritam.

He joined the front row of wolves and armored men. Keyel felt like a sunflower in the midst of carnations because of his blonde locks amongst the white hair of the Eritam. The men stirred restlessly beside him, and he wondered what the armies were waiting for.

Keyel could see the lake's shores stretching in front of him, but no one dared move to the beaches without the protection of the forest. To his right, also under the shelter of trees, were many hafif—including citizens of Nova. In front of the bridge were the Kinzoku. They would lead the main charge against the first tower. Behind the entire army were the Leici archers. All were waiting, breathless, for someone to make the first move.

A dragon roared above them, and the army unsheathed their blades. With a roar, the Kinzoku charged the golems guarding the first tower. Keyel and the Eritam waited breathlessly, wondering if they would be able to engage any soldiers.

Keyel saw their enemy first. King Toren had ordered some of his men to leave the protection of the tower and get into boats. As the vessels drew closer, Keyel heard a terrifying screech: the long howl of thousands of toothbreakers. The Eritams' wolves howled in response—melodic and haunting—conveying revenge against the toothbreakers.

Once the toothbreakers were ashore, Vartok gave the command. The Eritam left the protection of the forest to meet their foes. Men and their wolves sprinted from the forest. Keyel followed, exhilaration rushing through him.

Arrows were loosed from the Leicis' bows, arcing over the heads of the frontlines to the toothbreakers rushing the followers of Melchizedek. The toothbreakers who were hit whimpered. The Eritams' wolves took advantage of their cries, lashing out with teeth and growls.

Keyel unsheathed his sword and brandished his shield, feet pressing against soft earth as he rushed forward into the fray. His first opponent was a large toothbreaker, who lashed at him with snapping teeth and sharp claws. His shield blocked the claws, which squealed down the metal device. Keyel shifted and thrust his sword into the unprotected shoulder of the toothbreaker.

The wolf cried in pain, swiping at Keyel again with his other paw. An Eritam came up beside Keyel, his wolf using the opportunity to slice the werewolf's jugular. Blood flowed freely, but Keyel had no time to notice as he faced his next opponent. Never before had he battled Skazic in such chaos. He had always been alone, or with Jakin. Now, he was fighting beside wolves and masters who attacked like acrobats, spinning and stabbing with short swords or daggers, perfectly synchronized with their wolves. He tried to join the dance, stopping claws with his shield or blocking fangs with his sword. He sliced and twirled, his arm and shield an extension of himself.

The battle continued in the forest as more and more toothbreakers came to shore by boats. Keyel ran with the Eritam, joining them in fights against the toothbreakers, adrenaline pumping through his veins. With the others, he yelled a battle cry.

"For Melchizedek!"

KILOMETERS EAST, JAKIN and the Ningyo rowed silently across the lake. The waters stirred underneath them, even when they didn't paddle.

"These waters are not under our control," Andre said.

"Gabriel said the same once," Jakin replied. "I don't understand what they're waiting for, if there are Skazic in this water."

"I'm not sure I want to see," Andre said.

"Bring them on!" His grandson, Rafael, exclaimed.

"Be careful what you wish for," Andre censured, "and remember our task."

Rafael quieted, but he gripped his spear, looking at the water eagerly as the others rowed. The cliffs of Khartome soon came into view, and Jakin knew they were close to rescuing the prisoners.

Suddenly, the water rose around them. Scaly men and women appeared, riding the water like fish following a current. They screeched with guttural cries, and waves came crashing down on Jakin and the Ningyo. Jakin's boat flipped, and he found himself treading icy water.

The Ningyo still on boats fought their Skazic counterparts by throwing spears at the Skazic, who dodged the missiles easily. Somehow, the Ningyo wrestled control of Lake Khartome out of the hands of the Skazic. An all-out war of water erupted between both groups. Jakin found himself swimming frantically toward air pockets as warm and cold waves collided. Each side tried to drown the other, so it was like being in the middle of a typhoon.

Jakin could not dodge the attacks, and treading water with his armor was exhausting. He felt like he would soon drown if he didn't do anything, but his flames were extinguished by the water. He grabbed for the side of an overturned boat to keep from sinking.

"Jakin!" Andre shouted over the sound. "We will make a way for you to swim to the cliffs. From there, I'm afraid you're on your own!"

Jakin nodded, trying to keep his head above the surface. Even though it would make him more vulnerable, he shed his breastplate, boots and helmet, preparing to swim to the foreboding sides of the island. The opposing Skazic roared in fury as the Ningyo countered them, shoving the Skazic to the bottom of the lake with powerful arcs of water. This cleared enough room for Jakin to swim like he never had before. Even with his extra weight off, the chainmail made it harder.

Jakin burst out of the chaos—or so he thought. Just as he believed he was clear of the Skazic, an arc of water slammed into him and pinned him to the bottom of the lake. He tried not to gasp and swallow lake water as the Skazic pounded him, keeping him from floating to the surface.

Minutes that felt like hours passed. With each passing second, panic blossomed in his chest. When Jakin felt like he could hold his breath no longer, he prayed a simple prayer.

I come to you, Melchizedek and Tala. Keep Etania safe for me.

Then, he blacked out.

ETANIA AND SAIGON FLEW for a few minutes with their three-dragon escort. Then, they saw her dreaded enemy: the Soacroni! With their bat-like wings and scaled bodies, they rose into the air like a swarm of gnats. Surrounding one dragon and its rider, they stabbed and sliced with their claws until the dragon fell. Saigon cried out as he watched the Soacroni detach themselves from their prey and head for another dragon defender.

The dragons spewed their flames at the Soacroni, but the hot fire slid off the scales of their evil counterparts. The Draconian rider then attempted to shoot down the Soacroni with arrows. Saigon and Etania assisted as best they could. Etania used her crossbow to shoot arrows laced with Neuma, while Saigon used his bow and arrow to shoot their opponents. With the rolling motion of the dragon in flight, it was difficult to get a successful shot, and Etania had never tried to shoot a crossbow on a moving animal before. She briefly wished she had practiced on Sunset so that she might be better at gripping with her knees and shooting bolts. In the end, the combined efforts of the three of them only resulted in a few Soacroni deaths.

Another dragon succumbed to the horde of Soacroni, and they soon downed their second dragon escort. Etania and Saigon were close to their destination on the bridge from Nova to Khartome. They watched in horror as the Soacroni flew to the last dragon escort and started to overwhelm it. This time, Saigon urged his mount forward, hoping speed would be better than counter strike.

"We have to get you to that second tower, no matter what!" Saigon exclaimed. "My men know that more than anyone."

Etania couldn't open her mouth to reply. Instead, she felt hot tears against her face, their salty texture mixing with her sweat as they dived for the tower. Closer and closer they flew, a kilometer away, then half a kilometer. They were almost to the second tower when Etania felt something on her leg.

She yelped as she saw a Soacronis gripping her shin, his bat wings fluttering at high speed. She kicked him, sending him flying away, and then drew her dagger. Saigon drew his sword, and together they were hacking and slicing at the Soacroni attempting to overwhelm them. Etania tried to fire her Neuma at some of the attackers, but it was ineffective.

Saigon's dragon roared in agony as he was stabbed, sliced, and clawed at by hundreds of small Soacroni. Even though he snapped at them, they wouldn't leave him alone. Eventually, his wings collapsed. The three of them were suddenly falling together, like a boulder hurtling down a mountainside, heading straight for the second tower.

I have failed, Etania thought, bitterly.

DESPITE THEIR INITIAL success, Keyel and the Eritam were being pushed back from the shore of the lake, into the forest. For every toothbreaker that Keyel killed, it felt like there was another to take his place. The giant wolves that ran on all fours were difficult to kill, and each toothbreaker usually took two Eritam and their wolf companions to defeat. There was a sudden pause in the oncoming enemies, and Keyel found himself in the middle of the forest, far away from the other fighters.

Before he could think of what to do next, he heard a cry. He looked down and saw a soldier he recognized. Vartok was choking on his own blood, his wolf lying by his side and whimpering. Keyel knelt to see the damage and gasped. Most of Vartok's stomach was sliced open. Keyel sought to heal him, but Vartok thrust away his hands and pointed toward another man. This Eritam was as injured as Vartok, so both men needed immediate attention.

For a moment, Keyel hesitated. He had barely gotten his healing powers to work again, and now, Vartok was asking him to make a choice. As a descendent of Lord Thandor, he knew he might have stronger powers than an ordinary Leici. Members of the royal family possessed the ability to heal two people at once, so he could possibly heal them both. Yet he wasn't sure. Being a nothus meant he only possessed some royal blood. However, he couldn't hesitate, or both Eritam would die. Keyel sent a brief prayer to Melchizedek and decided he would try healing both of them. If Ivan had taught him anything, it was to never doubt the source of his Neuma.

Keyel began stitching the wounds together, working to make sure his repairs fixed the problem. At that moment, he was so grateful that Melchizedek had restored his Neuma. Only a descendent of the royal line could heal two men so gravely injured at once. Keyel finished healing both of them, leaving them to rest. It was then that he heard the call for a retreat. They were losing the battle!

What happened to Etania? He wondered.

Chapter Twenty-Nine

Jakin opened his eyes and coughed. Someone was patting his back, and he coughed again, realizing he was on his side. He spat out water and gasped as he came to his knees on the shore, the feel of sand and rock beneath his fingers. He continued to breathe deeply as he turned to thank his rescuer. Rafael met his gaze.

"Thank you," Jakin wheezed.

"It was Grandpa Andre's orders," Rafael said, gazing back at the water.

Jakin looked over, suddenly realizing how still it was, compared to moments before. The lake should have been choppy, and there were no signs of Andre or the other Ningyo.

"Where is he? Where are they?" Jakin asked.

"He's—" Rafael stumbled on his words, swallowing. "Gone. He sacrificed himself to defeat all of the Skazic in one fell swoop."

"What!" Jakin said, astonished. "How?"

"He called on Melchizedek, and the waters listened to him. They surrounded Grandpa in water like a funnel. I have never seen anything like it before," Rafael's eyes glistened as he spoke. "He commanded the waters to surround the Skazic, and all of them were captured by water and thrown up on shore, where our soldiers imprisoned them. The energy to do this ended his life."

Jakin couldn't speak. He knew the sacrifice of war from his years of experience, and the pain of loss never went away. He shook out the water from his clothes.

"The others carried Grandpa away and joined the battle at the bridge," Rafael explained sadly. "They told me to stay behind and revive you."

"Thank you," Jakin said, standing to his feet. He looked steadily at the Ningyo. "Give your grandfather a proper burial. He deserves it—his faith in Melchizedek saved us all."

Rafael nodded solemnly.

"Um, Lehrling," he said, after a pause.

"Yes?" Jakin replied, wondering what the young man wanted.

"I'm sorry about how I treated you when you arrived in Ningyo territory. I was really afraid," Rafael admitted.

"It's alright," Jakin said, giving him a reassuring smile. "Pretty soon, you will have at least one of your leaders back."

Rafael nodded again, and stepped back into the waters of Lake Khartome. The water then gently surrounded Jakin, warm like a blanket, and lifted him. Rafael used his Neuma to deposit Jakin on the clifftop; right next to the back wall of the castle. He waved down at the Ningyo, and watched Rafael swim away before turning back to the stone wall.

He had been right. Most, if not all of the guards, were at defensive positions near the front, leaving the rear castle walls lightly guarded. No one had seen the fantastic display of water Neuma except the Skazic who were now dead or captured. Jakin was safe for now. Shaking one more time and wringing his clothes, Jakin set off to find the secret entrance to the prison.

SAIGON JERKED HIS DRAGON so that it barely missed the tower, but Etania fell off. She didn't even have time to process her coming death before a bubble of green surrounded her. Instead of falling, Etania felt herself rising, and looked down to see Cephas controlling the Neuma that had saved her. He was riding on a raft on the lake, and she was elated to see Naymatua standing beside him. Instead of hitting the side of the tower face-first, she floated to the top. She stepped onto the stone surface and looked down to see Cephas waving at her from the raft. His raft was one of dozens filled with Naymatua, and they were sailing to join the rest of the army! Before Etania could cheer, she heard the groans and growls of Skazic behind her and whirled to face them.

These Skazic, with their pale faces and pointed ears, were remnants of Leici who had pledged their loyalty to Malstorm. Etania had no time to load her crossbow, so she used her Neuma as a projectile, throwing fireballs toward her incoming opponents. She felt like Melchizedek's Neuma was flooding her, and it was easier than ever to throw fire at them.

One after another, the Skazic fell beneath her Neuma. Screaming in agony, they lost their abilities and once again became powerless men and women. The horror of their loss caused them to flee in fear, and Etania finally had a moment to herself. Looking over the chaos of war below, she prayed.

Melchizedek, it's time, she said, feeling the coolness of the bracer combine with the warmth of the Neuma inside of her.

"Not so fast!" King Toren declared, and her concentration was broken. She must have been drowning out the noise when she concentrated on gathering her Neuma! She was surrounded by guards at the top of the small guard tower. Whirling in a circle and pointing her inadequate dagger at them, she wondered what she should do next.

"You can't use my gauntlet for good," King Toren said, lifting his own gauntlet and pointing it at Etania.

The bracer on her arm tingled but didn't respond. He cursed, trying again, but Etania's bracer didn't even react this time.

"What have you done?" He roared.

"Why don't I show you?" Etania retorted, deciding not to think, but to do as Melchizedek asked, trusting him with the results. The fire of her Neuma burst from her fingertips.

The Neuma burned brighter and brighter, expanding outward from her like a wave. It reached out in a wide explosion, just like when she had attacked Isabella. This time, however, her Neuma was warm and inviting. It was a fire after a long winter, caressing her skin, hair and arms. The white flames first consumed the Skazic around Etania and King Toren. Then, the Neuma swallowed the Soacroni attacking the Draconians in midair, and they dropped like flies. A cleansing flood of fire swept over the water Skazic who were imprisoned by the Ningyo, and disintegrated the golems that were attacking the Kinzoku. The toothbreakers cried in pain as the Neuma of the Vexli transformed them from terrifying creatures to helpless men.

All around the battlefield were cries of terror and strange noises as people transformed. Some surrendered to the coming army. Some fought back in desperation, only to be cut down by the armies of Melchizedek. All over the battlefield, a cry of victory rose as Etania fell to her knees.

She could hear Melchizedek's warning in her head about the bracer.

You will only be able to use it once, my child, and then you will be vulnerable to your enemies.

Etania's vision faded, the use of her Neuma completely draining her of energy as she fell to her knees. The image of King Toren's face, contorted with rage, was the last thing she saw before she lost consciousness.

AS IF TO ANSWER HIS question about Etania, Keyel heard dragons roaring in the sky. He ran forward, out of the forest, to the shoreline of Lake Khartome. There, he was able to watch the horrifying battles of the dragons and Soacroni. They infested each one like flies, forcing it to crash into the lake. He hoped that the dragon carrying Etania would make it to the second tower, as he saw it unhindered most of the way. But the Soacroni were not to be stopped. Keyel felt like his heart had leaped into his throat as he watched Saigon's dragon fall into the lake with a loud crash. He couldn't see anything after that, and he froze in place as questions sped through his mind.

Is Etania still alive? Could she have bailed at the last minute and survived? He had to find out, even at the risk of his own life. Keyel left the safety of the Eritam and sought to join the Kinzoku in their battle against the golems. The golems were forming a barrier on the bridge which the Kinzoku couldn't break through. Ramar saw Keyel attempt to join them and shoved him out of the fight.

"Leave us, boy! Your sword is useless against rock!" he said.

Keyel couldn't simply leave. Not now—not when Etania was so close! He had to find a way past the first tower on the bridge, to where Etania might lie. He had to see for himself whether she was alive or dead! He looked for another way forward, glancing from side to side, as desperate as a thirsty man in a desert.

To his surprise, the Naymatua pulled up on the eastern shore of the lake, Cephas leading them. Keyel knew this was his chance. Without even acknowledging the surprised group, he took a raft from them and paddled away.

"Wait!" Cephas called, but Keyel didn't heed him.

He was speeding away over the lake, his heartbeat increasing with every slap of water against the wood. He paddled, even as the burning in his arms intensified, until he was approaching the second tower. Most of Toren's soldiers were in front of this tower, trying to defend the bridge, so Keyel knew he could land on the island of Khartome without hindrance if he used stealth. He was about to do so when he saw a bright flash of Neuma.

He heard and saw the Skazic change from monsters into men.

"Etania!" he screamed, looking up toward the top of the second tower. He couldn't see anything, but he heard the soldiers retreating from the tower to the island of Khartome.

Keyel paddled quickly to shore and hopped out of his raft, stumbling as he regained his footing. He must reach Etania before King Toren could harm her! He entered the city of Khartome, grabbing a cloak from the display rack outside of a store to disguise himself. He would have to return it to the store owner later, as the man or woman was nowhere to be found. In fact, the capital city was quiet and still as normal citizens hid from the battle raging outside. As a result, Keyel had to stick to alleys and side streets while trailing the retreating army.

From his vantage point in one of the dark alleys, Keyel spotted King Toren. He was leading the way up to the pinnacle of the island, where his castle stood. Directly behind him, five guards carried Etania on their shoulders.

Keyel was pretty certain she was still alive by the slight rise and fall of her chest. There was no way he could rescue her without getting himself killed. Perhaps he should allow himself to be arrested—at least then he would be near her. No, that wouldn't work either. *They may kill me rather than keep me alive*, he reasoned.

Keyel's brain finally caught up with his actions. He needed to calm down. Etania was alive, and her mission a success. Most likely, the front lines were now rounding up the Skazic that had surrendered or pushing on to kill the rest. His Master was probably in the castle freeing the leaders and would soon have it secured. But what should he do?

He couldn't go back, since his raft was undoubtedly floating away by now. He would have to continue to tail the army to see if Jakin had succeeded.

Before he could decide, the army of Skazic was safe within the castle. He was about to curse, wondering what he would do next, when he heard the stomping of another army. Looking back, he saw a banner on a pole that made hope spring in his heart: a purple flame set in a black background.

JAKIN WAS GRATEFUL to finally feel some warmth seeping into his skin. Searching for the hidden tunnel had made him feel warmer, despite his wet clothes. It was well-hidden by moss and overgrown vines, but he managed to find it near the back wall. Cutting away the foliage, he wrestled open the grate-like entrance with minimal noise. He climbed inside, lighting an abandoned torch with his Neuma. The long tunnel stretched before him, leading directly toward the dungeons. He almost laughed in glee that it was unguarded, and that Toren had forgotten his lessons about old castle plans. This tunnel was originally dug by King Josiah and his men to escape the castle, and it had been abandoned during a time of peace. Now, it would be used to Jakin's advantage. The long tunnel led to a single cell, which usually stayed empty, acting as a museum of sorts for King Josiah's descendents.

Now, the hard part. Jakin had to make sure that no guards spotted him—an impossible task. Saying a quick prayer, he crawled through the last portion of the tunnel, and hauled himself into the empty cell. No guards were present, and the door of the cell was wide open. Jakin strode into the walkway between the cells, looking both ways for the guards. There was no one! He had to find one of the guards so that he could get the keys from them! Before he searched, a single guard appeared. Jakin smiled, trying to suppress a laugh. With his years of experience, he used his Neuma and combat skills to quickly disable the guard and take his keys. He jingled the keys, looking to see which cell he would open first. The first cell on his right contained a very pale Leici.

"Are you going to wait there all day or free me already?" Lady Maiya demanded.

Jakin was almost tempted to leave her there, but his friendship with Thandor compelled him to unlock the door. In the next cell was Larora, who quietly thanked him, and the cell across from her belonged to Adrianna, the Ningyo leader.

"You smell like my people," Adrianna said.

"You can tell from the smell of water?" Jakin replied.

"Of course! Can't you tell which flames are yours by scent?" Adrianna asked.

Jakin didn't reply to that, and shrugged. After all, he didn't want to tell her that both Andre and her daughter, Isabella, were dead. The following cell contained Calder, who was kept in a special cell made of wood.

"Finally!" Calder said. "Thank Melchizedek my Kinzoku helped you, Lehrling! I doubt you could've made it here without them."

"What, do you smell your people on me, too?" Jakin wondered, with a smile.

"No," Calder said, "I just know they would've joined the cause to rescue me."

Jakin bit back his protest about the trials they had endured to get the Kinzoku's support. He instead headed toward the last cell, where Jonida the Draconian was kept. She thanked Jakin, and all of them followed him back to the tunnel entrance. Each one slipped inside while Jakin kept watch. Another soldier appeared, and Jakin took care of him just as easily as the first. He hoped no one else would show up as he followed the diplomats into the tunnel. With the torch, Jakin led all of them outside of the castle to the back wall. Once they had, the entrance hidden again, they conferred together in whispers about their next move.

"Our only choice is to take the castle," Jakin said.

"Are you crazy?" Maiya exclaimed. "There has to be a hundred soldiers stationed at this castle."

"A hundred!" Larora exclaimed. "There is no way we could take on that force."

"Only twenty-five people for each of us," Jakin teased.

The leaders glared at him, and Jakin shrugged. Before they could come up with anything else, they heard the loud stomps of soldiers' feet. All of the diplomats flattened themselves against the castle wall. Jakin peeked around the corner of the wall, and saw King Toren's banner on one of the poles.

"It's the King!" he told the others, in a hushed voice.

Calder groaned, and Jakin wondered what they could do now that the enemy numbers had doubled. Shortly after King Toren's soldiers had entered the castle, however, another group of soldiers followed them. Jakin recognized the banners of their allies and quickly beckoned the diplomats to follow him.

The Kinzoku stood proudly in front, their metal clad soldiers pushing at the gate. The Eritam waited close by, snarls ready for when the door gave way. The Naymatua created slings from the earth and trees, building them so that they could be thrown at the wall. Leici hung back, bows at the ready, and a few of the unwounded dragons stood tall and proud behind them, ready to fire. Jakin smiled, feeling that the army would soon be victorious against the guards that remained at the castle.

"Maiya!" Thandor saw his wife through the crowd, and rushed out from his place among the Leici to embrace his wife.

Thandor wasn't the only one exclaiming in happiness over the appearance of their leaders. Suliman welcomed Larora back to her people, and the Ningyo cheered at having Adrianna back as a leader. Ramar slapped his brother on the back, and Ivan laughed, glad to have Calder in their presence again.

Jakin searched through the ranks for Etania. Instead, his eyes landed on Keyel, who made his way through the crowd of soldiers, to bow at his feet.

"I'm sorry, Master," Keyel said. "I've failed you again."

"What do you mean? What happened?" Jakin exclaimed.

"Etania was successful in using her Neuma against King Toren's Skazic. However, she was captured by the King. So far, he has not harmed her, and probably intends to use her as leverage. I hoped to find you in charge of the castle by the time we reached it."

"Well, that didn't happen!" Jakin retorted. "And stand up. You've not failed me. Etania and I knew this might happen."

Jakin pulled his apprentice to his feet.

"But we have to get in there!" Keyel exclaimed.

"I know," Jakin said, "and I have a plan to get her back—and an idea of where to find her."

"What is it?" Keyel questioned.

"You'll see soon enough. Let the army take care of the castle. We need to rescue Etania!" Jakin exclaimed.

ETANIA BLINKED SEVERAL times as the room came into focus. A lone candle, sitting on a dresser in the far corner of the room, barely lit the area. She could just see the outline of a bedroom; a mirror against one wall and a crib with a sleeping infant inside. She was tied to a large bed post, dressed only in her undergarments, and gagged with some kind of mouth cloth. She gulped, wondering what the King was intending. Surely he didn't want her for anything more than her Neuma?

"I'm telling you, this gauntlet didn't allow me to control her!" King Toren insisted, bursting into the room with his wife.

"And I'm telling you that's impossible," Jazel answered, bringing in a lamp that lit the room better than the candle.

"Here, I'll show you," Toren said, walking over to Etania and slapping on her bracer before reaching for his own. The king lifted his arm with the gauntlet and waved. Etania's arm did nothing.

"Let me try," Jazel said, slipping on the gauntlet.

Toren gestured for her to do so, but instead, she turned on him. She flexed her fingers, and the gauntlet extended a large blade from its center.

"Jazel, what's going on? It didn't do that before!" Toren said.

"I know. I modified it," Jazel said, taking a step closer to him.

"Why?" Toren asked, stepping forward.

In a single motion, Jazel thrust the knife into his chest. He stumbled to his knees.

"You failed me," she said.

Etania watched in horror as Toren stared at them both, wide-eyed.

"I loved you," he choked, in a hoarse whisper.

"I *didn't* love you," Jazel replied.

Two tears slid down Toren's cheeks as he fell forward. He breathed laboriously, blood flowing from his wound. Etania gagged on her mouth cloth.

"I hate it when things don't go as planned!" Jazel said, stepping over her husband's dying body. Walking toward Etania, she removed the mouth gag and wrist ties.

"You're freeing me?" Etania stuttered. "Why?"

Jazel whirled on her, the blade gleaming with blood in the candlelight.

"I didn't spare you, girl," Jazel said. "I only want you to take a message to your father: Jazel DeCamp will have revenge."

"Jazel DeCamp?" Etania repeated, wondering what the name meant.

"Yes, and I will not rest until you experience my pain!" Jazel said. "So I am not sparing you: I'm waiting until the right moment."

"Right moment?" Etania repeated.

Jazel didn't reply. She merely walked over to her wardrobe and removed a knapsack and cloth wrap. Etania was frozen, wondering what she should do. Jazel could still choose to kill her with the blade.

Jazel cleaned the gauntlet, putting it inside a box and shoving it into a knapsack. Then she went to the crib. She placed the baby inside of her wrap and walked to the door of the room, stepping outside.

"My husband! My husband is murdered by the Vexli!" Jazel screamed.

Etania's heart thudded in her ears. With that cry, she could hear the boots of the soldiers rushing to their king's room. She had nowhere to go, and her mind was still reeling from the violence of Jazel's actions.

She was going to die—the only one to know the truth.

Melchizedek, help me! She prayed.

Before she could complete the thought, she saw the amethyst from her mother's necklace glowing. The glow intensified and suddenly, she was wrapped in her father's embrace, to be swept away in a hurricane of flame.

When the soldiers arrived, they would find a dead king and the dying embers of a purple fire.

Chapter Thirty

K eyel watched as most of the soldiers filed out of Castle Khartome, their arms raised in surrender. Almost all of them tossed down their weapons and waved a white flag after realizing King Toren was dead and Queen Jazel had fled. Only a fraction fought to the death, refusing to give in, even in their weakened state. Within several hours, the battle was finished.

Etania returned to the army exhausted and unwilling to talk. Even though Keyel wanted to hold her and keep her within sight, he knew she needed rest. So he restrained himself, watching Etania ride away to Nova. Keyel would have joined her, but Adeline asked for his assistance as a healer. Together, they set up a healing house in the grand hall of the castle. Instead of resting, Keyel went from patient to patient, helping every injured person or animal within view. Eventually, he ran out of patients and energy, so he found an empty cot and slept.

He was shaken awake by a messenger boy.

"You're needed in the meeting hall," he said.

"Now?" Keyel asked, squinting against the bright light of day.

"In an hour," he replied, "for a noontime meeting."

"Noontime?" Keyel repeated, bolting upright.

The boy nodded and, crinkling his nose, added, "You might want to see the public bath before you attend."

"Thanks," Keyel grumbled, and the boy took off.

Standing, Keyel admitted he smelled like battle—a mixture of blood and sweat. He took the boy's advice and headed for the public baths, carrying a change of clothes a Leici healer had loaned him.

Finishing and hopefully smelling better than before, Keyel headed toward the kitchen. The kitchen was now run by a group of Melchizedek-following cooks, whose bustling and arguing resulted in many half-finished dishes. Keyel snatched a scone and an apple, getting out of their way before heading to the meeting hall.

When he entered, Etania and Jakin were the only ones present. He breathed a sigh of relief. Taking a seat by Etania, he noticed that she too had bathed and slept. Her hair was barely combed and her dress was more sturdy than elegant, but Keyel still found her attractive. However, he knew his thoughts shouldn't be on her appearance at that moment. He opened his mouth to ask her all the questions he wished to, but Jakin prevented it with his hand.

"Wait," he said.

Etania nodded in agreement, smiling slightly at him. Keyel's heart thudded in his chest. For that smile, he would do anything. Now that the battle was over, he could court her as he pleased. Suddenly, he felt guilty for feeling such happiness. He thought of all the men and women he had tried to heal. He thought of Andre, whose sacrifice would long be remembered. He knew then that Melchizedek had blessed them both by sparing their lives, and he would have to live with the consequences of being a survivor.

Etania reached over and squeezed his hand. Her reassurance sent a thrill through him.

Even if this was just the beginning, he knew Melchizedek had given him all he needed to find his way through it. That was enough for the Leici.

ETANIA WAS COMFORTED by the warm and calloused hand of her new beau. Keyel's presence was soothing after a night of restlessness. The image of the King's death had replayed itself in Etania's mind often, and she was unable to sleep well. She managed to debrief with her father about what happened so he could convey the truth to the council. But, her father refused to tell her why Jazel insisted on him knowing her last name. Jakin said it was a matter he would have to take care of, and that was the end of it.

Etania didn't like that answer. After the woman had stabbed King Toren directly in front of her, Etania felt like she deserved to know the truth. However, her own exhaustion the night before meant that she didn't want to argue. She might be able to ascertain the background today.

The rest of the council filed in: Vartok, Lady Maiya, Lady Adeline, Suliman, Cephas, Adrianna, Jonida, and Calder.

"Now that we're all here, I will begin the meeting," Jakin said. "The first order of business regards the King. Toren was killed yesterday by his wife right in front of Etania. She had modified the gauntlet to contain a blade and used that to harm her husband. Her reasoning and whereabouts are unknown, but Cephas has agreed to start a nationwide manhunt in Tamnarae."

Reasoning unknown? Etania thought. *But she told me! Why are you hiding it, father?*

Even though she thought this, Etania dared not say it for fear that his reasons for hiding the truth went far deeper than surface level.

"Because so many still hope that King Toren is alive," Jakin said, "especially the turned Skazic, I would like to bury him publically. I want an open casket so that all may verify his death. Does anyone disagree?"

Many of the council members shook their heads, but Lady Maiya voiced a concern.

"Should we bury him with the other Kings?" she asked. Jakin paused before answering her.

"I believe King Toren was manipulated by Jazel into his actions," he said, "so I think it is only right that he rest with his ancestors. Besides, I don't want to cause a riot with our new people."

Most of the table assented to this decision. Their agreement stood in stark contrast to their argumentativeness just months before.

"Speaking of those new 'people,'" Calder said. "What should we do with them?"

"What do you mean?" Jakin asked.

"Well, they're prisoners of war, and we don't have facilities to keep them..." Calder said.

"We should kill them," Jonida said matter-of-factly, grief adding to her words. "They killed our men. It is only just."

Etania's jaw slackened.

"We can't do that!" she protested, and all eyes turned to her.

"Then what do you suggest, Vexli?" Suliman questioned. "Since you turned them, they are technically your responsibility."

Etania gulped.

"I know it is just for them to die for their evil," Etania began. Nods of assent rippled around the table, and she swallowed. *Melchizedek, what do I say? I know you tasked me with keeping them safe.*

"Justice is important," Jakin agreed, "but so is mercy. I know that better than anyone."

He looked at Etania and she smiled at him.

"I think we should make this island their prison," Keyel added. "They lived here as Praytor, so their homes are already here. They just need to earn back their right to citizenship."

"If we do that," Adrianna said, "Then we will need a Leader, Captain, guards…"

"I will be the Leader," Etania volunteered. "As you said, I am responsible for them."

"And I will be her Captain of the Guard. I will train willing men and women," Keyel said, squeezing Etania's hand.

"I guess that means you'll no longer be my apprentice," Jakin said, with a wink. Keyel blushed.

"If you think I'm ready, Master," Keyel said.

"You're more than ready to be your own Master," Jakin agreed. "I volunteer to interview the former Skazic before they reintegrate into society."

"We want to reintegrate them?" Jonida protested. "None of my people will welcome a Soacroni back into their ranks!"

"I am also uncertain our people will accept a Skazic," Adeline admitted, looking at Keyel. "Especially since they cannot accept a nothus."

Jakin waved away their objections.

"We will cross that road when we come to it. In the meantime, we need to find a new place to meet, and a new capital to govern from," Jakin said.

"Why don't you come to my place?" Cephas suggested. "The valley is a perfect bridge between the mountains and Northern Tamnarae."

"I like any place that I can walk to," Calder grunted.

"It's so far," Maiya complained.

"I know the Draconians would transport anyone willing to ride," Jonida said.

"We could also help people on the rivers," Adrianna agreed.

"I'm sure my wolves could make it," Alpha Vartok said.

"Don't count us out," Suliman assented.

"Good!" Jakin was pleased. "Then the last order of business is trying to decide how we are going to govern. Do we find another King?"

"No," Calder stated, "I think this rebellion proves a king can't be trusted."

"I agree," Jonida added.

"Then what governance do you suggest? An oligarchy, like Northern Tamnarae?" Jakin queried.

"No way, you all argue too much," Etania said.

"A republic," Adeline declared, and all heads turned toward her. She shrugged, a light blush trailing her cheeks.

"I read that some countries overseas have a system of governance where leaders rule together. They make laws together and then agree or disagree on their implementation. They determine the outcome by amount," Adeline explained.

"What if we have a tie?" Suliman asked.

"Impossible with five leaders," Maiya replied, and then looked at Cephas and added. "At least in Southern Tamnarae."

"Six," Jakin corrected. "I would have to represent the humans without a specialized type of Neuma, like those in Nova."

"Then I will be the tie-breaker," Etania found herself saying. "Since I now represent a group of people as well."

The other leaders shifted uncomfortably in their seats.

"How about this?" Jakin asked. "I will write a basic charter, and then we can decide nuances in a few months from now, when we've settled back into our homes?"

Nods of assent once again went around the table, and each stood to exit the room. Etania waited until they left before addressing her father.

"Why didn't you tell them?" Etania questioned.

"Tell them what?" Keyel wondered.

"Tell them that Jazel said she was taking vengeance on you," Etania stated pointedly, at her father.

"Jazel said what? Why?" Keyel asked.

Jakin sighed, standing to his feet.

"I need to find some paper," he replied.

Etania crossed her arms over her chest and snorted.

"Well, are you going to follow me and get some lunch so I can explain, or are you going to stand there and huff at me?" Jakin questioned.

Her anger slightly deflating, she followed her father outside of the meeting hall, Keyel in tow. They walked to the library, and Etania felt a wave of familiarity rush over her. Only months before, she had stood in the library itself. As they went inside, the first thing Etania noticed was the silence. The record keepers and librarians had fled and they still hadn't returned. Then she noticed the cleanliness. Unlike its previous cluttered state, there were no half-written manuscripts rolled out on the table and no monocles sitting unattended. There was no smell of ink in the air, or quills scattered across the surfaces. Everything was neatly put away, the scrolls of fine vellum and papyrus tucked into shelves. Etania was saddened that this place, just like the citizens of Nova, had been negatively impacted by the battle.

Jakin went to one of the clean sheets of vellum and drew it out, fetching a quill and inkwell. He took a seat at one of the tables and looked up at Keyel.

"Keyel, would you mind getting us lunch? I would like to talk to my daughter for a few moments alone," Jakin said.

Even though Keyel arched his eyebrow at the command, he obeyed.

"Yes Master," he said.

"You don't have to call me Master anymore," Jakin said with a smile.

"Right. So what should I call you?" Keyel asked.

"Well, I think 'father' is a little too early, don't you?" Jakin teased.

Etania elbowed him, blushing furiously.

"Just call me Jakin. Everyone else does."

"Okay, Jakin," Keyel said, smiling.

Etania beamed at them both, her concerns about Jazel temporarily forgotten. Keyel gave her a kiss on the cheek and departed, leaving them both. Etania took a seat beside her father, her ankles tucked underneath her to stop her knees from moving up and down nervously. Jakin dipped a quill into the inkwell and began to speak.

"When you were around ten years old, I was called by Cephas to oversee a judicial hearing for a royal official in Northern Tamnarae," he said, scrawling the first line of the new pact. "The hearing was regarding the assassination of the King and Queen of the Pyros."

"Assassination?" Etania repeated. "I haven't heard about it."

"That is because Cephas and I strove to quell word of it. The oligarchy in the North is tenuous, at worst, and amicable, at best," Jakin continued. "We didn't want the others to start blaming each other, especially since it was a family matter."

"How so?" Etania wondered.

"The King of the Pyros had been with another woman before the Queen. From that relationship, a child was born. That child is Jazel Decamp." Jakin stated. The finality of Jakin's statement echoed with the ending thump of a sentence on the scroll.

"If Jazel is royalty, then how...?" Etania began.

"She isn't true royalty, just like Keyel," Jakin interrupted. "She was a small child when her mother witnessed the marriage of the King to his wife. Her mother was furious and took it upon herself to kill them both. During their marriage celebration, she poisoned them. They died within minutes, and she was jailed."

"This seems like a pretty straightforward case," Etania said. "Why were you called in?"

"Because the king's brother became king and wanted another man to evaluate the case. He wanted to see if I would disagree with Cephas' ruling," Jakin explained.

"What was Cephas' ruling?" Etania asked.

"He said she should be imprisoned for life. After being presented the facts, I voted for execution," Jakin said.

He sighed deeply, quill stopping on the page.

"I hated any sign of evil so much that I rushed to judgment," he said, pulling his hand through his hair. "My hatred had so many consequences."

Etania put a hand on her father's arm.

"You didn't know," she reassured him.

"I should have," Jakin replied. "Anyway, King Victor agreed with me. Jazel's mother was executed, and Jazel was entrusted to the care of Zamora, Victor's wife. When I saw her again, she was an adult who had caught King Toren's eye. I didn't know who she really was, having forgotten the case in my never-ending hunt of Skazic. I even thought Jazel Decamp had died when I heard about what happened to Zamora."

"What happened to Zamora?" Etania asked.

"She was supposedly killed in a fire," Jakin said. "I wonder now if Jazel was responsible."

"Jazel would kill her own guardian?" Etania repeated, and shuddered as the memory of King Toren's horrified face washed over her. "Yes, she would."

"I had no idea my actions would create so strong a desire for vengeance in another person," Jakin said. "I thought that a little girl could forget about her mother's death and move on."

"I don't think anyone could forget that," Etania said, feeling a slight bit of empathy. However, the knowledge that her mother had died because of Jazel quickly swept that feeling away.

"I didn't tell the council because they have enough going on without my personal problems," Jakin admitted. "We need time to rebuild, and that can't be done during a never-ending hunt. I know that better than anyone."

Etania wrapped her arm around her father's shoulders.

"I understand," she said.

"You do?" Jakin replied, leaning out of the side hug. "I think that's the first time you've agreed with a decision I've made."

Etania laughed.

"Well, it took a while for us to figure each other out," Etania said, "but I think Mom would've wanted us to put aside our differences and work together. It makes each of us stronger."

"Yes, it does," Jakin said, giving his daughter a kiss on the forehead.

"Anyone hungry?" Keyel asked from the doorway.

"Very!" Etania echoed, and Keyel brought in the food.

JAKIN LOOKED OVER THE document several times after they finished their food. His daughter talked to Keyel about Jazel while Jakin put the finishing touches on the charter. Jakin was glad that his apprentice was close-lipped. He didn't want anyone else knowing about Jazel's connection to him. He hid one thing from his daughter, however—he would not be staying long with them. He planned to hunt Jazel himself, without any help. He hadn't informed anyone of his decision, not even Cephas, who usually knew his travel plans. He knew time and disguise were of the essence, so he would have to leave as soon as the ink dried on the documents.

Even though he wanted to stay with his daughter, Jakin knew Jazel would escape if he didn't immediately go after her. Already, her trail grew cold. If he wanted any peace for their country, he would have to stop her. He prayed that Melchizedek would guide him in his hunt, making it quick so he could return. No longer did he seek Skazic for vengeance. This time it was for peace, for both him and his daughter.

Jakin also knew he was leaving Etania in good hands. Keyel would protect her from the turned Skazic and find good men to help the Changed. His Apprentice had grown more on their journey than during any of the training Jakin had given him, and he was very proud to give the Leici his freedom. Keyel's romantic interest in Etania would be closely monitored by Barick and Serena, and all would be well while he was away.

Even though his heart twinged at the thought of leaving Etania, he had to admit that he didn't want to return home. There, he would have to acknowledge that Tala was gone permanently. Without her, and with Etania now an adult, he wondered if he really had a home at all.

You do in Safarast. Melchizedek reminded him.

Jakin smiled. The discomfort of this earthly house was only a reminder of his true home with Melchizedek and Tala.

Reading over the document one final time, Jakin signed his name. He knew it was a basic document, but there was room for the leaders to add to it as needed. His work was done. He stood and called to his daughter.

"Etania, will you take this to the council? I should take our dishes back home before we meet there again," he said.

"Of course," Etania agreed, taking the document from him with some reverence. She also took quills and ink with her.

"I will escort her there myself," Keyel declared. Jakin slapped him on the shoulder.

"Keep her safe, you hear?" he said.

The words came out as a joke, so Keyel laughed, but Jakin was actually serious.

"I love you both," he admitted.

"We love you too, Father," Etania replied, looping her arm around Keyel.

Jakin gazed at them. This is how he would recall them on his long journey: standing side by side, stronger together. Etania, with wavy hair so like her mother's, her bright brown eyes like his own before Melchizedek's call, changing them to purple. Keyel, with his short blonde hair and striking, blue eyes. Gathering up the bowls and plates, he teleported away before he could change his mind.

ETANIA STRODE WITH Keyel back to the meeting hall and realized they were the last ones to arrive. The other leaders looked up at them expectantly, and Etania felt her palms start to sweat. She was one of them now; a co-leader in this new republic.

"Here it is," she said, handing the scroll and supplies to Lady Maiya first.

The Leici read it and added a few lines. Then she signed it, passing it to her daughter, Adeline. Soon, everyone had amended and signed the document, and Etania read everyone's additions and helped make changes where declarations conflicted. She let out a sigh of relief once it was done. She wondered what her father would say when he saw all of the signatures. She rolled out the vellum to read the first page of the declaration aloud.

"We, the members of the territories of Southern Tamnarae, hereby declare ourselves free from the rule of any King save the ultimate King Melchizedek, our ruler and authority. Together, we agree to enact laws of justice and mercy; laws that will promote peace, harmony and unity. We agree to free trade between territories and free protection between our people. We agree that all territories shall act if another is being attacked by the Skazic, and that we will remain unified against the evil that threatens our lands. We agree that all laws must be approved by a majority, ties broken by the designated leader. Most of all, we promise to honor Melchizedek first and ourselves second, seeking to serve our people and rule as well as any king. By signing this agreement, we come into an accord regarding all these things."

She paused, looking around the room.

"If there be any disagreement, speak now. If not, say Aye," she said.

"Aye!" the council echoed.

Etania smiled, and picking up her quill, wrote her name at the bottom. That was when she noticed her father's signature.

"Why did he already sign it?" she asked.

"We figured you knew," Adeline replied.

"Or that he had something he needed to do," Adrianna suggested.

"Yes, of course," Etania lied, looking pointedly at Keyel to support her bluff.

"Yes, he told us he trusted us to complete the council," Keyel said.

Etania continued, "Well, I think it is pretty complete. Do we agree to meet in six months from now regarding particular laws?"

"Aye!" they agreed.

"Then this council is dismissed. If you know any guards willing to participate in watching the turned Skazic, please confer with Keyel," Etania said.

The leaders nodded in agreement, and most trickled out of the room. Some spoke privately to Keyel about lending aid, and then they all left, save Cephas. Cephas, who had quietly attended the meeting but had not participated beyond giving advice, came up to Etania.

"Jakin is hunting again, isn't he?" Cephas questioned.

"I'm not sure," Etania admitted, "but I believe so."

"I thought Melchizedek would convince him that was useless," Cephas said.

"He did, but I think this time my father's hunt is different," Etania replied.

"How so?" Cephas asked.

Etania bit her lower lip. Her father had been okay sharing with Keyel, but she wasn't sure if she should tell Cephas.

"I don't think I can share that," Etania said finally. "He told me to keep it a secret."

Cephas arched his eyebrow at Etania but bowed his head in understanding.

"It has been a pleasure fighting alongside you," Cephas said. "But I think it is high time I return home to my family and let them know to expect visitors."

Etania chuckled.

"Say hello to Alondra for me," Etania said.

"I will," Cephas agreed.

They parted with brief hugs. After the Lehrling left, Etania rolled up the scroll of their new government and tied it with a leather strap. She shouldered the document and looked over at Keyel.

"Will you take a walk with me?" she asked.

"Of course," Keyel replied, offering his arm.

She wrapped her arm around his and led him up the stairs to the parapet of the castle, overlooking the forest and waters below. She took a deep breath.

"Your father is hunting Jazel, isn't he?" Keyel asked.

Etania nodded.

"I had hoped—" Etania hesitated. "I had hoped he would stay long enough to help me with the changed Skazic."

"I know. So did I," Keyel said, placing his hand over hers. "I think he believes we can handle it, though."

"I think so, too," Etania admitted, her heart warm with the thought. "If you had asked me months ago, I wouldn't have believed it."

"But now?" Keyel said.

"Now," Etania repeated, looking at the blue sky and imagining the castle of Safarast in the clouds. "I think I can handle them, with Melchizedek's help."

"And mine," Keyel said.

Etania squeezed his hand in return. Together, they would be able to face anything that life threw at them.

DAMIEN SHOULDERED HIS knapsack and followed Jazel's footsteps through the forest. The dethroned Queen had recruited him shortly after Toren's murder, telling him to help her escape the Vexli that had killed her husband. He agreed readily, not wanting to wait for the incoming army to take over Khartome.

"Your majesty, if I may be so bold, what is your plan?" he asked.

"We are going to escape to the Pyros. They will shelter me," she replied.

"That's hundreds of kilometers north," Damien said. "How will we get there unharmed?"

"We will have to be disguised. Which reminds me, I will need your help with my hair," Jazel said.

"My queen, I am no hairdresser," Damien apologized.

"It is a simple process, requiring herbs from the forest and water," she explained, picking an herb from the path to prove her point and showing it to him.

"I will do my best," Damien agreed.

"That is all I ask," Jazel said. "We are fugitives now, and I know that is not what you wanted when you became a Skazic."

"If you are questioning my loyalties, know that they lie with you, my Queen," Damien said.

Jazel let out a laugh.

"I am no Queen now, though I appreciate the sentiment," she replied. "I wasn't questioning your loyalty, but I am reassuring you that you will receive whatever you desire after I accomplish my goal."

As much as Damien desired to have his Neuma back, he wondered how Jazel would accomplish this feat. No longer fearing her wrath, he ventured to voice his concern, albeit politely.

"I don't mean to offend, but as you have stated, we are refugees. How are we going to gain any sort of power?" Damien questioned.

"So it is power you desire?" Jazel answered. "Don't worry; we will have power once I get my hands on Malstorm's monster."

A shudder ran down his spine at the mention of the beast. Something about the word whispered of evil and danger, like the gauntlet.

"I don't want mere power," Damien admitted. "I want vengeance."

"I understand that. Who is the target of your vengeance?" Jazel asked.

"The Vexli!" Damien sneered. "The woman who made me this way and murdered your husband."

His words only scratched the surface of how he felt inside. Oh yes, he wanted her blood. He wanted it so badly that it took all of his self-control to turn his back on the castle, knowing it was a lost cause to pursue Etania at this time.

Jazel chuckled again, a cold sound that sent another chill down Damien's spine.

"You may have her," Jazel said. "Now, gather some wood."

Damien obeyed, fetching dry branches and piling them together. Jazel withdrew flint from her bag and lit the pile. She lowered the babe to a bush nearby. Taking the herbs she'd picked while they walked, she crushed them with rocks. Walking to the river nearby, she filled a pot with water and tossed the leaves inside. She then boiled the mixture until it looked as black as the night sky above her. Putting the pot aside, she began stripping her clothing.

Damien looked away. As beautiful as the Queen was, he didn't want to suffer her wrath.

"You may look now," Jazel said.

When he turned around, her back was exposed—her blonde hair falling in waves to the bottom of her waist.

"Cut it to my shoulders," Jazel commanded.

Damien obeyed, carefully moving his knife across her hair so that it was shoulder length.

"Now pour the mixture over my hair and massage my head," she added.

He did so, working his fingers across her head, the water now a cool slop. Once he was finished, they waited for a while and then rinsed out the mixture. Jazel dried herself and dressed while Damien packed up their things, erasing any trace of their camp.

When she turned back to face him, Damien suppressed a gasp. Jazel was no longer a blonde- haired beauty. Instead, she had raven-black hair fixed in a pale face, her blue eyes staring coldly at Damien.

The new look suited her.

"Come," she demanded. "We have a demon to find!"

A Note for Readers

Dear Reader,
    Pastor Kyle, one of the pastors that I know, tells his youth group to leave saying they are wonderfully, beautifully, and uniquely made by God. He does this to remind them of their value and worth to God. My hope is that this book does the same for you. If you've felt it has spoken to you, please leave a review on your favorite retailer or on Goodreads. I love to hear from my readers.

Etania's journey is not over, and it only gets harder from here. In *Etania's Calling*, Etania will encounter a traitorous prince, a deadly curse, and whether keeping a secret is worth the sacrifice. You can buy the next book at any of your favorite stores or at mhelrich.com[1].

Wherever God takes you next, I pray his blessing upon you. May he keep you and guide you as you walk with him.

Sincerely,

M.H. Elrich

---

1.   https://mhelrich.com/

Glossary

Background Information:

<u>Lehrling</u> (LAIR-ling)- one of twelve humans who were the original followers of Melchizedek, each gifted with a unique ability in addition to their natural Neuma.

<u>Melchizedek</u> (Mel-KIH-zuh-deck)- a fictional representation of God the Son, or Jesus. An adult male with brown hair and brown eyes.

<u>Deo</u> (DAY-oh)-a fictional representation of God the Father; not a physical person but embodied through Melchizedek.

<u>Mark </u> (Mark)-God's invisible imprint on believers that is a fictional representation of the manifestation of the Holy Spirit.

<u>Malstorm</u> (MAL-storm)-a fictional representation of Satan, the enemy of God.

<u>Neuma</u> (NEW-mah)-God's unique gift or talent given to each human being as a special ability or power only held by that race.

<u>Skazic</u> (SKAY-zik)-human or humans who pledge their allegiance to Malstorm in exchange for more powers than they are already blessed with. They are corrupt and hollow versions of their former selves.

<u>Vexli</u> (VEX-lee)-a human with the unique Neuma to disable Skazic, removing their abilities completely.

<u>Nothus</u> (NO-thiss)-an illegitimate son or daughter in the Leici (see definition of Leici below).

<u>Toothbreaker</u> (TOOTH-bray-ker)-a Skazic who was once an Eritam (see definition of Eritam below).

<u>Soacronis</u> (So-A-kro-niss) Plural is Soacroni (So-A-Kro-nai) a Skazic who was once a Draconian (see definition of Draconian below).

PEOPLE GROUPS

<u>Hafif</u> (Half-EEF)- human or humans without any visible Neuma; live mainly in Khartome and Nova

<u>Leici</u> (Lay-SEE)-human or humans with healing Neuma, characterized by pale skin, blonde hair, blue or green eyes. They are governed by a Lady, who is unique in the fact she and her descendents have brunette hair.

<u>Eritam</u> (EAR-uh-tam)-human or humans with the Neuma of taming wolves. They have pale skin, silver or white hair, yellow, green or brown eyes. They travel in packs governed by Alphas, the highest ranking member of the pack. Each pack member is ranked by strength and ability, starting with Alpha and going to Omega in order of the traditional Greek alphabet. They have a council of Alphas which meet and make decisions for them.

<u>Naymatua</u> (Nay-muh-TWO-uh)-human or humans with the Neuma of growing plants. They have dark skin, brown or black hair, and brown eyes. They are governed by Chiefs.

<u>Ningyo</u> (NING-yo)-human or humans with the Neuma of controlling water. They have tan skin, black hair, and blue or green eyes. They are governed by a male or female elected by the people.

<u>Kinzoku</u> (Kin-ZO-Koo)-human or humans with the Neuma of manipulating metal. They have pale skin with red or black hair. They are governed by a Vizeheir, a male lord.

<u>Draconian(s)</u> (Dray-KO-nee-un)-human or humans with the Neuma of controlling dragons. They have pale skin with bright blue, red, or green hair, that matches the color of their dragons. They have yellow eyes that look like a snake's eyes. They are governed by a male and female lord and lady.

COUNTRIES AND CITIES

<u>Southern Tamnarae</u> (TAM-nuh-ray)-the area where Etania lives, the southern half of a large continent. Ruled by King Toren and Queen Jazel with a council of lords and ladies made up from the various people groups.

<u>Tearah</u> (TEAR-uh)-the name of the planet where Etania lives.

<u>Khartome</u> (KAR-tome)-the capital city of Southern Tamnarae, located on an island in the middle of a lake of the same name.

<u>Nova</u> (NO-vuh)-a city on the mainland outside of Khartome where Hafif live.

<u>Calques</u> (KAL-Kwez)-capital city of the Leici, in which they live in tree houses located at the tops of trees.

<u>Ligasha</u> (Lih-GAY-shuh)-capital city of the Naymatua, in which they live at the the bottom of the trees, inside a tree's roots.

<u>Milapo</u> (Muh-LAW-poe)-capital city of the Ningyo, in which they live on houses that are a few feet off the ground because of the river and floods.

<u>Azeeka</u> (Uh-ZEEK-uh)-the first city of the Kinzoku before reaching the innermost part, where the Kinzoku live in the mountain.

<u>Timane River</u>(Tih-MANE)-one of the rivers that flow from Lake Khartome and across the continent.

<u>Eriam River</u> (EAR-ee-yam)-one of the rivers that flow from Lake Khartome and across the continent.

CHARACTERS

<u>Etania Selali</u> (Eh-TAWN-yuh Say-LAW-lee)-daughter of Jakin and Tala Selali; eighteen-years old; brown hair and eyes.

<u>Jakin Selali</u> (JAY-kin Say-LAW-lee)-Lehrling whose original Neuma was and still is controlling fire. He is now blessed with the ability to teleport in addition to using fire. Over two hundred years old, with black hair and purple eyes, he wears an amulet with an amethyst that marks him as a Lehrling.

<u>Tala Selali</u> (TAH-luh Say-LAW-lee)- mother of Etania, wife of Jakin, with brown hair and brown eyes. A hafif blessed with long life because she married a Lehrling; around two hundred years old.

<u>Keyel Evant</u> (Key-EL ee-VAUNT)- son of Thandor and Shayna, brother of Adeline, with blonde hair and blue eyes. Twenty-one years old, with the Neuma of healing, and tremendous skill with a sword.

<u>King Toren and Queen Jazel</u> (TORE-in; Juh-ZELL)-the rulers of Southern Tamnarae. King Toren has brown hair and brown eyes. Jazel has blonde hair and blue eyes. Both are hafif.

Grace Stegel (GRACE STAY-gull)-Etania's childhood friend, daughter of Priest Alfred, seamstress.

Alfred Stegel (AL-fred STAY-gull)-the priest of Nova and Jakin's friend.

Barick and Serena (BARE-ick Suh-REEN-uh)- the husband and wife couple who are the Selalis' paid servants.

Damien (DAY-mee-in)- the first whom Skazic Etania changed, who is a commander in King Toren's army.

Lady Maiya and Lord Thandor (My-AH; Than-DOOR)-a husband and wife who rule over the Leici. Thandor has blonde hair and blue eyes. Maiya has brown hair and blue eyes.

Lady Adeline (AD-uh-line)-the daughter of Lady Maiya and Lord Thandor, with brown hair and blue eyes.

Shayna Evant (SHAY-nuh ee-VAUNT)-Keyel's mother and Thandor's one-time mistress. Shayna has blonde hair and blue eyes.

Kayne and Sarai (Cane; SARE-eye)-one of the Alphas of the Eritam, sent as representatives to the Council meeting.

Zeremu and Larora (ZAIR-uh-moo Luh-ROAR-uh)-the Chief of the Naymatua and his wife. They represent the Naymatua at the Council meeting.

Adrianna (AI-dree-AA-nuh)-a lady who represents the Ningyo at the Council meeting.

Calder (CAL-der)-the Vizeheir who represents at the Council meeting.

Saigon and Jonida (Sigh-GAWN; Jo-NEE-duh)- the lord and lady who represent the Draconian at the Council meeting

Vartok (VAR-tock)- Beta of Kayne and Sarai's pack of the Eritam.

Isabella (Iz-ah-BELL-ah)-daughter of Adrianna who was elected the temporary leader of the Ningyo.

Andre and Rafael (ON-dray; Ra-fee-EL)-older Ningyo and his grandson.

Suliman (SUE-luh-mahn)-the second highest ranking member of the Naymatua tribe.

Ramar (Ray-MAR)- brother of Calder; uncle to Bayanna.

Bayanna (Bay-AH-nuh)-daughter of the Kinzoku leader Calder. She has bright red hair and green eyes and is the fiery-spirited friend of Etania.

Ivan (EYE-vuhn)- ahe commander of the Kinzoku who is a wise man and brief mentor of Keyel.

Cephas (SEE-Fiss)-a Lehrling who has the powers of a Naymatua combined with the Neuma of creating shields. He has dark skin, bright green eyes, and black hair.

Alondra and Garel (Uh-LAWN-druh; GARE-uhl)- the wife and son of Cephas. Alondra has blonde hair and green eyes. Garel has brown hair, tan skin and green eyes and is about six months old.

Tevan (Tay-VAWN)-a Draconian with bright red hair, yellow slit eyes, and a dragon named Flamir (Fluh-MEER)

Works Cited

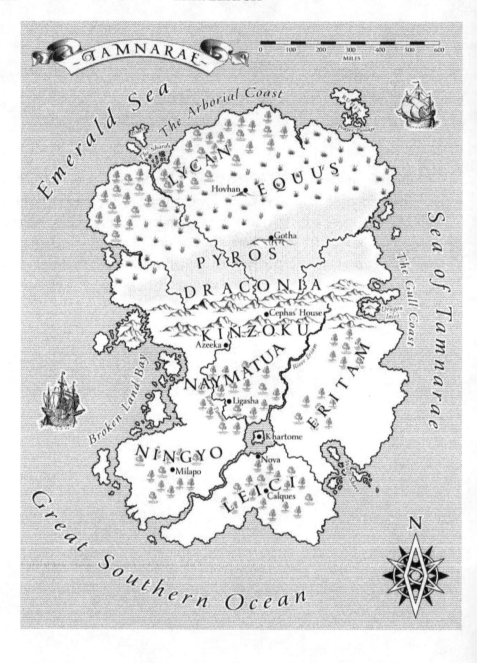

About the Author

M.H. Elrich is a Christian Fantasy author, reader, otaku, and teacher who wears too many hats. In her spare time (if she has any), she watches T.V. with her husband, rides horses, and travels to places with lots of trees. She has been published in The Write Word, Orpheus, Kern County Fair, and Short Fiction Break.

Printed in the USA
CPSIA information can be obtained
at www.ICGtesting.com
JSHW021025201123
52107JS00004B/16